Eleventh Hour • Book One

PUSH

IS THIS THE END?

Eleventh Hour · Book One

PUSH

IS THIS THE END?

MARK AMMERMAN
with E. Michael Rusten

BRIDGE STREET BOOKS
LANCASTER, PENNSYLVANIA

PUSH: Is This The End?
Book One of the Eleventh Hour series
Copyright © 2014 by Mark Ammerman and E. Michael Rusten

Published in the U.S.A. by Bridge Street Books

Editing and Typesetting: Marlene Bagnull,
www.writehisanswer.com/ampelospress
Proofreading and Copyediting: E. Michael & Sharon Rusten
Technical Assistance: Bart Palamaro, www.indieauthorsupport.com
Cover Concept and Book Design: Mark Ammerman
Cover Art: Daniel De León, www.lion-arts.com
Author Photo: Bethany Green, www.bethanygreenphotography.com

ISBN 978-0-9913844-0-2

Printed in the U.S.A.

Also by Mark Ammerman

The Cross and the Tomahawk series:
Rain From God
Ransom
Longshot

Roger Williams
John the Baptist
America: Built on Character, Founded on Faith

Also by E. Michael Rusten

The One Year Christian History
(with Sharon Rusten)

When & Where in the Bible and Throughout History
(with Sharon Rusten)

The End Times: Discovering What the Bible Says

To the wonderful women
(our wives)
who
know us fully,
serve us faithfully,
and love us anyway:

Terri Lynn Ammerman
and
Sharon Rusten

Matthew 24:4-14

Then Jesus replied to them: "Watch out that no one deceives you. For many will come in my name, saying, 'I am the Messiah,' and they will deceive many. You are going to hear of wars and rumors of wars. See that you are not alarmed, because these things must take place, but the end is not yet. For nation will rise up against nation, and kingdom against kingdom. There will be famines and earthquakes in various places. All these events are the beginning of birth pains.

"Then they will hand you over for persecution, and they will kill you. You will be hated by all nations because of My name. Then many will take offense, betray one another and hate one another. Many false prophets will rise up and deceive many. Because lawlessness will multiply, the love of many will grow cold. But the one who endures to the end will be delivered. This good news of the kingdom will be proclaimed in all the world as a testimony to all nations. And then the end will come."

Holman Christian Standard Bible (HCSB)

Preface

PUSH is the first book in a series of apocalyptic novels called Eleventh Hour. We have given ourselves to the writing of this fictional series because we feel that it's possible that we are living in that "eleventh hour" of the history of our world.

Though Christians since the first century have believed in the impending return of the Lord Jesus, the Bible foretells of specific events which must occur before the Lord comes back. Believers differ in their understanding of the prophetic unfolding, but we all look — with a joyous hope that will not disappoint us — to that day when Jesus returns for his Bride in the glory of his Father with the holy angels. That day could come a thousand years from now, or it could be soon.

Nobody can deny, amid the wars and rumors of wars of our day, that our world is fast (and desperately) becoming a global community in need of a global solution. There is genocide on a scale hardly known, drought and famine in many regions across the world, bankrupt nations and financial crises which affect us all, drug trafficking, human trafficking, and the disintegration of the family amid widespread sexual debauchery and confusion.

In all this, the Church knows that only Jesus can stop the stampede toward hell and bring about the consummation of a just and righteous worldwide Kingdom. How will that happen? When will it happen? Jesus said that the details of all of that are in God's hands. On the day of his ascension to the Father, Jesus told his disciples, "It is not for you to know the times or the seasons which the Father has put in his own power" (Acts 1:7 KJV).

So we don't know! But Jesus told us to watch, to work, to pray, to love, to evangelize, to make disciples, and to discern the times. PUSH, in the context of a page-turning contemporary thriller, proposes a scenario which we hope will help prepare the Church for whatever the Father has in mind for the last days. These are hard times already. Persecution of the Church of Jesus Christ is at an historic high around the world, and the Church in America surely faces its biggest challenges in the days ahead.

Our hope and our prayer for you, our reader, is that the words of this potent novel (and the novels which, Lord willing, are forthcoming in the Eleventh Hour series) will challenge and encourage you to take up your cross each day and follow Jesus, "come hell or high water," until he returns.

"May the words of my mouth and the meditation of my heart be acceptable in Thy sight, O LORD, my strength and my redeemer" (Psalm 19:14 KJV).

Your brothers in Christ,

Mark Ammerman
and Mike Rusten

The Cast of *PUSH*

Matthew Lyle Clifford (Matt) — Main character and narrator, journalist and columnist for the Philadelphia Bulletin

Aaron Stein — Owner/publisher of the Bulletin

Ahmed al-Farid — Al Quaida commander and 9/11 mastermind

Ali Ahkmed Baraki — Bulletin correspondent in Russia, Matt's colleague and close friend

Amnon Katz — Prime minister of Israel

Bradley Wall (Sleuth) — FOX News foreign correspondent and United States undercover agent

Cobalt Man — Mysterious stalker

Colonel Ivan Koval — Officer in Kazakh Air Command, father of Imanghari Koval

Deri Sesin — Jewish single mother on Kazakh train

Dr. Erkin Temirzhon and his wife **Aiday** — Family friends of Imanghari Koval in Kazakhstan

Magdalena Elizabeth Rivera (Magda) — "Cobalt Woman"

Ernie — Bulletin graphics designer

George Ognibini — Homeland Security agent

Gökhan Savas — President of Muslim Turkey

Imanghari Koval — Reluctant Afghani/Kazakh terrorist, friend of Ali Baraki, son of Colonel Ivan Koval

Kahmeel Kholani — Terrorist, brother of Rashid

Keith Sutton — Bulletin newsroom captain

Kevin McCarthy — Matt's best friend and member of Pancake Seminary

Jack Pascov — Bulletin correspondent in Israel, Matt's colleague and close friend

Jacqui Johnson — Bulletin broadcast news anchor

Jonathan David Clifford — Matt's father, western fiction author

Lisa Zimmerman — Matt's old girlfriend

Marco Gian Romano — Italian president of the Council of the European Union

Pancake Seminary Members — Doug O'Malley, Luis Ramirez, Tyrone Bates

Paul Yong Lee — Computer guru, Kevin McCarthy's friend and tenant

Rashid Kahmeel — Childhood friend of Ali Baraki, brother of Kahmeel Kholani

Rose Miller — Bulletin general news editor

Sam Wong Lee — Inventor, Batcave CEO, Kevin McCarthy's friend and tenant

Sanderson Dawud Clay — President of the United States of America

Siggy Roose — Bulletin camera man in Israel, colleague and partner of Jack Pascov

Stuart Jemmison — CIA agent

Terrorists — Arystan, Balta, Hafid Shameer, Tulegan, and Yusef

Tengiz Kobadze — President of eastern European nation of Georgia

Ulmes Malashenko — President of Kazakhstan

Ulzhan Kuandyk — Kazakh security guard and racecar wannabe

Vladimir Putin — Himself (president of Russia)

1

Blood Red Square

Thursday, July 3, Moscow. First week of Ramadan.

It was four o'clock in the morning.

Two stories beneath the ground, in a dusty basement laboratory, four men slept, weapons at hand.

On the floor above them, sitting nervously on an uncomfortable couch in an abandoned waiting-room, a fifth kept watch. Hafid Shahmeer fought sleep by quietly repeating Islamic prayers and periodically turning on a thin blue cell-ray to glance around his quarters. Occasionally, he stood up and carefully shifted a bulky weighted vest that was belted around his torso.

On the ground floor above the anxious sentry, the room was dark and cool. Silent as a tomb (for tomb it was), it sometimes seemed to whisper to itself as though its ghosts were restless.

Its floors and walls were covered with polished black marble. Red stone pilasters rose to the ceiling all around. Between each pilaster, the smooth walls were inlaid with a pattern resembling scarlet lightning, blood-red in the light of day but invisible now in the black of night. Only the faintest of a deep gray luminescence hung in the air, like a spectral mist, drifting out of the dim-lit stairwells at the front of the room.

To the normal eye, the only thing remotely visible was an ashen face, seemingly suspended several feet above the floor in the center of the room. A face, yes—and a pair of stiff, still hands. For there, lying in a crystal casket, was the embalmed corpse of Vladimir Lenin, the revolutionary founder of the United Soviet Socialist Republic. Ninety years he'd slept there—suited, blanketed, and carefully attended to by scientists who specialized in plastic surgery and the preservation of human flesh. Rumor had it that the real body had gone the way of all men, long ago, and that Lenin's climate-controlled casket housed a convincing facsimile. Rumor aside, the body of Lenin continued to be one of Moscow's largest tourist draws.

Viewed from the outside, Lenin's famous grave was a cubist pyramid standing upon the well-worn pavement stones of Moscow's Red Square. Its red granite façade was punctuated by a massive set of dark bronze doors. Above the doors, inscripted with red quartzite on black labradorite, was one simple word: "LENIN."

Behind the mausoleum rose the fifteenth century redbrick walls of the Kremlin, Moscow's ancient citadel. At the base of those walls was a mass burial site of Bolshevik revolutionaries who died in the battle of Moscow in 1917. Nearby, beneath bust-adorned memorials, and stored within the wall itself, were the bones and ashes of many of the former Soviet state's top leaders. Perhaps it was their disquieted spirits who whispered in the ears of comrade Lenin.

Whether it was the spirits, or the throbbing hum of the air-conditioning machinery within the mausoleum walls, Hafid Shahmeer heard voices in his head. He struggled with the nagging fear that he was not the only one awake within the cold pyramid.

But he was. His compatriots were snoring in the room below him.

The mausoleum guards had gone home early in the afternoon of the day before. They would not be back until 6:00 a.m. — earlier than usual for a Thursday, but security would be much tighter this morning. World-famous Russian president Putin was coming to pay a visit to world-infamous Russian dictator Lenin. Vladimir meets Vladimir, a carefully staged political photo-op, timed by Putin to throw a little cold water on an event taking place the next day over a thousand miles away in Jerusalem — the long-anticipated signing of the Middle East peace treaty.

But there will be no peace, Hafid mused numbly.

In a few hours, Red Square would be tightly cordoned off by the Russian government. Sharpshooters would be stationed on rooftops. Military helicopters would patrol the city in a two-mile radius of the Square. The president's Federal Guard would be thick as drones around a queen bee. But that wouldn't save the man. Not once he entered Lenin's funerary room. Not once Hafid was in the room with him.

"*Akhirah*," breathed Hafid. *Eternity.* Hafid would soon greet eternity.

According to the Prophet, if a man killed himself on purpose, he would go straight to hell. But if a man committed suicide for *jihad* — for holy war against the infidels — he went straight to heaven.

This is jihad. This is jihad, Hafid repeated to himself, within himself. But still he was scared. Life on earth was a precious and palpable thing. Family and friends. Food and sex. Love and laughter. Hunting in the mountains with his dog. Sunlight, moonlight, starlight. Sleep and dreams, and a new day each dawn.

Eternity was an unknown. Taken at the word of men who were still alive. Men who told other men what was true. Men who were sleeping in their own beds tonight.

He looked at his watch — 3:30 a.m. Two more hours before he would wake his brethren for the task they had trained for. And there were others with them in their mission, stationed strategically on the Square, waiting also.

Yusef was watching the Square from the steeple of St. Nicholas Tower on the eastern wall of the Kremlin — the western wall of the Square, the wall behind the Tomb. From his vantage point, he could see everything in the Square except for a small stretch of pavement on the far side of the Tomb. He had a very good view of the Kremlin Wall itself, until it turned from sight toward the Moskva River and the Bolshoy Moskvoretsky Bridge.

As Yusef thumbed a button on his cell-ray, Hafid's ray vibrated simultaneously, silently, in his underground hideaway.

Hafid jerked the cell-ray from his pocket and stared while its blue bulb flashed twice.

The blinking cell-ray was Yusef's signal that the Square's policemen — two of them — were strolling by the mausoleum on their normal nightly rounds. They would stop and try the front doors. They would walk around behind the Tomb and rattle the bars of the security door in back. They would smoke a cigarette and be on their way. They wouldn't bother to check the utility panel on the Kremlin Wall behind the memorial busts of the Soviet dead. And even if they had, it wouldn't have opened for them. It had been secured from the inside, after Hafid and his team had crawled into it, one after the other, at midnight. It was a narrow closet of pipes and wires attached to an underground air duct that led to the room where Hafid's compatriots now slept fitfully.

Hafid hated confined spaces, and the claustrophobic crawl through the damp, dusty duct had felt like hell itself. Cold metal crowding his shoulders on either side. His face to the feet of the man in front of him, his feet to the face of the man behind. Nose down, hardly room to lift his head enough to look forward. Shimmy like a snake in a flute. Try not to think. Almost too scared to breathe. Inch by inch. But he didn't have to go back out that way.

Normally, on Thursday mornings the Square was limited to visitors to Lenin's Tomb. Guards opened the Tomb at 10:00 a.m. and closed it up at 1:00 p.m.

The Square opened fully to the public at 2:00 p.m. But today, the Russian government had reserved the Square for itself. The only people in the Square all day would be President Putin, his Federal Guard, a sizeable contingent of Russian security forces and politicians, a hand-picked cadre of international journalists, and the media puppets of state-owned television network C1RW: Channel One Russia Worldwide.

Security would arrive early in the morning. The television crew would set up mid-morning. And then everyone would wait for Putin and his entourage to show up at one o'clock in the afternoon.

All this seemed like forever to Hafid.

Yusef chewed on a mouthful of almonds, swallowed, and yawned. It was standing room only in his reclusive observatory in St. Nicolas Tower. He had removed a half-inch pane of colored glass from an ancient stained-glass window to create a tiny porthole to the outside world. He watched the policemen emerge from behind the Tomb and amble across the cobblestones on their way to a cup of coffee and a shot of vodka. They would traverse the Square twice more before the dawn.

Arystan was hidden in the shadows near a small fifth floor window in the State Historical Museum on the western end of Red Square.

Face blackened, clothed in a dirt-gray jumpsuit like his compatriots, Arystan was almost invisible as he sat motionless on the floor beside a long row of dusty wooden cabinets. It was a neglected storage room with a solid oak door that Arystan had locked and bolted. He hadn't even looked outside yet.

Balta sat quietly in a dirty attic of the largest store in Moscow — the GUM Department Store — directly across the Square from Lenin's Tomb. The ornate Neo-Russian façade of GUM took up nearly the entire eastern side of the Square. Balta's lonesome post was in an abandoned garret on the top floor above the building's main entrance. The windows were small and cobweb encrusted. Balta wasn't going to clean them, but he would open one of them a few inches when the time came.

Tulegan was stationed at a tiny window in the Cathedral of St. Basil the Blessed at the southern end of the Square. In the tallest of the church's eight ornate domes, on a narrow plank catwalk in an attic with no floor (accessible only by a rickety wooden ladder and a leather-hinged trap door), Tulegan set up shop, lay down on an inflatable body mat, and waited.

From their posts, the four men commanded a comprehensive view of the Square in front of the Tomb.

Hafid buzzed the men below him at 5:30 a.m. Their cell-rays were set on mild shock mode. They were wide awake by the time they shut them off. After relieving themselves in their latex waste bags, they performed the Sunni *wudu* washings preparatory to dawn prayers. They unrolled their prayer mats, turned to the east, and very quietly prayed.

In half an hour, the Square and the Tomb would be filled with state guards. A few guards might descend to the unused floors where Hafid and his crew were hidden. If they did, they would find the metal doors unwilling to open to their keys. If they forced the doors open, they would find something quite a bit more troubling.

The sky turned yellow in the east, slowly pushing back the night. As the sun rose, it painted the city's skyline with the colors of the Orient. The Square came fully alive at six o'clock as Russian security forces arrived in military vehicles. They parked in regimented order in the large paved lot near the Bolshoy Moskvoretsky Bridge, then clambered out and deployed themselves in dozens of directions.

Men were soon stationed in all corners of the Square, near statues and monuments and at the doors and windows of the buildings that fronted all sides of Moscow's ancient marketplace. Armed men stood upon the Kremlin walls. Naval boats patrolled the Muskva for miles in both directions from the Square. Above it all, the rhythmic drone of military helicopters came and went on the wings of the cool morning wind.

Yusef saw it all and told it all in timed and practiced cell-ray signals to the rest of his compatriots. He was the designated watchman. There would be no action without his signal.

It was during noon prayers that someone tried the door to the chamber where Hafid was hidden. Startled into stillness, he heard brief conversation. Though his Russian was good, he didn't understand it all and couldn't really hear it all. Something about "secured." Something about posting a guard in the stairwell. A confusion of louder voices for a moment. Then the sound of retreating footsteps. And silence. Though not total silence, for the muted noise of activity above him came down the stairwell, through his door, and into his imagination. His heartbeat sounded louder within him than everything else.

Face to the stained-glass, Yusef had barely moved his head for an hour, though he slowly turned his arms at his side and continually flexed his fingers and his toes. His eyes alone roamed freely, taking in the outside.

Channel One had been set up since 10:30 a.m. No foreign journalists had yet arrived. They would come when the president came. They would not be allowed any cameras. They would see only what the president saw. They would tell only what he let them tell. That was Putin's protocol.

Yusef's fingers played upon his cell-ray, signaling his observations to the rest.

Ya Allah! Half-past twelve! Hafid sighed, more loudly than he had intended. Holding his breath for a moment, he stood up and stretched, silently exercising his legs, his arms, his neck, his torso. The weight around his torso felt like death.

He didn't think there was anybody in the stairwell. There had been no particular noises that would tell him so. He moved toward the door, listening intently. He was scared, very scared, and more nervous than ever. His head ached. He ate some almonds absently and fingered his automatic pistol.

Yusef observed a shift in the guard — a lineup at the Resurrection Gate.

A black limousine, the first in the presidential caravan, entered Red Square through the Gate.

Their cell-rays were set on shock. They felt it. The light was red. Engagement One: standby.

Arystan moved at last to where he could see the Square. No sunlight touched his window. He was still in the shadows, but the Square was a clear, framed picture before him, bright and vividly defined in the midday sun.

Tulegan's air mat lay discarded behind him. Tulegan himself lay upon his stomach, his rifle cradled in his arms as he sighted the barrel through the small glass pane in front of him.

Balta opened his window just enough to ready himself.

Yusef squinted through his gun scope.

The four men in the basement laboratory of the mausoleum were at their door, knives in hand, RPK10s on prime, stun grenades clipped to their belts. Russian military caps on their heads, Russian boots on their feet, Russian uniforms on their bodies—they looked just like the men stationed in the funerary room above them. One of them palmed his ray, and the door came unlocked. But he didn't open it.

Hafid's door was locked still. He wouldn't move until the men downstairs had made their move. Suddenly, he knew he didn't want to move at all.

Through the focused eye of his gun scope, Yusef watched the parade of black limousines move into the Square and park in formation in front of Lenin's Tomb. He saw Vladimir Putin step out of the backseat of the lead car and straighten himself in posed confidence before the cameras. The other cars were soon emptied of all but their drivers, and an ordered assembly, which included Putin's bodyguards, formed around the president.

Putin raised his right arm in an informal salute and began to speak.

Another cell-ray shock. Green this time.

Engagement Two: *Akhirah!*

There would be no more signals from Yusef. Everyone was on his own. They knew what to do.

The men in the basement came out of their room. Stealthily, silently, they ascended two flights of stairs, entered the funerary room, and quickly overcame the four guards who were stationed there. No shots were fired. They used their knives. It wasn't all quiet, but nobody outside heard a thing because of the idling limousines, the shuffling politicians, the chatter of Channel One, and the Sergei Rachmaninoff music being broadcast throughout the Square as background ambience for Putin's grand appearance.

But Hafid was frozen behind his door.

Maybe they could do it without him. Maybe he could

take off the belt, sneak downstairs, and squeeze back into the air duct. But, no. That would be worse than this. All alone in the Kremlin wall, hemmed in on all sides by the ashes, the bones, the ghosts of the infidel Soviets—stuck there, unable to move, unable to get out at the other side until everyone was gone. And what if he never got out?

Hafid opened his door, hands shaking, and started up the steps. He was a dead man already.

He stumbled into the funerary room, eyes blank, one hand gripping his pistol so tightly that his fingers were white. His other hand was at his belt. "*Akhirah!*" he whispered.

His companions stared at him in disbelief, motioning for silence, gesturing for him to take his place out of sight of the front doors.

"*Akhirah!*" he whispered again, not seeing them. He moved toward Lenin's casket, placing his unarmed hand upon the glass, staring stupidly at the ghostly face of the dead despot.

One of his companions moved swiftly toward him to speak to him quietly, but Hafid pushed him aside, falling backwards against the crystal coffin. "*Akhirah*, my brothers," he coughed.

Just outside the door, a guard heard the scuffling within. He peered briefly into the dim funerary room, then motioned to another guard. The two of them stepped quickly inside.

Yusef saw two guards enter the mausoleum. That wasn't supposed to happen, but all things had been considered. He wouldn't signal anyone. Everyone must make his own move now. Yusef's rifle was trained on Putin.

Hafid saw the guards coming, lifted his pistol, and began to fire. One guard died instantly. The other, wounded and screaming, turned and lunged toward the door.

Yusef didn't hear the gunfire, but he saw the guard stagger out and fall. Putin and his men were reacting.

So the job must be done from a distance.

Yusef pulled the trigger on his rifle. So did Tulegan, almost simultaneously. Arystan and Balta waited only a breath to follow suit.

In the crowd surrounding the president, men began to drop to the stones. Some were felled by bullets. Others took cover against the hail of gunfire coming from the unseen assailants.

Security snipers on the rooftops scanned the Square to see where the fire was coming from. Security on the ground scanned the rooftops and the buildings. More gunfire broke out. Russians shot Russians in a panic of self-protection. A sniper on the Kremlin Wall found Balta in his sights.

Putin's bodyguards fell upon the president, moving him toward the mausoleum on their hands and knees. Other guards stormed the Tomb ahead of them. Several limousines pulled up closer to the big bronze doors. Bullets strafed their rooftops for a moment, then the shooting slowed—and ceased entirely.

Hafid was on his knees, blood on his hands. His leg had been shot through. He couldn't stop the flow. Men were crowding into the room. Two of his friends were dead on the floor. Everyone was shouting. But nobody was shooting anymore. Men were staring at him, pointing guns at him, backing away from him.

Where were his other compatriots? *There!*—in the shadows behind him, moving toward the security door, their guns to the heads of two hostages. They were screaming, "*Akhirah! Akhirah!*"

His head cleared, and he struggled to stand. "Get back!" he ordered the soldiers in perfect Russian, one bloody hand upon his belt, the other waving violently before him. "Get back!"

And the Russian guards stepped back, massing nervously at the entrance.

For an instant, Hafid saw Putin's silhouette in the sunlit doorway. The president was kneeling, pistol in hand, grimacing, staring darkly into the mausoleum.

Hafid lurched toward him. He gripped a metal buckle at his belt and pulled. *Heaven or hell?* he wondered.

And then the funerary room was rocked and ripped by fire and glass and stone and a single, sense-shattering roar. Men were blown out the front doors like birdshot from a double-barreled shotgun. The carnage on the inside was ghastly. From the outside, apart from the dead and wounded, the Tomb appeared as always — solid, solemn, still and red — except for the thick black smoke that billowed from its gaping mouth.

In an astounding, swift display of efficiency and force, Russian police and security agents locked down Moscow in a radius of several miles, rounding up every possible witness to the drama of the day.

OMON — the Special Purpose Mobile Unit of the Russian police — was immediately on the streets, under the streets, on the water, in the water. Every building was searched, from basement to rooftop. Within fifteen minutes, everyone found within a half-mile of Red Square was taken into custody.

In four locations around the Square — the State Historical Museum, the GUM Department Store, St. Basil's Cathedral, and St. Nicolas Tower — empty rifle cartridges and rumpled gray jumpsuits were discovered in reclusive corners.

In an attic room at the GUM, the windows were shot to shards from the outside. Bullets had ripped the rafters, and there was blood on the floor.

Near a window in St. Basil's, there was a deflated body mat. It bore a tag in French which read: "*Fabriqué en Chine.*" No one, of course, suspected the French…or the Chinese.

Word of the event was shut down tight. The world would not know what had happened that day until the Kremlin wanted it to know. Putin's protocol.

The blood was washed from the Square, and the mausoleum doors were closed and locked when the sun went down at last.

2
No Safe Place

Friday morning, July 4, Philadelphia.

The City of Brotherly Love was dressed up for one long, hot and muggy Independence Day dance. But I had to work. Today was not just another Fourth of July—it was the day the Peace would be signed. And I, Matt Clifford, mild-mannered columnist for a great metropolitan news agency, had to think about it, blog about it, and sit in front of a camera and talk with others about it. For me, the party would have to wait until quitting time.

I was up at 6:00 for a shower, then a quick Facebook message to Lisa back in Lancaster—a tired habit that was rarely rewarded with a reply. Lisa was—well, I'll tell you more about that girl later.

The rising sun was barely squinting at the waking city when I hit the sidewalk at 6:30, but the day was already warm. A ragged red alley cat was the first living thing to greet me outside my apartment at Broad and Brown. Appearing from behind a row of overflowing trash cans, it pleaded for attention in a quiet, rasping meow. Cats are not my favorite mammal, but for the sake of being neighborly on a national holiday, I told it to have a nice day as I headed on my walk to work.

An early-morning breeze agitated the long, lethargic line of American flags hanging from the streetlights on

Broad. Windows fronting the street were checkered with yellow signs reading "Welcome Home Troops." A tired but determined patriotism had followed the recent ending of the catastrophic conflict in the Middle East.

Thousands of red, white, and blue plastic ribbons fluttered from a web of cable strung above the parking lot at Wilke Suburu, but there were no cars in sight. Wilke's fleet of foreign hybrids was locked safely in a windowless garage across the avenue. After the gas riots, nearly everybody took their vehicles off the streets. With prices hanging around $7.00 a gallon in the city, gasoline siphoning and resale was a profitable business for entrepreneurial gangs. Vehicle vandalism had become a pastime for youth out after curfew.

The youth curfew itself, federally mandated in all urban areas of fifty thousand or more, was an uncomfortable commentary on the state of American life. Gangs were rampant in the cities. Underground militias were growing in rural locations. The president's civilian security force (the National Service Reserve Corps) had been recently formed to bring order to the rising political discontent in America — or perhaps the militias were formed in response to the NSRC. To date, the NSRC had not been involved in any armed conflict, but it was certainly armed. It had legal mandate to seize shotguns and semi-automatic rifles in sixty-five designated American cities. It also had first-grab contracts on all American-made bullets. But the most troubling thing about the NSRC was that it answered to the president — not to the people or the Pentagon.

A block from my apartment, a handful of the poor and the jobless sat on the stone steps of Greater Exodus Baptist Church waiting for the breakfast kitchen to open. Some wore military camouflage — and not because it was the fashion. Our soldiers had come home to a devastated job market and the highest home foreclosure rates in a couple of decades. Philadelphia had more than its share of street vets. Downtown panhandlers and prostitutes were thick as flies on a garbage can. The police were too busy dealing with theft and violence to bother hauling in the beggars and the sidewalk barkers.

At the lonesome corner of Broad and Wallace, Mr. Allesandros methodically swept the walk in front of his Pizza and Grill. He never served breakfast. He was seldom open for lunch anymore. But he washed his windows, watered his walk, and weeded the flower boxes on either side of his awning-covered front door. He wore a black armband. A son or a daughter had not come home from the war. Or perhaps it was the riots. Or an indiscriminate bullet from gang turf crossfire, an overdose of diamond dust during recess, or a knife fight in a bathroom at school. But a crisp, new American flag rippled on a pole above his awning, and a banner behind his barred window read "God Bless America."

He nodded, mouthed a silent "good-morning," and stared past me at a police cruiser idling at the traffic light. Most city workers were still in bed on the 4th of July, resting up for the festivities later in the day, but not the Philadelphia police department. Not with the restless, ripening anarchy that was present on the back streets of our city—in fact, in all the cities of America. Times were tough, and American civilization was not as civil as it used to be. Nor as free.

Early as the morning was, a couple of black kids on bikes bulleted past me on a ride downtown. *Today, at least,* I thought to myself, *kids will have something to do besides play World War Z in the alleys.* The Freedom Festival would kick off at noon with food and music, a children's parade in the afternoon, a full-blown Independence Day parade in the evening, and then Philly's famous fireworks lighting up the night sky over the Museum of Art. For a few hours, community spirit—in a valiant effort to salute the heritage of America's past—would supplant the influence of the flat screen, the smartphone, the PS4...and the streets.

It was a brisk twenty-minute walk from my apartment to the Reading Terminal Market where I stopped in at The Four Seasons Juice Bar for my routine bagel and fresh-squeezed orange juice.

In the market's central seating court, hanging from the wooden rafters, was a large banner depicting American troops alongside the civilian soldiers of the NSRC. In the forefront on the banner was Philadelphia Mayor Brandon Black with city police and firefighters — and a contingent of Philly's new Security Alliance cops. The SA guys were Mideast War vets hired by City Hall as special urban security troops to maintain order in troubled sections of the city. The banner read: *A Safer World. A Safer City. A Safer Future, Now.* Lots of uniforms and badges. Lots of hats and helmets. Lots of guns. Everyone was smiling.

"Don't let them kid you, Matt," I said to myself, aloud. "There's no safe place on earth!"

"We're safer than we were six months ago!" said someone behind me.

I turned, startled, to see the dark and smiling face of Luis Ramirez.

"Hey, Luis!" I said, shaking his outstretched hand. "Today's not Saturday, is it?" I expected to meet Luis the next morning at the Dutch Eating Place, along with Kevin and the rest of the Saturday breakfast bunch.

"No, sir," he laughed. "I'm off work today — but not off duty! Friends and family will be coming over to the house for a Fourth of July picnic. The wife kicked me out of bed and sent me here to buy fresh produce while she starts the rice and beans."

"Wish *I* had the day off," I admitted, "but 'the news never sleeps.' And today is a day ripe with news."

"Hey, you gotta couple of minutes to talk?" Luis asked. "Let me grab a bagel, too! You find us a table, okay?"

I had time to spare — ten or fifteen minutes, then a twenty-minute jaunt to the Philadelphia Bulletin. I wanted to be at work a few minutes early today.

"Gonna be a crazy crowd downtown," Luis said as we settled into a corner of the court. A pair of young SA cops, recognizable in their crimson shirts and black pants, wandered past our table, eyes roving through the court. "The president will be talking live on those big outdoor news screens of yours, no?"

"Yeah. And on every other screen across America," I said, watching the SA guys saunter out of the market with their pistol-packed holsters strapped at their sides. They looked like a couple of gun-toting cowboys striding down a boardwalk in the old West.

"At 6:00 p.m. every major network will be carrying the speech. It's America's birthday—and more. The Peace gets signed today."

"Peace, baby!" Luis flashed the peace sign with one hand while stuffing the bagel into his mouth with the other.

I liked Luis. Mexican. Good sense of humor. A nice guy and a family man. He and his wife and four kids lived on the low scale edge of the upscale Bella Vista neighborhood of Philly. Luis worked for the Philadelphia Port Authority in the shipping yard at Pier 96. Special cargoes. Military vehicles—even tanks and planes. He was a supervisor there. Work hadn't slowed even though the war was done, but it probably would now that we were no longer selling war-wagons to Israel.

"Three dollars and fifty cents just for a bagel!" Luis grumbled. "Do you think prices will go down when the Peace is inked? Will the world economy stabilize? Will we get some relief?"

The Ramirez household lived plainly, frugally, but happily and well.

"No tax relief, anyway! Not while there's a Democrat in the White House," I said, forgetting that Luis was a Democrat. "And it'll be a couple of generations before we're done paying for the war."

The War.

Just six months earlier, on January 2, Israel sent warplanes into Iran to take out hidden plutonium reactors that Tehran was using in its clandestine nuclear weapons program. Almost immediately, in what must have been a pre-determined response to an Israeli attack, Iranian ally Syria launched a three-pronged counterattack on Israel.

Syrian troops near the Golan Heights fired North Korean Scud D missiles into Israel. Some of the missiles carried VX and Sarin nerve agents, spreading sickness and death throughout the Israeli countryside.

Russian-made MiGs took off from Syrian air bases to engage the Israeli warplanes. Within minutes, Syrian jets entered Israeli airspace heading toward Israeli cities and military installations with a mixed payload of missiles and bombs.

On the ground in the Gaza Strip, a large coalition of Hamas and Hezbollah jihadists crossed into Israel and headed for southern Israeli population centers.

In rapid response, Israeli troops moved in three directions. Some secured the West Bank, some headed toward Gaza, and others ascended the Golan Heights. Israeli planes took to the air to engage enemy MiGs and to hammer military sites in Gaza, Lebanon, and Syria.

Within an hour of the opened conflict, Iranian airpower joined the battle in a big way. The rest of us ducked under our desks and watched the warfare on TV and the Internet.

"When the war began, I wouldn't let the kids watch it on TV," said Luis. "They thought it was a reality show, and the wife said to them, 'It *is* reality, children, but it is *not* a show. It is happening right now, and people are being hurt. Children like you are dying. You must pray for the children who live where there is war.' We turned off the TV and prayed. I told the kids, 'The TV is off now, but war is still going on.' And they asked me if the war stopped for the commercials." Luis stared at the floor in front of us. "I didn't know if I should laugh or cry—so I laughed first, and then I cried."

"It's my job to watch what's going on around the world and write about it," I said, "But when I saw those nuclear mushroom clouds rising over Israel, I—"

"I know what you mean, Matt. We thought the world was coming to an end."

History will never accuse Iran of empty rhetoric against Israel. Former Iranian president Mahmud Ahmadinejad spent most of his term declaring the Jewish nation a "disgraceful blot on the face of the Islamic world that will be soon be wiped off the face of the map." To back up those words, and in abject defiance of a treaty Iran had recently signed in Geneva, Ahmadinejad's successors clobbered Israel with the Iranian nuclear fist that the whole world had been fearing.

Israel struck back with an atomic punch of its own, and the Middle East erupted in the planet's first nuclear war.

Cities disappeared in rubble and ash, and the international outcry was a howl and a groan heard in the heavens. The fear of widespread annihilation, and the immediate international call for a nuclear ceasefire, produced a momentary lull in the hostilities. But the lust for war and vengeance could not be quenched by either humanitarian prayers or diplomatic pleas.

Though the nukes stayed in their silos after that, the war accelerated with shocking intensity. Many Arab nations joined their brethren against Israel, while the armed forces of the United Nations, the European Union, and the United States—already present in the region—rose up in support of the Jewish state. Europe mobilized its armies in numbers not seen since World War II, and the United States packed its ships full of men and machines and plowed the seas toward the Middle East. One week into the war, rival forces were fighting on the ground in Israel and in nine Arab nations. I had a very good friend and colleague, Jack Pascov, on the ground in Israel, too. I worried about him the whole time.

"Your buddy in Israel," Luis said. "Pascov. He's going to be there where the Peace is signed, no?"

"He'd like to be. But the Peace will be signed in Brussels, and Jack's in Jerusalem."

"We watch him on TV. Watched him during the war — after the kids were in bed. The wife likes him. He's a New Jersey boy, ain't he? Him and that cameraman of his, Siggy Roose. I thought they were coming home after the war."

"I wish they had," I said. "But they'll be in Israel for another year. Jack's one of our best reporters, and the Peace will be news for a long time over there."

"Where is Brussels? I can't see it on the map in my head."

"Belgium. It's the capital city of Belgium, on the northern border of France. It's also the *de facto* capital of the European Union."

"God bless the European Union!" said Luis, putting his hand over his heart, and rolling his eyes. "Savior of the world, right?"

During the first week of the war, Uzbekistan, Kazakhstan, and Russia massed at their borders but stayed out of the fracas. China squinted, smiled, and polished its prized arsenal. Pakistani troops moved into Afghanistan in support of the US and the EU. In Pakistan itself, the world's sixth largest army hunkered down and pointed its guns, and its own nuclear warheads, in every direction.

In the midst of all the blood and fire, little Israel launched such a tactical, strategic, and power-packed counteroffensive that the Arab world was rocked on its heels. A series of unlikely battles put Israel and its allies at such an advantage that Syria sued for peace. Egypt had barely entered the fray when its forces were pounded to submission in the Sinai. Lebanon surrendered a few weeks later. This was in the third week of January.

"Crazy how that war went down," Luis commented. "Underdog Israel kicks butt again!"

"With a little help from its friends."

"God was on their side," Luis said emphatically, wagging a pointed finger toward the ceiling. "Father, Son, *and* Holy Ghost!"

"Yeah, maybe," I said. But I'd been thinking of a different trinity: the UN, the EU, and the US of A.

Iraqi forces, which had headed toward Israel with Iran's armies, found themselves increasingly pummeled by US airpower. Retreating back within their own borders, Iraqi soldiers encountered civil war against a coalition of Kurdish Iraqis, rebel Turks, and European Union forces. Iranian soldiers fled to Iran, leaving the Iraqis to their fate.

The rest of that month was relatively quiet, except for isolated skirmishes at the Iraq/Iran border. Even the voice of Al Qaeda front man Ahmed al-Farid—whose videotaped messages had been a constant call for *jihad* throughout the conflict—fell strangely silent. Surrounded by its enemies, Iran mobilized for national defense.

"Well," said Luis, draining his coffee cup with a prolonged slurp, "I'm trusting God to keep my kids outa harm's way, and I'm praying for everybody else's, too."

"Maybe the Philadelphia School District should distribute bulletproof T-shirts to its students," I suggested flippantly. "Or does Common Core only pay for condoms and hall cops?"

In the cold first weeks of February, a crack Italian army, supported by EU airpower, moved out of Iraq and across

Iran under the on-the-field leadership of General Marco Romano. At the same time, US and Afghani forces entered Iran from the east. Fighting their way toward a strategic rendezvous near the Caspian Sea, the allied armies met up outside Tehran and forced the surrender of the Iranian government. While the Iranian president was driving to the surrender site to meet with Romano, his convoy was ambushed by embittered soldiers of his own army. He died in a hail of automatic weapons fire. Grand Ayatollah Ali Mahmoud, the aged Islamic leader of Iran, was riding in a car behind the president. He died the same way.

"Bulletproof T-shirts!" Luis chuckled. "You don't need bulletproof shirts when you've got hall cops—and mall cops." He grinned, cocking his head in the direction of a young SA officer coming from the restroom, tucking in his shirt.

"Who's watching the halls while the cops take a leak?" I quipped.

The man shifted his holster as he walked. I thought about Romano.

In response to Israeli intelligence reports, Romano had pressed northward into Turkmenistan with a small and unsupported contingent of Italian special forces in pursuit of Al Quaida mastermind, Ahmed al-Farid. He tracked him down, fought a small-arms battle against his guard, captured him, and personally executed him! The terrorist chief's last moments were filmed in color and broadcast live via satellite. Al-Farid's blood ran red across the globe.

The demise of Ahmed al-Farid at the hands of an Italian military commander did more to demoralize the Muslim war effort than anything else that had happened on the battlefield. It was as if Mohammed himself had been killed. Though Osama Bin Laden had once been the face of Al Quaida, al-Farid had always been its brains. When the whole world saw those brains being blown to kingdom come, the enemies of Israel suddenly felt the effect of their combined wounds. White flags went up everywhere. Only the most dedicated terrorist enclaves continued to fight, and they were soon squashed.

Though smoke continued to rise into the grey skies over the Middle East and cold ashes fell for weeks upon the waters of the Persian Gulf, the Black Sea, and the crystal blue Mediterranean—the war was done.

"At least now we don't have to worry about our youth fighting and dying in a desert across the world," said Luis, swallowing his last bite.

"That's right," I said. "They can die right here at home. In school, on the sidewalk, at the park—"

"You're kind of negative today, Matt," Luis said sharply, soberly.

"I'm sorry, Luis. Sarcasm is a second language for political columnists. And, honestly, I have to say I'm not looking for anything positive from Washington just because of the Peace."

From the day the fighting ended, nearly four months passed while the final covenant of peace was negotiated by the nations that had been at war.

NATO was largely disbanded, with most of our European allies committing military allegiance to the politically ascendant European Union. EU forces were distributed heavily throughout the war-torn region as a peace-keeping presence. Under pressure from a war-weary America, President Clay pulled most of our troops out of the Middle East.

"At least our soldiers are home," Luis repeated.

"Yes." I nodded. "And I'm very glad of that. I'm just as glad that most of the world's nukes are now on the scrap heap."

Nuclear disarmament was at the top of the Peace agenda, especially for the principal warring nations of the Middle East. Syria and Iran destroyed their missile stockpiles, and Israel put a hold on warhead production. But the disarmament was wider. Pakistan shut down its nuclear-arms facilities. China forced a nuclear moratorium upon North Korea after petulant Communist dictator Kim Jong-un turned a deaf ear to disarmament.

Russia guarded its own atomic storehouse—nobody could tell Putin what to do with his guns and bullets. China and the US kept their holsters on. The EU weighed its options.

"Did you know my American grandfather was in the crew on the Enola Gay?" Luis asked.

The Enola Gay. The aircraft that loosed the first atomic bomb over the Japanese city of Hiroshima on August 6, 1946. Three days later the US dropped a second atom bomb on the city of Nagasaki. Terrorized, demoralized, Japan surrendered at last. World War II was over.

"You never told me," I said.

"Yeah," Luis said. "He was in that plane when the bomb went down. He wouldn't talk about it. But he had books with pictures. In his last years, he sat with those books in his lap—and cried."

I had been looking at old pictures of Hiroshima recently, comparing them with the horrifying images from the bomb-obliterated cities of the Middle East. I cried, too.

In the defeated Mideast lands, interim governments over-seen by Israel, the United States, and the European Union struggled to create a stable infrastructure in the region. Islamic nationalists were by no means dispersed, but they had bowed, submitted, and were going along with the program for peace.

The Saudi Kingdom was politically divided. The war

had increased Islamic solidarity among the masses while driving the elitist government more fully into alliance with western interests.

At least nobody was shooting at anybody anymore, oil production was back in boom, and the worst of the world's dictators were defeated or dead.

"Hirohito," Luis said, "was emperor in Japan during World War Two. His air force bombed Pearl Harbor. Hitler was dictator in Germany. Mussolini in Italy. Stalin in the Soviet Union. Evil men. That war was fueled by evil men. Demon-possessed men, I think. Hitler especially."

"Demon possessed? I don't know about that."

"Then how about deluded, inhuman, barbaric?"

"Yeah, I'm with you on that! And I'm afraid such men haven't gone out of supply in our own day, Luis," I said. *Gökhan Savas, for one.*

In Muslim Turkey, the fanatical religious mystic Savas ruled, and a deep anti-Semitism simmered. But Turkey held itself leashed by its desire to be part of the larger European community. During the recent war, Turkey maintained a strained military neutrality, partly because of traditional friendship with Israel and the United States, but mainly because NATO and EU forces were firmly entrenched in bases on Turkey's soil. When the war ended, Turkey's restraint and its long-time lobby to join the European Union were rewarded with EU membership. The Muslim country immediately quit NATO to warm a seat in Brussels.

From Brussels, nations were already working with one another to rise from the ashes of atomic war. This was more than a matter of burying the dead, bulldozing the rubble, and holding a barn raising. Whole cities, incinerated by nuclear strikes, were in the genesis of a decontamination process that would last for decades. Entire provinces were condemned and quarantined.

In the midst of it all, peace talks were complex but continual. Israel and the European Union were especially committed to a solid, clear, and practical plan that could be fully implemented—and enforced—by a league of the free and democratic nations of the world.

The United Nations—for generations an entity of international influence and power—had disintegrated internally, supplanted by the growing political leverage of a United Europe. It still held session, but it had no clout.

The United States was just plain tired—not to mention flat broke.

"The world's still full of loonies," Luis agreed.

"And our country doesn't have the money to fund an army if we have to fight any more loonies," I added.

"At least the new and improved Affordable Healthcare Act has got our kids covered in case they get sick or need a tooth pulled."

"You're joking, aren't you?" I asked.

"I wish I weren't." He smiled sadly.

In America, though domestic fuel production was back up and alternative fuel sources were growing in use, the cost of living continued to rise. Americans emptied their wallets at the gas pump and the grocery store, and broke their budgets staying warm that winter. President Clay blamed it on the cost of the War and pledged to fix the bank. But he couldn't because the bank was no longer run by hometown folks. The financial stability of America was tied to the political advantage of nations around the world—nations not at all interested in putting America back on its feet. And Clay remained more committed to an international financial solution than to a uniquely American economic comeback.

Social Security? Shot!

Inflation? Out of control.

In some parts of the country, folks were minting their

own coins out of silver. Communities were experimenting with creative bank and barter systems.

Unemployment was epidemic. Decorated war heroes worked at McDonald's. Unemployed teenagers wandered the streets. Gang violence and drug-related murder increased. There were tax riots, then gasoline riots. But that didn't stop Americans from buying new toys, going to the movies, eating out, piling up debt and—worst of all—reelecting the same bankrupt-brained legislators.

And, of course, there was the drought. Three years and counting in New Mexico, but bad all over the American west. Fires had devastated six thousand square miles of western forest, as far up as Alaska and throughout Canada. Other places in the world were just as dry—southern Africa, the Middle East, Central Europe, and a vast expanse of Russia's north.

Rain fell at sea, in the mountains of Brazil, in the jungles of Central America, in the southeastern United States, and in a deluge in northern Colorado, but seldom where it was needed the most. It was a thirsty planet. With the bread-basket of the world hoarding its crumbs, it was a hungry planet, too.

Would a peace treaty in the Middle East make a difference here at home? Everybody hoped so.

In the past few weeks, all the major Middle East states, along with the European Union and the United States—China and Russia watching at the table—had been huddling night and day to hammer out a final, comprehensive plan. And that plan was set for signing on the morning of the 4th of July.

"So why," Luis asked, "do you think they picked today?"

"I don't know," I said. "But I wish it weren't today. America needs to remember America. My grandfather used to say, 'Don't remove the ancient landmark.'"

"That's from the Bible," Luis commented.

"In there somewhere," I agreed.

"What's it mean?"

"I don't know. Some Jewish tradition, I guess. What Grandpa meant was that the past matters — history matters. We need to know it and talk about it and learn from it. He always said that 'those who can't remember the past are condemned to repeat it.' That's a quote from Edmund Burke or George Santayana — maybe both."

"Who?"

"A couple of philosophers. Eggheads, like…like news columnists."

"Eggheads!" Luis laughed, then quickly became serious again. "And how about the gas riots? Are they really over?"

They were recent. They were violent. They were on everyone's mind.

"The price has come down," I said.

"Topped ten dollars a gallon before the riots!"

"I'm glad we don't live in New York."

The riots started in Manhattan, then spread to other cities — Philly included. Gas stations were bombed, taxis and buses were vandalized. When a taxi-driver was pulled from his vehicle and beaten half to death outside Radio City Music Hall, Yellow Cab issued handguns to its drivers and the newly formed Metropolitan Security — made up largely of Mideast vets, like Philly's Security Alliance — began to patrol the city. Neighborhood citizen militias took to the streets against the gangs and the drug posses.

When Clay ordered federal troops to the city, the Big Apple resembled an urban army encampment. Thousands of arrests were made within a couple of weeks. A ground swell of citizen concern led to a city-wide neighborhood crime-watch coalition. Everyone bought locking gas caps. Garage rentals went through the roof.

"Nobody wants to own no car in New York today," Luis said.

"Unless it's a Renault O2," I added.

"Yeah, no gas to siphon! Not much drug money in compressed air and vegetable oil!"

The president rallied Congress and got on the phone to the Saudis, the United Arab Emirates, the European Union, and the major American oil corporations. Within a week, gas prices plummeted, the violence subsided, the riots stopped, and the nation heaved a massive sigh of relief.

That was a month ago.

Now it was the 4th of July — with reason to party. Whenever Uncle Sam gives us money for our birthday, America parties. It's what we do best. *Eat, drink, and be merry, for tomorrow we die.* Well...let's not talk about the dying.

"So where are you going to watch the fireworks tonight?" I asked.

"My penthouse suite," Luis said. "The wooden deck I built on the roof of my house. I told you about it. It should be condemned, but it's okay if everyone sits in the middle. The wife is afraid of it!"

"Taking the kids to the parade first?"

"Maybe, if supper is over by then and Clay is done with his speech. Hey, you wanna come over after work?"

Work! Lost in my conversation with Luis, I'd forgotten work. It was 8:00. I'd be late to the Bulletin — and with the Peace being ratified this very moment. Boy, would I hear it from the newsroom boss!

Suddenly the Market got very noisy. Just as suddenly it went ghostly silent, except for the amplified voice of popular Bulletin news anchor Jacqui Johnson exclaiming that the Peace had just been signed in the Middle East. Her words echoed loudly over the public address system.

A plasma wall screen flickered on across the court as Jacqui's announcement was replaced by the familiar voice of

my colleague and friend, Jack Paskov, Bulletin correspondent in Jerusalem — live and in color, the Temple Mount
behind him.

"Excuse me, Luis!" I lunged from our bench. "I gotta
go!"

Technically on call from 7:00 a.m. each day, I was in the
habit of turning off my phone on my walk to work. I pulled
it from my pocket, activated the wireless earpiece (in my ear
constantly, except when I shower, sleep, or swim), and
thumbed an auto-call to the Bulletin. As it rang on the other
end, I hurried out the Market door.

On my sprint to the Bulletin, people were bunched
around Bulletin Boards wherever there were Boards to
bunch around. The Bulletin had its hi-tech Boards all over
the city — at bus stops, in subway stations, and on the walls
of private businesses that receive special ad rates in return. I
wanted to stop and watch, but I had to get to work ASAP! I
could tap into the broadcast through my phone, but I
needed to talk with the newsroom first.

My call connected.

"Matt! Where are ya? I've been callin' and textin' and
hollerin' out the window for ya for the past half hour!"
shouted Keith Sutton, captain of the Bulletin newsroom
command center. Brooklyn accent, loud and clear — he
sounded more concerned than angry. We were lucky to
have this ancient New York Times veteran on the staff.
Competent, compassionate, and firm, he'd had his hands in
the ink since teletypes. But he could find his way around a
website and handle a satellite news conference with the best
of the Gen Zs.

"Sorry, Mr. Sutton!" I meant it. "I'm on my way!"

"Yer in the doghouse, Matt! The biggest story in months!
Ya knew it was comin' — and we needed yer commentary for
the 8:30 news. Yer too late for that! You'll have to edit a
fistful of stories for the print edition by ten o'clock and get

'em online and everywhere else at the same time. We're holdin' up the presses 'til mid-afternoon for late-breakin' news, and we wanna pull together as many op-ed pieces as we can before then. That's on yer slate, too! The big boss is hollerin' for all hands on deck."

We were lucky to have a deck. Most newspapers were spitting out the news from homebound laptops, sending their stories to a central office in cyberspace where editors in scattered locations put it all together without ever seeing each other's faces.

"I'm working up a sweat," I said, "heading west on Chestnut. Wish I was wearing P.F. Flyers. Hope my deodorant holds out!"

"P.F. Flyers! That's funny! Just exactly where are ya?"

"Coming up on the corner of Juniper. I'll be at work in ten minutes if I don't have a coronary."

"A towel and a bottle of mineral water'll be waitin' for ya! You'll have to take care of the armpits yerself. So shut up and run like hell!"

"Wait a minute, Mr. Sutton! Don't hang up! I haven't heard the news—just a bit of Jacqui's lead. Everyone's watching the Boards out here, but I'm running! What's Moscow saying?"

"We've got some stuff from the satellite service," Sutton replied. "Putin's high-fivin' the European Union—believe it or not! Praisin' his 'great friend and comrade' Italian Premiere Romano, and he's thankin' the US of A for steppin' aside and allowin' the peace process to proceed. As if Clay had nuttin' to do wid it! As if he's sittin' in the Oval Office watchin' the Cartoon Network! And since when did we ever see Putin and Romano goin' out to the movies together! More like sharpenin' their knives behind each other's backs! But no news of our own from Moscow, Matt. I know that's what yer askin' for. I'm waitin' on the same thing." He sighed sharply in my ear. "Ain't been able to get in touch with Ali."

"Probably at a Koran chant in the Kruschev Kafé in Red Square."

"Yer a laugh a minute! Ali ain't sleepin' at least—or whatever *you* were doin'! It's 4:36 in the afternoon in Moscow. Our satellite signal must be messed up. 'Atmospheric inconvenience'—or Putin's airwave police. I'd like to send some Irish cops to straighten them guys out. I've got all calls to Ali on auto-redial."

"The White House?"

"Clay's cheerin' the Peace also. He's gonna do an impromtu live holler from the Oval Office this mornin' as well as his scheduled address tonight. That's news."

"I just passed a posse of Orthodox Jews. I think they're break dancing!"

"Paskov was asking for ya. Wants to know if you can fax him a soft pretzel. You two're a pair'a jokers!"

"I'm coming down 15th."

"Michael Reagan dropped in—we got him on video. We're callin' Coulter, Thomas, Prager, Malkin, Gallagher. Tom Rice, too—for the local conservative Catholic spin. Dowd, Hitchens, Stewart, Moyers, Drum. The whole nine yards of 'em. The boss says ya gotta conference 'em all and moderate it. You'll need a gun and a sheriff's badge! That's by noon, remember. We'll have to clone ya! By noon!"

"I'm crossing Sansom, Mr. Sutton. Bunch of kids with firecrackers. Hear them?"

"Holy Hannah! We gotta listen to the crackin' all day and then cover the fireworks tonight! Wish I was in Manhattan on a Monday, drinkin' a beer at Dempsey's!"

"I'm done at 6:30, after Clay's speech. I'll buy you a root beer and we can go watch the fireworks from the Ramirez penthouse."

"Where? Yer done when I say yer done, Mr. Matthew Lyle Clifford! This is Philly on the Fourth, soldier. This is a new Roman holiday. A Jewish Jubilee. Christmas in July. This is the dawnin' of the Age of Aquarius, or somethin'.

This ain't the day for a stroll along Boathouse Row watchin' the bullheads jump!"

"Okay, okay! Can you have a stretcher ready for me at the front door? And forget about the bottle of water. I need a whole bucket—or a fire extinguisher! My feet are burning up. My shoes are about to explode. And I better sign off or I'm not going to have enough breath for the last half block."

"Okay, Matt! Over and out."

I darted across Walnut Street in the midst of the jostling taxis and stepped onto the sidewalk where a crowd was assembled in front of the offices of the Philadelphia Bulletin. People stared upwards in a unified gaze, as if expecting Superman to leap from a window at any moment. Weary from my twelve-block dash, I leaned against a light pole, lifted my eyes, and squinted at the massive video screen that stretched across the building's entire second and third stories. "Philadelphia's Largest Bulletin Board" we called it—and if you ever passed 1500 Walnut Street near Rittenhouse Square, you know the boast (and the pun) was a solid one. It beat the Inquirer's animated ad-board by a couple of dozen yards and about a billion pixels. Israeli technology. Aaron Stein, publisher of the Bulletin, was a Jew with connections.

"PEACE IN THE MIDDLE EAST!" scrolled repeatedly across the top of the screen in bold capital letters. Below the headline, the massive digitized face of Italian premiere Marco Gian Romano silently mouthed the transcribed words that rolled beneath his clean-shaven chin. A political victory speech, live from Jerusalem.

Romano the war hero. Italy's darling. Israel's idol. America's avenger. The man who chased down Ahmed al-Farid—and shot him dead.

Romano the peace prince. Europe's spokesman. President of the influential Council of the European Union. The man who helped engineer the first comprehensive

Middle East peace plan since modern Israel's birth in 1948. And today that plan had been signed by Israel, Turkmenistan, a dozen Arab nations, the European Union, and the United States of America. Nobody wanted more war in the Middle East. Not after the last decade and a half of blood and fire in that haunted region of the world.

Willing my aching legs to move, I pushed my way through the murmuring crowd to the Bulletin's front door — and went inside.

3

The News Never Sleeps

On the second floor of 1500 Walnut Street, the Bulletin newsroom was really many small rooms connected to the main news desk like spokes to a hub. Each room was a news department equipped to collect, collate, and continually release the news to the people of Philadelphia and to anyone who had the various technological toys needed to receive our information anywhere in the world. On-the-spot news came in from our own folks in the field in key locations around the globe. They worked out of their homes or from laptops and tablets while drinking latte at Dunkin' Donuts or eating rice in New Delhi.

The on-site staff of the Bulletin was half of what it was ten years earlier, but we delivered news in more ways than anyone once imagined possible. We had to, or we'd have been out of business like so many other big city newspapers in the cyberspace age.

Our city Bulletin Boards (our pride and joy) provided around-the-clock ads, movie trailers, public service info, entertainment bites, brief commentary on current events, and live breaking news. The same stream of information was available free online and could be accessed almost anywhere.

Every weeknight, tens of thousands of subscribers received a 24-page tabloid print edition of the Evening

Bulletin—a digest of local, national, and international news with general interest columns and a business section. No TV listings, no box scores, no comics (these were now online). Copies of the evening paper were also available in news boxes, newsstands, and private businesses throughout the region.

On Sundays, the Weekend Bulletin was delivered to 150,000 homes. It covered the news in more detail, as well as local and national sports, births, deaths, weddings. We still ran a couple of pages of color comics, an entertainment section, and a good bit of local advertising though our classifieds were online.

A daily top-story e-mailing (called The Bullet) went out to on-line subscribers around the world.

Interest in Israel was high in-house and among our readers, and the Bulletin was noted for its coverage of the Middle East. A large number of our subscribers were Jewish. Many were Zionists. My boss, Aaron Stein, the publisher of the Evening Bulletin, was both an Orthodox Jew and a Zionist. The Bulletin was something of a passion for him. He had deep investments in Israeli tech firms without which I believe the Bulletin would have gone belly-up—at least as a traditional newspaper.

On that 4th of July, we had two employees on the ground in Jerusalem—a reporter and a cameraman. We had three correspondents in the Middle East, one in the Balkans, and one in Russia. Some were Jewish, some Muslim, some Christian, one a self-professed witch. I lost sleep, many a night, worrying about them. No place on earth had been more dangerous than the Middle East in the past six years. Now, at least, the Peace was signed.

I struggled to juggle everything that Sutton threw my way, but I got it done. I spent most of the morning researching and writing a peace perspective for the Weekend. By 11:00 a.m. we still hadn't connected with Ali in Moscow. That was a troubling distraction as I hustled to coordinate the noon conference of national commentators. My head pounded like a drum machine as I refereed the one-hour live political boxing match. Afterwards, I stuffed my face with a cold Philly cheesesteak and faxed a color photo of a soft pretzel to Jack in Jerusalem. Then, worn out, I retreated to the bathroom and sat there for ten minutes worrying about Ali. It was my only break all day.

I read all the top social bloggers. I edited the incoming commentaries of a couple of dozen of the planet's most popular religion and politics editors. I typed up an op-ed digest for pixel and print that we spun into a live video spot to send flying through cyberspace at the same time that the Bulletin rolled out on newsprint at our presses in Upper Darby.

By 5:00 p.m. we all looked like we'd been playing football with the Philadelphia Eagles — except for Sutton. His sleeves were neatly and typically rolled up to his wrinkled elbows. His wide tie was nailed on with that New York Yankees pin that anchored every tie he wore. His thick white hair sat unruffled on his head in a perfect and perpetual Ronald Reagan wave. The sight of him alone refreshed me.

"Paskov on vid-com for ya!"

"And Ali?" I asked.

"Nuttin' yet. But he's all right, kid! I know he is. Don't worry."

Ali Ahkmed Baraki was born in the United States to parents who fled Afghanistan during the Russian invasion of the 1980s. A moderate American Muslim with a passionate interest in the democratic heritage of the west, Ali studied history and journalism at Penn State. We were in the same class, became best friends, and were hired by the Bulletin at the same time a few years after graduation.

As a reporter, Ali quickly made the Bulletin proud with

his diplomatic manner and his intuitive political analysis. When we started at the Bulletin, Ali spoke four languages fluently: Pashtu and Dari (the Afghani languages of his parents' native land), Egyptian Arabic (a dialect widely understood throughout the Middle East because of the popularity of Egyptian films and TV shows), and his own native English.

When the war broke out between Israel and Syria—and then everybody else—Ali was learning conversational Hebrew and begged the Bulletin to send him to the Middle East. We had Pascov on the ground in Jerusalem, so Ali accepted a placement in Moscow instead. Rising to the challenge, he hired a professor from Moscow State University to tutor him in Russian. He quickly became fluent enough to interview officials at the Kremlin. When the war ended and Putin pushed ahead with the Winter Global Games in Sochi (the Rusian Riviera on the Black Sea), Ali took a break from Kremlin politics to cover the international sports event. It was in the last weeks of February—with the daily Global Games broadcast—that America really came to know Ali Ahkmed Baraki.

I walked to the vid-com screen where Jack Pascov stared at me from a small dark room somewhere on the other side of the earth. I recognized the curtained window behind him. He was in his Old Quarter apartment, peering at his desktop computer.

"*Shalom aleichem*, Matthew! What a day! How ya doing?"

"An awful lot to do, but I'm hanging in here. And *aleichem shalom* to you, my friend. Did you get your pretzel?"

"Thanks, yes! But I can't *nosh* on fax paper! Besides, there wasn't enough salt. But good for a chuckle. I needed one. Thanks."

"Have you been to the Golan Heights?" I asked.

"Yes! The Jordan still trickles out of the ground up there. The Peace hasn't shocked it dry, though the drought may.

What is truly shocking is that Israelis and Syrians stand there together. They're still armed, but not pointing their rocket launchers at each other. They'll be turning all military weapons in to EU troops in the next few days. Israel's soldiers are de-arming by regiment, according to a published schedule—the first time they've retired their weapons since 1948. Only the prime minister's guard will retain Israeli arms.

"The matter of private handguns is being negotiated. I have two, myself. One is my grandfather's World War II German Lugar. That's an heirloom. I'll keep it no matter what. Want to see it?" Jack fumbled in a drawer off-screen, but I told him no.

"EU warriors everywhere here," Jack continued, scratching his thin black hair with his thick dark fingers. "They'll be returning to their own countries in pre-determined waves. But a good number are staying, especially in Israel, Syria, and Iran. After all, it's their job now to police the Middle East. Turkey has large numbers in Iraqi Kurdistan. And Italy plans to maintain a garrison on the Heights. Italy's deputy prime minister was up there today, lauding Italy's—and Europe's—golden boy Romano. It seems the Jews finally have true friends in high places."

"The United States has turned over its West Bank headquarters to the EU?" I asked.

"Yes, in a separate agreement. Clay and Romano will meet there one week from now—that's news only five minutes old. You heard it first, *goy!* I'm e-mailing it to the Bulletin at this very moment. You'll hear Sutton holler for Johnson any second."

"Johnson!" bellowed Sutton. "Get the White House on the phone. The president meets with Marco Romano in Israel next Friday! Send the story to the Boards and beat the Inquirer to the punch! Get it online, and we'll beat out the Associated Press!"

"There's a platoon of US Marines still here," Jack said,

"mostly posing for pictures and flashing the peace sign. Fireworks are planned tonight in Gaza, Tel Aviv, Haifa, Kieryat Shmona, Jerusalem, and Eilat by the Red Sea. The mayor of Jerusalem is traveling with the prime minister by helicopter to each city to light each display himself. Hey, you'll be seeing fireworks, too, won't you? Ben Franklin and the Fourth of July, right?"

"Yeah. But the Declaration of Independence has been a bit upstaged by the Declaration of Peace. Romano should have been an advertising mogul! He knows how to play the media to turn the spotlight on himself."

"He's upstaged the president of the European Council in the process. 'Who do I call if I want to call Europe?' Wasn't that Kissinger's question?" Jack asked. "I thought the president of the European Council was the man to call."

"Which president is which? I always wonder," I said. "The EU has so many councils, committees, and presidents! There's the European Council *and* there's the Council of the European Union. And then there's…"

"Von Kappel is president of the former, right? Romano is president of the latter—but that's only a six-month term."

"Von Kappel is supposed to be the voice of the EU, so why is he handing the phone to Romano lately?" I asked.

"Because Romano can talk on the phone and play chess at the same time," Jack quipped.

"Yeah, and right now he's the king, queen, bishop, and knight all rolled up into one."

"So who are the pawns?"

"Good question." I pondered.

"There are rifles stacked against the Wailing Wall," Jack said. "I'm surprised there aren't a few Muslim heads nailed there also, but the Peace seems to be sinking into hearts in a very deep way. Even women are praying at the Wall, and the Orthodox are praying right beside them! Strange day."

"Maybe you can say a prayer for Ali," I interjected. "We haven't been able to get through to him today. Been trying for…" I looked at the clock, "nearly nine hours."

Jack was silent for a moment, and I thought the audio might have gone down. Then he spoke. "I've tried also, but *gornisht*—nothing. It's not normal that all our connections be hampered. No cell phone connect. No land phone. No e-talk. Maybe there's a power outage. Russia isn't so well-wired, you know. And Putin—back on his old throne—likes to play with the switches to let his people know whose big fingers can turn the lights on and off at will. Ali can take care of himself."

"Sutton is waving wildly at me," I said. "I'd better sign off for now."

"Read my report," said Jack. "And e-mail me back when you've had a chance to rest. Don't call me on my cell. The solar battery's too weak. I've got it outside on the window sill soaking up the sun."

"The moon, you mean. It's almost midnight in Jerusalem, isn't it?"

"Yes," Jack laughed wearily. "And I must sleep. *Shalom aleichem*, my friend."

"*Aleichem shalom*."

Sutton held us overtime but let us go half an hour prior to the fireworks. Jacqui and her cameraman were already down at the Art Museum covering the concert and waiting for the big bang. We had everything programmed for a live webcast and an instant feed to the Bulletin Boards. Nobody was needed in the newsroom.

I begged a ride home with a weather intern who had just started with us. It was nearly 9:00 when he dropped me off in front of my apartment. Dusk was settling like a hot, heavy blanket although a cool breeze was rising with the moon. A thin curtain of a cloud—a cloud without rain—drifted in front of it, turning its bright quarter to a shadowed crescent.

A crescent moon! The symbol of Islam. The radical creed of

violence and religious intolerance that George W. Bush once called "a great and peaceful religion." He knew better even then! There are peaceful Muslims, but Islam has never been a peaceful religion. The horrific terrorist assaults on the Pentagon and Manhattan's Twin Towers on September 11, 2001, had been simply one more manifestation of an unholy war that began with the prophet Mohammed and had never ended.

The fundamental, historic doctrines of Mohammed have always moved his followers to violence against the infidels of the world — from the Prophet's massacre of the men of the Jewish tribe of Banu Qurayza in 627, to the brutal nuclear attack on Israeli settlements by Syria and Iran in the most recent war. When mushroom clouds started rising over Israel, Clay stopped calling the war on terror an "Overseas Contingency Operation." He cut off the civil chats with his "Iranian friends" and committed US troops to the battle against Mohammed's warriors.

Even when many of the major Islamic armies of the Middle East were defeated at last, the calls for bloody *jihad* continued to surface from secret terror cells around the world.

But those calls were now faint, weak, and universally disdained. At least that's what we hoped.

Too tired to walk, I took the elevator to the third floor. The apartment felt lonely but welcoming and safe. I plodded methodically toward the television, though the last thing I really wanted was to turn that intrusive thing on. I heard the pop of cheap fireworks somewhere in the neighborhood, and then the boom of the genuine article as the night sky exploded with brilliant colors outside my window. I pulled up the blinds, sank into my couch, and stared in private, thoughtless joy at the million-dollar light show that unfolded like a fantasy above the Philadelphia skyline. The city always had money for a party.

I cheered out loud at the fantastic finale and imagined the sights and sounds of the festive crowd that had begun to wander toward restaurant, nightclub, or home. I wondered what Sutton was doing at the moment. I laughed at the thought of Luis and his children on the roof of his house. Weary and hungry, I headed for my fridge and dug out the leftover lasagna that I'd brought home from the Olive Garden a couple of nights before. I stuck it in the microwave.

Then I heard, for the first time, the quiet tune my MagicMac was humming from the bedroom. A pleasant melody from the 1960s—some silly love song by the Beatles that my dad would recognize. That meant I had e-mail. Maybe Lisa. Probably not.

A ton of spam had escaped the filter. I could never figure how to keep all that junk out. There were exotic cruise offers, now that the war was over. Ads for medicine and cosmetics to improve the shape, size, and quality of every square inch of my body. Health foods that promised a life expectancy longer than anyone has ever lived. There were chances to gamble my wages away at Indian reservations and on fancy riverboats. And local single women were just dying to meet me.

Some real e-mail, too. A couple of notes from my dad. One from my sister. A long-awaited reply to a story I had submitted to a history magazine.

And…a Facebook message from Lisa!

I was hesitant to open it.

I almost deleted it out of sheer, prideful spite. That would have been the epitome of stupidity. Hope for half a year to hear from the girl and then trash her mail before even looking at it!

"Open Lisa Zimmerman," I said, and my MagicMac obeyed. Apple had the voice thing down pat. I was planning to buy a MagicPad next, but that would take a few more paychecks in the bank. Walking to work saved on gas, of course. Maybe the Peace would bring the price back down to $6.00 a gallon. Maybe lower. It cost a fortune just to drive to Lancaster on the weekends. But I hardly made that drive anymore. My car was stored uptown in a friend's garage.

Lisa's message was short. I hovered over every word and read it through four times. Then I went to the bathroom, brushed my teeth, came back to my bedroom…and read it again.

She'd been watching my broadcasts. She was worried about what was going on in the world—worried about "us." Did she mean Lisa and Matt, or did she mean everyone? She wanted answers. And she was asking *me!* I didn't respond immediately (not for a couple of days). I wanted to ponder it, rehearse my thoughts—and get it right. Tired as I was, I lay awake long into the night.

hi matt, she wrote. *saw your forum on my smartphone today. good job. great conference. especially moved by what prager had to say. when he quoted jeremiah ("peace, peace, but there is no peace"), it creeped me out. do u think they're right? do u think the peace won't last? and what will happen to us if it doesn't?*

4

Pancake Seminary

Saturday morning, July 5.

It was good to see Luis two days in a row. For almost a year now, I'd been meeting him every Saturday for breakfast at the Dutch Eating Place in the Reading Terminal Market—best Amish sticky buns in the city! We were usually joined by Kevin McCarthy, Doug O'Malley, and Tryone Bates. Ty didn't show, but the other guys were there. We gathered to eat a great, big, high-cholesterol breakfast...and to hold a Bible study.

I wasn't a charter member of the "pancake seminary" as Kevin dubbed our weekly breakfast gathering. I grew up in a highly churched community with a rich religious heritage (there were over seven hundred Christian congregations in Lancaster County—including the world-famous Amish with their horse-drawn buggies), but my parents never sent us to church. In fact, they never went themselves until I was halfway through college.

I learned some Bible stories at a neighborhood Bible club when I was a kid. I went to a church camp a couple of summers in a row before my teen years. I absorbed the Bible-talk and Bible-think of the Christian sub-culture around me. I hung out with a few church youth groups as a teen, and my belief in God was definitely shaped by those experiences.

I like religious folks. They were my neighbors. Many were my friends—some still are. And I have always been drawn to the person and the character of Jesus. But church? Organized religion? For me, personally, and for many in my generation, "No, thank you."

Inside Lancaster County you grew up thinking that the only true religion is the Christian religion. Most people there thought that was a very good thing—some didn't. There wasn't much room for debate on worldview. You learned to live with it, one way or another.

Outside Lancaster County, it was a different story entirely. You could breathe. You could think. You could drive down the highway without a billboard warning you to "Prepare to meet thy God!" You could turn on the radio and generally *not* hear Michael W. Smith or David Jeremiah or Tony Evans. You could eat at a restaurant and the cashier would *not* tell you to "Have a blessed day." There was no region in Pennsylvania (or anywhere else in America's northeast) so filled with overt Christian influence as Lancaster. That was one of the reasons I got out.

So I wasn't chasing God or seeking the purpose-driven life when I joined the Bible study. I was tricked into it. I was there because a co-worker invited me to breakfast eight months earlier. He didn't tell me I'd be chowing down with a bunch of Jesus freaks from a pocketful of theological camps.

Two months later, he quit his job at the Philadelphia Bulletin to edit a weekend journal in the Poconos. I stayed with the group because the food was good, the conversations were stimulating (inspirational fat for my Bulletin column), and I had begun to call these fellows friends.

For the past couple of weeks, we'd been discussing the book of Revelation. That's the last book of the Bible, and some folks believe it prophetically depicts our planet's grand finale. The basic plot is this: Jesus comes back, whisks all true believers to heaven, then sets his posse loose on the world in a last ditch battle against evil that's so gory that an entire Middle Eastern valley is filled with blood about three feet high. The world has seen a lot of blood over there in these past few years, but never *that* much! Revelation is not a funny story. I don't know what to believe about the book even now—but I don't think it's fiction.

Peace in the Middle East drove our discussion the morning of July 5. We were brain-deep in a lively political debate when our breakfast arrived—homestyle. Stacks of fluffy blueberry pancakes on a big platter, a plate of hot bacon, a steaming bowl of scrambled eggs, and a cold pitcher of organic 2% milk. We thanked our waitress then bowed our heads while Kevin thanked God. I kept my eyes open and fiddled with my fork.

When the prayer was done, I asked, "Does the Bible say anything about the Peace? Is this something that is supposed to happen? Something we're supposed to know about?"

"Peace, peace, but there is no peace," chanted Luis, smiling grimly.

I looked up from my eggs, intrigued. "Did you see my conference yesterday with the religious commentators? Dennis Prager quoted that verse. He was talking about why he thinks the Peace can't last for long."

"Wars and rumors of wars!" Doug slurred, his mouth full of bacon. "Jesus said so. They're getting worse all the time. We gotta have our bags packed 'cause he's coming soon!"

"There have always been wars and rumors of wars," Luis pointed out, reaching over Doug's plate for the pancake syrup. Real maple syrup, in a small pitcher, steaming hot.

"But never wars like now," Doug insisted. "Never with nukes flying back and forth!"

"I agree," Kevin said.

Kevin isn't pushy with his thoughts, but I could see he was itching to tell us something.

"I think we're closer to the end than any of us thought," Kevin said. "I think what happened yesterday was a specific fulfillment of prophecy. Daniel 9:27, first half of the verse, says that the Antichrist will make a covenant 'with many' — including Jerusalem — and there'll be peace. But the peace is not a real peace…not a lasting peace. Jesus said wars would continue, and that we're not to let anyone mislead us into thinking that someone has come in his name."

"Who's coming in his name?" Doug put down his fork and turned to face Kevin.

"The Antichrist!" Kevin said.

In spite of my skepticism, a slideshow of potential antichrists passed through my imagination — public figures, men and women, power players in the world of politics and religion.

"Right now?" Luis asked.

Kevin nodded.

"No way!" Doug challenged.

"How could the Antichrist mislead God's people?" Luis asked.

"He's slick," Kevin said, "and we're thick."

I prodded a pancake with my knife, glancing from Kevin to Doug.

"God's people won't be misled!" Doug insisted gruffly. "They won't even be around when the Antichrist shows up. The Antichrist can't come until the rapture of the church. All true believers will be gone from this hell-hole and watching the show from box seats in heaven by the time that dude comes on the scene!"

"Chill, bro!" Luis tapped Doug's arm with a friendly fist. "Kev is entitled to his opinion."

My curiosity was up. I ventured another question. "Who do you think the Antichrist will be, Kevin?"

"I think we saw him on TV yesterday when the Peace

was announced," he answered quietly. "I think the First Seal of Revelation has been opened—broadcast live from Jerusalem, announced live from Brussels—right before our eyes."

"Romano?" I coughed, unbelieving.

"No, sir! Nuh-uh! Can't be! He's the best friend Israel's had in decades!" Doug said, frowning darkly. He shoved himself to his feet, agitated and angry, then headed for the bathroom. In spite of the fact that our reason for meeting was to talk about these very things, we changed the subject to insure "the peace."

5

An Unparalleled Peace

Friday morning, July 11.

A week had passed with no word from Ali. The American Embassy in Moscow could tell us nothing. These were dangerous times and Moscow was a dangerous place, but why was there no news of Ali at all? I thought of him often, but the busywork of each busy day sometimes pushed him to the back of my mind.

There were other dangerous places in the world. Jerusalem was one of them.

My Jewish friend's square-jawed face was front-and-center on the screen, his dark, steady eyes pulling on the viewer as he spoke: "Philadelphia Bulletin correspondent Jack Paskov, live from the West Bank, Israel. Welcome to history in the making."

The scene shifted to a cluster of world dignitaries standing in front of a stately stone edifice. A brisk wind tugged at a few hats, as the camera rose to capture the poignant sight of an American flag dancing energetically upon a pole above the assembly.

"Good shot!" Sutton exclaimed. "Great shot! Who's on that camera over there?"

"It's Siggy," I said.

Most of the Bulletin's day staff was packed tightly into the news hub watching Jack on the main screen vid-com.

Someone started whistling the "Star Spangled Banner." Others joined in until Sutton howled, "Cut the orchestra!"

"One week ago, on Independence Day, the Peace we all have longed for was finally signed," Jack announced. His chiseled Semetic countenance and his clear, clipped English communicated the import of the event. "Today, the Commander in Chief of the American Armed Forces is turning over America's strategic West Bank headquarters — and its four military camps in the southern Israeli desert of the Negev — to the combined military forces of the European Union."

Jack held up a large pewter key. "Israel's head of state Amnon Katz, as landlord for the American holdings, will receive a set of keys from United States President Sanderson Dawud Clay, signifying the return of the properties to Israel. Prime Minister Katz will in turn present the keys to Italian Premiere Marco Gian Romano, who, as the current President of the Council of the European Union, represents the EU in this transaction."

Siggy's camera panned the three national leaders.

Amnon Katz — short, trim, solid and sound at eighty-six years — stood between Clay and Romano, both at least a half-foot taller than the spry Jewish leader. Though dressed in the camouflage khaki of an Israeli infantryman, Katz had never personally carried a gun in war. But at age twenty-nine, he held the position of Israel's Director-General of the Ministry of Defense and later helped develop Israel's atom bomb. Upon his head this morning, tilted over bushy grey eyebrows, sat a 1947 Hitelmacher hat — an army cap that had seen action (on someone else's head) during Israel's War of Independence nearly seventy years earlier.

To the right of Katz was Marco Romano, also dressed in military attire, his towering form erect and still as a statue, his bald head white and as round as a helmet. He wore the uniform, stripes, and medals of a much-decorated hero and Commander of the Italian Army. The clothes were not borrowed—they were his own, and they fit him well.

To the left of Katz, the straight, slim figure of Sanderson Clay stood in dark contrast to the white-washed stone of the building behind him. Wearing a crisp white shirt, red tie, black pants, and coat, Clay fisted a set of oversized silver keys in his left hand. The keys matched the highlights in the short-cropped head of hair that had been jet black only a few years earlier. Though Commander in Chief of America's military, Clay was the only leader in the day's lineup who had not served in his nation's military. Six feet two in his shiny black shoes, he was almost as tall as Romano. The Italian and the American looked like two pillars—one dark, one light—on either side of the Israeli statesman.

A full-front shot from our camera highlighted the somber visage of America's second black president. There was Caucasian blood in the man as well—and Arab blood, as his middle name attested, which gave him credence in the Middle East that few other American presidents have had. The world had come to know him as a man committed to international peace, a man committed to the good of all races, all nations—a "global president."

"Our world is weary of war," the president declared, "but it stands up tall on tired legs to cheer the Peace!" A wireless microphone programmed to an on-site public address system made his voice boom like a football referee calling a penalty.

The president continued, with the practiced oratory that had won him a presidential election and a Nobel Peace Prize. He talked about America's long, hard fight, beside our friends and allies, to defeat the terroristic nations that had plunged the Middle East into world war.

He talked about a new democratic beginning for the conquered lands now overseen by the free nations of the world.

He announced a coalition of Middle Eastern states committed to rebuilding the region. Arab oil money, Israeli solar technology, and advances in desalination would turn the salt waters of the Middle East into fresh water and transform that drought-parched, war-torn region into a land flowing with milk and honey.

"We have entered a new covenant—a covenant of demilitarization and peace," the president declared, turning to face Katz. "Mr. President," he said, "Israel and the United States have fought side-by-side in the past few years, heroically and selflessly, sometimes offering the ultimate sacrifice for one another. Now the Peace has come. America's soldiers have gone home. But our hearts are with you always. Our blood has mingled with yours and with that of our common allies," he gestured open-handedly toward Romano, "to further hallow this oft-hallowed ground."

"This is a reg'lar Gettysburg address!" Sutton said. "Hey, Ernie!" he shouted to our graphics man. "Work up a patriotic border and slap this speech inside it on a full page for the Weekend! Put it in the color section, after the comics. And tag it on page one."

"On behalf of the American people," Clay said, leaning his head toward the Israeli leader, "I thank you for all that Israel has provided for the military readiness and safety of our troops in this great conflict. I return to you the keys to our command posts and our camps. I trust they will not soon be needed in war again."

Clay handed the keys to Katz. As he did, a lone bugler played Taps while a quartet of United States Marines began lowering the American flag.

"AN UNPARALLED PEACE!" That was the Bulletin's headline that evening in print, online, and on our Boards.

For the first time since its inception as a modern nation, Israel lay down its arms in a unilateral regional demilitarization process. Many Israelis were against the dismantling of their national defenses and their nuclear arsenal, but the rest of the free world insisted upon it. Israel's most powerful enemies were defeated. And the planet's ascendant military force, the European Union, was committed by treaty to keeping the peace in the Middle East—and uniquely committed to the defense of Israel.

"I'm not confident that the EU can do it," Stein stated frankly at the end of Jack's broadcast. "But I'm praying that it can."

The newsroom was all but empty. On Fridays, most folks left at 5:00 on the nose. Sutton had said his good-night to me about fifteen minutes earlier. Jacqui was laboring in her department alone. She often stuck around to straighten up her desk and script her openers for the next day's newscast. I had hung around to check out some leads on the Internet and to talk with Pascov later on sat-com. An energetic maintenance man was mopping floors and singing songs in Spanish.

I saw the light go out at Jacqui's desk. I heard her sigh. A moment passed, and she stood behind me. I felt a hand resting on the back of my chair.

"Later than usual, aren't you, Matt?" A quiet question.

I swiveled carelessly and almost collided with her—she was standing that close.

"Sorry," we said simultaneously, and she stepped back. She wore a tired smile, but it looked good on her. A sadness in her eyes drew me, held me.

Jacqui Johnson was by far the most public face of the Bulletin. Our main TV anchor, she was young, single, smart, pretty—a natural brunette with a fading Virginia accent and a smile that invited love at first sight. I had a minor crush on her a dozen times in the two years we'd worked together. I took her out to dinner once and followed her home like a hungry puppy, but we parted at the door. I'd had dreams and visions ever since.

Still, Lisa always trumped her in my heart. But, why? I

had begun to ask that question of myself. After all, Lisa barely acknowledged my existence anymore, while Jacqui leaned over the fence to be friendly.

"I'm waiting for Jack to get home so we can go face-to-face on sat-com," I explained. "He eats late on Friday, then gets with a bunch of other news stringers. A night owl, you know. Doesn't get back to his apartment 'til midnight. That's just about now over there."

"Oh." She smiled wearily. "Well, say hi to him for me."

"I will." I returned her smile, rather self-consciously. It probably looked just as weary.

She turned away, hesitated, then turned back. "He'll be okay, won't he, Matt?"

"Jack?"

"Ali," she said, a tremor on her lips. "It's been a week."

I nodded slowly, leaning toward her. It had been nine days, actually, since I had contact with him. E-mail on the 2nd. Nothing since.

"I'm sorry," she said.

"You don't need to be sorry..."

"Sorry for you," she explained. "You care about him so much. The two of you—best friends. And we don't even know where he is. His wife didn't want him over there to begin with. Five kids, wondering why their daddy doesn't call home. I'm...I'm sorry." Her eyes held a question but looked sad enough to cry.

It surprised me, this empathetic moment. Clever, sarcastic remarks were more the norm for Jacqui Johnson. She flirted. She joked around. She made light of things in a way that made a person think, but she seldom bared her soul. She was professionally passionate about human needs in her casting of the news, but this was a far more personal disclosure.

"Thank you, Jacqui," I said, dropping my eyes to avoid hers. "Yeah, it's hard," I admitted, relieved to be able to say so to someone else who knew Ali. Someone who cared.

"I think about him," she said. "I think about his family."

I looked up, attempting an optimism that I couldn't feel. "Well, we're searching for him. I'm sure he's okay. I think I'd know it if he wasn't. Do you know what I mean?"

Hope lit her face. She nodded, and with that sad, tired smile she said, "Yes, I know what you mean."

A silence held us as our eyes held one another. My turn to talk, but my mind went blank, my tongue dumb. Jacqui waited for me patiently. "Good-night, Matt," she said at last, backing out of the room. "I'll see you Monday."

I watched her walk away—watched her leave the office and close the door quietly behind her. I wondered how it was that I had worked with her for all this time and yet I hardly knew her.

I had Jack on two-way. He was back at his place in the Old Quarter.

"It's always good watching you work, Jack," I said. "Great job today. Tell Siggy that he handles that camera like an artist. Seeing our flag come down, Sutton had tears in his eyes."

"It's not about the job, Matthew," he replied. "It's about the news. We have to tell it while it's happening. We're all part of it, you know. And the world turns faster than it used to."

"We still have no news from Ali."

"*Zeh loh tov!*" Jack spat. "That's not good!"

I stared at Jack across the miles. He stared at me.

"I'm very worried," I said. "Even Sutton is grim about it. The American Embassy in Moscow can't find him. Something is happening over there. The foreign press has been shut out of the meetings of the Russian legislature. Putin is on Channel One, the state-owned TV station, talking every day about Russian solidarity and threatening reprisal against subversive elements in the state. But no one has seen him publicly for over a week. The tabloids say that his TV image is old footage. The political pundits say he's brewing some kind of power-play or military action. But what? Why? Where? And what's happened to Ali?"

"*Oy, a klug!*" Jack sighed. "That means 'Woe!' The Hebrew prophet Jeremiah said that a lot. But you know that. You're a Bible man, aren't you?"

"It's my job. But," I added, "my dad's the real Bible man. And my friends, Kevin and Luis—you've met Kevin. I've not read much of the Old Testament, your Torah."

"Nor have I," Jack laughed. "My grandmother used to call me a *shaigetz ainer!* That was her rebuke for all irreligious Jewish boys."

"The Yiddish version of backslider?" I mused. "I know one thing, though—Jeremiah was also the dude who said, 'Peace, peace! But there is no peace.'"

"*Feh!* It all stinks! We have peace in one place and holocaust in another. Bright lights in the kitchen, shadows in the hall. I've been talking to a friend, an Israeli newsman in the Russian town of Gubkin, five hundred kilometers south of Moscow, on the Oskolets River."

"Five hundred kilometers?" I don't know my metric.

"That's about three hundred miles, maybe a little more. Anyway, this guy in Gubkin says they won't let him out of town. Foreign jounalists all over Russia are being restricted from traveling. So my friend gets free room and board at Hotel Ruda. He can watch TV, play cards, fish in the Oskolets. But stuck in Gubkin! He is, however, in touch with some peers in Moscow. Not Ali, but some other international guys—CTV, Univision, Omni, BBC—they've got cell phones. Something's going to break soon. The government is promising hard news and a longer leash for the foreign press."

"Does your friend know Bradley Wall?" I asked.

"The FOX News guy?"

"Yeah. Wall's a digger and a muckraker. Ali calls him Sleuth. A microphone in his wedding ring, camera in his tie tack, that sort of guy. Intuitive, awake. Guts, good looks, and good luck. He found his way through Kazakhstan, Uzbekistan, and Turkmenistan to the Iranian border right after Israel hit Iran back with the nukes. Iranians fled to Turkmenistan in droves.

"Wall interviewed refugees—soldiers, politicians, farmers, and imams. Recorded and filmed them. Sent the stories to FOX via satellite. Then he got out, back across the Stans to Moscow where he landed an audience with Putin himself. The only interview Putin gave during the war!

"Wall's a friend of Ali's. If anyone can dig up what's happening with Ali, he can. I have no way to get a hold of Wall myself. FOX won't connect us—professional conflict of interest or some such baloney! I've tried everything from my end. Asked the embassy in Moscow to put him in touch with us if they can, but nothing so far.

"Can you check with your guy in Gubkin? Have him contact Wall if he can. And see what Wall can find out about Ali."

"I'm on it, Matthew, as soon as we say good-night."

"Don't you mean *shalom*?"

"Yes," said Jack, and I could see his weary grin in the dim light of his apartment. "I do mean *shalom*."

I had messaged Lisa twice that week. Once on Monday and again on Thursday, but no reply. It was Friday now, a week since she'd e-mailed me on the 4th. What was wrong with the girl? Or was it me?

I read my messages to her over and over and argued with myself about every phrase that she might have misconstrued. But really, I'd been very careful.

I thanked her for her kind words. I sympathized with her feelings about the days we lived in. I briefly shared my thoughts about the Peace and about the social and political situation in America and elsewhere in the world. I said I didn't think that any peace could last forever. But maybe it would last a good long while. I didn't know how to answer her question about what would happen if the Peace failed soon.

I thought of writing down some thoughts that the Bible study guys had discussed, but I didn't want to start talking about God with her. That was one door I wanted to leave closed. So I simply said, "I don't know." And maybe that's why she didn't reply. Maybe M.L. Clifford — the fast-talking, big-city newspaper answer man — had let her down again. Good for clever news copy and smart-aleck commentary, no good for coming alongside a friend in real life and for offering the answers that *really* count. For Lisa, it was all about the God-answers.

6

Sherlock Sheetrock

Saturday morning, July 12.

It was a pancake seminary morning, but I slept in with the blinds shut and the curtains drawn. The morning sun stayed outside where it belonged. It was 9:00 a.m when my MagicMac alarm woke me to the rolling guitar intro of one of my dad's favorite classic rock songs, "Sweet Home Alabama." I lay there listening. Southern rock is an art form.

I felt bad about missing breakfast with Kevin and the guys, but I had Ali on my mind. I didn't feel patient or pious enough for pancakes or platitudes. Cornflakes and the morning news would have to do me.

I reached for my phone and slipped the wireless on my ear while bustling out of bed. One voice mail. It was Jack.

"*Boker tov*, Matthew."

"Good-morning to you, too, Jack," I said to the recording.

"Check your e-mail, *goy!*" the message continued. "My man in Gubkin says you should have a note from Wall in Moscow. Nothing solid on Ali, I'm sorry to report, but Wall has promised to dig. You can take it from here. Keep me posted. *Shalom!*"

There was nothing in my in-box but spam. And my spam box was crammed with crap. Sometimes real mail gets sidelined there, but if Wall didn't use his own name on his e-mail address, how would I sort out the wheat from the chaff? No Wall. No Bradley. Nothing in Russian. Nothing that hinted of Russia. No "fox"—no clever wordplay on animals of any kind. I figured I'd better open everything that was not an obvious Trojan horse.

Wu Yi Tea for sale. Great rates on re-financed mortgages. Free tuition to a culinary school in Oregon. Karate lessons online. How about a career in fashion design? This was ridiculous!

I laughed out loud when I saw an untitled piece from a source named Sherlock Sheetrock. Then I caught myself. The Sleuth! Wall!

When I opened it, the e-mail address read info@ mercurymail.com. Its message was nothing but a text-garbled link. I grit my teeth, clicked, and opened to a secure site with a blank mail form and a send button at the bottom.

I typed, "Wall?" and sent it.

I hit the back button to return to Mr. Sheetrock, sent the same one-word question to Mr. Info, and then went and poured myself a cup of coffee.

I was very tired. Tired of the rat race of chasing bad news all over the globe. Tired of worrying about Ali, Lisa, gas prices, urban violence, and nuclear annihilation. Would anybody miss me if I drove off to Utah and went mountain biking? Lisa might not see me on TV, but so what? Sutton would understand…well, no, he wouldn't.

Two cups of coffee later, I heard the Beatles. E-mail had arrived.

Another untitled piece, this one from Sameday at nonesuch@aol.com. The note contained a series of numbers and another link. I wrote the numbers down, hit the link, and ended up at a FedEx package-tracking site. What now? On a whim, I clicked the tracking link and typed in the numbers. A message came up: "Your package has been delayed. To facilitate delivery, call 1-800-HURRY-UP or contact us via e-mail."

"This is nuts," I told myself, but I had nothing else to do at the moment. If it narrowed the search for Ali, it was worth the hassle.

I called Mr. Hurry-Up and spent fifteen minutes working my way through a dozen prompts while telling a machine about my personal life. The machine put me on hold when I was finally able to ask for a real person. After five more minutes of bad music and annoying company promos, I talked to someone named Jugal who told me (in a staccato Indian accent that I had to close my eyes to understand) that a pre-paid, numbered package with my name on it had been picked up at a FedEx drop-box in New York City early that morning. It had been processed and shelved because it had no delivery address. It also had no return address. If I provided my own address, it would be delivered to me by six o'clock tonight.

"Tonight!" What was in the package? Ali's press badge? Ali's right hand? What was I getting into? Where would it all lead?

Saturday evening, July 12.

At 6:03, FedEx pulled up in front of the apartment building. I was on the street waiting. "No signature needed, sir," said the black man in the black and blue uniform.

I went back into my apartment, opened the package, and found a small red cell phone inside. This was like living in a Lee Child novel!

The phone was a slick little item, about the size of a book of matches. It slid open vertically. The instant it was opened, it automatically called an unknown number. It rang for a long time on the other end, without an answer. I was almost afraid of an answer, and I finally cut the call. I considered a redial, but there was no keyboard. No way to manually call anyone. I talked to it, but that didn't work. I closed it, tried to turn it off, but it wouldn't power down.

I sank into my couch and stared at the tiny gadget in my hand. I thought of calling Jack on the Mac, texting Kevin, or ringing up Sutton or my dad. But I just sat there, weary and wondering. Twenty minutes later, at exactly 6:30, that little phone rang!

"Hello," I said quietly. Then I said it again, a little more confidently.

"Are you alone?" said a voice that sounded like Bradley Wall.

"Yes," I answered.

"I've got two minutes. What I'm telling you now will be known all over the world by the time we're done speaking. The news is right now being released to national and foreign journalists at a press conference in the Kremlin.

"Nine days ago, on the afternoon of the third of July, there was an assassination attempt on President Putin. At least eight armed Muslims and a suicide bomber in an attack at Lenin's mausoleum. The Red Czar's crystal casket was blown to smithereens as were a few Russian politicians and some of Putin's bodyguards. The bomber, too, of course.

"The president was injured, but that's hush-hush. He's healing well. You've seen him on the newscasts over the past week. He looks fine because he's fit and quick — a judo expert, you know. Trains daily with his bodyguards, moves as intuitively as they do. He pulled a gun along with the rest of his men — then disappeared like a ghost into the midst of his guards, into the mausoleum, and out again. He survived the bomb, got into a car, and was gone in a blink. He knows how to stay alive.

"At least two of the terrorists escaped. They took two hostages: a Russian official and a foreign journalist. The Russian was found dead in a wooded area inside the Kremlin, a short distance from the mausoleum. The journalist…is Ali."

"No!"

"He hasn't been harmed."

"How do you know?"

"I know."

"You've seen him," I said.

"I was at the mausoleum when it happened. I have news of him since."

"Why haven't we heard of this before now?"

"Eyewitnesses were under arrest until today. The story was suppressed. The killers are being tracked."

"But you know Ali's condition. Where is he? How did Paskov's friend get in touch with you?"

"The Russians didn't net me. I skipped out of Red Square unscathed—played the ghost also."

"Where are you now?"

"Kazakhstan."

I was astounded.

"You can't call me," he said. "I'll call you the same time tomorrow if I'm able. The phone is solar, and it's fully charged. Ten minutes in the sun will power it up for forty-eight hours. It can't be turned off on your end. Its signal is almost impossible to intercept. Make sure you're alone when we talk. Tell no one anything unless I say so. E-mail Jack Pascov that you didn't hear from me after all. I don't want to die. I don't want Ali to die."

"Is Ali in Kazakhstan?"

"I'll call you."

"Are you really a FOX reporter?"

"Of course I am."

"You…you trust me with all this…"

"I choose to." The call ended.

7

Kidnapped

The news hit the media before Wall hung up, and the Bulletin staff was summoned immediately. "All hands on deck!" bellowed Sutton when I answered his call.

The word of the failed assassination was international. No one agency had scooped another—it was broadcast everywhere at once. Of course, some media venues had men and women on the ground in Moscow, and they were able to trumpet things loudly. But the Bulletin, even with our voice silenced in Russia, was headlined all over the world because Philadelphia Bulletin correspondent Ali Ahkmed Baraki was a hostage in the hands of Muslim terrorists.

Though it was late, the Bulletin was a beehive. We launched into a special edition of the Weekend, highlighting the events in Russia, highlighting Ali himself—a Muslim captive among Muslim captors. A gentle, religious man—an Afghani-American of unquestioned American patriotism— Ali had courageously covered Middle Eastern, Asian, and European events (from the Russian sidelines) throughout the Israeli-Iranian War. Though dedicated to his work, he was a family man who returned home during Muslim holy days and traditional American holidays in order to be with his wife and five children. I had spent many a wonderful evening with the Barakis in their home in the suburbs of Cherry Hill, New Jersey, across the Delaware River from downtown Philadelphia.

While the Bulletin staff frenetically assembled the Weekend, my employer, Aaron Stein, along with Sutton and a couple of our editors met behind closed doors with officials from the CIA, FBI, DHS, DPP, and even (we were told) the White House and the Pentagon. All the time, I kept thinking of Bradley Wall whispering into a cell phone somewhere in Kazakhstan. I prayed nobody would ask me anything about anybody.

Then Sutton called me in. I felt lightheaded as I stepped into the crowded quarters of Stein's opulent office. Were the lights brighter than usual? Was my heart wired for sound? What did they want? What would I say?

Stein spoke first. "Matthew Lyle Clifford, religion and politics. One of our best," he said, half in greeting, half in introduction. He held out his hand to me. It was a comfort to feel that honest grip.

He nodded to the others in the room. "Matt is a friend of Ali's. Perhaps his closest friend among our staff. He has been especially concerned about him during this past week in which we've had no contact with Mr. Baraki."

He looked at me then. "These men and women, Matt, would like a minute with you—in our company, of course." And he sat down. There was an empty chair next to him, and I took it. I felt much better just sitting beside him.

"When was your last contact with Baraki?" asked a thick-spectacled man in a disheveled grey suit. He flashed a badge, in a tired gesture that seemed as natural as winking. "Stuart Jemison, CIA."

I laughed. Inappropriate perhaps, and certainly not because I was in a good mood. I was nervous. This was so unreal. Like a movie—a bad movie. "Sorry," I said. Jemison nodded. Sutton frowned. Stein smiled sympathetically.

"Last contact with Ali was on Wednesday, July 2," I said. "We exchanged e-mail. I've been working on a series discussing the morality of limited nuclear warfare. Locally, I've been polling spiritual leaders from various religions.

But I wanted a bigger picture response. I have some first-hand material from the Pope and from the Archbishop of Canterbury. Ali was trying to get something fresh from the Primate of the Russian Orthodox Church. He hadn't landed anything, and that's what we talked about."

"Did he mention anything about plans to cover any events involving Russian president Vladimir Putin?" asked a woman standing behind Jemison. She didn't identify herself.

"Nothing," I said.

"Anything about Putin at all?" Mystery Woman again.

"No," I said. "He sent me some comments about a nuclear disarmament discussion he'd had with other journalists in his hotel — that was all. And he asked how the Phillies were doing." Nobody even so much as chuckled. This was worse than the movies.

"Has he ever interviewed Putin? Is he close to anyone who has?" Jemison asked.

"He rooms in a hotel full of international journalists," I said carefully. "And the Kremlin handpicks those guys to cover political events. The Kremlin tells us only what it wants us to know, when it wants us to know it. Sometimes the press gets to sit in the same room as Putin. Most of the time it doesn't. Until last week, I'm not aware that Ali has ever been among the chosen few."

Sutton chimed in uninvited. I thought he must be pyschic because he said what I had been avoiding. "The only guy who ever personally interviewed Putin is that crackerjack reporter from FOX News, Brad Wall."

"That's right," I added, nodding casually.

"Scoops us every time!" Sutton said.

"Any thoughts, any guesses, where Mr. Baraki may be?" asked a very short, dark-skinned man to my left. I thought he was sitting, but he was not. He looked Arab, but might have been Hispanic. He sounded British. "My name is George," he said, breaking a lopsided smile.

"I have imagined a hundred scenarios," I answered. "Who are his captors? Nobody has claimed responsibility. Al Quaida? Taliban? They barely exist anymore. So who would attack so brazenly in Russia? The Caucasus Caliphate Jihad maybe, or some new group from Latvia, Lithuania, Georgia, Estonia. Why hostages? What can they gain? Where would they take them? I don't know." I sighed. "I don't know."

"Of course you don't," Mystery Woman said. "Of course he doesn't," she said to the room full of somber speculators.

Nobody spoke for a long moment. Then I asked, "Have *you* any thoughts, any guesses, where Mr. Baraki might be?"

Mystery Woman stared at me as if I were suddenly naked. Stein chuckled. Sutton said, "Of course they do, but they're askin' the questions today, Matt."

"That's my job, too," I said quietly.

"Yes, it is," said Stein, sitting forward in his big leather chair. "And you do it well, son."

"We appreciate you sitting with us, Mr. Clifford," George said abruptly. "We are sorry about your friend. We are doing everything we can, in cooperation with Russian authorities, to find him and secure his release."

"Thank you," I said sincerely.

George nodded. "We'll contact you if we need you. We'll keep you all informed of any information that national security protocol allows us to release."

I got up. Stein smiled as I left the room.

"They checked all our e-mail before they even got here." Jacqui Johnson poked my shoulder to get my attention. "They've got folks a thousand miles away from here reading our phone texts right now—looking at the inside of our computers from the outside of theirs."

I hardly heard her. I was thinking about Ali—about all these people trying to track him down.

"They know more about us than we know about

ourselves," she said. "Especially the little guy. George Ognobini. Homeland Security. He wears NSA headphones to bed. He's got his eye glued to the global telescope to make sure nothing evil comes our way. He knows what Marco Romano ate for lunch today."

"You think they've really hacked into our computers?" I asked absently.

"Of course," she said, "and they've read all our love mail."

I looked at her. She was wearing that coy smile of hers.

"I don't write love mail. And nobody sends me any," I said.

"Well, you can bet they've read all your columns. Remember 'Who is the Antichrist?' Your parody on the hysteria that preachers whip up by pinning '666' on any politician they don't like? You named names—Putin included."

"World leaders always get fingered for Antichrist status," I argued. "When Ronald Wilson Reagan was president, some people thought he was the Antichrist because there were six letters in each of his names: 666. So, I hit Obama with the same claim."

"Under the subtitle 'Obama-nation of Desolation,'" she reminded me, eyebrows arched in mock disdain.

"That header was a play on Jesus' own words about the Antichrist," I said in my defense. "I took Barack Hussein Obama's eighteen letters, divided them by three—and *voila!*—three sixes."

"That's really stretching things, Matt!" Jacqui laughed.

"Okay, okay…" I chuckled, enjoying her attention. "But controversy is good for sales. Folks read the paper for the commentary—not the news. They like a good fight better than a good story or a pretty face."

The smile went out of Jacqui's eyes for a moment—then returned, with a steely glint. "You're a better fighter than a storywriter?" she fired back.

"I think I write a good story!" was all I could say because suddenly it struck me that I wanted to impress this woman with my wit, wow her with my words, and woo her to want to hear more of them. And the realization slowed me down, weakened my punch. But the girl was quick on her feet.

"A good tall tale is more like it!" Jacqui quipped, screwing up her lips and rolling her eyes. "Like when you wrote that Ali had been invited to supper with Putin, with the Beast sitting at Putin's right hand!"

She shot me a mock, scolding stare. But all I could think about was that Jacqui Johnson was quoting something I wrote months ago. I didn't know she read my columns.

"And you wonder why the FBI thinks you might have some inside information on current Russian events?" she said with a smirk.

"A joke!" I protested. "Like the rest of the column. A tall tale, like you said. It came from a humorous discussion I had at a Bible study. I wrote about 'roast beast' on Putin's menu. Dmitri Vlostek, one of Putin's favorite cronies, is nicknamed the Beast. He ran a KGB torture house in Moscow, under Brezhnev. Personally strangled political prisoners because he enjoyed killing them. A beast! These intelligence guys should have enough intelligence to know political satire when they read it."

"They'd have to read the Bible first to know what it was you were satirizing," said Jacqui, smiling. "And, of course, they would have to have a sense of humor."

We could see them all bunched together in Stein's office. The glass door was closed. We couldn't hear the conversation, but mouths were moving and fingers were talking. George was sitting. Nobody was laughing.

Jacqui's smile faded also, and the sadness returned that I had seen the night before.

"It's awful, actually," she said to me quietly, staring intently through the glass into Aaron Stein's room. "Ali kidnapped—and even those guys don't know where he is."

It was nearly midnight, but I was still awake. Camped in my living room, I'd watched every breaking newscast and searched the web for any fresh leads on Ali. Nothing.

It was cooler than it had been for a couple of weeks, and my window was open to let in the late night breeze. The neighborhood was unusually quiet. There were no human voices on the wind. A cat was crying somewhere. Cars passed occasionally.

I turned off my light and lay upon my bed for a few moments thinking about Lisa—and Jacqui. But I knew that wouldn't help me fall asleep. I thought of Ali, and my heart ached with a numbing sense of helplessness and loneliness. The whole world seemed lonely and lost. Was I depressed that I felt such weight? No, I was thinking like a realist.

The world is not a happy place.

It's an amazing place, where the hope of happy moments draws us from one day to the next—but mostly it's filled with sorrow and longing, death and loss, hunger and war. Tears are more common than laughter. *Blessed are those who mourn,* Jesus said, *for they shall be comforted.*

"Oh yeah?" I mused aloud. "So where's the comfort?"

8

Roman Warrior

7:30 a.m., Sunday morning, July 13.

Kevin called. "You awake, bro?"

"I am *now*." I yawned.

"I wanted to check on you before I go to church. You okay?"

"Oh, sure," I said. "The Central Intelligence Agency, the Internal Revenue Service, and the Girls Scouts of America all want to know what I know about Ali. And I want to know what they know, but…they can't tell me, of course, so…"

"The guys in the pancake seminary are praying for you, praying for Ali. We missed you yesterday. I believe Ali's alive. God is present wherever he is. We just need to pray for his protection—pray that Ali will call upon the name of Lord himself."

"Which name of the Lord should he use?"

"There's only one name."

"Yeah," I said. So Ali had it wrong. But didn't God understand Ali's heart? "Hey, Kev," I said, "maybe we can take a late walk around the city sometime soon. To talk about stuff."

"How 'bout tonight?"

"Okay. Tonight. Supper somewhere first? I'm up for a nice, juicy flat iron steak."

"Public House at Logan Square."

"Medium rare!"

"Six o'clock."

"Let's make it 7:00—no, 7:15." Brad Wall might call at 6:30.

"It's a plan, man. See ya there."

It was something to look forward to. With Ali missing in action, college buddies scattered across the region, and family busy with their own lives back in Lancaster County, I was glad for Philadelphia friends. I enjoyed some of the crew at the Bulletin, but I'd not grown very close to them.

Kevin McCarthy and I had hit it off right away though, and in just a little while he had become something of a best friend. He was a level-headed guy, great intellectual company, and I could talk to him about most anything. An evening out with Kevin would be just the diversion I needed from the drama that had overtaken me. The thought of a nice steak dinner and a long evening stroll woke me up fully and energized my day.

I e-mailed Jack and told him that Wall had not yet contacted me. Maybe the Sleuth couldn't find anything, I suggested. I'd keep waiting.

It was an easy lie. Besides, I *was* waiting.

I messaged Lisa on Facebook—for the third time since she'd contacted me a week ago. It was still too early in the morning for church, so she'd be home.

She'd know all about Ali by now. I didn't want her to think I needed her advice or her emotional support. I didn't want her to think I needed anything. But I knew that I did. I knew that I was over my head in water deeper than I could stand up in. Maybe I was blowing things out of proportion because of my fears for Ali, but I felt that the events of the past day had catapulted me into some strange new world. I needed help—whether I wanted it or not.

I asked her for prayer. Plain and simple. "Crazy days!" I wrote. "I know you are praying for Ali—and for me. Thanks. Keep it up."

Then I thought, "The more the better," and I e-mailed Dad and texted my sister Bethany. I didn't mention my James Bond cell phone or Bradley Wall or the Mystery Woman or the White House or the CIA. I just asked for prayer.

You would think I'd had enough of the news all the work-week long without having to check it out on Sunday, too. But the drama I was a part of wouldn't let me rest. Television on, I paced back and forth from my front window to my apartment door. I ate lunch with my eyes glued to the screen. And I swam.

The apartment building was only a few years old, built just before the global recession, with a brand new constant-current spa-canal in every apartment living room. Ten feet long by five feet wide by four feet deep, the pool was a great workout. Far better than the old exercise bike my dad had, it was worth the extra rent. When not in use, it had a hardwood plank cover—as sturdy as the floor that it matched—that slid over the top.

I had the TV programmed so that every time a commercial came on, it would switch to the next news channel. I heard the Russian story played out dozens of times. A couple of Ali's pictures—a smiling family photo and a gritty portrait from the streets of Moscow—caught my attention every time they flashed on the screen. Around 5:00, I was beginning to look at the clock every few minutes in an anxious countdown to 6:30. Would the Sleuth call? If he did, I knew I must ask only the most important questions. I had a mental list prepared.

At 5:15, the news anchor at WorldNewsNow announced a live broadcast with Marco Romano coming up next. I climbed out of the spa, toweled myself dry, donned some light sweats, poured myself a glass of Dr. Pepper, and sat down to watch.

And there he was, standing in partial military dress in front of a wide bookcase in his presidential office in Quirinale Palace in Rome. He almost always interviewed standing.

His clothing was perfectly tailored, never twice the same. Six feet three inches tall, head shaved bald (he was nearly bald anyway), his deep hazel eyes sometimes changed to brown with the colors that surrounded him. Face shaved as smoothly as his head, his dark frowning eyebrows drew a strong thin line over a sharp beaked nose, giving him the look of a vigilant eagle or an ancient Caesar. Athletic, erect, and solid, his movements were confident, smooth, graceful. They reminded me of a cat. *A wildcat. A panther,* I thought as I watched.

Marco. It means "warrior" or "hammer." It's Latin originally, from the war god Mars. Marco, Marcus, Mark, Marcellus…they all mean "dedicated to Mars." Pleasant thought.

Romano means "citizen of Rome."

Marco Romano. Roman warrior. Hammer of Rome. A Caesar—he was born in the wrong age of history. But he was certainly making the most of the political opportunities of his day.

As the camera panned his high-raftered office, it settled briefly on two flags secured to the wall above a set of thick oak doors. Side by side were the banners of Italy and the European Union.

I turned on the digicorder when Romano began to speak. His eyes were angry, I thought. They stared through the TV screen like a twin-barreled laser gun.

"Some dogs," he said, "die hard."

What a line! No American politician could start a speech that way. Clay wouldn't dare. No matter where Romano went from there, his words would headline every news source in the free world—and probably everywhere else.

"For nearly a decade and a half," he continued, "Italy, the United States, and much of Europe have faced the rabid attacks of the wild Islamic packs of the Middle East. We defended ourselves against the mad dogs here at home, and we returned their violence by chasing them down in their dark desert dens. We captured or killed the leaders of the packs. We bared our arms, crawled into their caves, faced their fangs, wrestled them to the ground, broke their teeth — and then broke their necks! We emancipated those held captive to the tyranny of these depraved philosophies.

"In equity and mercy we sat at the table with the peace-loving nations of the free world in order to create a plan for Middle Eastern restoration that would heal the land and bless the whole earth. And then, in the very hour that the European Union, the United States, and the nations of the Middle East pledged a final, sacred peace with one another, more demon-driven dogs were running toward blood in the heart of ancient Europe! Murderous, misguided, intolerant, and without any civilizing instincts, they tried to assassinate the elected sovereign of the state of Russia, killing many of his guard and kidnapping a fellow Muslim who rejects the bloodthirsty, unenlightened tenets of fundamentalist Mohammedism."

Romano lowered his head for a moment, took a sharp breath, then braced the camera with his eyes again. "We cannot, *we will not* allow the dogs to run free any longer!"

Beware of dogs! It says that somewhere in the Bible, I think. Jesus said it — or was it the apostle Paul? Or maybe it was Shakespeare and not the Bible at all. I don't know which — or what it meant. But I knew what Romano meant, and I'd never heard such a vehement denunciation of radical Islam from the lips of a world leader. Not even from Israel. Certainly not from Clay. Not even while the world warred against Syria and Iran.

But Romano was right. The world had too long ignored the threats of a religion whose most fundamentalist followers simply echoed their own deity's declaration:

"Convert or die!" It took the horrors of 9/11 to move the United States to warfare against radical Islam. Even then, we were hesitant to trace the source of terrorism to the mouth of Mohammed. We said that evil men had hijacked a peaceful religion. We were afraid of offending key Muslim allies like the Saudis. And afraid of offending Muslim Americans like my friend Ali who practiced a form of Islam that ignored (or somehow explained away) much of what Islam's founder actually said and did.

Romano knew what he was talking about. He had witnessed the ravages of the wild dogs in his own backyard. Wherever Muslim immigration and the Muslim birthrate outstripped native European population growth, Islamic terror also increased. Throughout Europe, the howling Mohammedan hounds ran the same path of blood that the Prophet ran when he was alive and well on planet earth.

Many nations—Italy first among them—closed their borders to Arab immigration. The European Union armed itself and joined the war against Iran, Syria, and the multinational Islamic militias.

Marco Romano, a seasoned Italian military commander and a one-time mercenary with the American-backed *mujahideen* resistance against the USSR in the Soviet-Afghan War, fought beside his men in the mountains and the deserts of the Middle East. He knew, from experience, that the way to stop the howling was to kill the dogs.

In February, one month after the start of the war, General Romano—at the head of an Italian special forces team and guided by Israeli intelligence and his own sharp hunting instincts—hounded down Ahmed al-Farid in northern Iran. The elusive mastermind of 9/11, a man with a twenty-five million dollar price on his head, was forced to flee into Turkmenistan.

Romano and his men, without air support or mobile artillery, followed al-Farid across the border, trapping him in the sandy foothills of Mount Shahshah in the Kopet Dag

Range. A pitched battle followed. Al-Farid was wounded and captured.

Romano had cameras. He took pictures of himself and his men standing around a bloody, dirty, and dejected al-Farid. Photos of the hated and defeated terrorist lord were sent via satellite to news sources around the world. Romano was an instant hero. One hour later, a live video broadcast from Mount Shahshah was also filling the newsroom screens. It riveted all who saw it. Ali was home for a few short days, and he and I—along with the rest of the Bulletin news team—watched, transfixed, as the scene played out before our eyes.

The video was 52 seconds long—crisp, clean, in brilliant color. No audio. Just al-Farid rising from his seated position, standing wearily, resolutely, facing the camera. He was speaking in Arabic, and Ali could read his lips. *"Allahu Akbar."* Allah is the greatest. And then, "Glory be to Allah. Praise be to Allah. There is no god but Allah, and Allah is most great, dearer to me than everything on which the sun rises."

"I don't like this," said Ali, wagging his head, distressed. "This is a prayer invoking the help of Hazrat Isra'il—upon whom be peace—the angel of death and resurrection!"

We saw Romano then. Through the eye of the camera, he walked up to al-Farid, raised a pistol to the man's head, and fired once.

The outcry around the world was unanimous and condemning. This was brazen, unadulterated murder—against every tenet of the Geneva Convention concerning war and prisoners of war. And to broadcast it across the globe! Romano must be crazy! He must be brought to justice himself and tried for murder.

But this was a world war. And Ahmed al-Farid was in many ways the Hitler who began the war, the man who—from his hidden enclaves in Pakistan and Iran—had so lately fanned the flames of war. Violence, hunger, poverty, terror, suffering, and death had covered the earth because of al-Farid and his ideological compatriot Bin Laden. Nations had been torn apart, blown apart. Hundreds of thousands had died. Many more had lost loved ones because of the twisted hatred of these men and the terrorist troops who followed their lead and spread their creed.

Sentiment quickly swung from horror at al-Farid's cold-blooded execution to near-euphoric exultation at his death. The New York Post incited popular sentiment with a front-page graphic image of the Twin Towers with al-Farid's face on it. It was the famous 9/11 shot of the second jetliner exploding in the South Tower. The al-Farid photo was a stark, bloody shot of the final second of his life. The jetliner entered his head where Romano's bullet had punched a hole. Behind al-Farid's head, his blood and brains were collaged with the conflagration caused by the impact of Flight 175. A terrible image, but the justice of it was inescapable. The Post ran no copy with the graphic, just the full front-page image with a biblically-inspired headline: "LIVE BY THE SWORD, DIE BY THE SWORD."

There were immediate hearings, and Romano wept passionately. "I have shot a man in cold blood, and his death is upon my soul, so help me God." But he vehemently denied losing his mind before blowing out al-Farid's.

"Some say I went mad once we caught Ahmed al-Farid," he said in his defense, "but I was never so clear-headed. If I was mad, I was mad with the blood of the world, and I knew it. I followed a trail of blood to catch the man—a long and bitter trail of innocent blood—the blood of children and women, old men and civilians, and soldiers of the armies of the free world from Italy and France, Germany and Poland, the brightest and best of the youth of many lands. I swore upon their blood to catch the man, and I knew that I would. God led me to the man and gave Italy the victory—gave the world the victory. When we had the man at last, I only had to look into his eyes to know there was no man left to kill—

no human in that frame. I didn't kill al-Farid. I simply pulled the trigger that closed a dead man's eyes!"

Israel called for leniency. The man had helped defeat their enemies, had personally executed one of their greatest foes, and was rumored to have some Jewish blood flowing in his veins besides. The nations of the world held public debate. Sentiment ran high in the Italian commander's favor.

Romano was exonerated. Italy held parades in his honor. The only discipline he received was removal from official military command. Even so, he continued to wear his uniform, and many Italians continued to call him General.

Directly after his trial, the war being done, he returned to the Middle East in the capacity of Italian ambassador at large. His mercenary years of fighting with Afghani nationalists against the Soviet Union had made him many friends among the warriors of the Afghan mountains. His foreign relationships had expanded during the latest Mideast war as—entirely against all modern military protocol—Romano was often found with his own men on the field of battle. On the front lines, behind enemy lines, in the heat of the conflict, he made friends within the allied nations' commands and with Iranian warlords fighting on the side of the Allies.

His many friendships opened doors for him now—and for the peace process itself. Competing warlords were willing to come to the peace table because of Romano's persistent and courageous dialogue across the lines.

After a month of decisive diplomacy, he flew back to Italy like an ancient Roman conqueror, full of the victories, full of himself. Politically embattled Italian Prime Minister Vittorio del Vasto nearly crowned him prince. He quickly became an internationally sought expert on world events. Satellite transponders rocketed his commentary across the earth. When the *Popolo della Libertà*—the People of Freedom party—asked him to run for office in del Vasto's place, we all knew he was a landslide winner before the campaign even began. On July 1, it was Italy's turn at the half-year helm of the Council of the European Union, and newly-elected Italian premiere Marco Romano was the man.

I stood in the center of my living room, absorbing Romano's words as the broadcast continued.

"The people of Russia and the nations of the European Union are united against the terror of the dogs," Romano declared, talking with his fingers as much as with his tongue. Italians are bi-lingual that way, and Romano used his hands with the skill of an orchestra conductor.

"President Putin and I have spoken of an alliance against the forces of terrorism. Together we will assure the Peace by taking violence to those who assail the Peace. Violence is the only language that terrorists speak or understand. The armies of Italy, and indeed the nations of the European Union, are committed to the restoration of peace and order in all of Europe—and indeed in all the world. We shall not live in fear. We shall not bow to terror. We shall take up the hunt, track down the dogs, capture the captors, and set the captives free."

He turned from the camera, which followed his gaze to a massive bronze map of the world covering half a wall in the spacious office. The map was a work of art in itself, polished and ponderous and sculpted topographically. It was not marked in any way by national borders or any indication of human habitation—except for Rome. The city wasn't labeled, but its location was polished in such a way that it shone brighter than anything else upon the rippled maze of oceans, rivers, hills, and plains.

"The people of my native Italy, the people of the nations of a united Europe, the people of all the civilized lands of the earth desire peace, deserve peace, and will be given peace. Pray for peace, my brothers and sisters," Romano said. "No matter who your gods are, pray for peace. And we shall have peace."

The red cell phone rang. It was Wall.

"Are you alone?" he asked.

"Yes."

"Two minutes again."

"Is he alive?"

"Yes."

How did he know? Was he near them? Did he have contact with them? Did he know somebody on their inside? I wanted to ask, but…

"Are you still in Kazakhstan? Is Ali in Kazakhstan?"

"You'll find out soon, I believe, where he is and how he is. The world will see him. He is Muslim. He is Arab by blood. He's no fool, as you know. His captors will use him, but he will use them, too."

"Every American intelligence agency and military command is looking for him. Putin is looking. The Italians and the European Union are looking. Do they know where to look? What happens if they find him? Will there be more violence?"

"This is a game of hide and seek. Violence is an option, but not an inevitability."

"Do you…do they know where he is?"

"Some may, some may not. The manhunt is more of a competition than a coalition."

"Are you alone?"

"Very much."

"The terrorists wanted Putin dead," I said. "They're after a power shift in Russia, or they're baiting Russia, or they're seeking Muslim solidarity in the region. Why do they need hostages? What can one isolated terror cell accomplish against a whole world that has risen up against radical Islam? We've just ended a war that obliterated the world's major Islamic terror groups and three of the world's most powerful Muslim nations!"

"There are more."

"More what?"

"Groups, nations."

"But the Peace…"

"Was not signed by everyone."

"You are in Kazakhstan." Which had not signed the Peace.

Wall sighed. "But Ali is not, as far as I know. As I said, this is a game of hide and seek."

"What are they after…?"

"Blood. Yours, mine, Putin's. America's. Israel's. Their own in holy martyrdom. And then…Islamic Armageddon. The coming of the Islamic Messiah. The world conquered by and conformed to Islam."

"What are you after?"

"Truth."

I thought of saying, *What is truth?* but I remembered that was Pontius Pilate's line. "Why are you talking to *me* about this?" I asked. "Why not the CIA or the Pentagon?"

"You are Ali's friend," the Sleuth said, "and you may be key in events as they unfold. I'm sorry to be so elusive, but I can't tell you what I don't know. I do know that we haven't seen the end of war."

"Wars and rumors of war," I quoted Jesus. Figured that was better than Pilate.

A moment of silence, then, "Yes, that's right."

"But the end is not yet," I quoted Jesus again.

"Not yet," the Sleuth affirmed.

"You'll call tomorrow?" I asked.

"Hopefully." And the call ended.

9

Cold Crew

We ate at Public House on Logan Square, then hiked down Arch Street through the historic district to the river. The flat iron was weighing on me, and I was glad to be outside walking it off. It was a hot night, but a breeze came off the Delaware as Kevin and I strolled Columbus Boulevard beside the boat docks. That part of town was heavily policed. Folks felt safe. They came out at night to waste their time and spend their money.

"So we're in the end times," I said, pressing into a discussion that I knew Kevin was itching to have.

"Absolutely," Kevin affirmed. He was the Revelation man in the Bible study. It was his idea that we study the book. Lately, we'd not had much time for that.

"And, in spite of the Peace, the war to end all wars is just around the corner?" I was anxious for his thoughts. I had an idea for a column, but my interest was increasingly personal.

"Yes," he sighed tersely.

"So what part does the United States play in it?"

"Why do you ask, Matt?"

"Because we live in the United States! And because you said last night—and at the Bible study the day after the Peace—that you think Bible prophecy is coming true right now! And that the Antichrist is the premiere of Italy and the president of the Council of the European Union."

"So what if he is?" Kevin smiled grimly.

"So what if—!" I got it. He was trying to get me to talk about Jesus! The guy was jumping out of his shoes to tell me about the Antichrist, but he was baiting me to talk about the condition of my soul. I wasn't biting. "Just answer the question about America, will you?"

"Okay…America," he echoed. "Some prophecy scholars say the U.S. is Revelation's 'Babylon the Great,' a culture of great wealth, international influence, and moral decadence. Babylon will be destroyed by the Antichrist. But I don't think that America is Babylon. We're bad, very bad, but not *that* bad. I think America will always fight for freedom, always try to stand up for the right. I think we have a calling on God's side, not Satan's. A calling that hasn't been revoked even though we're a nation that has fallen far from the Lord."

"America! America! God shed his grace on thee, and crown thy good with brotherhood from sea to shining sea," I sang humorlessly. "Brotherhood! More like Cain killing Abel, every day, everywhere, coast to coast."

"God's grace is still upon America."

"Why? How? Can a nation have a calling? Like Billy Graham? Where's that in the Bible?"

"Israel had a calling. Still does."

"Yeah, that's in the Bible. That's clear," I admitted. "But America?"

"God is the maker of the nations. And America's origins are remarkably Christian. You know our history as a nation."

"Yes, I do," I said. "And it damns us."

"Our sins don't negate our calling. We've got to look to the nation's inception."

"Origins," I said thoughtfully. "Maybe," I conceded.

"We haven't lost the calling."

"Well, we've lost sight of it! We haven't lived up to it. Slavery. The subjugation of the Native American. Racism. Rampant materialism. Corporate greed. Pork barrel politics. Abortion. Pornography. The current social landscape is littered with moral pollution from sea to stinking sea. America doesn't deserve God's grace."

"Grace is always undeserved."

"My father says America deserves judgment," I said.

"Of course we do."

"Is God judging America now?" I wondered aloud.

"We reap what we sow."

"You've got a scripture verse for everything!"

"And you've got a song," he said.

"Is America in the Bible?" I asked again.

"Nothing obvious. Not to me, anyway. But some end times guys say the Antichrist will be handpicked by the United States to head the UN and then rule the world through the United Nations."

"Not likely," I piped. "The UN still barks, but it hasn't any bite. It can barely pay its rent. Its reputation is a tarnished badge of anti-Semitism. It can't pawn *that* to a world that just helped Israel win a war. And if the United States isn't in the Bible, how do these guys find the United Nations in there?"

"You can find anything in the Bible that you want to find," he said, "but that doesn't mean it's really there. God didn't give us the Bible so that we could cut it up into little pieces and make a collage that looks like what we want it to look like."

"Maybe I should read it more often," I confessed. "My dad reads it every day." *So does Lisa,* I wanted to say, but I was avoiding what I really wanted to talk about.

"Some folks say that Iraq is Babylon," Kevin said (he was on a roll), "because Iraq is where the ancient city of Babylon actually was."

"Iraq is now history, too—since the war."

"Yeah," Kevin said. "But some interpreters of Revelation believe that Babylon is Rome, or that Babylon consists of the European nations that now make up the geographical reach of the ancient Roman Empire. I used to hear about the European Common Market being Babylon—ten European nations linked in political alliance. But when I look at Revelation, I don't see Babylon as any particular group of nations...certainly not America. I think Babylon is a commercial system—a carefully structured world economy like the one Clay keeps preaching. Like the one that we're increasingly becoming with a religious philosophy opposed to God himself."

"A world financial system based on false religion. Is that it?"

"In God We Trust," Kevin quoted, stooping to pick a penny off the dirty sidewalk. "These copper circles are worthless," he mused. "About a year ago, I started throwing my pennies in my recycle bin! Then I thought that we'll probably stop minting them soon, so now I'm collecting them in a big glass bottle."

"Big glass bottles are collector's items," I noted. "You think that penny will be worth anything anytime soon?"

"Nope," he answered, handing it to me. It was scratched and badly worn. I squinted at its date. 1997. Minted in Denver. I gave it back, and he put it in his pocket. "Some believe that Babylon is the Roman Catholic Church," he said.

"Yeah, that's Doug's line—always ragging on the Vatican. 'The Whore of Babylon!' he says."

"He left the Catholic Church when he got saved, and he thinks everyone else should, too."

"Come out from among them, saith the Lord!" I laughed. "Touch not the unclean thing. What fellowship hath light with darkness?"

"Who's quoting scripture now?" Kevin grinned. "Or misquoting!"

He bent over again, this time to pick up a stone and toss it into the river. It was getting darker, and Columbus Boulevard veered away from the river a block or so ahead.

"Babylon will kill Christians," he said. "I don't think America would..."

"No?"

"I don't know," he said. "We'll have to wait and see."

"So you really believe we're living in the last hour of history, Kevin?"

"I do," he said soberly. "In fact, I think—according to Daniel 9:27—we're in the last *week* of history. We've got exactly seven years left."

"Seven years!" I was astounded, more by Kevin's matter-of-fact manner than his words.

"Three and a half years from Romano's declaration of the Peace until his politically heavy hand makes it obvious that he's the Antichrist. And then three and a half more until Jesus returns."

"Anything important you want to accomplish between now and then?" I asked sarcastically.

"Wake up every morning and follow Jesus," he answered sincerely.

"Romano's only on his little EU throne for five more months," I said, remembering my talk with Jack. "Then it's Latvia's turn to put a man in, then Luxembourg's. And what about Von Kappel? He's the official P.R. man of the EU."

"Sidelined by Bell's palsy—and sideswiped by Romano. Von Kappel's been there nearly five years, and he's out of office himself in five months."

"Exactly! So we'll get a whole new slate of EU top guns."

"God watches over his word, and he is ready to perform it," Kevin quoted enigmatically from somewhere in the Bible.

"Every generation since Peter and Paul believed they were living in the end times," I argued. I'd been doing my homework.

"Yes, but the signs…"

"Sign, sign, everywhere a sign! Christians have been jabbering about signs for two thousand years."

"Yes, but Israel makes all the difference," he insisted. "Until God gathered the Jews together in their own homeland in 1948, after twenty centuries of being scattered throughout the world—until then, all the signs weren't really signs. Now they are."

"Israel…" I thought of Jack in Jerusalem. I thought of Ali…somewhere. I didn't want to think of Ali. I'd been thinking of him almost every waking minute.

"But Christians aren't going to be around to see it all happen, anyway," I said. "Are they? I mean…if we do happen to be counting down toward midnight, isn't Gabriel supposed to blow that horn of his and launch all true believers into the clouds before the Antichrist takes his mask off and the Great Tribulation opens up in a theater near you?"

"Let's take North Penn," Kevin said as he angled us back toward the river.

North Penn was an old street, newly-paved, that ran between a wall of boarded-up warehouses and a row of new waterfront high-risers that separated the noisy, neon city from the quiet, shadowed Delaware. Scrawny saplings fenced the sidewalk at the perimeter of a dark, empty parking lot. Tiny groves of oak and sumac competed for life closer to the river. Not the safest part of town.

"Yes, Gabriel is going to blow his horn," Kevin said, "but I don't expect to fly until Jesus comes back himself."

"Planning to be left behind?" I quipped, as we started down the lonely avenue.

"Kind of," he said. "I think the Church is going to go through it with everyone else."

"Through it?" I asked.

"Through the Great Tribulation. Through the hard stuff. Right up to the end."

"Sweet," I said. "Sounds like fun."

"Is this what you wanted to talk about," Kevin asked, "when you suggested we take a walk tonight?"

"Well, sort of."

"You want to talk about Jesus?" He grinned.

I did, but it bugged me that he was pushing. So I said, "Well, no."

Kevin sighed. Taking off his Phillies cap, he wiped his forehead with the back of his arm. The night was humid, hot in spite of the breeze.

North Penn ended. As a street, that is. It continued as a paved walkway through the empty lots that butted into a seedy concrete block warehouse next to an acre or two of grass, rocks, and trees (which the city loosely maintained) called Penn Treaty Park. We followed the walkway.

Other than Jesus, I wanted to talk about Lisa, but I came back to politics. It was easier. "What do you think of Romano and Putin in political partnership?" I asked.

I knew what I thought. The two would rather drink poison than drink a toast together. But that's politics. It would be better for the EU to have the Russian bear at the dinner table—and even in the war room—than prowling outside the house rummaging for food. In truth, though, Europe would have been a safer place if Putin were dead and a more moderate man was president in his place.

"Marco Gian Romano, publicly pledging fidelity with Vladimir Putin," Kevin mused. He followed the news closely. He was single. Spent a lot of time reading up on current events, history, theology. A lot like my dad. A lot like me. Only Kevin did it for God so that he could pray for people. I did it for my job so that I could pay the bills.

"It's a power play," he said, "but if it plays out like he's calling it, it won't be the first time Romano has pulled off a political miracle."

"'No matter who your gods are, pray for peace.' Did you hear him say that? What's that about? The 'gods'! We're used to that from Oprah the Divine, but not from a world leader. Weird."

"Yeah, and from a lapsed Italian Catholic."

"Maybe he's really a New Age Jew," I joked. "An anti-Islamic Eurabian New Age Jew. I feel a blog comin' on!"

"He's the Antichrist, Matt!" Kevin's eyes were narrow, grim. "He's Clay times ten."

I laughed. Kevin wasn't being funny, but I laughed.

"Clay, like Obama before him, has been pushing spiritual tolerance and the privacy of religion," Kevin said passionately. "Says he's talking about freedom of religion as the founders meant it, but he's really talking about freedom *from* religion. What he really wants is to push traditional religion out of the public square—especially Judeo-Christian religion. If tolerance means that all religions have an equal claim on the American conscience, then why are the Clay courts, the Clay Congress, and the Clay executive pushing judgments and laws that increasingly declare Christianity intolerant? And all this on top of Obamacare's pro-abortion mandates!"

"My dad used to say, 'It's a free country' when somebody said anything 'intolerant.' He doesn't say that anymore."

"Because he's changed his mind on what's intolerant? Or because it's not a free country anymore?"

I shrugged. "Now he talks about the demise of truth. The divide between Christian truth and postmodernism—"

Kevin interrupted me. "Clay claims to be in the Christian truth camp, but just like Obama, he calls the Koran the 'Holy Koran.' He calls Islam a 'revealed' religion—as if it descended from heaven. And he's practically outlawed any overt Christian expression in the military, even telling our chaplains they can't name the name of Jesus when they minister or pray!"

"I wrote a column during the holidays last December," I said, "about the truth claims of the world's major religions. I didn't bash Jesus—I would never do that—but I didn't put him up on the one-and-only truth pedestal either. That got me more boos and hisses from Christians than any column I'd ever written."

"Yeah? Well, you can handle it, Clifford," Kevin said tersely. "That's what you get paid for, isn't it?"

"I guess so," I admitted.

"When Christians speak up for biblical truth in the realm of moral behavior in America today," Kevin continued, "we're called 'haters.'"

"Yeah," I chuckled. "Look at how A&E tried to spank the Duck Dynasty's Phil Robertson for quoting the Bible about homosexuality. They thought he was just a backwoods quack, but they didn't realize they were wrestling with an alligator!"

"Guys like Phil—and me—are dubbed 'backward fundamentalists.'" Kevin snorted. "When Obama was president, he said that people who believe in biblical morality are stuck in 'worn arguments and old attitudes.' My pastor was sued earlier this year for preaching about homosexuality from the scriptures. The case went in his favor, but it was Clay's recent gay rights legislation that dragged him into the courtroom."

"What do you think of the European Union?"

"A petulant dictatorship of nations! They took Poland to court because the Polish state school system—and Poland's Catholic president—tried to keep gay propaganda out of the schools."

"And Romano?"

"Biblically literate, spiritually rhetorical. Rants and raves like an Old Testament prophet. But like I said, he's Clay times ten. Same politics, same spirit—but deeper, wider, definitely more brutal…and slicker."

"An antichrist," I mused.

"Yes," Kevin said, and his eyes flashed.

"I'm not a prophet, Matt, but I read the prophets. I didn't make this stuff up. I've studied it for years."

"Why Romano?" I asked.

"It's not about Romano, as if he's got the political profile to make the perfect Antichrist. It's about all the prophetic pieces. Daniel 9. Revelation 6. Jesus' words in Matthew 24. And by the way, I'd like to be wrong—really, really wrong!"

"Putin, at least, says what he means concerning religion," I offered. "The man's a twenty-first century communist king in a judo toga. He hates religion—and he says so."

Kevin nodded his agreement. "Clay and Romano wear religion like fine clothes, but they've got dirty underwear!"

"You should be writing my column," I said. The mention of Putin reminded me of Ali. "I think he's alive," I said.

"Ali?"

"Yeah, I think he's alive. Something tells me—"

"Some*one* tells you," he interrupted. He meant God.

"Yeah…" *Someone named Wall.* I was too full of the real story to talk about it any further. I knew I'd let something slip, so I suddenly went where I'd been afraid to go all along.

"Lisa Facebooked me a week ago Friday. The day the Peace was signed. I've messaged her back three times, but it's like…it's like…"

"We're praying for Ali," Kevin said as though he hadn't heard me mention Lisa.

"I asked Lisa to pray, too. I thought she'd at least respond to that."

"God will respond to that." He sighed. "So…why *did* she Facebook you?"

"To say she watched me on her smartphone. Doing my job. A commentator forum for the Bulletin. And she was troubled about what could happen if the Peace doesn't last. About what will happen to us…to all of us, I guess. Sometimes," I said, "I wish I'd never taken the job at the

Bulletin. It pulled us apart." I threw my hands in the air in an angry gesture. "No, I'm lying! I moved to Philly because I couldn't stand the fact that she and I were no longer together."

"You're talking to the wrong guy," Kevin said quietly, and he stopped for a moment in the middle of the crabgrass-tufted field.

Wrong guy?

"Why?" I was frustrated. "Are you gay?" It was a bitter jab, but I was upset. I wanted advice about Lisa. I finally worked up the guts to ask. And Kevin clams up!

"You can be such an ass, Matt," he said.

"Hey, dude," I shot back. "I don't mean are you *really* gay! I mean…can't you help a guy figure out his girl problems? You've been around a decade longer than me."

"Long enough to mess up a handful of lives. And to break my own heart in a hundred pieces."

"We all mess up." I gestured awkwardly.

"I never told you this," Kevin said, "but I was married once—for ten years." He pursed his lips, bobbed his head. "Great gal. Two kids. It fell apart. A disaster. I bear the blame. I was a self-centered idiot…worse than a self-centered idiot.

"I know God has forgiven me, but I haven't sorted it all out yet. Court won't let me see the kids. Maybe when they're eighteen, if they're not too embittered by Katie's own bitterness. Kyle will be eighteen in four years, Kristen in five. It tears me apart."

His eyes were on his feet as we walked.

"That big house I live in on Spruce Street," he continued. "It didn't always have Korean families renting from me. I bought it for Katie and me. Our children were born there." He took a deep breath. "And I didn't always go to church a block away at Renewal Presbyterian, but I wish I had."

"I'm sorry…"

"Give Lisa her space, Matt. From what you've told me in

the past, she loves God. God will lead her. If he wants you and Lisa together, he'll tell her."

"He already knows I love her!"

"Do you?"

"I've never loved anyone else!" I insisted. "Ever since I first saw her back in junior high! We dated in our last couple of years of high school. Kept in touch throughout college. I had a fling or two during that time, and a few more since, but it never changed how I felt about Lisa."

Kevin just stared at me.

"She was friends with some other guy from her church, on and off, for a few years after college," I said. "They both work at the church—same church my dad attends. She's a secretary and he's a youth pastor or something. But it never came to anything. He married someone else. She and I reconnected. Had some really fun times—good, clean Christian fun! I even went to church with her once or twice a month! I bought her a ring and asked her to marry me." I looked off across the field toward the river. "She said no."

"She loves God, Matt."

"She can't love God and me also?" I spat.

"She's playing by the rules, Matt. 'Do not be unequally yoked with an unbeliever.'"

"I'm not an *un*believer!" I argued. "I just don't need to sit in a big, stuffy stained glass house to talk to God or sing about him or hear some guy with a pastor's 'anointing' tell me what I need to do to stay out of hell."

"You don't love God," he said bluntly. "And you love yourself more than you love Lisa."

Then I saw the car. I'd seen it half an hour earlier, parked about a block from where we'd eaten supper.

"Hey, that grey car over there! There's a guy sitting in it, watching us. I saw him back on Arch...way back on Arch. Saw the car, I mean. Don't let him see you looking! He was at the curb, opposite side of the street from the Holiday Inn. Maybe a few blocks west."

"How could it be the same guy?"

"Same car. I know cars," I said. I used to play the car game with Frank Rogers when we were kids. You had to know the make and model, the year, too, from the front, the back, or the sides. He always beat me, but only because he would shout it out first. I always knew, but he always said it first. I hated losing. It got so I made up new rules. We had to remember all kinds of details about all our neighbor's cars including dings, dents, hubcap styles, and license plate numbers. "That car over there *is* the same car."

"Why would anyone be following us?" Kevin asked.

"Let's go ask him," I said on a whim. The welcomed lights of Frankford Street were coming into sight. Penn Treaty Park was only a block away, on the other side of the dark-walled warehouse at the end of our path. City Police patrolled the parks on a regular round, and the Security Alliance vets were out at night on bikes with headlights. I was up for an adventure. "Let's just walk over toward the car, carefully, and see what happens."

I thought Kevin would try to talk me out of it, but he said, "Okay, let's go. But not too fast."

As we headed toward the vehicle—a 2010 Chevy Cobalt, slate grey, two-door, no rims, busted gas panel, blue-light GPS on the dash—it pulled away slowly and headed up the street. We followed, keeping the car in sight.

"Kinda glad he's moving on," I admitted.

"I wonder what he wanted?" Kevin asked. "Money?"

"Wouldn't get much, would he?" I chuckled. All we had was a dirty penny and Claybucks—our national bank credit cards secured against identity theft and unauthorized use.

"Nothing at all, if I could help it," Kevin said, eyes on the drifting Cobalt.

We walked beside the warehouse and out of the shadows into the white blaze of the sol-power lights of Penn Treaty Park. Israeli technology again. Most cities still didn't have these yet. Sol-power cell lights absorb the sun all day

long and turn on automatically at dusk. Their special
filaments duplicate natural daylight so well that I felt like I
had stepped out of a darkened movie matinee into the mid-
afternoon sun.

The Cobalt still crept ahead of us, about half a block
away. At the other side of the park, bunched around a
Bulletin Board near some benches at the river's edge, a late-
evening crowd was gathered. Suddenly, the Cobalt sped
away.

Kevin and I stood silently, staring up the street. Lost in
my thoughts, I hardly heard the rising sound of voices
behind me. But I felt Kevin's hand on my shoulder, an
urgent grip. I turned to face the gang that had crossed the
park to confront us.

Teens. All black. Twelve of them. All male but one. They
were talking, if you could call it that. More like growling, I
thought. Or the grinding of some gigantic, out-of-synch
gears. It wasn't a comforting sound, mixed as it was with the
coarse shuffling of feet as the gang spread out in a semi-
circle in front of us. I heard the dull clank of metal against
metal—chains, or something worse.

Kevin was the first to challenge their approach. "Yo," he
said, loudly and clearly, "what's out with the pride
tonight?"

"Cold crew," said a big bruising dude with an Afro
twice the size of his head. Interpretation: *We're chillin'—and
we're doin' just fine, thank you.*

"What's the score?" Kevin asked, thumbing his hat to
point out his allegiance to the city's team. He knew they'd
been watching the baseball game live on the Bulletin Board
across the park.

"Seven to four, Phillies!" the girl piped. She was sucking
on a cigarette and blowing the smoke into the night sky.

"Fifth inning," said one fellow, a lighter-skinned black in
a long white T-shirt that hung so far over his knees that I
could barely see his black shorts beneath it.

"Rod hit it blast hard, over the top. Three runs. Then…then *you*." He laughed as he said it, and the rest of them chuckled. I didn't think it was funny.

Everybody was dressed in black and white except for Cold Crew who wore a green shirt over black straight-leg jeans. He said, "Sh'up," and everybody shut up.

"Bet on it?" Kevin said. Bet on what? The game? Kevin was stalling for time, playing these guys, feeling them out.

"Got it anyway," Cold Crew said.

Oh! So they wanted whatever we had on us. More than Mr. Chevy Cobalt wanted it. Or maybe the Cobalt was in with these guys. Scout out two white dudes leaving a classy restaurant, follow them, keep in touch with your crew by phone. Hit them and take what they have. Suddenly, I wished I'd opted for those self-defense classes in college.

The gang pressed closer, and Cold Crew put his hands in his pockets. "Loaded?" he asked. Was that a signal to his gang? Was he talking about weapons? Was he asking if we had money?

"Wired," Kevin said. And Cold Crew stiffened. Kevin had just told him we were miked for sound, maybe video.

"Ya laughin' me? Or ya straight up?"

"Wired," Kevin repeated. "Double," he said, jerking his thumb toward the warehouse behind us. I glanced and saw the cameras. City surveillance. Every park was watched now—or at least filmed—round the clock. Urban security. I had almost gotten used to the fact that Big Brother was watching.

"Bet on it?" Cold Crew said through a wide, white grin. Was it a challenge, or did the guy just have a good sense of humor?

"Know this face?" Kevin said, pointing to me.

Everyone stared.

"Yo!" shrieked the girl. "The Bulletin Board guy!"

Everyone leaned forward and stared all the more.

"Wired," I said. Figured I'd get in the game, too. I had

turned on my smartphone recorder as soon as Kevin had started talking. Thumbed a call to the Bulletin also, but all I was getting were automated prompts.

Then suddenly the police came. No sirens, but the flashing lights could almost knock you over. Cold Crew didn't move. Nobody moved. Four cars. Eight cops. Where had they come from? What brought them? Talk about timing!

"Everything okay here, folks?"

"Fine," said Kevin. "We're just discussing the game." He pointed to the Board at the other end of the park.

"You see Domonic's home run?" asked one of the cops.

"Yo, three men in!" said Cold Crew. He took a pack of cigarettes out of his pocket. "Gotta pen?" he asked me. I fumbled for one and found it. "Autograph!" he said, holding out the cigarette pack. I signed it, trying to stop my hands from shaking. "M.L. Clifford," read Cold Crew with a grin, "Board Man! Mister News! Line up, kids!" And the gang pulled out scraps of paper and candy bar wrappers for me to sign. One guy had me sign his arm, just above a full-color tattoo of a coiled rattlesnake.

"Jesus loves you," Kevin said, as one after another they faded into the darkness along the river.

"You want a ride?" asked a policeman.

"Yes!" we said in grateful unison. "The 4000 block of Spruce," Kevin added.

As we pulled away from Penn Treaty in the back of a police cruiser, I shook my head in weary disbelief. "Man," I said to Kevin, "you've got the street lingo down! But what would we have done if the cops hadn't come along?"

Kevin leaned toward me in the darkened seat and opened his shirt. Under his left arm was a shoulder holster and a gun. "It's licensed," he said quietly.

"So much for 'What Would Jesus Do?'"

"I'm not a Mennonite from Lancaster County," he said.

"No kidding!"

"I know how to turn the other cheek when it's appropriate," he said.

"What about love your enemies?"

Kevin was silent.

I wasn't playing fair. The guy loved God. He loved his neighbor. He would never pull that gun unless he absolutely had to, and then probably only to protect someone else — someone as foolhardy as me!

The cruiser's speaker crackled on above our heads, startling me. "Spruce Street?" asked the cop who was driving.

"Yeah, 4620 Spruce. Corner of Spruce and Farragut," Kevin said loudly. "My friend lives up at Brown and Broad. Can you drop him off at his own place after you take me home?" I guessed Kevin didn't want to talk anymore.

"Sure," said the cop. "Were you really chewing about the Phillies and the Mets with those guys?"

"Yes," said Kevin, "and other things — like talking our way out of an armed robbery. Let's just say we're glad you showed up!"

"We got a call," said our driver.

A call? I looked at Kevin. He shrugged, puzzled.

"911 dispatch," said the cop. "A report of trouble at Penn Treaty Park. We pulled a few cars together and swung over. The gangs are wild lately."

"Those guys were looking for dope money, and they might have tried to roll us for it," said Kevin. "We're very glad you came along!" He turned to me. "Want me to pick you up for lunch tomorrow?" He smiled. "I'll treat, and we can finish that talk about Lisa." He was trying.

"Thanks," I said, "but no. I need some time to process everything. And with all that's happening in the news, I'll probably eat lunch on the job."

Kevin nodded, then turned to look out the window at the streetscape and the passing cars. When we got to his house, he shook my hand firmly, stepped out of the car, cupped his hands to tell me he was praying, and tipped his baseball cap as we drove away.

The ride to my apartment was a quiet one.

My phone rang. I heard it in my dreams before it woke me up. It could have awakened my neighbors first—I was so deep in sleep. I fumbled in the dark, knocked my clock on the floor, then finally got my fingers on the phone.

"Yeah," I mumbled thickly before the phone was even to my face. "Matt here—more or less. Who's this?"

"Lisa."

"Lisa," I repeated numbly. Was I still asleep?

"You okay?" she asked.

"Uh…yeah," I said. "Just kinda sleepy…asleep. That is, I was. What time is it?"

"Four o'clock in the morning, Matt. Awful early. I'm sorry."

"Lisa…"

"I had a dream," she said.

"I was having one, too," I said, fuzzy-headed and annoyed. *Idiot,* I said to myself. *Say something nice, something gracious.* Lisa hadn't called me once in the two years I'd lived in Philly. A few e-mails were all I'd gotten. I'd practically sworn to God to go to church for an actual phone call from this girl. "Tell me about it," I managed. "And are *you* okay?"

"Yes," she said, suddenly guarded. "I just wanted to…to talk to you…about some things. I had a dream—a nightmare—but I'm not looking for comfort, Matt."

Why did this call have to be in the middle of the night when I couldn't think?

"I just can't sleep with all that's going on in the world," she said. "I mean, I've been praying for Ali…like you asked in your message. Praying for Jerusalem, for peace in Jerusalem, and now…"

"Now there's peace," I said.

"Yes, but…"

I could hear her breathing.

"Go ahead," I said, easing toward sympathy. "I'm a little bit more awake now."

I wanted to say, *It's good to hear your voice*, but was it? Why was she calling? Because she cared about me? No—she wanted to pick my brain. Matt has a good brain. He's got his fingers on the world's pulse. He knows the news. He can make sense out of current events, as long as the events aren't personal.

"I really don't want to talk over the phone," she said.

So why call? At 4:00 in the morning! I didn't know what to say, so I said nothing.

"Could you…you know…once you get a few more hours of sleep… drive home in the morning?" she asked. "Meet me somewhere for breakfast? And just talk?"

Drive home? Lancaster wasn't home anymore. Even with Dad there. Even with my sister Bethany and her husband and kids.

Breakfast with Lisa? My God, I'd run barefoot to Panama for breakfast with Lisa! But now that she was asking, I was surprised at my resistance.

"I'd have to call in sick to the Bulletin," I explained. With the news of Ali's kidnapping, Sutton would expect more of me than usual. But we had plenty of capable hands on call, and my column didn't run until Wednesday. "I've got personal days coming, and I can…" *Sutton won't let me go*, I argued with myself. *He'd beg me to come in even if I was sick!*

"I don't want you to tell any lies or get in trouble for playing hooky from work."

"No, it…it won't be like that," I fumbled. "I can take time off when I need to," I lied. "And I can make it up throughout the week." *Like hell I can!*

"Then, you'll come?"

"Yes," I said, in spite of myself. "I'll meet you at the Neptune Diner on Prince Street in Lancaster City around

8:00. There's a non-smoking room in the back. "

"No," she said. "That's too small…not private enough. The tables are too close to each other. Everybody can hear everybody else. How about Shady Maple? You love their breakfast buffet."

"Yeah," I said. "I do."

"And how about nine o'clock?"

"What about *your* job?" She worked at her church.

"I've got the morning off. The church is helping with a week-long tent revival. That's in the evenings, so I'm working afternoons. I'm going to the tent meeting tonight. Maybe…but, never mind that. Nine o'clock at Shady Maple?"

"Yeah," I said. "Sure."

"Thanks, Matt. Sorry to wake you."

"No…it's…I was… Yeah, well…we can talk in the morning. It's already morning, of course. But…that's okay." I noticed then that the connection was dead. I sat in my bed for a long time, staring at nothing. "Good night, Lisa," I said at last to the phone and the walls and the dull, dark silence.

10

Dreams and Visions

Monday morning, July 14.

I didn't sleep at all after Lisa's call. In fact, I got up around 5:00 to pace my living room in the dark. I showered, shaved, dressed. I put some things in a knapsack and walked to Kevin's where my car was in storage. His garage was a safer place to park than at my own apartment, and I seldom drove during the week. It was cheaper, and healthier, to walk to work.

With a password Kevin had given me, I turned off his garage alarm and quietly rolled my car out. That was around 6:30. A few minutes later, I called the Bulletin and left a message in Sutton's voice mail. I told him I was worn out and sick. I told him I was turning off my phones in order to sleep. A couple of the newsroom guys could handle my regular Monday workload, and they could rope in the weather intern to help if need be. I could put in some late hours on Tuesday, Wednesday, and Thursday if I was feeling better. At 6:55, I turned on my phone to call Kevin and tell him I'd taken my car for a day trip to Lancaster.

"Lancaster?" he asked.

"Breakfast with Lisa. I'll be back tonight to park this machine in your garage again."

"Lisa," he echoed.

"I don't know what I'm doing," I admitted. "I'll tell you about it when I get back. Or maybe tomorrow."

"Have a good day," said Kevin. I think he meant it.

My route wound westward out of Philadelphia through a monotonous jumble of urban sprawl until, connecting with US 30, a half-hour drive through Chester County brought me to the Lancaster County border. Almost immediately, the view from the highway opened into vistas of beautiful gardens, well-kept houses, whitewashed barns, and verdant pastures filled with fat cattle. The rest of the world was turning yellow for lack of rain, but Lancaster looked as if it was watered from within.

The rural landscape was interrupted occasionally by small towns, home-grown restaurants, historic roadside inns, and a stretch of train rails still in daily use by Amtrak. North of Route 30, the click-clack of horseshoes on asphalt became audible as I passed the horse-drawn buggies of the Amish who populated a good portion of the county. In front of me, cornfields rose thick and green on either side of the road. My dad always said that a good crop of corn is "knee high by the fourth of July." This corn was high enough to hide an NBA basketball team! The farmland of Lancaster is some of the best soil on earth.

Another couple of miles and I'd be at Shady Maple Smorgasbord—and breakfast with Lisa. I still had no idea what I would say when I saw her. I'd rehearsed a half-dozen openers about a hundred times—none to my satisfaction.

Shady Maple. Parking lot filled as always. Lisa's little yellow hybrid near the middle of the lot. She wasn't in it. I pulled over next to her car, got out, and walked toward the restaurant. It was a sunny Lancaster summer morn, humid and heading toward hot. I could smell the fertilizer in the fields.

"Hello, Matt!"

I turned, startled at the sound of my name—but even more by the voice that spoke it. It was Dad!

My father, Jonathan David Clifford, was a tall, good-looking guy in his early 70s. Something in his genes had kept the color of his age out of his thinning hair. (I hoped those genes had been passed on to me.) His short-cropped sideburns sported most of the obvious grey, but even his scruffy goatee was still predominately dark. Steel-blue eyes danced behind a pair of contemporary wire-rim glasses—you only saw the wrinkles when he smiled. And he had done a better job of keeping his belly under his belt than most men his age. He played tennis. When he and I played against each other (which was very seldom those days), he usually won.

J.D. Clifford used to teach American history to middle-schoolers. You'll recognize his name if you read cowboy novels. His short story, *Rio Rancho*, was picked up by Hollywood and filmed as *Blood on the Water*, starring Ewan McGregor as a nineteenth century Scottish immigrant in New Mexico. Dad was a steady contributor to American Heritage magazine, and he authored a couple of non-fiction books about the American west. Dad's father, Joseph Richard Clifford, was a small-town Pennsylvania newspaper editor. Dad's mother, Jean Margaret Clifford, was a published poet. My sister, Bethany Joy Clifford Wasman (who edited a popular regional homeschool magazine), liked to say that "the ink is in the blood" of the Clifford family. She was referring to printer's ink, and she was right.

Mom had been gone for five years. Cancer took her. But during the year and a half that she fought the disease, she got religion. Dad came out of a spiritual coma at that same time, and they started going to church. They joined a congregation of holy rollers that spent Sunday mornings clapping, shouting, singing, and dancing to the accom-paniment of a spiritually sanitized rock and roll band. They called it contemporary worship. A perfect fit for a couple of ex-hippies. I was in college at Penn State at the time and only went to church with my parents when I was home on holidays. Lisa went to the same church.

I got to know their pastor, Rick Randolph, because he and Dad played a lot of tennis together. Sometimes Bethany and I played doubles against them. A year or two before Mom's death, I backed out of church altogether. If God is everywhere, then why pack yourself into a building to worship him? Maybe I've got too much Woodstock Generation in me from my parents. Maybe I'm just a black sheep on the fields of salvation. Maybe I'm a goat—and not a sheep at all. I don't try too hard to figure it out.

"You by yourself, Dad?"

"Meeting someone," he said. "Same as you."

We crossed the parking lot and found Lisa waiting in the restaurant lobby. A quiet greeting, a sad smile, a brief "thank you for coming." No hug, no kiss. What did I expect? I felt numb.

We asked for a booth—Lisa and Dad and I. "You've ganged up on me," I said. I wasn't happy. This was not the intimate moment with Lisa I had envisioned. This was some kind of set-up, cooked up by my father and the girl he'd once told me was too good for me.

"There's no conspiracy, Matt," said Dad. "Lisa called me this morning, distressed. She said you were coming because she asked you to. But she chickened out. She didn't want to talk to you alone."

"So you're the chaperone," I said coldly.

"Matt!" Lisa said sharply.

I almost lost my cool right then, but I glared at her instead. Looked her up and down—which wasn't very nice of me. Her slight, trim figure curved where it counted. She wore a modest blue summer dress. Her naturally blonde hair fell a few inches over her shoulders in a bright, lively wave. When I looked into those clear blue eyes that mirrored the soul of the girl, something gripped me. This was the woman stuck in my heart, but did I really want her in there? Did I really love myself more, as Kevin had said? Dad put his hand on my shoulder. I turned toward him stiffly.

"Let's eat," I said, starting toward the buffet tables. I wasn't happy, but I was hungry.

Lisa's dream, like most dreams, was a crazy quilt of changing actors and shifting scenes. She'd had the same dream several times—two nights in a row recently—and it frightened her.

I was in it. So was Dad. So was an old childhood friend whom I couldn't recall when Lisa mentioned him. The four of us were riding bicycles on a forested path that led to a rambling mansion by a riverside. Lisa and I went inside, but Dad and the other guy weren't with us anymore.

We climbed a winding staircase to a door that opened on an outside balcony without rails. It leaned precariously out over the river, which became a waterfall, loud and raging. The stairwell behind us became a wooden ramp with men on horseback ascending—four men. At first they looked like people Lisa knew, but she couldn't place their names. Then a voice said, "Come and see!" and the shape and clothing of the horsemen changed.

A man on a white horse carried a bow and a quiver of arrows on his back. A crown was on his head. A man on a red horse wielded a great sword, sharp and bloody. A man on a black horse rode with a pair of weighing scales in his hand. And the fourth rider sat upon a pale horse. This last rider's name was Death, and the dead were following him.

As the horsemen came closer, the balcony became a wide floating dock, pitching to and fro upon the waters above the falls. Then it was loose upon the waters, a raft without moorings. The dead stopped at river's edge, but the horsemen waded into the river toward us. Dad was on the shore—with Ali!—shouting to us. We could hear their fading voices as our raft tipped and we tumbled over the falls. Then Lisa awoke.

I had no idea what the dream was about, or what Lisa wanted from me. But I wasn't enjoying my omelet anymore.

"It may mean nothing," Dad offered. *No kidding!* "But to dream the same thing twice?"

"Look," I said, pushing my plate aside. "I sometimes dream the same thing for a couple of nights. Doesn't everyone? Maybe young men will dream dreams and old men will have visions, like the Bible says. Maybe daughters will prophecy. But I don't know anything about this stuff. I'm not Joseph telling Pharaoh what his dreams mean. You've got folks in your church who do the Holy Ghost thing, don't you?"

"Matt…" said Lisa. "I'm afraid for you."

My spite softened. All she had to do was say my name.

"Afraid for me!" I frowned. I was a little afraid myself, given the events of the last few days, but I wasn't about to get into that.

"Yes," she said. "The reason I wanted to talk to you is that God has been asking me to pray for your protection."

"My best friend carries a gun," I said glumly.

"It's not about Philadelphia," she said. "It's something else. Something that's happening in other places in the world. Something about Ali—you asked me to pray for Ali. Something about the four horsemen."

I knew who those horsemen were. We'd talked about them at the pancake seminary. They were from Revelation. Lisa knew that, too, I was sure. Dad also.

"What about them?" I asked.

"I don't know," she said. "But it's…it's big. And your best friend's gun won't help one bit!"

"I appreciate the prayers," I said. "You can talk to God about me all you want. I'm okay with that." I looked at Dad.

"But this other stuff is too weird. I've got enough to deal with while I'm awake. Real wars. Real mysteries. Real friends lost in the real world."

A waitress cleared our plates while I played with a half-empty glass of fruit juice. I looked at Lisa. "Did you ask me to meet you today just to tell me this dream?"

She bit her lip and dropped her eyes. Probably wished she'd never called me.

"Well, I took the day off," I said fumbling, "so…maybe we can drive around the county later and…and talk about the dream some more." I wanted to drive straight back to Philly.

"I have to work," said Lisa, her eyes lifting to mine. "I have to get ready for the revival tonight."

"Oh, yeah, I forgot about that." I was feeling pretty stupid and getting really irritated.

Dad tried to help. "Lisa thought…we thought…that maybe God had been speaking to you lately."

"Oh, sure! God and I have a little talk every night before I go to bed. I tell him thanks for another day, and he says, 'No problem.' Come on, Dad! It's just a dream!"

Lisa was staring at the table.

"Matt," said Dad.

"Dad," I said, more sarcastically than I meant to. He ignored it.

"Matt," he repeated, "I'd like you to join me tonight for the tent meeting."

Hell, no! came to mind. *Honor thy father* came to mind next. I snorted and stared at my plate. "Well, I took the day off. When's this tent meeting? And where?"

"Seven o'clock, at County Park," said Dad. "Up in that big stretch where the old ball fields used to be before they bulldozed them over and let the grass grow up *au naturel*."

"You can see the city from that hill," I recalled. "I'll meet you there," I muttered reluctantly. "Save me a chair if I'm late."

"I'll bring you a Bible," said Dad.

"Actually," I admitted hesitantly, "I've got one in a knapsack in the backseat of the car. I read it every Saturday morning at the Dutch Eating Place in the Reading Market. That's my weekly devotions."

"Devotions?" Lisa asked, her eyes widening.

"Just a Bible study I got roped into by a former co-worker," I explained tersely. "It's not a religious thing. Bunch of guys from different churches. Regular guys. That's why I like it. That...and the pancakes!"

Outside I said good-bye to Dad, then walked Lisa to her car. She got in, closed the door, and opened her window. "I'll look for you tonight," she said.

"I'll look for you, too. Hope your afternoon goes well."

She smiled, but the smile froze when she saw the startled look on my face. "What's the matter?" she asked.

"Nothing," I lied. "Thought I saw someone I knew. I used to live around here, you know!" I grinned awkwardly. "But, it's nothing. Nobody." I stepped back from her car. "See you later," I said with a little shuffle. "I'm going to go drive around the countryside with my windows down—take in the Lancaster County dairy air." I held my nose for a second, smiled again, waved, and walked away.

The slate-gray Chevy Cobalt! In the shade of a row of maples at the edge of the parking lot. I headed straight for my car. Climbing in, I saw Lisa drive away. I pulled out of my spot, cruised the lot, and came up alongside the Cobalt. Yes, it was the same car! But...not exactly. The scratches and the dents were identical—I was positive—but the wheels now had hub caps. There was a white ribbon tied to the radio antennae. I hadn't seen that yesterday. Several of the cars in the lot had ribbons like that. I think churches give out the ribbons on Pro-life Sunday or Anti-porn Sunday, or something like that.

I got out of my car and circled the Cobalt. Nobody in it. Nobody heading toward it. It wasn't even locked. I thought of opening the door and rifling the glove compartment. But, what if it had an alarm?

I checked the license plate. Pennsylvania. DLR 1882. Current registration. No dealer's identification. A normal plate. I hadn't memorized the plate last night, but this one looked familiar. Was I going paranoid?

I got in my car and drove to an empty spot between a pickup truck and an antique station wagon. I could just see the Cobalt from there. I settled back in my seat and chewed at my fingernails while I watched folks coming and going from the restaurant.

Finally, a middle-aged white man, wearing a green John Deere cap, came out, walked toward the Cobalt, got in, and drove away. He never so much as glanced in my direction, never looked anywhere else either. *I must be going nuts.*

I watched him leave the lot, and gave him a full minute to head down the road. I drove out onto the road myself, but only after the Cobalt disappeared over the hill in the distance. He couldn't have been the same guy as in Philly! Then again, if he was, he couldn't have had anything to do with Cold Crew and the Penn Treaty Park gang. And if he had nothing to do with them, but he was the guy from last night, then who *was* he? What was he doing in Lancaster... and at the same restaurant as me? If he trailed me from Philadelphia, why did he drive away and leave me here now? Or did he have a partner who was dogging me instead?

Was there someone else? Another car? Was my car bugged, so that he didn't have to follow me to know where I was? What was going on? Why would anyone want to shadow me?

Did this have something to do with Ali? With the under-the-radar world of political intrigue and government intelligence agencies?

I remembered Jacqui Johnson's comment about the people who questioned us at the Bulletin: *They know more about us than we know about ourselves. Especially the little guy – George Ognobini.*

Was one of George's agents tagging me? Did they have my apartment bugged? Did they know about my contact with Wall? Did somebody else know about Wall? What if some Russian secret agent was on my tail?

"Humbug!" I scoffed. "Damn it!" I added. This morning's version of Cobalt Man was probably just some local farmer enjoying a breakfast spread before heading back to the farm to shovel manure. But I drove down the road in the opposite direction that the Cobalt had gone. And I watched my tail.

In my rearview mirror there was nothing but an old produce truck that pulled off the road into a farm. Even as I watched, I half expected the driver to lean out his window and stare at me through dark sunglasses and a pair of binoculars. He didn't. I swung off the main drag and hit the back roads.

At a totally un-peopled intersection, I drove onto the grass shoulder, stopped the car, and opened my glove compartment to see if Cobalt Man had stuck some high-tech homing device in there. I looked under my dash. I swore at myself as I dug dirty coins out of the cracks of my car seats. I checked in my trunk, under my hood, on the underframe of the car. Nothing, of course. Sweating and calling myself demeaning names, I crawled back into the driver's seat and headed east toward the Susquehanna.

It's all just a weird coincidence, I told myself. *Can't be the same car! Wasn't the same car. Will never be the same car. I'm upset about Ali, and I'm imagining the whole thing!*

I finally convinced myself and threw the puzzle to the wind. I turned on the radio and found a 1960s classic rock station. Soon I was belting out the songs I'd heard my dad sing all my life.

I spent the afternoon by myself.

I rolled up and down the hills surrounding Pequea Creek, swung over to Tucquan Glen, and hiked the woods along the water. Then I drove up toward Millersville, bought a Big Mac, and headed back down to River Road to wind my way up to the Pinnacle. There I parked on the windy ridge that gazes down upon the whirling waters of the wide Susquehanna.

The view from the Pinnacle was spectacular. The high wooded hills of York County rose like walls of a fortress on the other side of the river. Looking down at the river itself, I saw a lone fisherman in a rowboat—tiny as a pin from my vantage point—heading downstream past a spate of small islands. There were no other signs of human life, upriver or down, as far as the eye could see.

Once upon a time, Lisa and I used to drive to the Pinnacle alone. We found places to hide—crevices in the rocks, grassy shelves halfway down the massive cliffside— where we laughed and dreamed and did things our parents said we shouldn't do. Then Lisa got religious. Or maybe she was always religious, and it was me who got un-religious. That was years ago.

I scrambled carefully down the steep incline and found one of our old hideouts. Sitting in the late afternoon sun, memory singing sadly to my soul, the wind whispering in the trees below me—I actually dozed.

I awoke with a start.

I glanced at my watch. It was nearly a quarter to 6:00. And Wall would be calling—I *hoped* he'd be calling—at 6:30.

I climbed up to the overlook, jogged to my car, and drove back down the mountainside.

11

Sideshow

I pulled into County Park from the east side and drove down a wooded lane where an old covered bridge crosses the Little Conestoga. Just beyond the bridge, I found a place to park and turned off the ignition. The little red phone rang a moment later—6:30 on the nose.

"Yes," I said. "I'm alone."

"Two minutes," Wall said. "And good news."

"News of Ali?"

"You're scooped again, and I can't tell you how, but you'll find out tomorrow. FOX at Dawn—7:00 a.m. Don't miss it. Absolutely don't miss it. Record it."

"He's well?"

"Yes."

"He's where?"

"I don't know. I don't think he knows."

"How do you know what he thinks."

"I don't know what he thinks."

"Where are you?"

"Hiding."

"From who?"

"Any number of suspicious parties," Wall said. "Russians, mostly. Arabs of assorted national origin. Maybe an American or two. I can run fast if I need to." A moment's pause and then, "There's work for you to do. It will help Ali.

It will help many. Don't miss the broadcast. FOX at Dawn—
7:00 a.m. Record it."

"OK. And then what?"

"I'll tell you when I know."

"The manhunt?"

"It continues, as you know from official Russian sources."

"But you have other sources?"

"I have eyes. I have ears."

"More than one pair?"

"Hands and feet, too."

"Are you safe?"

He laughed quietly, ironically.

"You'll call tomorrow evening at 6:30?" I asked.

"What does the Good Book say? *'Lord willing.'*"

"And the creek don't rise," I added. That one wasn't in the Good Book.

The phone went dead. *Lord willing.* Who was this fellow, this Wall? This Sleuth? More than your average, mild-mannered reporter, obviously. But how much more?

I drove further into the park. Past the tennis courts. Past the fenced-in garden plots rented by city residents who raised their own vegetables in the battle with rising inflation. Past the gate to the upper fields—a gate usually locked to anything with four wheels. Tonight the fields were jam-packed, from tree line to tree line, with parked vehicles— everything from solar-electric SUVs to one-horsepower Amish buggies. A line of horses was tethered to a rope beneath two tall sycamores. This was Lancaster.

On a flat rise in the middle of it all stood a massive yellow tent, its canvas sides rolled up. It was packed with an overflow crowd seated outside on folding chairs. More people stood behind them. Folks sat in the backs of pickup trucks and on top of vans in order to get a glimpse of the goings-on inside the tent. I circled the tent twice, looking for

Lisa and Dad, but couldn't find them. I worked my way inside and settled on the matted grass against one of the canopy's main supporting poles.

A band was playing on a central stage—guitars, drums, keyboard, a saxophone, and a violin—leading the crowd in songs of worship, but the music was so loud I couldn't understand the words. The crowd was engaged in the experience in a variety of distracting ways. Some folks sang. Some shouted. Some jumped up and down in place. Others clapped their hands or raised their arms.

Near the stage, a few women danced gracefully, expressively. Some waved large nylon flags that dipped and whirled in front of the band in an ethereal blur of muted colors. Children played on the grass at their parent's feet. Amish men with their hats off sang through their beards. I closed my eyes and gave my mind to the rhythm of the amplified instruments, the thunder of hands and drums, and the incoherent syllables of song.

At last, the strains of a calming and familiar melody drifted through the tent, and I found myself on my feet, singing along to Amazing Grace. I scanned the crowd again for Lisa, for Dad. Couldn't find them in the mix.

The band stopped playing. The instruments were moved to the back of the stage, making room for a small podium. A man and a woman stood side-by-side at the podium, taking turns thanking various people for their part in making things happen. A brief prayer followed, then a brief introduction, and evangelist John Brunk was suddenly all alone on stage. Short, squat, and bearded, with an Amish accent and a strong tenor voice, Mr. Brunk started preaching.

Brunk was an engaging speaker, but where was Dad? I tried to follow the sermon, but I couldn't keep my mind from wandering.

I remembered playing little league baseball on that hill as a boy. Dad never missed a game. The mayor of Lancaster always came out to throw the first pitch of the season. Local clergy took turns saying a prayer before each game, and then the umpire hollered, "Play ball!"

Lancaster! Where else could a tent revival be held in the county's largest public park? The event might be shut down if it were happening elsewhere in the country. America wasn't as church-friendly as it used to be. Tax-free status was under review by the IRS. House churches and home Bible studies were losing ordinance battles in many cities. Church buildings were being locked and chained in some states. So-called hate-crimes legislation and restrictive urban zoning were challenging the free-speech rights of Christians and hampering their ability to assemble publicly. But not in Lancaster. The county was a haven. An oasis. An anomaly.

Brunk was shouting. Quoting Revelation. It seemed like everywhere I went folks were talking about the end of the world. He was railing about trumpets and seals and a pregnant woman in heaven who was standing on the moon. She was clothed with the sun and crowned with twelve stars. She was Israel, Brunk said, and Satan was out to kill her. But God was protecting her, and so the devil was looking for someone else to persecute. He was going after the Church, because the Church was the offspring of the woman. If you can't hit mom, then hit the kids!

"The day is here," Brunk practically yodeled, "in which the devil has his sleeves rolled up! He's sowing tares in the fields of the righteous, undermining the foundations of the faith, tearing down the temples of the faithful. Like a hungry lion, he prowls and leaps, and he devours. Some turn tail and run from the lion. Some stand firm, as God has called us to, even when it means our lives! When a Christian dies for his faith," Brunk sang, "he does not lose the battle against the enemy. He overcomes the enemy! John the Revelator wrote that 'They have conquered him by the blood of the Lamb and by the word of their testimony, for they loved not their lives unto death.'"

Gory story! But I remembered church camp. I saw myself sitting with a circle of ten-year-old boys at the foot of a bunk bed while a counselor (whose name and face I wish I could recall) read us the story of Stephen, the first Christian martyr. The tale gripped me. What faith Stephen had! To stand there, looking up into heaven, face shining like the sun, and let men stone him to death because he wouldn't back down from his love for Jesus.

That was church camp. This was camp meeting. *No difference, actually,* I thought. Except that I wasn't ten years old anymore. And I wasn't "in love" with Jesus.

"Are you ready for the return of the Lord?" Brunk shouted. "Are you washed in the blood of the Lamb? Can you stand up to the devil and defeat him by the word of your testimony? Do you have a testimony? Do you know God? Will you be able to stand when the evil day comes— and, having done all, remain standing? Will Jesus find faith on the earth when he comes to rescue his Church from the tribulation that is coming? Will you be ready to meet the Lord in the air? Or will you be left behind?"

I thought of Kevin. He'd be ready, come what may. *And I'll be ready, too,* I told myself stubbornly. *God knows my heart.*

"If you're not living for Jesus," Brunk said quietly, "then you're not ready."

"What must we do to be saved?" a man cried out poignantly from the center of the tent. I coughed. Was this staged? I didn't think so, but it was a damn good show!

Brunk fired back his answer. "Call upon the name of the Lord, and you will be saved!" And then he began to talk about Jesus.

Jesus.

I was drawn to Jesus as a boy. He was my hero. I thought he was so cool. He always had an answer for the religious hypocrites, and I still like that about him. He always had time for the lowlife and the leper. He hung out with everyday people, and he told great stories. His miracles made him a superhero in my eyes. And the way he stood up to the Roman governor Pontius Pilate, even after he'd been beaten within an inch of his life—that took *macho!*

I wanted to be like that. Able to take the hit, spit out the broken teeth, turn the other cheek, and still come back with the perfect one-liner. Then cast out another demon just to show the world who my Father was!

Brunk was talking about the cross. About the blood of Jesus shed as payment for the sins of the world—a sacrificial price for the ransom of our souls. I used to believe that. Kevin still did. The pancake seminary guys did. Maybe I did, too, but I wondered how we'd gotten from a bloody cross on a hill outside Jerusalem to a circus tent on a hill outside Lancaster?

The tent grew strangely still. On stage, next to brother Brunk, was another Amish man, tall and thin, with a dark, gaunt face and a white, wispy beard. He raised his eyes to the canvas ceiling and began to speak. Without a microphone, his deep, sonorous voice carried his words to the crowd. He wasn't really preaching. He was prophesying, shouting "thus saith the Lord!" I was gripped by the moment and stood up to hear him.

"My people," he said, addressing the crowd as though he were God himself, "a flood is coming, like the flood of Noah, but not like the flood of Noah. A flood of darkness, not of rain—a darkness that will cover the face of the earth like the waters cover the seas."

Darkness. That was certainly an apt description of the world around us. Danger, deceit, destruction, despair, death—darkness.

The Bulletin marketed darkness daily. The tragic tales we told. The terrible images we broadcast. The hurricanes, famines, and floods we covered. The greed and violence, hatred and corruption. The senseless acts of violence and betrayal that filled the pages of our newspaper and flashed across the city on our Boards. It made me wonder whether the Peace would be good for the news — or not!

My thoughts moved on to Ali — to the bloody events of Red Square. What had really happened there? Who planned that terrible attack? Why was Ali there? Why had he been kidnapped? Why did the terrorists kill the other captive and allow Ali to live?

Ali spoke their language. What had he said to them? What had he promised? Did he beg for mercy as a husband and a father whose life was precious to those who loved him? Was he talking with his captives even now? What was he plotting? What was he praying? I didn't know…I couldn't see. It was all darkness.

The tall Amish exhorter kept his face uplifted while he spoke. His hands moved expressively. I couldn't see his eyes, but I had the impression they were open wide.

"Don't be surprised by the fiery trial that will come upon you," he cried. "Blessed are you when men revile you and persecute you and say all kinds of evil things against you falsely for your stand with Christ. Rejoice! And be exceedingly glad, for great is your reward in heaven, for so they persecuted the prophets who came before you."

He lowered his eyes at last and let his piercing gaze wander through the tent. "I know your works and your labor and your patience, and how you can't bear those who are evil," he continued. "How you have tested those who say they are God's messengers, but they are not, and you have found them to be liars. And you have labored for the name of Christ and have not fainted. But God has something against you!"

He does? I asked myself. *What?*

"You have left your first love!" the prophet thundered.

The book of Revelation again. We had read the "first

love" passage the week we started studying the book. I recognized myself in the words — or at least I saw the child I had been, the boy who once-upon-a-time was captivated by the person of Jesus Christ.

The prophet's words rolled on: "Therefore, remember from where you have fallen, and repent! Do the things you did in the beginning. Or else I will come to you quickly, and I will snatch away the candlestick from where it stands."

"Repent!" shouted Brunk, an abrupt exclamation point at the end of the thin man's exhortation. And then again, "Repent! Repent!"

And suddenly, as though the entire congregation took this for a cue, folks began to get up from their seats — inside and outside the tent — and walk toward the stage. I'm not normally claustrophobic, but a panic gripped me. I felt like I was caught in the current of a spiritual riptide, drawn into a whirlpool at the center of the tent. I might go under and never come up again!

Then Lisa was at my elbow. I couldn't hear the preacher anymore for the up-swell of music as the band struck up a loud crescendo to this bizarre reality show.

"Is my dad here?" I shouted.

"Over there!" she yelled. I saw him, maybe twenty feet to my right.

"Has he been there all night?"

"Yes," she mouthed, though I couldn't hear her.

Only twenty feet away! Weird how one face can so easily melt into a crowd.

Or jump out of a crowd! *That man! — standing just beyond my father.* The man who had gotten into the Cobalt at Shady Maple. He wasn't looking at me, but he was definitely scanning the crowd. His hat was off. But it was the same man. I tried to get closer.

The current was moving slower. The preacher and the prophet were praying for folks near the stage. The sound was deafening. I lost my man, saw him, lost him — then saw

Dad, moving with the masses, then out of sight.

I elbowed a small boy — unseen in the press — as I pushed toward my father. "Sorry," I shouted, stopping to see if he was okay. He rubbed his forehead, forced a smile — and I realized I was utterly without a compass in the sea of moving bodies. The waters parted for a moment, and there again was Dad. He saw me, turned toward me. But Cobalt Man was gone from sight completely. Had he moved forward with the crowd? Dad and I connected clumsily.

"Did you see a guy with a green John Deere hat?" I yelled.

"John Deere hat? No."

"Without the hat, then! White guy, five o'clock shadow, a little shorter than you, green shirt, long sleeves rolled up. Looks like a farmer."

"No."

"He was here a minute ago — on your right!"

"Somebody you know?"

"Not really, but…" I pressed forward to the prayer line. People were weeping. Falling over. Catching each other. Babbling in tongues. Shouting. On their knees. On their faces. On their backs. Too weird for me! And my man wasn't there.

I went to the back. Went out into the darkening field and stood upon the grassy knoll that peered out over the city I'd once lived in. The lights of Lancaster could be seen above the tree line, golden on the horizon. *You are the light of the world. A city on a hill cannot be hidden.* I was lost for a moment in a sense of *déjà vu*. Then Dad was with me, and I had nothing much to say.

I wanted to get out of there. Get on the road. Get back to Philly. Go hide in my apartment.

I told Dad I loved him and I'd call him sometime soon. He gave me a hug. I held on for a moment before breaking loose, then wandered off through the dark field to find my car. When I found it, I found Lisa.

"Good-bye, Matt," she said from the shadows.

"Yeah, well, it was good to…to be with you…and with Dad today."

"Thanks for coming," she said. She took a step away from the car, away from me. The headlights of a pickup truck threw her familiar figure into sudden silhouette. "We'll be praying for you."

"And Ali," I said. "Pray for Ali."

"I will. And I'll be in touch, Matt."

"Why? Why now? Why not before now?" I was tired. If I kept talking, I might say things I'd regret.

"Remember from where you have fallen," she said. And the truck moved on, sending Lisa to the shadows once again.

"Lisa," I said. But she had walked away. "Good-night, Lisa!" I shouted. And I thought I heard her say good-night in return.

That was it. That was all. The long-anticipated reunion with the woman I loved. Expensive breakfast—with my father at the table. A burger for lunch—by myself in my car. No supper. Awkward words. Prophetic dreams. Apocalyptic sermons. Cryptic farewells.

I felt like I'd been strapped to a pew and preached at all day! The only intermission I'd had was my private tour of the county and my moments of aching reminiscence overlooking the wide Susquehanna.

From where I've fallen! I'd rather jump off the Pinnacle than consider from where I'd fallen. *More like from where I'd escaped!* Lancaster County—for all its wonderfully quaint and old-fashioned ways—was a great place to visit, but I was glad I didn't live there. What a strange day! A schizophrenic daydream in the midst of the essential drama of the real world. But every day had seemed a dream lately.

I needed to get home. Get some sleep. Wake early for FOX News—like Wall had said.

The moon was a little past full as I drove east toward Philadelphia. It hung low upon the horizon, inflated and orange, hovering above the fields, watching as the drifting fireflies decorated the dark landscape in a silent winking display of nature's fireworks. Long-fingered tassels, silhouetted in the lunar nightlight, waved mystically at the top of an endless wall of stalked corn. It was a calming scene, almost mesmerizing, but I found myself continually glancing at my rearview mirror. And I checked out every car that passed me on my ride back to the City of Brotherly Love.

12

Fox at Dawn

Tuesday morning, July 15.

I woke abruptly and sat up in bed. Had I overslept? No, it was not quite 6:00 in the morning. I'd been dreaming, but I couldn't recall my dreams. My conscious thoughts were only on Ali. The room was dark, but outside my window the world was growing lighter in the east.

I dozed again. My alarm went off, startling me. I got out of bed, headed for the living room, turned on the TV, and tuned in FOX News. I went to the bathroom, stuck my head in the shower to wash my hair and wake myself, and returned to the television. I powered on the digicorder, though I still had fifteen minutes until the show. Grinding fresh coffee, I made a pot of Green Mountain and sat down to wait.

Two cups of coffee, three local news stories, and five commercials later, I was edge-of-my-seat anxious for FOX at Dawn.

Wall. From somewhere in Russia, I thought at first—but he wasn't telling us where.

And FOX wasn't telling us where he'd been for the last week and a half. He just pops up, on the air, live from the other side of the world. He could be in Arkansas for all we knew. Except for the Central Asian steppes rising behind him.

Does he have a camera crew? A tech assistant? Is he filming this himself?

Wall didn't look like he'd been running and hiding. But then what does that look like for a guy like the Sleuth? He must have worked out when he was younger—maybe still did (lifting rocks to look underneath for clues). He reminded me of Clark Kent—without the glasses. Was he Superman? Tall and fit. Dark, piercing eyes. Sculpted eyebrows. Coal-black wavy hair. A chiseled chin. And all this packaged in a pair of faded blue jeans, a yellow button-down shirt, and a brown leather jacket of recent Russian cut.

"Bradley Wall for FOX at Dawn," said the Sleuth with a grim smile. "The sun is up on another day." His trademark opener, in spite of the fact that where Wall appeared to be standing it was ten or eleven hours ahead of Philly's Eastern Standard Time. "But these are perilous days," he added. "Ten days ago, on the fourth of July, the first and hopefully the *last* limited nuclear war in modern history ended officially with a peace treaty in the Middle East. On the previous day, a quartet of Islamic militants attempted to assassinate Vladimir Putin, president of the Russian Federation, in a bloody battle inside—and outside—of Lenin's Tomb in Red Square."

Familiar footage of Putin and his entourage on the day of the violent event replaced Wall on the screen. This was the film Russia released the day they broke the silence about the attempted assassination. The Russian president's fleet of black limousines rolled into Red Square, pulled up outside Lenin's Tomb, and Putin stepped out first. In a moment of staged drama, he stood facing the Tomb while other Russian dignitaries joined him in choreographed order, rapidly surrounded by the president's military guard.

"Putin survived," said Wall. "But contrary to Russian news releases, FOX News has evidence that he was wounded in the attempt." *Wall should know,* I thought. *He was there.* "He is recovering well."

Photos of the chaos that erupted at the mausoleum faded one into another as Wall continued his monologue. These were not official Russian shots, certainly not taken with the Kremlin's permission. They were Wall's own photos, I was sure — broadcast now for all the world to see. Wall had *better* be able to run and hide! What a slide show!

A close-up shot of Putin, staring dark-eyed and intent into the mausoleum.

Another Putin face shot, head turned back toward his entourage, mouth open in astonishment, eyebrows bent in an angry frown.

A third shot, Putin wincing, teeth clinched, eyes closed.

A fourth, a full body shot of Putin twisting, hands clutched over his left hip.

Then Putin on the ground, covered by his guards.

Politicians hugging the bricked pavement of Red Square, a dead guardsman on the perimeter.

Guards shooting.

Putin, pistol in hand, bleeding, crawling with his guards toward the Tomb.

An explosion within the Tomb, viewed from outside, men blown backwards out of the mausoleum's entrance, flung into the square like dolls.

A dead Federal Assemblyman. Smoke billowing from the Tomb's front doors.

Three consecutive images of Putin's cavalcade driving away, pocked with bullet holes.

And, lastly, a view of two gunmen, dressed as Russian guards, fleeing with two hostages — Ali among them! The photo caught them running at the foot of the Kremlin Wall behind a row of tall evergreens.

"Twelve men died in the botched assassination: three members of the Federal Council, six members of Putin's elite guard, and three terrorists. Eight others — politicians and police — were wounded. The famous glass-covered casket containing the mummified corpse of Russian revolutionary leader Vladimir Lenin — first head of the Communist Party and first ruler of the former Union of Soviet Socialist Republics — was utterly decimated by a body-bomb strapped to one of the terrorists."

A brief, choppy video aired (filmed by the Sleuth, I'd bet), depicting the gory, bomb-blasted insides of the Mausoleum. A severed arm lay upon a pile of rubble, its hand extended, blue and wax-like — the bloodless hand of comrade Lenin! God only knows how many death warrants it signed. The political decrees it penned led to the subjugation of nations, the murder of millions, and the enslavement of multiplied millions more.

"Two of the armed Islamicists, shouting '*Akhirah! Akhirah!'* — 'Eternity! Eternity!' — escaped with two hostages," Wall continued. "The captives were Russian Federal Councilor Georgy Marianenko and American journalist Ali Baraki." Pictures of each of the men flashed as Wall mentioned their names.

How had he constructed this broadcast? He had to pre-script it, prep his graphics, and program the separate media pieces to follow his monologue. He could use an online solar Flapjack computer for that — and a program like Apple MediaBox. He must have had someone working with him. Probably *more* than someone. FOX had the money, and the Sleuth had the savvy and the connections to make it happen, even in the Russian wilderness.

"Marienenko was murdered within minutes of the escape," Wall announced. "His body was found in a wooded park inside the Kremlin walls, about a quarter of a mile from the Tomb. Baraki and his captors disappeared.

"Putin put the lid on the incident for eight days," Wall explained, "while an organized military posse spread out through the region to track down the terrorists. It's now eleven days since the kidnapping, and in spite of an extensive search by the Kremlin's crack brigades, captors and captive remain at large—somewhere in these rolling steppes…"

Wall turned his gaze to the sun-soaked mountains in the distance. Where were those mountains? They could be anywhere in Central Asia. Anywhere in Eurasia. Most likely down in the Stans.

"Official Russian spin claims the terrorists moved west from Moscow into Ukraine, then south toward Georgia. FOX News believes they are elsewhere."

Was Wall still in Kazakhstan? It would be just past 5:00 p.m. there—or 6:00 p.m., depending on where he was in that big country. But where in the world was Ali?

"Now," Wall announced pointedly, "the Big News."

A dramatic, melodious sound bite punctuated his words, FOX's cue that a breaking headliner was coming up. The words "BIG NEWS" scrolled repeatedly across the screen below Wall's face.

"The Big News is that FOX News has attained footage of the remaining captive, Philadelphia Bulletin correspondent Ali Ahkmed Baraki."

Ali's portrait again. I put my hand over my mouth and stared at the screen.

"The video you are about to see was filmed thirty-three hours ago. Monday morning in my part of the world. It is an anti-Western, anti-Zionist propaganda piece—but beyond that, its purpose and its message are unclear."

I got up and paced impatiently in front of the TV. "Just show it to me, Wall!" I demanded.

"It does not identify either the captors or their cause," he said, "but it's all we have right now.

"It was released by the kidnappers ninety minutes ago— sent in VN3 format to several cyberspace addresses—and FOX News has reason to believe this video was scheduled to be broadcast first by the official news media of the European Union. But FOX is wily, FOX is fast," said Wall, flashing a sober grin. "Bradley Wall with the scoop…again."

Wall faded out, Ali faded in! I sat back down and leaned toward the screen.

He looked weary but well.

He was in the woods, a fairly thick woods. There were cypress trees and underbrush hidden by mist, fog, or smoke from a campfire drifting behind him. There were voices, Arabic voices, barking in the background. Ali shook his head and answered them. Then he stared into the camera. It would be something around 9:00 a.m. on Monday in the Stans, if Wall was right about the time of the filming.

"Ali!" I cried, gripping the TV on both sides and peering into the screen as if it were a vid-com and Ali could see me, too. "I see you! I hear you!" I wiped tears from angry eyes.

The mist faded behind Ali for a brief moment. I was sure it was smoke now. Through the trees, in the hazy distance, stood an old stone building—a castle or monastery—tipped in red sunlight, surrounded by towering cypress, stark against a snow-capped mountain range. The Caucasus! Then the smoke obscured it all and Ali began to speak.

"My captors are my brothers in Islam," Ali said almost casually. I touched the screen, to touch Ali. "They have treated me very well. They have fed me well, and there has been no violence toward me at all."

Almost blowing you to pieces in a mausoleum! Dragging you away at gunpoint! That isn't violence?

"The only violence I wish to talk about is the violence of the world against the Muslim people and the Muslim lands," he continued. "The people of Islam are not asleep. They are not all dead. They know they are the target for the aggression of the Zionist-Crusader alliance."

This was not his heart, not his mind. *They were using him.* But he will use them, too, Wall had said. Ali was strong. Ali was smart. He'd play the game, but not by their rules.

I studied his face, his mouth, his eyes. Was he sending a

signal through his body language? Something he wanted others to read? Nothing moved upon his face except his lips. Even his eyes were unblinking.

"America, Britain, and the European Union are to blame for the violence in the Middle East, for the pogroms against the Muslims. Israel is to blame for the suffering of the Palestinian people, for the warfare that has raged in the Muslim lands that surround Israel."

Ali didn't believe that. The whole earth, the Arabic world included, had seen the true and terrible face of fundamentalist Mohammedism. Everyone was united in opposition to the jihadist's violent vision of the world. Ali's tired script might win a few cheers from the Al Qaeda choir (wherever it was hiding), but even in the few remaining autonomous Islamic nations, no one was waving the banner of *jihad* anymore. At least no one who wanted to live for very long! But, then, our greatest error had been in believing that the jihadists *wanted* to live when, in fact, it was *akhirah*, the next life, that motivated them to kill and die in the name of Allah.

Then Ali fingered Russia for the troubles in the lands of the Muslim peoples in the Balkans and in the lands of the former Soviet Union. I leaned back and listened intently.

"These lands have been surrounded by the wicked or occupied by wicked armies. These are lands in which my people simply wish to live. But they can't simply live. They must suffer under the heel of the oppressor, hide from the siege cannons of the aggressor—or they must run. And if they must run, they must either be the hunted…or the hunter. My captors are both. My captors are my brothers in Islam. They will treat me well."

Ali paused, closed his eyes, took a deep breath, blinked, and continued.

No! He didn't blink—he winked! Twice. His little way of saying, "Just between you and me," to whomever he was talking. And to whom was he talking now? To whom was he winking now? Who, besides his closest friends, knew that habit of his?

"What?" I shouted to Ali and the TV and the haunting video. "What are you trying to tell me?"

"All praise be to Allah," said Ali.

Of course, you blessed Muslim monkey! But what are you trying to tell us?

"We seek his help and ask for his pardon."

Pardon for lying about America and Britain and…?

"We take refuge in Allah from our bad deeds and wrongs."

We? Meaning who? What bad deeds? Murder? Kidnapping? A bad script?

"Though all men lie, Allah is true. We…"

Ali hesitated, touching his heart with his hand, blinking his eyes as though sorrowed by his own sin…whatever sin he was confessing to the world. And he winked twice again. The winks were mixed with the fluttering blinks, and I wondered if I'd really seen them at all.

"We," he hesitated again, "lie all… And I…" Another hesitation. "We must look to the Perfect One in the hour of trouble." He took a sharp breath then and chanted: "All praise is due to Allah. I bear witness that there is no God except Allah—no lesser gods with him—and I bear witness that Muhammad is his slave and messenger."

The video ended. Wall returned briefly to the screen, but I hardly heard him. I cut the broadcast as soon as Wall bid the viewer farewell. I didn't want to hear any commentary just then—I only wanted to listen to Ali again.

I hit the playback on the digicorder, and there was Ali in the woods, smoke drifting behind him. I played him through a dozen times. I skipped the diatribe against the infidels and listened carefully to the words he spoke after the winks. Then I went back and played it all over again, writing everything down, word for word.

I knew that his talk was already transcribed and under

the microscope at every intelligence agency in the free world and that the media was buzzing with commentary and conjecture. But I wanted to get it all down for myself, while by myself, alone with my thoughts, my questions, my personal musings. Wall had wanted me to pay special attention to this, so that meant Ali wanted me to pay special attention. "Don't miss the broadcast," Wall said. "There is work for you to do. It will help Ali. It will help many."

I had work to do. To help Ali. To help others. Who? How? What?

And I was late to the Bulletin again…with another global headliner shouting for attention: "Ali Ahkmed Baraki is alive!"

But where?

13

Georgia on My Mind

"Here!" Putin pointed to an area in the Caucasus Mountains just south of Russia's border on the Black Sea. He stood beside a large, colorful globe of the world. Lit from within, it cast a mottled glow upon the stern, settled face of the Russian president.

At five feet, five inches tall, Putin was a trim, solid-bodied man in his early sixties. Thin blonde hair, streaked grey around the temples, was combed back from a serious brow. His shrewd yet somewhat childlike face would have been dominated by the long nose that sloped toward his spare chin, if not for the magnetic blue eyes that were always aimed at you like bullets.

Making a fist while staring grimly into the camera, he rapped the globe repeatedly with his ashen knuckles. "This is where the killers have fled," he said. "This is where we'll find them."

Georgia! Bordered on its south by Turkey, Armenia, and Azerbaijan, on its north and east by several Russian provinces, and on its west by the Black Sea itself, Georgia is about the size of West Virginia. Formerly folded under the widespread wings of the Soviet Union, Georgia was given its independence from Russia in 1993. But Russia had never surrendered its desire to oversee the affairs of this fledgling democracy in the Caucasus.

During the inaugural celebration of the 2008 Olympics in China, while the world was glued to its TV sets in anticipation of the global games, Russia rolled into Georgia and battered the little republic in supposed defense of two Georgian provinces that had pledged their allegiance to Moscow. Russia pulled its forces out only after a week-long display of terroristic military bullying.

When Moscow announced its recognition of the independence of the Georgian provinces of Abkhazia and South Ossetia, Georgia complained loudly and bitterly about this unabashed annexation of its territories—but to little avail. Russian authorities continued to declare Georgia's strategic importance to Russian national security, raising the possibility that Russia might someday simply sweep the independent republic back into its empire.

War with Georgia! That was what Putin was itching for. And now he had a reason to scratch.

I turned away from the Russian president and the big screen. The Bulletin newsroom was a beehive. Sutton was buzzing loud enough to take the mic and do a live commentary of his own.

"Ali's not in Georgia!" he shouted. "If Wall says he's not in Georgia, he's not in Georgia!" Sutton's street-level candor would have been too much for the newsroom if not for his genuine affection for us all. He was often like a drill sergeant, but we knew he deeply cared about each one of us.

"Those are the Caucasus behind Wall!" Jacqui declared.

"But not in Georgia," I said. "Not *necessarily* in Georgia," I added quickly. "The Caucasus cover a lot of territory in that part of the world." My head was spinning from all that had happened. I had to remember that I knew more than anyone else was supposed to know. But what did I *really* know?

"The church!" general news editor Rose Miller piped in. "What about the church in the woods?"

Rose hates churches. She's very anti-religious. If she had

her own column, she would probably use it to argue against everything in mine. She thinks I'm a church boy, even though I sleep in on Sundays. It must be the smell of Lancaster County on me.

"The one you can see through the trees," she continued. "The one all the networks are saying is in Georgia."

"The monastery is in Georgia," Jacqui stated flatly.

"What do you say, Matt? You're the history guy." Rose pushed the question at me.

"Sure looks like Georgia," I admitted. I had extracted a visual file of the church from Ali's video and done an online SeeSearch. "It appears to be the Bodbe Monastery, which contains the tomb of St. Nino, patron saint of Georgia. She was a young slave girl who converted Georgia's Zorastrian King in 334. The monastery is near the Azerbaijan border, on a steep hill overlooking the Alazani Valley."

"But Ali ain't there!" Sutton insisted. "Wall's never wrong. I've been in this business since Guttenberg, and I've watched Wall hit the bull's-eye time after time fer longer than some of you've been outa grade school!"

"It's like bait," said a man who seldom joined us in the newsroom. The buzz faded as the big boss, Aaron Stein, stepped out of his office. "Any fishermen here?" he asked with a grin. "Or fisherwomen?" he added with a flourished bow to the ladies who were present.

"Bait is not always what it appears to be," he said. "I used to fly-fish for trout up in Pine Creek, Tioga County. My father had a cabin up there for a while, but there was no synagogue. And so we sold the place." He shrugged. "When you go fly-fishing, you don't use real flies. You use a shiny little handmade fly with a sharp hook worked into it. The fish doesn't know the difference, of course. And he ends up in the frying pan. Fresh trout! It's been a while."

Smiling, he walked back into his office.

"Hey, Ernie!" Sutton shouted, summoning our graphics man from his private den where he often hid in his creative

dreams, even during lively discussions like the one the rest
of us were having. "Let's look at Ali's film again. Get it up
on yer wall-screen, Rembrandt! Check out the smoke scene.
We're lookin' fer bait!" He eyed the rest of us. "When I said
we," Sutton explained, "I meant Ernie and me. The rest'a
you squirrels get back to yer trees and start gatherin' nuts!
And work like yer getting' paid!"

I turned toward my cubicle, but Sutton hailed me.
"Clifford!" he said. He seldom called me by my last name,
except when he was angry or excited. He hadn't talked to
me yet about the day I'd taken off, and I was afraid I was in
for it. "You feelin' better, fella?" he asked.

"Yes, Mr. Sutton," I answered nervously. "Thank you, I
am."

"Good!" was all he said about it. His eyes were bright
with strange fire, and it made me even more anxious. "I got
a hunch about this Ali thing, Clifford! It ain't somethin' I can
pin down. It's just a naggin' hunch."

"A nagging hunch, sir," I echoed meekly. But I began to
see that he was in earnest.

"That's right! I shoulda been a cop like my old man. He
was a Brooklyn detective—a not-so-private eye—who had
hunches like a drunk has hiccups. And the hunches always
led him to his man. It's in my genes, too. But I ain't a cop,
and I ain't in shape to run down alleys anymore. But *you*
come to work in runnin' shoes even though you come in
late! When you come in at all!"

"I'm sorry about yesterday, Mr. Sutton. I..."

"Never mind yesterday, Matt. I'm talking about today,
about my hunch...and I'd like to give ya some detective
work. Are ya game?"

"I'm game," I said sincerely. I was already in the game, if
he only knew!

"Politics is like a mystery movie," said Sutton, gesturing
with his hands, which he seldom did. "There's always
somethin' happenin' to keep ya guessin', to throw ya off, to

fool ya for a while — until..." He rolled his sleeves up tighter and loosened his tie. "You and me are sittin' here eatin' popcorn, watchin' the show, writin' reviews, seeing only what the producer wants us to see — 'cause he's hopin' we won't figure it out until he's used up all the special effects and the award-winnin' dialogue is delivered. Then he's got us...and bang!"

"Life feels like that sometimes," I said.

"Don't get philosophical, son! Never mind the commentary about the Great Screenwriter or the Grand Producer. I'm not talkin' about God. I'm talkin' about this Georgia thing! I'm talkin' about Ali and Putin and Romano...and who knows who else! I'm talkin' about diggin' a little deeper to find out what's really goin' on 'cause I just know some of this stuff has been scripted out in a smoky back room, and there's folks just hopin' we'll keep eatin' popcorn and chewin' Milk Duds while the actors take us all for a ride!"

"I wasn't talking about God either. I was..."

"Never mind that. I want ya to come look at this Ali video with Ernie and me, and then I'll tell ya what I'm thinkin'."

Ernie had it cued and got it running. "That's smoke," I said. "I thought it was fog at first, but it's not."

"No, and it ain't the Boy Scouts," said Sutton. "It's staged. It's scripted, I tell ya. Pretty slick, but it's only B movie stuff. These guys don't have George Lucas workin' with 'em."

"They wanted the mist to part for a moment? Is that what you're saying, Mr. Sutton?"

"That's what I'm sayin', my dear Watson," Sutton said, staring at the video as the monastery appeared through the trees. "Somethin' screwy in this scene, but I can't figger it..."

Ernie paused the video, his finger wagging.

"Whaddya see, son?" Sutton asked.

"The light source," Ernie said. "It's coming from two

different directions. The sun is shining on Ali from the east because it's morning, right? And the sun is shining on the monastery from somewhere else...more like the west."

"Yeah!" I exclaimed. "It's really hard to see through the trees, but the shadows are wrong, and the red glow on the roof of the monastery is more likely the setting sun than the rising sun."

"Two pieces of film, together as one," said Sutton.

"Actually," said Ernie, who had started the video running again. "It's only one piece of film. The back shot—the monastery and the mountains behind it—is a still. It's a photo, probably swiped from an online image cache and melded seamlessly with the video. They made the clouds behind the monastery look like they're blowing across the sky in the same direction as the fog—as the smoke—but they animated them."

"How can ya tell?" Sutton asked.

"The clouds aren't breaking up at all like they would in a real wind. Not shifting in shape. Whoever worked on this simply moved the cloud portion of the photo across the sky to give the illusion of wind. It works well, because it's such a brief moment in the overall video."

"Sonuvagun!"

"Simple stuff," said Ernie. "Anyone can do it."

"Slick, but not so slick, after all! I'd fire the guys!"

Ernie re-ran the smoke scenes several times, backwards and forwards, while Sutton and I talked.

"So," said Sutton, "let's say Ali ain't in Georgia like Wall says he ain't. But these kidnappers want us all to think he is...to think that they are, too...and that Georgia is responsible for harborin' terrorists."

"Or training terrorists..."

"Or exportin' terrorists for its own purposes, like killin' presidents, fomentin' revolution, stackin' the political deck, overthrowin' governments...and those kinda things."

"Are they trying to stir up Russia against Georgia? Is this

a group from one of the other Islamic nations down in the Stans, trying to light a fuse in Russia?" *Maybe Kazakhstan, where Wall has been hanging out?*

Sutton was silent, chewing on a pencil. "I dunno. That don't quite make sense to me. I got a hunch, but I'm still lookin' at it through the trees. Ya know what I mean? Too much smoke! C'mon, Clifford, let's get back to the pundits."

He led the way into the newsroom to the main screen near his own desk. From his shirt pocket, he unclipped a universal remote control. As he thumbed it, news channels blinked at us in rapid succession until he settled on one. "There y'are, ya bald eagle!" he said, speaking to the image of Marco Romano as the Italian president's presence filled the screen. It was a live Italian broadcast—with English subtitles—direct from Romano's office in Rome.

Romano was standing at his bronzed wall map, reminding me of Putin at his globe. Like Putin, he was pointing to the Caucasus Mountains, south of Russia. Unfamiliar Latin phrases poured artfully from his thick lips, while his fingers talked and his arms swung like swords before our eyes. Romano was using his bully pulpit to tell his countrymen that the would-be assassins of President Putin were hiding out in Georgia and that Italy would head a special EU troop deployment to help Putin find them.

Sutton recited out loud the English text that marched across the bottom of the screen: "And we will hunt down the dogs in their hidden den and haul them out for all the world to see…dead or alive! Then the Peace will be stronger, the world will be safer, and Italy can lift its head higher in a world grateful for heroes such as the sons of Rome!"

"This guy likes to rail against dogs, don't he?" Sutton said. "And he sure don't mince words over what he plans to do with the dogs when he catches 'em!"

"Heroes such as the sons of Rome!" I repeated, shaking my head. "Romano sounds like Pope Urban II preaching the Crusades in 1094."

"Pope who?" Sutton snorted. He stared at the screen as an Italian commentator came on, then muted the broadcast. "As if Putin needs Romano to help him shovel up dirt in his own backyard! Both those boys have muddy boots already. The Bulletin needs somebody over there to do some diggin'! Ya wanna go look for Ali, Matt?"

"Yeah, right!" I scoffed.

"I ain't kiddin', Clifford," said Sutton.

"Me?" I was astonished. "I'm still working on my English. The only European language I know at all is French, and that's from hearing my dad repeat little phrases he learned in high school."

Sutton stared at me, grimly, but there was humor in his eyes. "And I'm pretty good at pig-latin," I said weakly.

Sutton laughed. "English'll do, just fine!" he said. "And ya probably won't even have to leave Philadelphia! I want ya to shift gears, is all. Put most of yer regular chores on the side and give this Ali thing top drawer priority. No more waitin' for the news to come flyin' in our window! We're gonna start diggin' for it ourselves. Dig, dig, dig until we find out what's really goin' on over there."

"Yes!" I declared. "That's what I want!"

14

Mysteries

Within the hour, Sutton and I were digging into the mystery together. I was amazed at the energy with which the old man wielded his shovel.

"You can never guess what these presidents and kings are thinkin'. Maybe I'm nuts," said Sutton passionately, "but I don't trust most of 'em farther'n I can throw my livin' room couch! Putin is an out-of-the-closet commie who wants to resurrect the Soviet Union. Romano is a war dog who'd like to be standin' in front of a couple'a million goose-steppin' Italians willin' to sell their souls to their general-in-chief. But these two hate each other! Putin doesn't want Romano beatin' any Russian bushes. Romano doesn't want Russia in the European Union. So what's with the dog-chasin' alliance? Somethin' stinks, and it ain't dog poop in Georgia!"

Sutton thumbed his remote. WarnerWorld flashed on the screen with digital video of Georgian president Kobadze live from the Georgian capital of Tbilisi. He was chest-pounding mad, bitterly denouncing the rumors of terrorist enclaves in his nation and vehemently denying any connection between Georgia and the failed assassination of Russian president Putin.

WarnerWorld then took us to Washington D.C. where the Russian ambassador claimed that evidence was mounting of a Georgian conspiracy. The monastery in the terrorist's film was Georgian. One of the dead attackers at Lenin's Mausoleum was wearing a Georgian military shirt and other typical Georgian attire underneath his Russian disguise. Russian intelligence had been tracking the attackers through various means as they made their way toward Georgia. They lost them just north of the Russo-Georgian border but had reason to believe they crossed into Georgia.

"It's a ruse!" Sutton blustered. "Putin's makin' up the whole dadblasted thing!"

"Or playing it for what he can get out of it, at least."

A quick survey of international news channels, as well as the Bulletin's first-hand sources, showed Russia and Georgia in full-blown argument. Meanwhile Marco Romano (speaking for the EU and, presumably, Italy) pledged solidarity with Putin. In response to White House concerns for Georgian sovereignty, Romano promised complete and open communications with Kobadze concerning the manhunt. "We will not enter Georgia until the Georgian government opens their door," Romano promised Clay in a continent-to-continent phone call between the two presidents.

"Until?" I said. "What about 'unless'? Romano seems pretty confident that Kobadze will cooperate."

On CNN, the Georgian ambassador to the United States defended Kobadze's outrage and piled up oaths concerning Georgia's ongoing commitment against terrorism within its borders. We watched the Kobadze video again—the one we'd seen first on WarnerWorld. It was now making the rounds of all the networks.

"Kobadze doesn't know anything about Ali's kidnappers!" Sutton declared. "He's boilin' mad, and he's boilin' over the top for the whole world to see because…" Sutton looked me in the eyes. "Because he's scared stiff."

"No wonder," I said.

"He's dead if the Russians come in," said Sutton. "Georgia's a goner if Russia rolls into Kbilisi. And if the EU comes along for the ride…"

"Romano's a radical, but a multinational EU force may be a moderating presence," I suggested. "More of a peace-keeping force than an aggressor."

"With Romano callin' the shots? He'll jump in a tank and ride right into Georgia with his own head stuck out the top, shoutin', 'Ride 'em down, boys!'"

"Bait," I said, troubled by the rumors of war.

"Yeah! So, who's baitin' who? Georgia ain't baitin' Russia! That's like David baitin' Goliath — without his slingshot!"

"Without God," I said.

"Who's baitin' who?" Sutton asked again. "What's the game? Putin wouldn't try to kill himself just to have an excuse to hit Georgia. And what does Romano have to gain besides more headlines?"

"If Ali isn't in Georgia, then where is he, and what do his captors want?" I wondered. "Why did they try to kill Putin? Why did they release that video?"

"Now yer usin' your noggin, Clifford!" Sutton said. "That video is like a smokescreen itself. Just keeps us coughin' and holdin' our hands over our eyes."

"Why was it supposed to be released first by EU news sources? Who arranged *that?*" I asked.

"And what does Wall know?" Sutton interjected. "This ain't 'news,' Clifford! This is a crisis rollin' toward all of us! We gotta get down on the ground and run with this thing, and — "

Jacqui tapped Sutton on the shoulder. She held a pot of steaming coffee.

"No more fuel, Johnson. Push my gas pedal any closer to the floor and I'll go through the wall!"

I had never seen the old newsman so agitated. But he was enjoying the agitation.

"Let's talk to Pascov!" Sutton started out of his seat and headed for the vid-com. "See what his take is on this...see what's happenin' in Jerusalem. Pascov knows some news guys in Russia, right? Get Stein in here, Johnson! I mean..." He quieted himself for a moment in front of the vid-com and took a deep breath. "Jacqui, would you please ask the boss if he's got a few minutes to talk with us over here?" Sutton smiled apologetically. "Thanks," he added.

I went numb. We were about to get hold of Jack and ask him about his contacts in Russia! The only correspondence between Jack and me in the past week were a couple of e-mails in which I continued to tell him that Wall hadn't contacted me after all. But I'd said nothing to anyone at the Bulletin about any of that.

I'll let Jack bring it up, and then I'll lie about it again, I thought frantically. It would seem strange to Sutton and Jack that I hadn't mentioned anything to the Bulletin crew about trying to track down Ali through Wall, but...

We found Jack in his Jerusalem apartment, alone as he usually is when he's at home. "*Tzohorime tovim,* my friends." He grinned at us across the miles.

"Good-afternoon, Jack," I said nervously.

"Good to see ya, Pascov!" Sutton said.

We spent a few minutes on small talk about Philadelphia and Jerusalem, the weather, and the sports. Then Jack headed straight to Wall—but not as I'd expected.

"What do you think of that Wall?" Jack said. "Ali on film! Thank God he's all right! And where has Wall been all this time? Not a public word since the attack on Putin, and now he surfaces with a terrorist video in hand! Who can figure this guy? He's like James Bond. Or Frodo Baggins with an invisibility cloak! Matt knows who I mean."

I was sweating it. Was Jack hinting something to me, or just ribbing me about my fanaticism over J.R.R. Tolkien?

"I know who Frodo is, too, ya Jewish beanbag!" Sutton laughed. Jack was rather pudgy, and Sutton always kidded him about it. "I was readin' *Lord of the Rings* in journalism school before ya knew how to turn on a DVD player—in fact, before there were any DVD players!" Sutton paused. "Glad ya mentioned Wall. I wonder if ya can track him down yerself, through Petrescu in the Balkans or some of those guys ya know in Russia. You were buddies with an Israeli stringer who got himself shipped into Russia a year or so ago, weren't ya?"

I was *really* sweatin' it.

"Yeah," Jack said, "but he's back in Israel now. I don't know anyone else in Russia personally, but I'm following every trail I can to find Ali. I talked yesterday with Petrescu—"

"Did you?!" Sutton fired. "He's truckin' through a corner of Turkey right now, did ya know that? We wanna get him out on the Black Sea—closer to Georgia—but not too close! We're negotiatin' a berth for him on a Greek merchant ship."

"He was in Istanbul when we spoke. Headed to the shore at Zonguldak. But he has no news on Ali."

"Ya think Ali's in Georgia?" Sutton pressed.

"Nobody here thinks so," said Jack. "Israel's new Prime Minister, David Tabeel, is appealing to the European Union to pull on Putin's coattails in regards to Georgia. There is even doubt about the authenticity of the video."

"How so?" Sutton asked. He glanced at me.

"Oh, there's no doubt that it's Ali," Jack returned. "At least with those of us who know him. But some of the Mideastern news vets don't think it's Georgia."

"Even with the Bodbe Monastery in the woods?" I asked.

"Why would they release a film that gave even a *hint* of where they really were?" Jack said.

"The monastery is a fake," I said.

"We think so, too!" Jack said.

"So, where are they really?" I wondered aloud.

"I think we'll all find out before too long," said Jack darkly. "I just hope Ali is alive when the truth is discovered."

He never even hinted about his contact with the Gubkin reporter, nor said a word about our previous conversations about Wall. I was relieved, but troubled. I had been prepared to express my own angst in not being able to contact Bradley Wall. I was prepared to lie. I was not prepared for Jack's silence on the matter. *Did Wall get word to him to keep quiet about it?* He must have! So how much did Jack *really* know about Ali? And who could I trust if not my friends? This stuff was really getting to me!

"So then—" Jack said.

"So then we gotta dig deeper, run faster," Sutton interjected. "Now that Wall has surfaced, we gotta get ahold of him ourselves. He and Ali knocked elbows over there—I know that much. I've got an old colleague or two at FOX. I'm gonna tap 'em on the shoulders to see if they can scare up this Sleuth for us. Thanks, Jack! We gotta go. Got stuff to do!"

"*Shalom,*" said Jack as Sutton shut down the connection. He got up and started pacing back and forth in front of the screen.

"We gotta get into Georgia somehow," Sutton said through his teeth. "Or wherever Wall is. Get down on the ground somehow, through someone who's already there, and *snoop*. We gotta find Ali! We gotta do more than noodle up the news! We gotta bag some bad guys, head 'em off at the pass, save some skins!"

I'd not seen this side of Sutton. He was riled. I swiveled in my chair and noticed Aaron Stein sitting just behind me, smiling. He was watching Sutton pace and enjoying the entertainment.

"Keith Sutton and I go back a few years," said Stein quietly, calmly. "We worked together at the New York Tribune in the mid 60s before the paper folded. That's fifty years ago! Keith was a poor Catholic cop's kid who wanted to be a gangbuster with a typewriter. I was a silver-spooned Jewish media brat who wanted to boss a newspaper. We butted heads. We sweated the news. We took on some giants of graft together. We grew up some in the process. We became friends. And, I'd like to believe...I do believe...we helped clean up some dirty corners of New York in our own little way."

"You bet we cleaned up some dirty corners!" Sutton insisted. He sat down and rolled his chair back where he could take in the whole room. "I got inta this business, Matt," Sutton said, "to rake muck! I wasn't big enough to be a cop. New York cops hadda be six feet tall in them days, and I never made it over five foot eight! But if I couldn't wear a badge, I'd find another way to bag the bad guys — with a press card!"

Sutton got back up and started to pace again.

"I followed my hunches, like my father did," he said, "and I smoked out the bad guys with front-page headlines. I went after crooked politicians, water-pollutin' corporations, highbrow college presidents with their private body-guards — even went after a precinct of dirty New York cops, with my dad's help. Won some investigative journalism awards. Won some enemies, too! But Stein always backed me, and the good guys always came out on top. I believe they always will. But now..." Sutton stared at his old colleague, Aaron Stein.

"What now?" Stein prodded.

"Now my bones are too brittle to be chasin' down hunches!"

"But the hunches don't leave you alone, do they, Keith?" said Stein.

"Y'oughta know, y'old mockin' bird!" Sutton laughed.

"I'm in," said the big boss.

"Clifford can do this with us, Aaron," said Sutton to the old Jew. "When this boy looks at the news, he sees the insides of the men and women makin' the news. He hears 'em thinkin'." He turned to look at me. "Yer a sleuth, too, Matt! We've just never let ya loose where it's dangerous…or where ya can do the kinda damage that matters."

"Mr. Sutton," I said. "I just want to find Ali."

"So do we," said Stein. He wasn't smiling.

"I'll start tonight," I said soberly. "I've already got some… some hunches that I was planning to follow."

"Do yer homework, Matt," said Sutton. "And we'll pick this conversation back up in the mornin'. But keep this under yer hat. The rest of the Bulletin crew has nothin' to do with this unless I say so. Got it?"

"Got it," I said. *Got more than I can handle!* I thought.

"You've got a raise, Matt," said Stein, "and anything else you need — hardware, software, influence, money — anything at all that will help you track down Ali and 'dig up the dirt,' as Keith would say. Meanwhile, I'll be making some phone calls of my own, and Keith will keep me informed on your progress." Then he smiled.

Jacqui caught me on my way out the door. "What's up with the Ali hunt?" she asked sincerely.

Jacqui was a sleuth in a class of her own. Sharp, inquisitive, on top of the job. She wasn't satisfied to simply read a script. She had to know what she was talking about before she got in front of the camera. She wanted to "say something," as she put it. To make people think, to move them to care. A good-looking, smart-talking, deep-thinking female news anchor was good for ratings. Good ratings were good for Jacqui Johnson's ego. At least I'd always thought that's what she was about. I was changing my mind on all that lately.

"We're turning over every stone," I said. "Looking behind every bush — that kind of thing." I hoped I didn't sound evasive.

She touched my arm. She was always touching guys. It

seemed disingenuous, but I suppose I wouldn't have minded so much if I was the only one she touched. And if there had been no Lisa in the picture.

But was she in the picture after all? Or was she more a snapshot from another day, another life? In a photo album on the shelf—dusty, dated?

Jacqui pulled her hand back, held it suspended between us. She seemed to be searching for something else to say.

"Maybe tomorrow we'll know more," I offered.

"I hope so," she said thoughtfully. "Tomorrow," she repeated optimistically, smiling.

I opened the door for her, and she walked out into the hallway alone. The elevator came. She got on. She punched a button, and then looked across the hall at me. I hadn't moved from where I stood, still holding the office door open. Jacqui waved—fingers wiggling as if they were playing notes on a piano—and the elevator closed.

"Sunday-school-sweet," said a voice behind me. "That's what she says about you."

"Rose!" I barked. "You surprised me."

"Why do you put her off, Matt?"

"Put her off?" I echoed. "I don't know anything more about Ali than what I just told her," I lied. "We're all hoping—"

"Of course we are! And I hope we find Ali *before* tomorrow," she said, almost indignantly. "But I'm not talking about Ali. I mean Jacqui herself. What's wrong with her, Matt? Or what's wrong with you, that you don't just take her home? She's crazy about you."

I didn't believe her. Rose was always trying to trip me up. Prove me some kind of a hypocrite. God knows how often I'd thought about taking Jacqui Johnson home! But wasn't she crazy about everybody?

"She's fascinated by you," Rose continued. "You're so straight! So squeaky clean. I think she wonders if you've ever slept with a woman."

"What?" I coughed. I glanced around to see if anyone else was listening.

"You too good for her, church boy?" Rose jibed.

"I don't go to church, Rose," I said stiffly. "But if I ever start, I'll let you know—and maybe you and I can go together."

"You are out of your freaking mind, Clifford! The day I go to church is the day they stick my open casket up front with me laid out all waxed and cold!"

"And, no—I'm not too good for Jacqui Johnson," I added. "Maybe she's too good for me." I found myself wanting to defend her from all the talk about her that seemed too obviously true. The girl needed to be rescued from herself.

"Just trying to do you a favor," Rose stated bluntly, frowning.

"Thanks, but no thanks," I said acidly.

Rose was a small woman, fair-faced, thin, small breasted, with her hair cut short like a man's—except for a long braid on the left side of her head that always lay across the front of her shoulder. She had an elaborate heart tattooed up high on her cheek, near the left ear. Some people thought she was a lesbian. But she had two kids and a boyfriend. Or, rather, two kids and a slave. Looking at her standing in front of me—diminutive, defiant—I couldn't stay mad. I smiled. She frowned all the more. I stepped back and held the door open wider for her.

"I like working with you, Rose," I said. "I like working with Jacqui. With the whole crew. We've got a great team. I didn't mean to offend you. I appreciate you thinking about me…and Jacqui. I'm just not looking for a relationship right now, short term or long. I've got…" What did I have, in terms of relationships? Lisa? Hardly. Some friends in a Bible study. Some friends on foreign soil. Some friends lost somewhere. Family in…Narnia. "I've got too much on my plate—covering the Peace, looking for Ali…"

"You're weird, Clifford," said Rose, loosening her frown enough to speak. She tossed her braid and crossed the hall.

She got on the elevator. I took the stairs.

Too good for Jacqui Johnson, I thought, as my feet echoed in the empty stairwell. *Too religious for Rose Miller. Not good enough for Lisa Zimmerman. Maybe I should just head over toward Girard College, buy a burger, and have a few beers at the North Star Bar. Listen to some live rock and roll. Find some cute chick and dance all night.*

"No," I said as I came out of the stairwell into the lobby. "I can't." I had a calling now—find Ali! Voices were pleading with me. Wall's. Sutton's. Stein's. Jacqui's. Jack's. Ali's wife and kids. Everybody, everywhere, who was wondering, praying. Ali himself.

I walked down the wide steps in front of the Bulletin. The city was full of the rush-hour flow—noisy, busy, harried, tired, anxious to get home and forget about the rest of the world.

I walked through the flow as a man in a dream.

My door was locked and my blinds were shut. I paced the living room nervously. I'd seen Cobalt Man again. On my way home from the Bulletin. On one of several routes I often took. There he was, ten feet in front of me, with a two-day beard, a three-piece suit, and a leather briefcase. He wasn't in his car, but sitting at a sidewalk table at Rouge, a French café on the 200 block of South 18th Street across from Rittenhouse Square. A woman was with him—pretty, Hispanic. They were talking, but they looked up at me. I was shocked, but I tried not to show it. I passed right by their table, quickly turned a corner onto Chancellor Street, and walked halfway down that alley before glancing over my shoulder to see if I was being followed.

I wasn't.

I doubled back and peeked around the corner at the tables. The two of them were gone. Had they been almost done eating? I hadn't noticed what was on their table—I was too surprised by the sight of the man himself. Was it really Cobalt Man? He couldn't possibly be a Lancaster farmer dressed up for a business dinner in downtown Philly. I had no way of knowing if he was the man in the Cobalt whom Kevin and I had seen during our walk. I hadn't seen the man's face that night…only his car. Was I losing my mind?

Anxiously, fearfully, I hurried home, ran up the stairs to my apartment, locked myself in, and drank half a liter of Mountain Dew while peeking through my blinds at the street below my window.

The red phone rang at 6:30, startling me in spite of the fact that I'd been expecting it.

"I'm alone," I answered, still looking out the window.

"This will take a little longer tonight. But not much. It's too dangerous to keep the signal open for long."

"Ali is well?"

"Yes."

"He is where?"

"I don't know."

"The tension between Russia and Georgia?"

"Unfortunate situation. Very troubling. Do you pray?"

"Yes. Sometimes," I said. "But not for political sorts of things."

"It wouldn't hurt."

Where was this going? I was crazy curious about Jack and his connection with Wall, but I didn't want to flat-out mention Jack's name either. "Jerusalem?" I probed.

"Don't fret it. More on that another time."

"You know what I mean?"

"Probably. More on that another time."

"Okay, okay," I *was* fretting. "I've watched Ali's video— a million times! Where *is* he? What do you want me to do?"

"He's well, and as hard as it is, we must be content with that for now," said Wall.

Content! Are you out of your mind? "Where are you? We're trying to track you down. We—"

"Don't meddle," he said with an edge in his voice that I'd not heard before. "I don't want to die. I don't want Ali to die. You don't want to die just yet, do you?"

"No," I said quietly.

"Listen to me carefully, and don't talk until I ask you to. We have only a few precious minutes."

I sighed.

"Watch the video again," Wall said. "See John in Philadelphia."

John who? I wanted to ask, but I kept my mouth shut.

"See John in Philadelphia," he repeated, as if he knew my question but knew he couldn't tell me. "John will tell you what to do." He was silent for a few seconds. "You may now ask me any questions *not* related to what I just told you."

"Will Ali be released?"

"I don't know. But this is bigger than Ali."

"I'm being followed," I said tersely. "Do you know anything about it?"

"I know a lot about being followed," he said, though it wasn't an answer to my actual question. "Has anyone approached you to speak to you?"

"No," I said, "but I've seen the same man—I think it's the same man—in different places, in different clothes, in different situations…five times now. Once today—with a woman."

"Have you seen anyone actually shadowing you? Has anyone attempted any contact with you? Does this man seem to pose a threat of any kind?"

"No threat that I can figure," I said. "And I've not seen him following me. In fact, it seems like I'm following him. That is…when I'm going places, he's already there." How ridiculous this all sounded when I said it out loud!

"Don't fret it," said the Sleuth. "Perhaps it's just a

coincidence. Or it's not the same man at all. You are under a lot of pressure. But…" Wall paused for just a breath, "you would be wise to be wary. If you see this man, or anyone else, actually shadowing you — chasing after you to keep you in sight — then you may have something to worry about."

"Oh? So what do I do?"

"You know Philadelphia well, don't you? And you can run, can't you? You can call the police if need be — to tell them about being followed if you feel in danger. But don't tell them anything about our conversations. Do you own a gun?"

"A gun! What are you getting me into?"

"I don't exactly know. But you'll find out, Lord willing."

Lord willing!

"And we'll talk. Please follow through with this. There are lives on the line, my friend — more than mine or Ali's…or yours. Many, many innocent lives — women and children, as well as men."

"Ali wants me doing all this?"

"I must say good-bye," said Wall, and the phone went dead.

See John in Philadelphia! How many Johns were in Philadelphia? How many did I know? How many did Ali know?

I wrote down all the Johns in Philadelphia whom Ali might know. I could think of only half a dozen. I looked them up in the online Philly White Pages and jotted down phone numbers and addresses. Then I Googled each of them and wrote down any pertinent information that I found.

I called Ali's wife, Jumana, and we talked for a while. I had called her three times since Ali disappeared — once during the first few days, once when the kidnapping was announced, and again when his video aired. She was receiving a lot of support from her local mosque but was always grateful to hear from me. I told her nothing about

Wall. But I told her I was working hard to find out all I could about Ali and that I needed to speak to somebody named John whom I thought was an acquaintance of Ali's. She knew only one John that Ali spoke to often—John Simmons, a reporter at the Inquirer. She also suggested I call the imam at the local mosque. Maybe there were some Johns in the congregation.

I called Simmons first.

"John in Philadelphia?" I asked, as he answered his phone.

"Uh...yes," he answered. "John Simmons at the Philadelphia Inquirer, as I just said. May I ask who this is?"

I told him. We talked. He knew absolutely nothing about Ali's whereabouts, though he was very worried about him. He hadn't talked with Ali in a couple of months. They'd had lunch back in April when Ali was home for a week for his daughter's birthday. When the conversation was over, I was sure Mr. Simmons was not the John I needed to talk to.

Ali's imam reported only two Johns in his congregation—a Jamaican named John Jeffrey Jackson, and a fellow whose first name was Muhammed and whose last name was John. I called both. Mr. Jackson was an incoherent Islamic convert who wanted to argue about religion. Mr. John was an elderly maintenance man in a downtown apartment building who didn't know Ali personally but was aware of his kidnapping. Mr. John was praying for Ali. I thanked him for that kindness.

I called the rest of the list, starting each conversation with my secret password, *John in Philadelphia?* Nobody had a counter password. Of course, I didn't know if there even was one. Nobody knew anything in particular about Ali, except for what they'd heard on the news. One man hung up on me twice after I asked for John in Philadelphia. The third time, he stayed on the line long enough to tell me what he thought of prank callers who won't leave a guy alone in his own home.

I watched Ali's video again, several times over. By then, I could recite every line, and mimic every blink, wink, and nod. Still, I had no clue as to what Ali was trying to tell me — if he had any message for me personally.

I Googled "John in Philadelphia," and up popped a list of 94,500,000 entries related to my search! Everything from Papa John's Pizza to Philly Port-a-John, Inc.

I Googled "John in Philadelphia + Ali Ahkmed Baraki." Google wondered if I'd misspelled Ali's middle name, and gave me a list of fifty-four items related to its suggested revision.

I Googled "John in Philadelphia + Russia," and got another list with several million possibilities. I did advanced searches, narrowing the options to try to find Johns with a reasonable connection to anything related to Ali and his present situation.

I scrolled and scanned the lists, jotting down categories of Johns that could be used for further searches.

Then I bottomed out. This was too big!

It was nearly 9:00 p.m. and I had pretty bad headache. I was working on my third cup of coffee when the phone rang.

"John in Philadelphia," I answered wearily. I was dead tired.

"Matt?"

"Kevin! Am I glad to hear your voice!"

"Just called to see how you're doing. And to hear about Lisa in Lancaster," he said. "So what's up with John in Philadelphia?"

"Can you come over?" I begged. "Can you call the seminary guys and ask if they'd come over, too?"

"You okay?"

"No," I said. "But I don't need Jesus." *That's not what I meant!* "I don't need to get saved tonight! I don't need to have you guys pray with anyone to get saved, either," I explained. "I need help finding Ali. And I need help finding

John in Philadelphia. And I can't tell you exactly what I
mean, but if you guys can help me figure out a mystery,
then lots of people will get saved from lots of trouble…and
maybe I'll believe in miracles."

"Figure out a mystery?"

"Yeah," I said, carefully, wearily. I had to be guarded
concerning Wall. "Top secret sort of stuff that I'm
investigating for the Bulletin and…for Ali, you know. I have
reason to believe that Ali's video contains a coded message
that is very important to…to the safety of many people. The
video may even contain something Ali wants *me* to figure
out. I think it does. But I'm so tired…and I've worn myself
out trying to decipher it."

"I'll be glad to help," said Kevin. "But do you really
want me to rouse the whole gang?"

"Yeah…I mean, I think so. I'd appreciate just having you
all here for a few hours. I need the camaraderie. And two
heads—or three or four or five heads—are better than one."

"There's wisdom in the presence of many counselors,"
Kevin said. "That's Solomon, from Proverbs."

"Thanks," I said. "I can't think of any song to go along
with this just now."

"How about 'One Is the Loneliest Number'?"

"Three Dog Night!" I said. "I went to see them in concert
with my dad a few years back. At the American Music
Theater in Lancaster."

"Are they still a band?" Kevin asked.

"Yeah. Just three of the original members. Balding and
grey, but they've got some young bucks playing along and
they sound great…if you like that classic rock stuff."

"Well," said Kevin, "put on some classic rock and order
some pizza. I'll see if I can get the guys to turn off their TVs
and join us for a late-night mystery at M.L. Clifford's.
Maybe you can roll back that living room floor of yours and
get that pool ready for a swim, too!"

"Yeah," I said, "maybe I can."

15

Who, What, Where, When, Why, and How?

Kevin arrived first. He brought ice cream. The pizza came next, with Doug right behind it. Luis and Tyrone came together in Luis' car. They lived pretty close to each other in South Philly, and they brought a couple of liters of soda.

I'd never had the guys over all at once. In fact, Doug had never seen my place at all. It was good to have their voices bouncing off my lonesome walls.

"I forgot my bathing trunks," Luis laughed, stepping around the opened pool to put the sodas in the fridge.

"You could go skinny dippin'," Tyrone joked. "Like we useta do in the Schuylkill when we was comin' up. 'Course thet was gen'rally after dark, and we was mostly dark ourselves!"

We all laughed. It was good to laugh.

Tyrone was very dark — a short, stout African-American with Caucasian facial features and graying hair trimmed like a Marine's. Ty was in his early forties. He worked downtown for the Philadelphia County Board of Elections. Married twenty-two years, with three kids, his family attended the historic Mother Bethel African Methodist Episcopal church over on south 6th Street. He was raised in that church. His family went back several generations there.

He was natural and easy about his religion. I liked him a lot.

"Hey, you boys want a beer?" Luis shouted from inside the fridge. He held up a bottle of Rolling Rock Extra Pale.

"What's that in there for?" Doug asked, frowning.

"Oh, that's just one of the leftovers," I said. "I had the other four for breakfast."

"Winebibber!" Kevin quipped.

"Glutton!" said Luis with a grin, holding up a box lunch from Chick-fil-A.

"Friend of sinners," I added, as we laughed some more.

"No, really," Doug pressed. "Why do you have booze in your refrigerator?" Little things were big to Doug.

"For friends," I said. "Friends who drink," I added with a chuckle.

"I thought—" Doug said.

"I seldom drink," I explained, a bit upset that I had to explain at all, "and never alone. Some of the guys from the Bulletin come over once in a while. One of them likes Rolling Rock. I do, too, I guess."

"I like a beer every once in a while," Kevin said evenly, "with steak or a home-grilled burger."

Doug kept frowning. Frowns seemed to fit him. In fact, he had those kind of eyebrows that frowned all by themselves, even when he was smiling. Wiry, red-haired, hazel-eyed, with a face that fairly shouted of Ireland, Douglas O'Malley, at twenty-six, was the youngest of the pancake seminarians. He and his wife lived in an apartment above Rittenhouse Hardware at the corner of Pine and 20th. Doug worked in the store and was a partner in the business. An ex-Catholic, Doug attended Kensington Independent Baptist in a part of town that most folks didn't like to travel through even in the daylight. His wife didn't go with him. She was still Catholic. It was a sore spot in their marriage.

Luis handed Doug a plate for his pizza.

"Thanks for coming, guys," I said. "God bless our mess!" And I opened the pizza boxes. "Help yourselves."

Luis said "Amen" real loud, and then I heard the sound of water splashing. Tyrone had taken off his shoes, shirt, and pants and was making himself at home in the pool. He had his swimming trunks on underneath!

"Livin' large!" he sighed, treading water gracefully. "Could one of you fellas git me a glass of thet Kutztown Orange Cream Soda? On the rocks, please."

Kevin dug out some ice from the freezer and poured Tyrone's soda. He delivered it to him on a tray, and with a British accent said, "Your orange pop, sir." Somehow it struck Doug funny and smoothed the frown from his face.

"So," said Luis from a dining stool in the kitchen. The living room and kitchen were one large room, partitioned only by a marble-topped counter that served as a table for as many people as you can line up on either side of it—eight or ten, max.

"Yeah, *so*…" said Tyrone from the tub.

Kevin handed me the television remote.

"So, I'm over my head, guys," I said with a tired sigh. "This has been a whirlwind couple of weeks for me. And today, I…I need your help."

With no mention of Wall, I told them that I'd been given a four-word key—by a source I couldn't name—to help decipher a special message that Ali had worked into the video that the terrorists had released. The hidden message was for me alone. And by figuring it out, I would be on my way to solving a mystery that could help save lives.

"That's all I know," I said. "I'm convinced this is a matter of life and death for a large number of people. Maybe it has to do with Russia and Georgia. Maybe it's something in the Middle East. Or something here at home. I don't know…but it's real, it's imminent, and I've been trusted—by my friend Ali and my unnamed source—to do what I can about it. Whatever *it* is!"

I turned on the video and then immediately hit pause. Wall was standing there, the Central-Asian steppes in the background. "This is Bradley Wall," I said, "FOX News correspondent in Russia. You guys have seen him on the air for years. You've probably seen this broadcast already today. It's been replayed on FOX a number of times and excerpted on other networks. Wall…"

I wasn't sure how to tell it without telling too much. "Let's watch this thing all the way through. Then I'll tell you the key, and we'll watch it again. Then we'll talk and watch Ali's segment…or something like that."

Suddenly, abruptly, I powered it off and turned to face my friends squarely. Would Wall want me taking these guys into my confidence? What would Ali say? I didn't know, but if we were going to work on this together, I needed to impress upon the guys the peril of the situation, the need for absolute secrecy.

"Look fellas," I said gravely, "not even my bosses or co-workers at the Bulletin know what I'm going to share with you tonight. Like I said—life and death are on the line here. This is big stuff. This isn't a theological debate about the book of Revelation while we pass the butter and eat pancakes. This is…"

I thought about Cobalt Man. About Wall's talk of carrying a gun. About Ali tied up somewhere in the Caucasus. I thought about the ghastly, severed arm of Vladimir Lenin lying in a blood-spattered mausoleum. I saw the Four Horsemen of the Apocalypse riding up to the banks of a dark river.

"You can't tell *anyone* about what we're doing here tonight. Not your wives. Not your dogs. Not your pillow. Not your priest. Not even each other, after you leave here. So help you, God! Got that?"

Luis said, "Amen."

Kevin said, "Yeah."

Tyrone said, "Got it, man."

Doug indicated *yes* with a grim shake of his shaggy-maned head. Then he said, "My priest is Jesus Christ."

"You can tell *him*," I conceded. And I turned the video back on.

We watched. I told them the key: *See John in Philadelphia.* I told them about the winks in the video. We watched again— and again.

I told them about my name searches and my phone calls. I got out my long lists and tried to put things in context, but I began to feel as confused and overwhelmed as I had earlier in the evening.

"Okay, okay," said Tyrone. He was out of the pool and all dried up and dressed. "That key phrase of yours don't say '*talk* to John.' It says '*see* John.' So let's jest 'liminate anyone you think you need to talk to—'cause you *don't* need to talk to 'em!"

"That narrows it down," said Luis with a grin.

"Right!" said Tyrone seriously.

"So what kinda Johns can you only *see?* A statue 'round town of some famous colonial John Someone-or-other. A portrait of John Street, our ven'able mayor emeritus! Somethin' like that."

"Yeahhh," said Kevin, kind of long and slow. He was already making a mental list.

"Landmarks," said Luis.

"Land*johns*," corrected Doug.

"Does the Liberty Bell have a nickname?" asked Luis. "Is it John, maybe?" He was kidding—I think.

"Port-a-johns," suggested Doug, smiling wryly.

"This is great!" I laughed. "Really...I mean it," I said, re-invigorated. "Let's brainstorm. Nothing is stupid right now. Everything will help narrow the search—focus the search."

"And see John *where?*" Doug said. "In Philadelphia," he answered himself. "So let's keep our brainstorming right here at home."

"But does 'in Philadelphia' have to refer to the city itself?" Kevin asked. "Or is there some other 'Philadelphia' somewhere in the city? Another landmark? A work of art? Maybe a building, a business, a restaurant?"

"Or a ship!" Luis said. "There's a USS Philadelphia. It's a submarine!"

"Down at the docks?" I asked. Luis works at Pier 96 where they ship military vehicles in and out of the country.

"No," Luis said. "Her homeport is Groton, Connecticut. But she's active. She's been in the Mediterranean. She collided with a Turkish merchant ship in the Persian Gulf about nine, ten years back. Remember that? It was in the news. Minor damage. Back in action soon afterwards. Don't know where she is now."

"Can you find out?" I asked. "And whether she has a commander named John—or anyone else on board by that name?"

"Yep," said Luis, and he pulled out his smartphone to search it out on the Internet.

"Well, then," Doug said, "if we're not stuck in Pennsylvania, what about other cities named Philadelphia?"

"There are at least four that I can think of," I said, and I jotted them down.

"The movie!" Kevin blurted. "There's a movie named *Philadelphia*. It was an Academy Award winner about twenty years ago."

"The homo movie," Doug said. "It was about queers and AIDS—and Tom Hanks was in it."

"M'man Denzel Washington, too," Tyrone said. "Plays a lawyer."

"Anyone named John in that film?" I wondered, getting up and heading toward my bedroom. "I'll get my MagicMac out here so we have another option for going online to check this stuff out. Ty, can you Google for information as we hand you clues?"

"Barney Google, at your service, sir," said Tyrone. "With them goo, goo, googly eyes!"

"Where'd you find this guy?" Kevin said to Luis.

"Oh, he was just walking down the street, singing old spirituals, and I thought it would be fun to bring him over here tonight to help us keep perspective on things, you know," Luis joked.

Everyone was laughing when I came back with the Mac. I set it on the floor next to Tyrone. He was reclining in my electric La-Z-Boy, staring at his BlackBerry. Luis had split-screened the TV and was already online on one half, while Ali's video was paused on the other half. "I forgot we could do that," I said.

Kevin motioned me to sit next to him. "The winks," he said, "and the touching of hand to heart in Ali's address. These are keys in themselves…or signals to you, Matthew Lyle Clifford. This may sound ridiculous, but when Ali says, 'We…lie all…and I,' could he simply be saying, 'We, Lyle and I'? Could he be talking about you and him?"

"Oh!" I said, astonished by the thought but instantly convinced. It fit!

And the hand on the heart! I suddenly remembered Ali doing that when speaking about his wife and his children, when expressing his love for them. "He's telling me that I'm his friend, Kevin. That we are friends…" My eyes teared, and I couldn't speak for a moment. "And that he loves me." *Ali! Kidnapped!* "But his captors are his *brothers* in Islam," I muttered bitterly, sarcastically, "and they will treat him well."

"So the winks and the hand on the heart," Kevin said quietly, "they make sense. And they mean that what Ali said right after the winks is most important."

"Yes," I said, sitting up straight. "After the first winks, Ali's words are a double-entendre. There are two meanings hidden there. He's saying my name—but he's also more obviously saying that everybody is a liar. He's apologizing for lying! Anyone who knows Ali would know that his diatribe against Israel and America is neither his heart nor his mind. And then after the second winks and the hand on

the heart, he wants me to hear everything he says until…
well, probably until he pauses to praise Allah the second
time."

"We—Lyle and I—above all, we must look to the Perfect
One in the hour of trouble," Kevin quoted.

"So what about the key?"

"Hey!" Doug said suddenly. He had been quiet for a few
minutes, sitting by himself, thumbing through his King
James Bible. "What about the apostle John? He wrote about
Philadelphia in the book of Revelation!"

"See John in Philadelphia!" Tyrone shouted, trying to sit
up straight in the horizontal recliner. "See the words of John
in the letter to Philadelphia in Revelation! You got it, Doug!
Where's m'Bible?"

"Would Ali be using the Bible?" Luis asked. "He's
Muslim."

"He reads all kinds of things," I said, "including the
Bible. Maybe he reads it more than I do. He knew we were
studying Revelation because he and I talked about it."

"Then maybe this Revelation stuff *is* key," Kevin said.

"Yeah," I said. "Let's hear it, Doug."

Doug began to read the passage aloud. "And to the
angel of the church in Philadelphia write: These things saith
he that is holy, he that is true, he that hath the key of David,
he that openeth and no man shutteth, and shutteth and no
man openeth. I know thy works. Behold, I have set before
thee an open door and no man can shut it, for thou hast a
little strength and hast kept my word and hast not denied
my name. Behold, I will make them of the synagogue of
Satan (which say they are Jews and are not but do lie)—
behold, I will make them to come and worship before thy
feet and to know that I have loved thee. Because thou hast
kept the word of my patience, I also will keep thee from the
hour of temptation which shall come upon all the world to
try them that dwell upon the earth. Behold, I come quickly!
Hold that fast which thou hast, that no man take thy crown."

Doug looked up, and with an air of authority said, "Revelation, chapter three, verses seven through eleven." He closed his Bible.

I was silent. Angry. Overwhelmed. What could these verses possibly have to do with what Ali was trying to tell me? *The key of David. The synagogue of Satan. Jews who weren't Jews.* What was all this to Ali? Or to me? *The hour of temptation* — at least that sounded like the "hour of trouble." But did it relate to Ali's message? We could be running down a rabbit trail, far from the path that Ali wanted to take me on. I was weary, and I felt like sending the guys home and taking a fresh look at it all the next day.

"Let's pray," said Kevin abruptly. "Will you pray for us, Luis?"

"Dear Lord," Luis prayed, "you open doors that no man can open. You close doors that no man can close. We don't know which doors are which. We don't know nothing! Please, Lord, show us the way. Help us to help Matt, for the sake of those in danger of their lives. We thank you and praise you in the powerful name of Jesus Christ. Amen!"

In danger of their lives… And what could I possibly do to save them?

"Okay," Kevin chimed with finality. "Let's not get tangled up in the end-times theology of what Doug read. Let's not try to guess where Ali might be. We've got to figure out what Ali said to Matt!"

"Look, guys," I sighed, "maybe tomorrow…"

"But," Doug insisted, "this all fits. There's a key here, too. The key of David." He gestured impatiently, trying to make something of David's key, but he couldn't. "And Philadelphia is the sixth church in the list of churches in Revelation. That means something." He pulled a wrinkled chart out of his Bible, unfolded it, and held it up for us to see. It was an historic chronology of prophetic events, and each of the seven Revelation churches were there, representing periods in the history of the Church.

"This shows that the church of Philadelphia is the church from about 1800 until today," Doug declared. "That's us! Right now. The church right before the Rapture. Before the hour of temptation comes. Before the Antichrist is revealed. Before Jesus takes us out of all this."

"Ali's not a theologian," Kevin said in slow, measured syllables. "He's not a Christian. He's not waiting for the Rapture...whenever it will be."

"It could be *tonight*, dude!" Doug argued.

"Maybe tonight isn't the time to try to figure out anything at all," I inserted, "about Ali or..."

"We can do this," said Kevin, facing me. Then he turned to Doug. "We can debate end-times stuff on Saturday mornings at the Dutch Eating Place. Let's focus our time tonight on what can best help Matt hear what Ali is saying to him."

A reasonable appeal, but Doug wasn't hearing it. Not at all.

"Who died and made *you* pope?" Doug's green eyes flashed. "Let's ask Matt what he thinks. This is his party!"

"Whoa, bro!" Tyrone cautioned. "Whussup? Kevin's jest tryin' to help us stay on track."

"Sometimes I think you guys don't even care what the Bible really says!" shot Doug.

"What?" Luis laughed nervously. "Is it past your bedtime, gringo?"

Tyrone laughed also—then covered his mouth. "Sorry for thet. I think it's past m'own bedtime. Hey, I'm willin' to keep workin' here. But, let's bless one another, brothers— not git into a rumble over what time of day Jesus is comin' back!"

"Doug's hit on something, though," I said, seeking peace. "I do think there's something in those verses. 'Hour of temptation' sounds like 'hour of trouble.' And Ali sometimes used that phrase when we talked about the wars in the Middle East. Write that down, Ty, will you?" I nodded at Kevin, who was sitting back in the couch next to me, stiff-lipped.

"Gringo," Doug repeated darkly.

"I don't mean nothing negative by the comment," said Luis. "Just a little joke."

"Maybe…maybe I'm rankled over other stuff," Doug confessed. "The hardware store is understaffed. We had to lay off a long-time worker because of the cost of Claycare. Home Depot and the other big-box stores undersell us every day. Even WalMart's got a hardware department—and who can compete with them? Things aren't too good at home, either. I've been growling around the apartment too much, and Emily is threatening to stop cooking for me if I don't stop being so mean." He sighed. "She should talk!"

"Hey," Luis leaned toward Doug, "why you didn't say so before, man? We're your friends! Ain't nothing more important than your marriage. And we can talk about it with you…pray about it."

"I don't want to load you guys up with my problems," Doug said, staring at his hands, clasped tightly on his lap. "But it would be good to talk to someone about it…sometime."

"How 'bout right now?" said Luis.

Oh, God! I thought. *Not now!* But I needn't have worried. Luis was thinking for us all. "Do you guys mind," he said, "if Doug and I call it a night? We'll take a ride around town—and talk. I can come back later for you, Ty, or maybe Kevin can take you home. Would that be okay, Kev?"

"Okay with you, Ty?" Kevin asked.

"Fine by me," Tyrone replied. "We'll pray for ya, Doug. And y'all pray for us thet we can solve this partic'lar puzzlement."

Doug got up and sullenly shook hands all around. "Sorry I got upset," he said to Kevin.

"Don't worry about it."

"You do a good job leading," Doug said deliberately.

"You did a great job finding John in Philadelphia."

"Text me, Matt," said Doug. "Let me know what you guys come up with."

They backed out the door into the mid-summer night's heat.

In a moment of tense reflection after Luis and Doug had departed, I glanced at the clock on the wall. It was almost 10:00 p.m. I had a headache. Coffee didn't help. I really wanted to call it a night myself. But Kevin was a night owl— a morning bird *and* a night owl. *Does he need sleep at all?* I wondered.

"Back to business," he said.

"Amen," said Ty.

"Something occurred to me while Doug was railing at me," Kevin said. "Maybe it was the Holy Spirit. Maybe it was an undigested bit of pizza. But I thought about the fact that there are a few churches here in the city called Open Door. Like in the verses Doug read."

"There's a Church of the Open Door north of the city, in Fort Washington," said Tyrone. "Independent fundamentalist, Bible thumpin' folks…like Doug's church. Big church, and it's been 'round awhile."

"Yeah," Kevin said. "And there's a storefront Baptist church called Open Door Baptist, near Girard College, I think. There's also the Sanctuary Church of the Open Door, not far from my house, on Walnut Street. It's a grand old Gothic structure with a Christian school right next to it."

"Here's a couple more," Tyrone said. He had taken Luis' place at the split screen. "Googlin'," he said.

"Anybody named John pastoring one of those churches?" I asked the same tired question.

"Save that church info for later, Ty," Kevin said. "Write it down, or copy and paste it in a Word document." He stood up and stretched his long arms toward the ceiling. His fingers touched it, even with his feet flat on the floor.

Kevin is about 6′3″ and as fit as a basketball player. He used to play in college and came close to being drafted into the NBA. Then he badly broke an ankle on the court, and that was the end of a promising career. He took up karate a couple of years later to strengthen the ankle and have something else to aspire to. In better shape than I'll ever be, he still played pickup at the city playgrounds. The urban boys could dribble circles around him, but when Kevin shot that ball, he never missed the bucket!

"Let's get back to Ali's words," he said. He was standing at the window, blinds open, looking out. I got up to take a look myself.

"Empty street this time of night," I said, closing the blinds again. I didn't see Cobalt Man. Or anybody else.

"Perfect one. Hour of trouble. What could that mean, Matt?" Kevin asked. "What would it mean to you and Ali?"

"The hour of trouble…that's been sticking," I said. And I started pacing my well-worn path between the window and my front door. I'd covered up the pool shortly after Tyrone had climbed out.

"Ali and I talk about the days we live in — that's our job," I said, thinking out loud. "We talk about how bad things are around the world. And Ali is like you guys — he thinks we're near the end of things. He believes that we're in the last days…the 'hour of trouble' he calls it." I stared at Ali's figure on the television screen, paused in mid-sentence, hand on his heart. "So, what are you saying to me, Ali?"

"Muslims have their own version of Armageddon, don't they?" asked Kevin. "They call it *Al-Malhamah Al-Kubrah* — The Great War."

"Yes," I said. "How do you know all this stuff, Professor McCarthy? I thought I was the guy with the Muslim friend!"

Kevin shrugged and sat back down. "I watch the History Channel. I read World magazine, Summit Report, the Bulletin commentary pages…"

"Ali is interested in Armageddon — like we are," I said,

resuming my pacing. "It's a Shia Islam belief that the last battle will take place in Syria. Shiite clerics preach that the Imam Madhi—twelfth grandson of the Prophet Muhammad—is going to return to the Muslim people and usher in a worldwide Islamic revolution. The signs leading up to the Imam's return are similar to the biblical signs prior to the return of Christ. Chaos and rampant violence in the Middle East will precede The Great War in which the Imam will return to lead Shiites to victory."

"Plenty of thet rampant stuff to go 'round!" Tryone interjected.

"That's what Iranian president Ahmed al-Farid wanted," Kevin said. "That's why he started the war with Israel. He believed he could usher in the return of the Imam."

"Yessir," Tyrone commented. "But now that's one dead Iranian president, no Imam Madhi, a lot less chaos—and a gen-u-ine peace treaty on top of it all."

"No Imam," I murmured.

"They even believe that Jesus is coming back to earth," Kevin said.

"No way!" coughed Tyrone.

"Uh-huh," I grunted. "Some Muslims believe that Jesus is the Messiah, but not the Son of God—not the savior of the world. His role as Messiah was a prophet, a messenger of Allah—like Moses before him and Muhammad after him. They call Jesus *Isa*."

"In the *name* of Isa!" Tyrone chanted.

"According to some Islamic scholars," I continued, "Isa only seemed to die on the cross. Somebody else was nailed there in his place while God took Isa to heaven. But he's coming back. He's going to whup the Antichrist, confess Islam, slaughter every pig in the world, break every cross…and then get married, settle down, and have kids for a thousand years."

"Well! Is all thet in their Koran?" Tyrone asked.

"No," I said, "but it's in the jumble of their traditions."

"The Bible has Jesus returning on a white horse to destroy the nations of the earth who are allied against God," Kevin said. "Shia prophecies have Isa devastating the infidel armies of Europe before restoring peace and brotherhood to the planet."

"The Imam Mahdi comes in there somewhere," I added. "Maybe Isa is the Mahdi. Different Muslim scholars have different ideas. And there are different traditions that go way back."

"Sounds a lot like the different idees we have in our little pancake sem'nary," Tyrone noted. "Also sounds like them Muslims was readin' the end of the Good Book but kinda changed things around to give 'emselves a happy endin'." He pushed up out of the recliner to help himself to the last of the pizza.

"So Doug was right," Tyrone said, "thet this here is thet hour of trouble. And Ali might say so, too."

"The 'hour before midnight,'" I mused. "That's another of Ali's phrases."

"The 'leventh hour, Mama useta say." Tyrone crushed the pizza box and stuffed it into my trash can. He opened my cupboard to take down some bowls.

"But what would Ali mean by that?" Kevin asked. "We have to look to the Perfect One before the end comes? Look to God? Look to Allah? Why would he ask you to do that? Is he concerned for your salvation?"

"No," I said. "Ali's a liberal Muslim. He believes in Allah, but not in a big way. Not in an exclusive way, I should say. He thinks that all the People of the Book—the Jews, the Christians, and the Muslims—really worship the same God."

"Let's forget the spiritual clues," Kevin said, stretching himself out on the couch. "Let's chuck out the end times stuff, too. That's too complex. Ali isn't trying to pass on a spiritual message. He wants to tell you something with his words that you can discover right here, right now. A plot to uncover. A story to write. A warning to sound. He's pointing you to something or somebody he wants you to see. John in Philadelphia. The Perfect One. In the hour of trouble."

"Yeah," I said. "Who, what, where, when, why, and how? All the questions reporters are supposed to consider while working on a story. All the questions we're supposed to answer when we write a story. But what *are* the answers?"

"You said *when?*" Tyrone asked rather loudly. We looked at him digging the ice cream out of the freezer. "Did you say *when?* How 'bout thet hour of trouble being the 'leventh hour? For real. It's comin' up on us pretty soon. Mebbe you're s'posed to meet someone, somewhere, at 'leven o'clock." We just stared at him. He smiled and shrugged. "And mebbe not," he said, filling a bowl with chocolate marshmallow ice cream.

It was 10:15.

"And here's a silly one," he added. "Really a stretch! But you said nothin' was stupid tonight, right? So how 'bout messin' with some numbers?" He put the bowl down and stuck his fingers up, like he was going to count on them. "Mebbe the word 'perfect' means the number 'seven'...like in the Bible. Like in the passages Doug read us. Seven letters to seven churches. Seven's the Bible number for perfection, ain't it?"

"Yes," I said, remembering something else about Ali.

"So mebbe it's a street number of one of them Open Door churches, or mebbe a street number of a church with a *John* in it, like St. John's Lutheran or St. John's Catholic."

"If Doug were here, he'd say St. John's Catholic would fit the 'synogogue of Satan' verse," I said. "But Ali wouldn't think that way." I started pacing again. "But you know, Tyrone, Ali *would* think about the number seven as the perfect number. At least, he might use that to clue me in on what he wants me to figure out. We had a talk about that

once because of a story he covered about Islamic doctors in
Chad who used numerology and the Koran to heal people.
Muslim witch doctors! We talked about biblical numerology
also."

"Okay," said Tyrone. "So let's *add up* the 'perfect one.'
'Perfect' means *seven,* and 'one' means *one!* Do the math—
seven plus one—and you git eight."

"Look to eight at eleven o'clock!" I said cynically,
kicking my couch.

"Verse eight!" said Kevin, holding up his Bible. "Maybe
it's the Holy Spirit after all. Verse eight in the Philadelphia
passage in Revelation specifically says, 'I have set before you
an open door.' So, we're back to the Open Door."

He was serious. We were all serious. Seriously confused!

"Let me get this straight," I said, trying to pull
something together out of all that we'd discussed. "When
we see John in Philadelphia—that is, when we have seen the
passages he wrote about Philadelphia in his Revelation—we
are to conclude that Ali wants us, above all, to look to some
Open Door Church at 11:00 p.m."

"I don't know," Kevin said flatly, somberly, pressing a
pillow to his face.

"What if he meant 11:00 a.m., when church normally
starts on Sunday morning?" I asked.

"The 'leventh hour is the hour 'fore midnight!" Tyrone
insisted. "You said Ali talked about the hour 'fore
midnight!"

"Who? What? Where? When? Why? How?" Kevin
recited.

"Okay, who?" I asked.

"John," said Ty.

"What?" I asked.

"The book of Revelation," Kevin said, sitting back up.

"Where?" I challenged, getting louder.

"In the verses 'bout the church in Philadelphia. Some
church of the Open Door!" Ty said, pounding his fist on my

counter. His ice cream bowl fell off, and he had to catch it. The spoon clattered on the hardwood floor.

"When?" I shouted.

"Eeee-leven o'clock p.m.!" declared Tyrone, bowl in hand. "Pretty doggone soon!"

"Why?" I fired, staring wide-eyed at my friends.

"Life and death," Kevin uttered grimly, "for many people."

"And how?" I asked, throwing up my hands.

"That's for you to figure out," Kevin said quietly. "Ali is counting on you to figure it out."

"Right," I said wearily. Then I straightened up and hollered, "Let's go church hopping! We've got about half an hour to get to one, maybe two, of those Open Door places before eleven!"

Kevin got up, saluted me, and headed toward the door. Then he said, "I better use the boy's room first."

"Mind if I stick here and ketch some sleep?" Tyrone asked. "I'll call the wife and tell 'er I'm puttin' m'feet up over here fer the night."

"That's okay with me." I said. "Let's move, Kevin!"

"My car's right outside," he said from behind the bathroom door. "We'll head for the church on Walnut. I can find it faster than any of the others."

"Y'all want 5923 Walnut, to be exact," Tyrone said from in front of the split screen. "Google says so!"

I started laughing. It was all crazy. But anything was better than sitting there knocking our heads together until we were punch drunk and dizzy. I followed Kevin down the stairs.

We pulled out onto Brown, worked over to Broad, headed down to Vine, and drove straight east across the Schuylkill River toward our mysterious destination. I didn't see the Rolls Royce tooling along behind us about three blocks back. I didn't see the driver, or his partner sitting next to him, as they talked to some third party through the two-way sat-com built into the dashboard. I'm glad I didn't, or I might have told Kevin to turn around and take me home.

I never would have met Rashid.

16
Rashid

As Kevin and I sped westward on Walnut Street, I watched the city slide by beneath the streetlights and the neon glow of fuel station signs and fast-food marquees. At bus stops and an occasional street corner, the bright, shifting colors of the back-lit Bulletin Boards enlivened the otherwise tree-shadowed avenues.

I'm a country boy, but I love the city. I grew up with my feet in the Pequea Creek, but I'd rather walk the sidewalks of New York or Philadelphia any day. Lisa hated the city—one more reason why we'd grown apart. Day and night, I soaked up life from the noise and the bustle of the never-resting metropolis. Lisa said there was no real life in speed and light—it's all a thing of the senses. It feeds the flesh, but starves the soul. She may have been right, but I couldn't imagine making my home beneath the trees again, with nothing to stir me besides the crickets, the katydids, and the cold wind in the brittle autumn leaves.

Immediately over the Schuylkill on Walnut, the big city faded into an eight-block cruise through the center of the University of Pennsylvania where state-of-the-art hotels and campus buildings competed with four-floored Victorian frat houses postured behind a haphazard picket of young maples. Beyond the university, Walnut morphed into an unkempt corridor of post-World War II homes, stores, and office buildings, with an occasional school and some new development. A redundant façade of two-storied row houses followed, standing solid and stiff on both sides of the street, behind wide, cracked concrete walks and small, well-kept yards.

The late night traffic was sparse. We'd seen more police cars and SA vehicles than anything else on our short journey. Once past the college, the pedestrian presence practically ceased, and the neighborhood grew darker, more compact, as we rolled through the remaining blocks toward our destination. Kevin and I were silent as the gothic spires of the historic church came into sight above the residential rooftops. Pulling up in front of the massive Sanctuary Church of the Open Door was like approaching a medieval castle.

The formidable ecclesiastical structure, and the school that grew out of its side, took up half a city block. No spotlight lit its chiseled black exterior, but a dim radiance stretched across the dark avenue from streetlamp and porch light to kiss the cold stones. A few parked cars, scattered up and down the street, were not yet put to bed in safer quarters for the night. Two orange rectangles of rippled glass glowed contemplatively in a corner of the shadowed school that sat back off the street behind a wide grassy lawn and a cobblestone courtyard.

On the right, a wing of the old school reached out to the sidewalk again. It was an open corridored hallway, reminiscent of an old English university, colonnaded and porticoed, roofed in thick slate. All it needed to transport it to another time and place was a cover of ancient ivy and a drawbridge. A man was standing in the shadows of the porch, smoking. I could see the flare of his cigarette as we drove slowly past. Was it "John"?

"Too weird!" I whispered. The sound of my voice was almost startling in the quiet confines of our automobile. "Pull around the block, Kev," I said, "and park out of sight of the church. I'll walk back alone and check this out."

"Are you sure you don't want this?" Kevin asked, patting the shoulder holster under his shirt.

"I'm sure," I lied. I would have liked the gun firmly in hand, but I was afraid I wouldn't know what to do with it.

When Kevin pulled over a block and a half away, he opened his glove compartment and rummaged for a moment. "Take these," he said. "A friend left them here a couple of days ago. Pretend you need a light." I took the crumpled pack of Marlboros and put them in my pocket.

I got out, quietly and cautiously, and closed the door. Kevin signaled me with cupped hands. He'd be praying.

I started up the street toward the corner, halted, then strolled onto Walnut to pass in front of the church and toward the darkened portico. A dog barked somewhere down the street, a door opened on a cavernous porch, a woman barked back at the dog—and all was silent again.

I'm on a mission, I told myself, and the truth of it kept me walking, kept me wary, kept me thinking—kept me scared enough to pray.

I fumbled in my pocket, pulled out the opened pack of Marlboros, and fingered a single cigarette. I'm not a smoker, but "John" was. I put the cigarette in my mouth. As I approached the stone porch, I patted my clothes as though looking for a light.

"Oh!" I said, when directly in front of the porch. "I didn't see you there until I saw your fire just now." I chuckled amiably, turning toward the silent figure. "Have you got a light? I thought I had a lighter, but I can't find it." I stepped toward the porch. "Sorry to bother you."

The man took a tentative step toward me, and his features came out of the shadows. Arabic?

He didn't speak, but as I leaned my head toward him, cigarette between my lips, he held out the lit end of his smoke. His hand was shaking slightly. I fired up the Marlboro—the way I'd seen it done in the movies—and inhaled carefully so as not to cough my head off and give myself away. "Thank you," I said thickly—and smoke escaped me with my words. The man simply nodded and stepped back into the shadows.

"Hot night," I said, drawing another blistering cloud into my mouth. I blew it back out slowly. My eyes were tearing, and I bowed my head to wipe them discreetly. "Muggy. *Close*, my mother used to say. Makes you sweat just walking down the street."

The man grunted.

"Well," I said, turning away without moving away, "thanks again." I wanted to walk off, but I knew I couldn't.

"You're welcome," he said, in a northwestern American accent tinged with something foreign. It wasn't strong, more of a distant echo of another land, but I knew it— Afghanistan!

I shifted on my feet carelessly. "This church here," I said nonchalantly, "is it St. John's of Philadelphia?"

He straightened sharply—but didn't reply.

I tried again. "Is this a church that looks to the Perfect One in the hour of trouble?"

"No," he spat. "It reads the wrong book."

Now I was the silent one. But he wasn't done. "Do you know Wrong Book?" he asked, his voice quivering.

"Ali!" I said, barely loud enough to hear myself. I couldn't help it. The stranger heard me.

"Ahhh…" he sighed, and his body relaxed.

Ali had a nickname among the Pancake Seminarians. Doug had dubbed him Wrong Book because of the Koran. Ali knew the moniker because I told him. This man knew it, too—because Ali told him.

"You are Matthew Clifford," said the man. "I know you from the news boards and TV, though I had no idea it would be you who found me here."

"Yes, I am Matthew Clifford," I said. "You are John?"

"Rashid," he replied, and then his reserve fell from him.

He took my hands in his, shaking them almost violently. "Do you know where he is?" he cried.

"No," I said bluntly. "I had hoped that you would."

"Come," said Rashid, leading me further into the darkness. "I have been waiting here for you every day since Ali was taken. I have smoked more cigarettes than ever in my life!" *So have I,* I thought. "You are Matthew Clifford," he said again.

"Yes," I said. "And Ali's friend."

I was getting used to the shadows, and could see Rashid's animated face. There were tears in his eyes, on his cheeks. But he was grinning—sadly, anxiously. He would not let go of my hands.

"Before he was taken," said Rashid, "he told me to come here. If he did not die, but was taken, I was to come here. At eleven o'clock. Every night. To wait and watch for you, dear friend of Ali! Though he couldn't tell me who you are. And I never guessed, though I tried hard to guess. *Al-Hamdu lillah!* Thanks be to God! You are here!"

"Before he was taken?"

"Ah, yes! He knew he could be a prisoner someday—or a dead man! Because of what he knows…for what we know together…for what he was seeking to know. But he didn't know when or how this might happen—or if it would happen at all. Oh, Ali!—my brother! Will we see you again?"

This was incredible. I knew, without knowing, that Rashid was a treasure chest full of all that I was seeking. And suddenly I had hope that I could do all that Wall hinted I could do. But I must get Rashid out of that dark hallway and into Kevin's car. We needed to have a long talk—somewhere safe where the shadows didn't have ears and eyes. Where we wouldn't have to run.

"Rashid," I said, shaking his hands as he had shaken mine, "will you come with me to my home tonight? Will you…trust me?"

"I will. I do."

"Do you have a vehicle nearby?"

"No. I walked."

"Another friend of Ali's is with me," I said carefully. "In a car, around the corner."

"His name?"

"Kevin McCarthy," I said. "He's my best friend. He's been helping me to find you. He...he prays for Ali every day."

"A friend of Matthew Clifford," said Rashid resolutely, "is a friend of Ali, is a friend of Rashid. For whom else do I have?" He let go of my hands and said, "Let us depart."

We walked together, briskly, to the car. I offered him the front seat. He got in, sat down, and immediately reached to shake Kevin's hand. "You are a friend of Matthew Clifford," Rashid said, looking Kevin in the eyes. "I am Rashid Kholami, cousin to Ali Ahkmed Baraki, ally to Matthew Clifford and to you. I've been expecting you. Thank you for coming to see me." It was as if he were welcoming us into his home. I liked this man already.

As I climbed into the back seat, the headlights of a lone vehicle came around the corner and caught me in their glare. I ducked quickly out of the spotlight and pulled the door shut. The car drove by and continued down the street. It was a black Rolls Royce with tinted glass. I could see it was tinted from the way it reflected the streetlight above us. I saw no one inside, but my imagination conjured a well-heeled drug lord—or a steel-eyed man in a baseball cap—staring at our vehicle as if to burn its image in his mind. "Let's get out of here," I said.

We drove to Kevin's. I thought it best not to take Rashid back to my apartment where Tyrone lay snoring in the recliner. It was just past midnight when Kevin locked his door behind us and offered Mr. Kholami his choice of seating in his spacious living room. Rashid waived his rights, so I took the couch. He accepted a hot cup of coffee but didn't sit down until he had inspected every picture on Kevin's walls, every knick-knack on display, every book upon his shelves. At last, settled nervously in an antique rocker near the window, he burst forth with all that was within him.

"I am Ali's cousin on his father's side," he said. "We've known each other since we were newly born, being one week apart, Ali the older. His father and mine are brothers who came to America together — to New York City — when they were young men seeking opportunity in the land of the free."

"Why didn't Ali ever tell me about you?" I wondered aloud.

"Ah! Because we were reunited only very recently, and we were torn apart when we were only boys," he said. "Our fathers became foes when Ali and I were very young. It was a small thing, a foolish thing, that divided their hearts. They both applied for a job they wanted. One of them was hired, the other was not. It became a big matter in their pride, and it was a wall between them. My father regretted it, grieved deeply because of it, but the wall never came down. Ali's family moved to Trenton, New Jersey, when we were but five years of age. My family moved west to Oregon. I carried Ali in my heart, all those miles and all these years, but I never heard from him in all that time until…"

He got up again and walked over to a small corkboard next to a shelf packed tight with books. There was a computer print of a photo on the board. It was Ali and his family.

"Matt e-mailed that picture to me the day after the news of Ali's kidnapping," said Kevin. "I pinned it up there to remind me to pray for Ali and his wife and children."

Rashid looked at Kevin with a question in his eyes, then back at the photo again. "May I…hold it?"

"You may have it to keep, if you wish."

Rashid smiled widely, took the photo from the board,

and sat back down, staring at it as if it might speak to him.
Then the smile faded. "I never heard from him again," he
continued, "until one day in June of this year when I came to
Philadelphia to visit my brother Kahmeel who moved here
two years ago.

"When Father died, Kahmeel was a young man
with restless friends. Upset by Father's death, he sought
fellowship with a small community of Muslim idealists
dedicated to Sharia law. The group was radical. They called
themselves the Sons of Islam. They had a website called
Western Jihad. We thought it was just youthful zeal.
The government thought otherwise and arrested several
members. Khameel's community fell apart, but a few of the
young men moved here to Philadelphia. Kahmeel came with
them."

Rashid sat up, setting the photo on the coffee table
between us. His dark, expressive eyes found mine. "I came
to Philadelphia only to visit, but I have stayed. Because
when I arrived, I found Ali!"

I stared, fascinated, at the friendly stranger on my couch.
He was an olive-skinned Afghan-American, clean-shaven,
with dark, squared eyebrows and a close-cropped head of
hair. He resembled Ali with his long thin nose, strong chin,
and wide mouth full of straight white teeth. But there was
more of the Mongol in Rashid's eyes than in Ali's—more of
the Asian steppes and less of the European hills. A hand-
some man, but haunted.

"I didn't find Ali himself of course," Rashid explained,
"but his image on the Bulletin Boards—standing in the
Kremlin, in Russia!—telling the world about what he was
seeing and hearing. My cousin, my brother! Ali Ahkmed
Baraki! I saw the boy in the man. I felt reborn. I praised
Allah for his goodness and his mercy, and I knew that I
must contact Ali. I thought first of phoning the Bulletin, but
I know a friend in Moscow so I e-mailed him instead. He
found Ali, Ali e-mailed me—and we were brothers once

again! We talked by cell phone the second day, by sat-com the next. That was the end. This was only last month, you see!"

"Exactly when?" I asked. "What was the date that you last connected with him?"

"It was June 31."

"Two weeks ago," Kevin commented. "Less than a week before the kidnapping."

"When we were done rejoicing…done with telling our lives to one another, Ali became sad," Rashid said soberly. "This was in our last talk, when we spoke face-to-face by sat-com. He became very serious and asked me to swear that I would stand with him in something that must be done.

"I told him that if I must swear, I would swear by Allah or remain silent. This is the Koran. And so I swore by Allah."

Kevin sat forward on the couch. I nodded silently, anxious for Rashid to continue — hoping that he would.

"Ali has uncovered some things," said Rashid, hesitantly. "He…he is not just a newsman anymore."

"What do you mean?" I thought of Wall. He was not just a newsman either.

"I trust you because Ali trusts you," said Rashid.

I'd heard that before. I thought again of Wall.

"I know only what Ali told me," said Rashid. "Our hearts were as one when we were children, and they became as one again. He told me something about my brother Kahmeel that he thought I might not already know. I did not. It was hard for me to hear it. He talked about Kahmeel and the Sons of Islam. Ali was convinced they were a terrorist cell, connected to other cells in other cities in America, in Russia, and in other nations. I didn't want to believe it, but I also couldn't doubt it. I knew somehow that it was true."

Terrorist cells! In Philadelphia. In other cities. Networked internationally. What were they up to? What was their plan?

Was it connected to the assassination attempt on Putin? To Ali's kidnapping?

"I don't know how Ali knows these things," Rashid confessed. "I don't know who he's working with."

"Not the Bulletin!" I said. "Not on this cell stuff." *Wall?* Who *was* the man? I suddenly felt sure that he and Ali had been working together. Perhaps they still were. But why? For who?

"I don't know why he was kidnapped," Rashid said, "or what it has to do with the Russian president, but he told me, only a week before he was taken, that if he was captured—or killed—that I was to go to that church every night at eleven o'clock and wait there for a man who would know Wrong Book. He would ask for John in Philadelphia. And he would be a trustworthy friend. A man of Ali's heart."

Rashid looked at me. "And he is you! I have watched you on TV. I knew you cared for Ali. I could hear it and see it in you when you reported about him. But I didn't know it would be you who came to the church tonight."

"What now?" I asked.

"Now I must tell you what Ali wants of you, because he told me what to tell you. But we must be very careful. *You* must be very careful." And he nodded also to Kevin.

"I am being followed," I said. "Do you have any idea why?"

Rashid was silent for a moment. Kevin shifted on the couch and stared at me.

"No, I don't," said Rashid. "But I don't like it, if it is so. I don't believe that I've been watched. I would know it—I think."

"I *do* know it," I said. Or did I?

"Kahmeel knows nothing about my contact with Ali!" Rashid said. "He isn't a bad boy—not a killer. He wouldn't strap a bomb on. He wouldn't lie in wait to harm a man. But he walks with men who would…and who will if they are able."

"What does Ali want me to know?" I asked bluntly.

"He…well…Kahmeel tells me some things," Rashid continued cautiously. "He trusts me. I'm his elder brother. He wants me to say to him that he's doing the honorable thing by pouring his life into this…this radical service to Allah. And I listen to him, but I don't say, 'Kahmeel, you are right.' I simply say, 'Kahmeel, you are a man.' And so he knows that I love him and respect him as a man."

"And what about Ali?" I pressed.

"Kahmeel tells me some things," he repeated, "but not the big picture. Little hints…but I know there's more. Something is going to happen. Something big. Something everywhere at once. Ali told me that murder and terror is being planned. Right here in Philadelphia. But I am convinced it is elsewhere, too. And that is what we must find out about. We must start with my brother Kahmeel and his group! And you, Matthew Clifford, are the man Ali picked to find out the more. Now I know why. Because you love Ali…and because you—just like Ali himself—know how to uncover things that need to be uncovered…and then tell them to the world."

17

Ellsworth Street

It was 8:00 in the morning, Wednesday, July 16.

Rashid had stayed the night at Kevin's. So had I. We talked until a couple of hours before dawn, strategizing our next moves in this convoluted mystery. Around 4:00 a.m., Kevin offered Rashid a bed in his guest room. I had already fallen asleep on the couch.

Tyrone woke me with a call on my phone around 6:30 a.m. wondering where I was, worried. I told him we'd "made contact," to make himself some breakfast if he wanted, and to lock my door on his way out to work. I felt like I was in college again, waking up in strange places, wondering if I'd missed class.

I got my car out of Kevin's garage and drove Rashid to my apartment. It was 7:30 when I called Sutton to beg for a few hours respite before coming into the Bulletin. I told him I was following some leads on Ali—couldn't tell him what, but would fill him in later in the day. He gave me the go-ahead. It was 8:00 when Rashid and I pulled away from my apartment and headed toward his.

Rashid roomed with Kahmeel in a small flat on litter-strewn Ellsworth Street in the Grey's Ferry neighborhood of Lower North Philly, a couple of blocks from the Schuylkill Expressway. Some of Kahmeel's compatriots in the Sons of Islam lived in the same neighborhood, but none on the same block or in the same house. Others were scattered around town.

Rashid and I rolled into an alley behind Kahmeel's place and left my car in a vacant lot that served as an unofficial parking area for the neighborhood. Kahmeel would already be at work. We let ourselves into the house through a padlocked back door that yielded to a key Kahmeel had lent Rashid. This opened to a dingy, narrow hallway leading to his brother's apartment.

Kahmeel worked as a waiter in the Sahara Grill on Walnut Street in Washington Square West—only a block and a half from the Bulletin. He earned a good wage, plus tips. Most of his money went into an account for the Sons of Islam. It certainly didn't go into his seedy apartment on Ellsworth.

In the kitchen, an efficiency sized refrigerator-freezer sat next to a greasy gas stove, an old cast-iron sink, and a narrow counter with shelving above and below. The dining area was adequate, but the only furniture that graced the cracked and faded linoleum floor was a card table and a couple of chairs. The bathroom had a shower, a toilet, and a sink—and wasn't much bigger than a walk-in closet. The shower faucet dripped incessantly.

There was a bedroom with a single bed, a closet, and some wall shelving. A compact metal computer desk and a folding chair crowded a corner of the room near the apartment's only window—two weathered frames of glass that fronted the house and served as a dusty lens to the run-down world outside. A small computer terminal and a smaller television shared the top of the desk. On the floor, half under the bed, sat an old portable typewriter.

"Look at this!" I said, pulling it out to examine it more closely. The machine was in pretty good shape, and the ink ribbon looked new. "My dad learned to type on one of these—before computers. Does your brother use this thing?"

"Yes," said Rashid, an amused smile upon his face.

"Mother gave it to him when he was young. He used to write poems with it. He brought it from home. He types poetry on it still. He doesn't want the poems saved on the computer, for some reason. He says they must be one-of-a-kind creations. He types and types…and tears most of them up. But if he likes one enough, he sticks it in a big manila folder with the rest of his poems."

"Crazy," I said. "I'd never want to go back to using one of these to write my stories."

"It is the artist in him," Rashid laughed.

"Where do *you* sleep?" I asked.

"On the kitchen floor, in a sleeping bag on top of an air mattress. Kahmeel's bedroom in our mother's home in Oregon is bigger than this whole apartment," Rashid commented with a wave of his hand. "He is not happy here, but he is afraid to go home. We have talked about it, but 'the mission' holds him here."

"Does it?"

"It is more likely that fear holds him—fear of his *friends.* And they are not so very friendly. I have met a few of them, knew a few from back in Oregon. They don't talk to Kahmeel when I am here, except to joke with him, to insult him. When they come, he usually leaves with them. Kahmeel is a sociable fellow. I can see it is hard for him to be stuck in such a small box with such tight-lipped and narrow-minded company. It is pride that keeps him rooted to the cause. Pride…and fear."

Rashid led us back into the kitchen. He opened the refrigerator. It was nearly empty. "Sorry," he said. "I was going to offer you some soda, but…"

"Does he have any friends outside the Sons of Islam?"

"At work, there is a young woman. He is quite interested in her—though he has a girlfriend back in Oregon. He doesn't date the girl from work very often for fear of saying too much about his 'real' life. I have seen her picture on his computer, but I have never met her."

"I'm sure he's never brought her *here*," I added, running my fingers across the dirty kitchen counter.

"He used to be so tidy," said Rashid, a pained and puzzled look in his eyes. "He likes nice things. I don't understand how a man falls from good habits to bad."

"No?" I said. "Isn't it much more rare to see a man go from bad habits to good?"

"His clothes are new because he needs them for work. But his money, like his life, is no longer his own."

We moved quickly into the bedroom where Rashid turned on his brother's computer.

"He spends time in here, with the door closed, each night before he goes to sleep. He goes on Facebook. He tells me that he e-mails a few friends in Oregon and sometimes chats with the girl from work. But I know that he communicates also with the Sons of Islam. They have a secure website of their own. I can hear him talking to them through his headgear as he types.

"One night he left his door open a crack, and I listened. That was when I heard him talking about something big happening soon…all over the world. And that night he came back out and sat with me. He was troubled, and he talked more than he usually does. No details—just a vague, meandering monolog of impatience and anxiety.

"He loves me. He knows I love him. I think he would like me to take him away from here. But he won't say so. He is not happy."

The computer was on. The screen's desktop background showed the Cascade Mountains of Oregon. Kahmeel Kholami was not a city boy at heart.

"He told me that I could use the computer when I wanted and not to worry about his 'private business' because he erases all communications. He used to hide things from mother this way…when he looked at girls online."

"Mothers are pretty good at finding things out," I said.

"And computers don't forget so easily as we do," I added, kneeling beside the machine and inserting a hack-drive into the USB port. Kevin had given us the hack-drive and told me how to use it. He's an electrician by trade, but he's also really good with computer tech stuff—and he's got a couple of guys renting from him who are bona fide computer geniuses.

In a few minutes, I passed through several levels of digital memory, digging deeper into the computer's trash files than the computer's own brain thought possible. Like rummaging through a garbage heap, most of what I found was corrupted or unrecognizable. We were looking for files with people's names and identifiable tags. There were a few. I saved them onto the hack-drive to check them out later.

"I don't see anything that really jumps," I said. "Do you? Nothing obviously related to the Sons of Islam or any coded missions stuff."

"Can you go deeper?"

"I think so, but…" Then we heard a heavy door slam shut in the hallway on the other side of Kahmeel's bedroom wall. That would be the front door. There were three other apartments in the house. Two upstairs and one on the same floor as we were. I muted the computer, pulled the hack-drive out, and shut the machine down.

Footsteps sounded in the hall. If they went upstairs, we would hear that also. They stopped. Someone coughed, setting something down on the bare wooden floor. Had Kahmeel come home unexpectedly? Or perhaps it was another tenant putting down his things to open up his door. The other apartment on the first floor was directly across the hall from Kahmeel's. There was no way in or out of Kahmeel's apartment, except that hallway…and the window beside us. I positioned myself to open it. Rashid motioned that he was going to step into the kitchen, which he did, closing the bedroom door behind him.

I heard a door open in the hallway. Was it Kahmeel's? I

forced the window up a crack. It didn't want to open any further. It had no screen or storm window on the outside, but it was definitely stuck.

"Hello?" That was Rashid. "Who is coming?" he demanded, I heard a man reply. What he said, I didn't know. I was suddenly inspired to greater violence with the stubborn window. I pushed, pressed, heaved, and finally banged on it a few times until it gave. As I wrestled with it, I heard an angry interchange in the kitchen. Should I stay? Did Rashid need my help? I already had my head and shoulders out the window.

"No, you will not!" said Rashid, emphatically, from the kitchen. He didn't sound cowed. I suddenly knew he could take care of himself. Out the window I spilled, collecting myself more nimbly than I thought possible—and barreled down the sidewalk toward the first alley I could find between the ramshackle row homes.

Out behind the houses once again, I sprinted to my car, tumbled in, slammed the door…and then sat a few seconds breathing hard and heavy. I could hear my heart pulsing in my ears. I could see the back door of Kahmeel's house, the padlock hanging open. Would someone burst out of that door any minute? I started the car and drove away.

I called Kevin on his cell. The call went directly to voice mail. I left a message.

I called Sutton.

"When you comin' in, cowboy?"

"Around noon, boss."

"What'd ya rope?"

"I've got some leads…which may open up to more leads. Nothing direct. But I'll know more by the time I come in." I couldn't tell him everything. I didn't know what I'd tell him. I didn't know what to think!

I called Kevin again. Voice mail. I didn't leave a message. He'd see my number and call back when he could.

I arrived at my apartment, parked directly in front, and hurried upstairs. Why hadn't I heard from Rashid? No cell call, no text, no message. We had exchanged contact info during our long session at Kevin's. Maybe he had e-mailed me. But there was nothing in my MagicMac account. The landline? I hardly ever checked it, hardly ever used that dinosaur—but there were no messages. What should I do? This was no longer simply an issue of working for Ali's rescue from the hands of foreign terrorists. There were terrorists on the other side of town! Would they harm Rashid? Would they come after me?

Should I call the police? Should I buy a gun? Borrow Kevin's?

Should I call Rashid directly? Should I go back to his apartment? Or should I wait to hear from him?

I had to calm down. It had only been half an hour since I'd left him. He was probably sitting in Kahmeel's kitchen, talking to whoever had surprised us, resolving whatever quarrel they might have had. If the man had heard my banging, Rashid would have already given an explanation. And the open window…maybe it wouldn't even be an issue.

Perhaps Rashid was out walking somewhere, processing all this himself. He was no fool. He'd been thinking through this whole situation longer than I had. Maybe he would go to the Bulletin to meet me. He was probably getting ready to call me right now. The talk we had at Kevin's showed me that Rashid was an able ally in the present danger we faced.

But what exactly was that danger? What kind of terror and murder had been planned? When? Where? Ali and Wall—and now Rashid—were counting on me to find out. Sutton and Stein had no idea how big this might be. Or did they?

I had a wireless laptop, also borrowed from Kevin, for communicating with him directly and securely. I'd been thinking about Jacqui's quip about the CIA hacking into our e-mail, and so I wasn't going to trust my MagicMac on this one. I hooked Kevin's hack-drive into the laptop. Within a few minutes, I was able to recover and open almost all the files I had saved from Kahmeel's computer. Only two—a graphics file labeled "Liberty" and a word file labeled "Independence"—refused to open. Something told me they were two of the most important files of all. I opened a new e-mail account to send them to Kevin, with a note to do what he could with them. I also typed him the morning's adventures and asked him to pray for Rashid.

Of the files I was able to open, none were of any import except an enigmatic message that made mention of "the Russian push." It was created on July 3rd, the day before the Peace. The day of the assassination attempt on Putin and the kidnapping of Ali!

The missive was short. In full, it read:

Concerning the Russian push: when all is ready, it will go forward. First the push, then the pull. All eyes will be there, then here. Nobody will expect either the push or the pull. Nobody will expect what happens next. For your part, remember the silversmith.

It contained no details that connected it to any person or place other than that phrase "the Russian push," a repeated reference to "there" and "here" and a mention of "the silversmith." I assumed that "there" was Russia, but where was "here"? Some other nation? The United States? Oregon? Philadelphia?

I e-mailed the file to Kevin. Asked him his thoughts. Maybe we needed another pancake seminary session to figure it out. But I was too tired for that. I knew Kevin would think about it...and pray.

That afternoon at the Bulletin was torturous. I had no word from Rashid. I finally called him myself, from a secured Bulletin landline—but all I got was a busy signal. Not even a voice mail option. I e-mailed him a simple "You okay?" I used a secure Bulletin account when I sent the message. No answer…all day.

There was nothing from Kevin either. I started imagining that the Sons of Islam had gotten him, too. I couldn't work. I managed to shuffle papers, delegate a few things to others, make some contacts with out-of-office freelancers, but I couldn't think straight and I couldn't write. I finally had to pull Sutton aside, lock him in the conference room with me, and tell him something, anything. I needed help.

"When Mr. Stein said that I could have anything I needed to track down Ali, did he mean…anything?"

"You've been puttin' me off all day, Matt. And now ya drag me in here and pant all over me like yer havin' a cow! What's up?"

"I don't know how much I can tell you, Mr. Sutton."

"Look, kid! Ya can tell me everything ya danged well need to tell me…or anything ya wanna tell me. It don't matter to me. As long as we find Ali and pull him outa the fire! But this assignment wasn't supposed to push ya off the deep end of the dock. What'd ya find out that has ya in such a tizzy?"

"I found out that there is a potential terrorist cell operating here in the city."

"What?!"

"Yeah. And I met someone who knows about it. Someone who knows Ali. Someone who Ali was in touch with just before the assassination attempt. And Ali, before he was kidnapped, wanted to get in touch with me through this man—not through normal channels—to tip me off about this cell…and bigger things, too, it appears."

"How did ya—?" Sutton sputtered. "I deputized ya for this posse only yesterday! Where ya been ridin'?"

"I can't tell you everything, Mr. Sutton," I said, feeling as frustrated in the midst of the confession as I had before it. "I had some leads already—some contacts that gave me leads—and it just happened that things came together last night. But I don't know what to do about it."

"Follow your leads!"

"I have been. I am. And I'm concerned that somebody… maybe more than one somebody…may be in danger of their lives right now."

"So that's why y'asked if Stein can help with *anything*…" Sutton said slowly.

"Yes. I'm not so worried about Ali…well, of *course* I am…but—"

"But we've got a situation right here in town," said Sutton. "Is that what yer sayin', Matt?"

"Yes."

I filled Sutton in on the morning's adventure. I told him about Rashid, about Khameel, and I told him where the Kholami brothers lived—but I didn't tell him about the message I'd discovered in the computer file. I didn't tell him about Wall.

"It might be nothing to worry about—the incident this morning," I said. "But this is sensitive. I mean…this is bigger than Rashid. We can't just have the cops busting into Kahmeel's apartment. That would scatter the rest of the rats. We've got to see if Rashid is okay somehow, but we also have to keep things under cover… sniff out this plot…whatever it is. That's what Ali is after. Maybe it's why he was kidnapped. There's something going on around the world, connected to this. Or…*this* is connected to something going on around the world. We…"

"I know who to call, Matt," said Sutton, his hand on my shoulder. "You've met him already. Let's go see Stein about it."

My phone vibrated as we headed to Stein's office. It was Kevin. "Hey," he said, "you at the Bulletin?"

"Yes," I gasped. So he was all right! He hadn't been shot

by snipers or captured by men in ski masks. Maybe the
world was not really coming to an end.

"Can't open those files you sent, but I've got someone
else on it...someone I trust. You on your way home soon?"

"I don't know," I said. "But I'm heading into a meeting
here right now. I'll call you when I'm out. Can we get
together again tonight?"

"Of course. I'll wait to hear from you."

"Hello, Matthew." I was looking into the clay-brown eyes of
George Ognobini, MidAtlantic Director of the National
Office of Homeland Security of the United States of
America. He was smiling, somewhere, on the other end of
the two-way vid-com.

I told him what I'd told Sutton. I felt that he knew that I
knew more—but he didn't press me. He thanked me, kept
smiling, and said the situation would be taken care of.

What will you do? I wanted to ask. And I would have, but
I realized all of a sudden how small I was and how little I
really knew about all that went on in the shadows and the
cracks of so-called civilized society. I suddenly didn't *want*
to know what he would do. Instead, I said, "Rashid is a
good man. And his brother Kahmeel is not a bad man."

The office was empty of everyone but Keith Sutton, Aaron
Stein, and me. We had been talking for a long while after the
conversation with Ognobini. The early evening sun, linger-
ing above the Philadelphia skyline, washed the room white.
Stein's office windows were good old Philly plateglass, no
tint, no curtains—just solid wood Venetian blinds pulled up
high and opened to the light of day. Stein liked the sun. The
wrinkles around his clean eyes, around his chiseled lips and
thoughtful brow, were etched by many a year under the
sun. A man of light, not darkness. Honesty, integrity, and
principled goodness—but not a man to trifle with, not a man
to try to fool. He could see you wink a mile away.

"You can't carry this alone, Matt," he said gently but with steel in his stare.

"I don't want to, Mr. Stein," I said truthfully.

"But you are," he said.

"I have to, some of it," I answered. "At least for now."

"Ognobini will move mountains to check out what you told him," Stein said. "And nobody will feel a tremor, though some may disappear beneath the earth without a trace. Your new friend, Rashid Kholami—if he is alive at this moment—will be safer under the eyes of Ognobini's men than if he climbed into a bank vault and closed the door. And you can move about with little fear as well, though not without caution. If you want to continue our hunt for Ali, I'll give you all the help you need—as I said already—and you can carry on your work knowing that Ognobini is watching your back. Whatever you tell him will aid him. Whatever will aid him will help Ali…will help all of us."

"Has he been watching me all along?" I asked.

"Not that I know of," Stein said. "Why?"

"It's just that…" I hesitated. "All of this is making me wish I had rearview mirrors attached to my head." I didn't want to mention Cobalt Man. I was afraid of talking about Wall. I had a copy of the "Russian push" message in my pocket, but I hadn't shared it with either of these men. I knew I probably should, but I hadn't yet put all the pieces together in my own head. Who to trust. What to tell. *Don't tell anyone what I am telling you,* Wall said. *I don't want to die. I don't want Ali to die.*

I didn't like this triple agent role—but it was mine for the moment. It was making me wonder who else was hiding a superhero costume or a semi-automatic handgun under a business suit. If I had x-ray vision, what would I see beneath Stein's cotton turtleneck, beneath Sutton's crisp white shirt?

"How do you know Ognobini?" I asked, as if I had a right to straightforward answers while withholding so many of my own.

"I met him the same day you did, Matt," said the old Jew. "The day we all found out about Ali's kidnapping."

"How do you know we can trust him to do all that we hope he can do? How do we know his guys are that good? They're just cops with a license to operate without uniforms. They have to go to the bathroom like everyone else. They can't always be staring through their binoculars. Some things they'll see, some things they won't. Sometimes they'll shoot straight, sometimes they won't. And bullets don't know the difference between the good guys and the bad guys."

"I know," said Stein, so sincerely that I suddenly knew that he'd seen bullets fly in his day. "But I've got friends in Homeland Security. Guys that go back to the days when the agency was first created and Tom Ridge stepped down as Pennsylvania governor to head it up. Guys that worked with Sutton's father before that, undercover in the New York streets. Guys who Sutton and I would trust with our own lives. They believe the right things. They're for America. They care about people. They don't like to shoot anyone. But they *can* shoot—and they will if they have to."

"I'd like to go home," I said.

"I'll drive ya." Sutton got up, stretching.

"I drove myself today," I said.

"Okay." Sutton sat down again. "Sleep in tomorrow."

"I don't think I can."

I texted Rashid. No reply. I drove past the apartment on Ellsworth. No one was outside. The window was closed. I didn't dare stop and go to the door. Ognobini would be tracking Rashid, protecting Rashid. Stein said so—and I trusted the old Jew.

I drove home, distracted and distressed, and parked in the semi-security of the apartment house's open basement garage. I turned on the auto-alarm and set it to alert my phone if anyone tried to get into the car.

It was not quite 6:30 when I settled into my couch, little red phone in hand. But 6:30 came and went—with no call from Wall. I couldn't believe it. Maybe the phone had died. But I'd had it by the window all day. It was actually warm from the rays of the sun. Its power light was on, a pencil-point of backlit green in the middle of the phone's front panel. I slid it open, closed it, opened it, closed it. Of course I couldn't turn it off—or make it do anything at all. 6:40. 6:45. 7:00. No call. I thought I'd go crazy. Wall—though I'd never met the man face-to-face—was my only real connection to Ali. Even Rashid seemed ethereal compared to Wall. The Sleuth was my savior in all this. He was the only omnipresent player in the game. Why hadn't he called?

Kevin showed up at my door. I'd been so intent on the call from Wall that I'd forgotten to get back to him. He came anyway. Brought a liter of cold Mountain Dew, caffeine in green. Maybe Kevin was the superhero in the story. *Strange visitor from another planet with powers and abilities far beyond those of mortal men.* Maybe he could fly. I wished *I* could. I would have taken off right then and headed through the starry skies toward Russia, zipping over the Asian steppes, gliding through the Caucasus. Too fast for anti-aircraft fire. Too small for radar. Too smart for any anti-missile missiles. I'd find Ali. Fly him home in the moonlight. Slip him down his chimney like Santa Claus on Christmas Eve. Tuck him into bed beside his sleeping wife—and they'd wake up together in the dawning of a new day. If only life was like the comic books.

Kevin couldn't get the files opened…no way, no how. Gave them to one of his Korean tenants…a genuine computer wizard…a guy from his church named Paul Yong Lee. In his younger days, Lee had hacked into a Pentagon office system, just for fun. They didn't know anything about it until he sent them all their own secrets, bundled in a hyper-secure e-mail circular. The FBI started looking for him, but he knew all about their search before they had the first clue where to find him. Instead, he turned himself in by making a personal appointment with FBI director Robert S. Mueller III. He was accosted, arrested, fined, cleared, released—then offered a job. He turned it down, but the FBI continued to call on him from time to time. Another secret agent? Living in my best friend's house?

"Those files you sent me are tough nuts to crack," Kevin said. "And if Paul can't crack them, nobody can. But he already knows where they came from—the one you opened, too."

"How?" I asked. "Where?"

"Everything sent into cyberspace has a cyber launching pad. Every file has a track-back code, though it's not easy to decipher. It can't tell you that Matthew Lyle Clifford sent the file from his apartment in Philadelphia, but it can tell you what e-mail address it originally came from…what server it first came from, what server it next bounced off. A file can be forwarded a hundred times, but the track-back code can trace it all the way to square one. Attempts to cover the tracks can confuse the code, but they can't fully wipe it out. A really good tracker—and they are rare—can follow a file backwards to home base."

"Where's home base?"

"The e-mail account was private, unlisted, not connected to any known browser or mail provider. The server was in Brussels."

"Brussels?"

The doorbell rang.

I went to the window. There was a mirror just outside, a cylindrical magnifying lens that captured—in strange distortion—the front stoop and anyone on it.

Rashid!

But not alone.

I watched him ring again, look around. The light above the door caught the face of the man with him. I knew in an instant that it had to be Kahmeel. I ran down the steps and threw the door open. Rashid grinned widely, glanced once more into the quiet street, took his brother by the arm, and came inside.

18

Kahmeel

"Where have you been all day?" I blurted at Rashid, hurrying the brothers up the stairs and into my apartment. I closed the door—and locked it.

"Sit here," Rashid said to Kahmeel, pointing him to my recliner. Kahmeel sat down, reluctantly. Kevin was seated on the couch.

Rashid pulled me aside into my bedroom. "The man at Kahmeel's apartment was one of the Sons of Islam," he explained quietly. "He said that he had come to work on Kahmeel's computer—to add some software and fix his printer. But I told him, 'No, you will not! Not unless I hear from Kahmeel himself.' And he didn't like that. We argued, and I thought he might try to force his way past me. So I said, 'Let me call Kahmeel at work and ask him.' And all that gave you time to get out of the house."

"But…all day?"

"The guy stayed to fix the computer, and I stayed while he was there," said Rashid, seating himself in the center of my couch. "I offered him lunch. We did noon prayers. He wasn't mad at me any longer. In fact, he thanked me several times for being protective of my brother's property. We had a nice lunch, and he left."

"I waited for your call. I sweat bullets. I finally texted you."

"I saw it."

"Then why didn't…? I even drove by your place, but…"

"To be on the safe side," said Rashid, his hands in the air in apology. "So that nobody could trace you from me," he explained, "I decided not to answer your calls or contact you directly. I waited for Kahmeel to come home from work and then invited him to go out for dinner with me. We went to eat, had a good meal and a good talk, and then we took a walk. At last, I told him about you…and asked him to come here with me. He came willingly. He wants to talk to us." We stepped back into the living room.

Kahmeel and Rashid were obviously brothers—almost twins in appearance, except for the grey in Rashid's hair and the fact that Kahmeel was thinner and an inch or two taller. The faces were the same, the mannerisms and inflections in their speech as well. But Kahmeel was far the more nervous one, and he could hardly stay seated.

But he talked. Even when afraid to tell us everything, it was obvious that he was relieved to be telling us something.

And he cried. It was hard to see the man weep as he did. Then he'd pull himself together, and he and Rashid would converse in Arabic for a while. Then it was English again, with all of us talking. Then he'd break down in tears and go through the process again.

Putting it all together—minus the Arabic—it went something like this:

"You should go back to Oregon, Rashid!"

"No, *you* should go back to Oregon, Kahmeel!"

"I can't!"

"What is going on here, Kahmeel?"

"If I tell you, you must go back to Oregon."

"I already know more than you think, Kahmeel, and I cannot go home knowing even that much. But I…we…must know the details in order to help you. To help Ali."

"I don't *want* your help!" Kahmeel cried. "I don't *need* your help. And I don't even *know* Ali!"

"He was a brother to me before you were born."

"Then why was I born," Kahmeel wailed, "if you had brothers enough already?" He wiped his eyes with his sleeve, set his face like a stone, and paced back and forth from my dining counter to the window. He squinted through the blinds each time, though Rashid repeatedly asked him not to. I looked outside once or twice myself, but saw no one.

Where were Ognobini's men? Had they tagged Rashid to my apartment? Were they out there somewhere, watching, listening?

Cars passed. Neighborhood kids rode scooters down the sidewalk. The shadows were long in the street. The rooftops were red with the setting sun.

"Father loved Ali," Rashid said to Kahmeel, "and he loved Ali's father, though they never reconciled. Father repented of their differences before his death—you know he did."

Kahmeel nodded his head in sober agreement. "What would Father want?" he asked earnestly.

"He would want us…you and me…to do all that we can to help Ali."

"I know very little, and I don't see how it could help Ali in any way."

"A little is much under the circumstances," I offered.

"I am afraid, Rashid," said Kahmeel, ignoring me.

"There is no shame in fear, Kahmeel," said Rashid. "I am afraid myself."

Kahmeel stopped his nervous pacing to look at his brother.

"There is only shame in giving in to fear," said Rashid.

"Then what shall we do?" Kahmeel asked.

"This is our country, is it not? The country that Father chose for us—in which to live free and grow old."

"Yes," said Kahmeel, "this is our country, though it's filled with infidels and wickedness."

"Are we not all sinners? Are not the infidels our neighbors and our friends? America has been good to us, Kahmeel. Good to Father and Mother. It is not the devil's hole that the Sons of Islam say it is."

Kahmeel was silent.

"I have seen how the Sons of Islam treat you," Rashid continued, anger in his eyes although his voice was calm. "They take your money, and they make you the butt of their jokes. They put software on your computer to spy on your e-mails to Mother, your love letters to Evie, your poems to that pretty girl at work."

"Leave my love life out of this! It's because I'm the youngest among them that they treat me this way. It's because Mother isn't a Muslim."

"And you let them put you down because you are the son of your mother? I'm the son of your mother, too. Father wouldn't want you to put up with such prejudice…or such bullying. You were never treated this way by your family. If anything, you were spoiled."

"I know who my friends are," said Kahmeel stubbornly, but without conviction.

"I am your friend," said Rashid pointedly. "I am your brother. I am begging you to choose life, not death."

Kahmeel sat down hard upon a stool, though only long enough to bluntly say, "We've planned some bombings." Then he resumed his pacing.

"Where?" I interjected. "When?"

Kahmeel flashed a sharp glance my way, then stared at the floor as he paced. "They'll kill me if I tell you," he said.

"You will die no matter what!" said Rashid. "We will all die someday. But this is our country! What would Father say? If we were at home in Oregon, would you let the Sons of Islam endanger our neighbors? Would you put a bomb at the post office to kill Mrs. McGinnis as she's sorting the mail? Would you blow up Oxbow Elementary where Evie teaches?"

"Stop it! I don't want to kill anyone! It's not about killing people anyway. Maybe nobody will die. Only the idols will be destroyed! The idols and the icons of this damned and decadent culture! Then the people will have to look to God, and we will tell them who He is. Praise be to Allah!"

"Idols!" spat Rashid angrily. "The Sons of Islam are your idols, and you are their slave!"

Kahmeel leaned back on his heels. I thought he was going to strike his brother, but instead he sank down into a squat and covered his head with his arms. "I don't know where to run! I don't know where to hide!" he groaned.

"We can hide you," I said, thinking of Ognobini. "And then make it so that you have no need to hide."

"I can hide you," Kevin also offered. "I have friends all over town."

"No need to hide…" Kahmeel echoed in a voice muffled by his own enfolding arms. "But how—?"

"By throwing the Sons of Islam into jail," I said, "and then throwing away the key."

Kahmeel would tell us nothing more. He was afraid of the Sons of Islam. Afraid of the police. Afraid of going to jail himself. Afraid of dying.

But he was equally as ashamed as he was afraid. Ashamed of his involvement in a scheme that had become bigger, meaner, and more violent than he had dreamed. Whether it was big from the onset, or whether it had grown since his first involvement, I don't know. But he was in too far to simply run out the door.

I offered Kahmeel my couch if he wanted to stay the night, but he insisted on returning to his apartment before dawn.

"I'll drive you," I said.

"No, I'll walk."

"Then I will walk with you," Rashid said.

I pulled Rashid aside and quietly told him about

Ognobini's agents. "You may never see them—and that's just fine. Don't tell your brother. Until we can pry him loose from the Sons of Islam, we can't let him know too much. It wouldn't be safe for him, it wouldn't be safe for us, and it wouldn't be safe for the 'guardian angels' who are watching us."

"I will contact you later today, I promise—and we will meet somewhere," Rashid said, as he and Kahmeel headed out into the streets in the pre-dawn darkness. Kevin left shortly afterwards. It was 4:30 a.m., Thursday, July 17.

I managed to sleep a couple of hours and still make it to work on time. I reported the previous night's events to Sutton. Of course I made no mention of my failed connection with Wall—nothing at all about Wall. I was beginning to get dizzy from juggling secrets. Sutton took me to see Stein.

"Bombs!" Aaron Stein declaimed grimly. "All across America, no doubt, if Rashid is correct in what Ali told him. Our very own Ali Ahkmed Baraki, uncovering an international plot. And right here in our own city is a terrorist cell with a man in it whom Ali knows. Incredible circumstance. And if we can hook these fish and scale them clean, maybe we'll find Ali in their belly, still alive and well—God will it! I'll contact Ognobini as soon as we're done talking. He'll pass the word to the other agencies. Philly will be buzzing with invisible bees." He stared out the window toward the Philadelphia skyline. "And our very own Matthew Lyle Clifford, with a magnet in his pocket, I guess. Picking up clues as he walks down the sidewalk!"

"I wish it were that easy," I said quietly.

"And what else can we do to uncover what the big boys aren't already finding?" He leaned forward over his desk. "That's the question, men. What can we do? I want to know, and I want to do it. Not for the news—we can't print this yet, God knows!—but for civilization itself."

"You suppose Ali was kidnapped 'cause he knew about these Sons of Islam?" Sutton wondered aloud. "Or was he simply in the wrong place at the wrong time?"

Wall would know! I thought, but I didn't dare say so. I could, however, offer something else. I handed Sutton the Russian push memo. His eyes widened.

Stein was staring out the window, his back to us.

"What is this?" Sutton asked me.

"An e-mail message, buried in Kahmeel's computer. I extracted it," I said nervously, "yesterday." Suddenly, two sets of very serious eyes were trained on me. "But I didn't know what to—"

"Clifford!" Sutton roared. "You can protect yer sources if ya have to in an investigation like this, but ya gotta come clean with every little thing ya find or we're not gonna find Ali in time to save his hide! And who knows what else is at stake?"

Wall. Ali himself. No, I couldn't tell all. Not yet. The memo would have to do for now.

"I'm digging!" I said bitterly. "I was digging before you commissioned me to dig—and I've got big blisters, and I'm in over my head. The ground is hard—but it's breaking. I'll do everything I can to find out where Ali is. I'll tell you everything I can." *But not everything I know.* "I love Ali like a brother. The lives of many brothers are on the line here. I may not be a pro at this game like you guys, but…I won't let you down."

Stein sighed, looked at the memo in Sutton's hand, and nodded.

"*Concerning the Russian push,*" Sutton read the memo aloud, "*when all is ready, it will go forward. First the push, then the pull. All eyes will be there, then here. Nobody will expect either the push or the pull. Nobody will expect what happens next. For your part, remember the silversmith.*"

He laid the memo down where Stein could read it for himself.

"Was the assassination attempt the push?" asked Stein. "Was Putin going to die and then something else happen elsewhere?"

"Will the bombs in the States be the pull?" wondered Sutton.

"All eyes there: Russia; then here: the States," suggested Stein.

"What's it all about?" Sutton puzzled, drumming his fingers on the thick plateglass that covered Aaron Stein's big wooden desk. "What's happenin' next? And who's the silversmith?"

"Paul Revere, perhaps," Stein said, smiling coldly, "warning us that the Reds are coming."

"Nawwww…" Sutton frowned and shook his silver-maned head. "Not the commies."

We had the memo. We knew it was sent the day Ali was kidnapped. We knew it apparently originated in Brussels, though it was in perfect English. But we didn't know what it meant or if it had anything to do with Ali at all.

We had the knowledge that bombings were planned by the Sons of Islam. We didn't know when, where, or whether the cell was ready for action.

We knew from Rashid, who heard it from Ali, that terrorist activity was being coordinated internationally, and that the Sons of Islam were somehow connected. So perhaps there were acts of terror planned consecutively in America and around the world.

I knew that Ali wanted me on this case—though I hadn't told anyone other than Rashid and the seminarians. I knew that Ali wanted me to work with Rashid. I knew he and Wall were in this together somehow. And I knew—or thought I knew—that they had been in contact even after the kidnapping.

We knew that Rashid's brother was on the inside of the Sons of Islam here in Philadelphia. We even had pictures (supplied by Rashid) of some of the guys in Kahmeel's cell—digital shots of the boys hanging out together, goofy pics of young men having fun. But not so funny considering the nature of their true game. Those pics had already been e-mailed to Ognobini. And we knew that Kahameel wanted out. We just didn't know how badly. We had to get him out—for his own sake, and because we had to know what he knew.

My phone vibrated. A text message. Three words: *Got a light?* Rashid!

I called Kevin. He was wiring a private residence while the family was on vacation. He packed up his toolbox, drove to the Bulletin, picked me up, and together we headed west toward the Sanctuary Church of the Open Door.

It was broad daylight this time, and Kevin walked with me as we ascended the few steps that fronted the portico where Rashid and Kahmeel stood waiting just out of sight of the street. Rashid wasn't smoking this time. Kahmeel's face looked pale even in the shadows.

"Kahmeel has something more to tell you," Rashid stated.

"I'm going back," Kahmeel said quietly, his voice raw, as if he'd been shouting. I wondered if he'd been crying.

"Back to Oregon, he means," Rashid explained.

"They're sending me back," said Kahmeel.

"Sending you? Who? Why?" I asked.

"The Sons of Islam. I asked if I could return."

"And they said yes?" Kevin interjected. "Don't believe it! Don't go back."

Kahmeel looked up in amazement. "I thought you wanted me to get out of this before the…" He bit his lip. "And now that I have a chance…"

"Yes, get out," said Kevin hotly. "But get out alive!"

"I'm worried about that, too," said Rashid. "I told you, Kahmeel, that Matthew and his friends could help! Please listen to them."

"Don't go back," Kevin repeated. "Come home with me. Matt can get you protection, get you out of the city, get you somewhere safe."

"Why would my brothers want to hurt me?" Kahmeel said painfully. "I told them I'll go back to my home and my girlfriend and my job. I'll send them money. I'll recruit for them if they wish. They said that might be a better role for me. They said I could go."

"Something ugly is going to break out in the city, isn't it?" said Kevin. "Your 'brothers' may kill people. They may be killed themselves. They'll surely be caught, and if they've murdered anyone, they'll be convicted and sentenced to die themselves. This is bigger than you've told us, Kahmeel, and nobody on 'your side' can afford to let you wander back to Oregon after what you've seen brewing here."

"What can you do for me?" he asked stiffly.

"The government can hide you, move you, protect you. And after the Sons of Islam have been taken out, maybe then you can go home."

He stood still in the shadows, the mid-morning breeze moving his hair, his shirt sleeves. He wiped his forehead with the back of his hand. "Nobody can 'take out' the Sons of Islam," he said slowly. "There are too many sons, with more being born every day. Even the American government can't keep me safe if the Sons are looking for me. No," he said sadly, "I must go home now. I will stay a Son, but I won't have to…to kill anyone." He looked away, toward the church sanctuary with its stained-glass sparkling in the sun.

"Go home with Kevin," Rashid pleaded.

"No," said Kahmeel, "I'll go home to Mother. I'll work hard and help her keep the house. I'll make love with Evie. I'll send money to the Sons."

"Kahmeel," I said, looking the man in the eyes, "as long as the Sons have plans to make bombs and money to make bombs, they will kill people. As long as you are a Son of Islam, no matter where you are, you're helping them kill people. I live in this city! People I know and love live in this city! People that you know and love live in this city! Can't you help us at all?"

"No, I can't!" he said. "Not today! Not..." He grit his teeth. "Damn it!" he blurted, then lurched off the porch and walked hurriedly up the street.

Rashid ran after him. "I'll contact you!" he shouted back at me.

I called Sutton. I told him of the meeting with Kahmeel and Rashid. Stein called Ognobini. I hoped that the long arm of the undercover angels extended to Ellsworth Street—and anywhere else that Kahmeel and Rashid Kholami might wander in the next few days.

Kevin drove me to the Bulletin. I went back to my desk and my computer. He went back to his wires and his volts. Rashid texted me once: *I'll call tonight.*

When the day was done, I walked home in a daze. But every few blocks, I woke from my stupor to look around me. The evening was hot. The sun still painted the upper stories in bright warm hues. The city teemed with people. The streets and the buildings were familiar, but the noisy mass of humanity was one big stranger.

I wondered if there was a face in the crowd who knew me, watched me, tailed me, chatted about me on a cell phone—telling someone that I was walking up Such-and-such Street, at the crosswalk on Bla-bla Boulevard, passing the Bulletin Board at the corner of Whatchacallit Avenue. I imagined someone else sitting at a sidewalk café, a few blocks closer to my home, listening to the play-by-play, waiting for his turn to watch the show live.

But I got home without incident. No Cobalt. No men in false whiskers. No secret agents smoking cigarettes under the streetlamps.

"Thank God!" I said aloud, as I locked my door behind me. Then I stiffened.

A noise in my bedroom! Someone breathing! I stood still for a long, anxious moment.

"Oh, man!" I cried suddenly, realizing that the breathing was the sound of my MagicMac set on waves. The sound bites of nature whispering through the Mac's speakers helped me sleep. Sometimes I set it on wind—a steady drone, like a bad air conditioner, which muted the noise of cars and kids and the human drama in the apartment next to me. But usually I set it on waves, and the rhythmic sighs of the surf played over and over until I was snoring in unconscious abandon. I hadn't shut the doggone thing off that morning, that's all. "Off!" I shouted angrily, as if the Mac had misbehaved on purpose. It heard me, and off it went.

6:30. 6:35. 6:40. 6:45.

I took the red phone into the bathroom with me. I had the runs, a bad case of them. I was in there for a while.

7:00. 7:05.

Where was Wall! Why didn't he call? I had unscrewed the battery panel on the back of the red cell a dozen times the night before. I replaced the solar battery with a top-of-the-line Eveready rechargeable at 6:15, in time for Wall to call.

The phone lit up as always—the little green light that indicated everything was go. The battery was fine. But no call. Nothing. Two nights in a row.

I was praying—sort of. More like, "God! Come on!" But that's still prayer, I think. And the phone rang. Not Wall's phone, but the phone on the wall. That almost never happened anymore unless it was telemarketers—or my dad.

"Hello?" I expected the telltale telemarket silent moment, but instead someone just laughed…and hung up. "Oh!" I said, and my eyes flew to the window. Something had passed by my third floor window! There! Again!

Crows! Lousy crows! I looked out quickly as a loud, raucous flock of blackbirds settled into the only tree on the block across the street from my apartment. A couple of Asian kids shouted at them, and the flock rose as one from its sylvan perch, circled the rooftops noisily, and landed in the branches again. They looked like black leaves waving in a wind. The kids shouted again, and the game continued until the kids wearied and wandered off down the street. The crows stayed.

I closed the blinds.

Who had called?

A phone rang again, startling me. This time it was my cell. I didn't recognize the number on my caller ID. I flipped it open.

"Yeah," I said tersely.

"Matthew," said Rashid.

"Holy cow!" I said. "Where are you?"

"I'm calling from a pay phone outside the Sahara Grill. I'm waiting for Kahmeel to get out of work. I called you a couple of minutes ago from another phone a block away, but it went dead. And then I couldn't get a dial tone."

"Did you call me on my home phone?"

"Yes, but we got cut off."

"Did you laugh?" I asked.

"Yes, I think I did. I saw a man trip and fall into a hot dog stand. It wasn't really funny. The man hurt his head, and some good hot dogs were ruined, but you know how you sometimes laugh at such things. And then we got cut off."

"Yeah, yeah," I said, shaking my head in disbelief. "Crows laugh, too."

"Ah, yes, they do," said Rashid hesitantly, not sure of the joke. "C-haw, c-haw, c-haw!" he said, chuckling.

"That's right," I sighed. "Are you okay? Is Kahmeel

okay? Has he changed his mind? What's happening?"

"He is going home on Saturday."

"Oh no," I groaned.

"He has his tickets already," he said bitterly. "The Sons bought them for him. But he wants to see you before he goes. He has something for you—he won't tell me what. He asks you to meet him here tomorrow, at the restaurant, at closing time. It will be his last night here. A Friday night—a late one. He will probably get out around midnight. I'm going to eat my supper there tomorrow and then stick around nearby until he quits. He doesn't want you to come early. So I will text you when it is time. Just be somewhere near. I will text *good-bye*, and you will know to come. I will look for you."

"You are not in any eminent danger?"

"Not that I know of. I have seen no cloaked Arabs with sharp scimitars. Nobody is following me, that I can tell. And I haven't seen any of the Sons today at all, except for the one named Mufti who brought the airline tickets to the apartment this morning."

"You'll be back at the apartment tonight?"

"Yes."

"You'll be walking there?"

"No, we will take a taxi."

"Text me when you're in and safe. Just say *home*."

"I will text you in the morning, too. Something nice to start your day. A morning prayer, perhaps."

I laughed. It hurt to laugh. "Thank you, Rashid. I'll pray for you, too."

I went to bed.

"God! God! God!" I whispered, as the wind whistled softly from the MagicMac. That was about all I could say. I figured God could figure out the rest.

The room was dark. I faced the wall. That's how I fell asleep.

19
Hit and Run

Friday morning, July 18.

I woke up with Jacqui Johnson in my bed. I'd been dreaming about her, that is—and it wasn't the kind of dream to chat about around the water cooler at the Bulletin. But it made me realize that she'd been on my mind. On Wednesday, while searching for Sutton to tell him about Rashid, I had poked my head into Jacqui's office to see if he was there. Jacqui was at her desk, head down, arms wrapped around herself. Rose was talking with her quietly.

"Oh," I said, almost in a whisper, backing out to let them have their privacy. But Rose heard me, saw me. I waved my hand, apologetically, trying to exit graciously. But Jacqui turned her head toward me. That's when I saw the tears. "Sorry to interrupt," I said. "Just looking for Sutton."

Later I found Rose to ask her what had upset Jacqui.

"What's it to you?" she fired back. Then she pulled her lips into a humored smirk and said, "Ali's kids. Jacqui's nuts about them. Absolutely loves them. She was over at the Kalami's house this morning before work, comforting Jumana. And the kids were crying. They miss their father. They're worried about him. And Jacqui can't stand to see kids cry."

So she brought that sorrow to work, I thought, as I lay in my bed, waking from the dream. *And she cried at her desk.* Silly? Sentimental? Compassionate? Her time of the month? This was the woman who was on the air only half an hour after her sob-session, make-up in place, smile on her face, her blouse arranged strategically to grab the attention of Joe the Plumber as he walked through his living room on his way to a can of beer.

"She went to see Jumana," I said, sitting up in bed. How often, I wondered, did she do that?

What did I really know about Jacqui Johnson? What did I really know about women? Kids? The draw of the domestic? The mother instinct?

I thought of Lisa. I imagined her with children—pushing them around Weis Markets in a grocery cart. I'd hardly thought about her since my trip to Lancaster. And as I lay beneath the sheets in the grey morning light, I realized that I didn't even want to think about her. Was I waking up from more than a dream?

Seeing Lisa on Monday had been like hearing an old song that had once been a favorite...but which I hadn't heard for a long time. Hearing it again, and listening to the words anew, I didn't like them quite as much as I thought I did. It was a catchy tune, but the memory was better than the melody...and my taste in music had changed.

And Lisa's nightmare. She only called me about it because she couldn't sleep at night. She was worried about me, not because she wanted me, but because she couldn't bear to see me get hurt, or be deceived by the Antichrist, or go to hell. It wasn't love that invited me to Lancaster, it was religious obligation. If I "got saved," then the Matt-and-Lisa sins of the past could be washed away. Lisa could go to sleep—and to church—with a clean conscience.

Matt and Lisa? Oil and water! I was greasy, used oil... and the girl didn't want to get her hands dirty.

I thought about Jacqui Johnson again.

But it was time to get up.

FOX News at Dawn. No Wall. FOX was reporting him missing in action. His last broadcast had been the Ali video. His last connect with the network had been the following day. I wondered if I had been one of the last to talk to him. It was Tuesday night when he called me, three days ago—but it seemed like forever.

Where was he? Did FOX know more than they were saying? Were FOX and Wall working an undercover game in collusion with American intelligence? Or was Wall just...Wall?

Somehow I felt he was on the loose, slipping through an alley in some exotic Asian city, running through the woods on some far-off fabled mountain. Chasing terrorists. Snapping photos. Practicing his lines. Laughing. Waiting for the perfect moment to upstage us all.

Meanwhile, Russia was massing troops along the Georgian border. Putin insisted that his would-be assassins were harbored in the Georgian province of Khevsuretti, the ancient "land of valleys." He claimed that an Islamic militia was holed up with them.

Smack in the center of Northern Georgia, Khevsuretti was home to a few thousand highlanders in scattered mountain villages. Some of the villages were medieval stone fortresses. Many had been abandoned during the Soviet years when native Khevurs were forced to leave the mountains to live on the arid plains. Ancient Georgian Orthodox churches stood upon the high horizon, and stone crosses sat like lonely sentinels on the short-grass hillsides.

The EU was moving soldiers through Turkey toward Georgia's southern border. They had ships in the Black Sea to the west. Russia had ships in the Caspian to the east. Romano said he wouldn't put up with any trouble between Georgia and Russia. But he also would not allow the terrorists to escape.

Clay pontificated for peace.

The UN wrung its hands and looked the other way.

The president of Georgia railed against the world, sent troops to all his threatened borders, and surrounded himself with priests.

Putin and Romano! A strange marriage. If they were a pair of black widow spiders, which would be the widow? For one would love to eat the other.

Putin, though a renegade in international politics, was surrounded (and thus somewhat mollified) by nations that had no love for Russian nationalism.

And Romano was only one man among many in the overall leadership of the European Union—with a representative presidency limited to six months.

But both men had great influence and wielded great power.

America, I mused, was no longer the world's policeman. We had passed the baton to the EU. What would that mean in the days ahead?

Rashid texted me. It was my "morning prayer":

In the Name of Allah, the Most Beneficent, the Most Merciful. All the praises and thanks be to Allah, the Lord of all that exists. The Only Owner and the Only Ruling Judge of the Day of Recompense. You Alone we worship, and You Alone we ask for help for each and every thing. Guide us to the Straight Way, the Way of those on whom You have bestowed Your Grace, not the way of those who earned Your Anger, nor of those who went astray.

I knew, from Ali, that "those who earned Allah's anger" were the Jews. "Those who went astray" were the Christians. So what about Jesus and the "narrow way"? Maybe it was *too* narrow.

I had promised to pray for Rashid. "God," I said as I picked up my briefcase and my umbrella before heading out my door, "keep my friend Rashid safe. He's a brave man. He's a good man. Amen."

Kevin called while I was walking to work. I turned up the volume on the earphone. A soft rain was falling, and the patter of the rain on my umbrella made it hard to hear him.

"Louder, Kev!" I shouted.

"Not so loud yourself, Matt," said Kevin. "I can hear you just fine."

I filled him in on last night's call with Rashid. "Can you join me tonight for the meeting with Kahmeel?"

"It doesn't sound like I'm invited."

"I'm inviting you."

"No," he said. "We'd better play it Kahmeel's way. Just make sure Stein tells Ognobini. I've got to be elsewhere anyway. But I'll be praying. And I'll call the seminary guys if you want me to. Not with details…just to be praying for you as you head to the front lines."

"I guess that's okay. I'm feeling a little out on my own."

"You've got Stein and Sutton pulling strings. You've got undercover cops watching your back. You'll have Rashid on red alert, right there with you. You've got Kahmeel planning a meeting that he wouldn't plan if he wasn't sure of his own safety—and his brother's and yours. You've got a genuine guardian angel of the Lord—believe it or not. You've got our prayers. And God doesn't sleep."

As I walked up the steps to the Bulletin, I knew that something had changed within me. Some new resolve had settled in. It was a strange feeling, and it wasn't that I had made any conscious decision to turn some corner in my soul. I just felt different. I knew I would find Ali. I knew I'd be talking to him soon. I knew that I had a key role—in part, at least—in uncovering a terrorist cell in one of the largest and most historic cities of America. My meeting with Kahmeel, the day before he would fly back to Oregon, would provide the information needed to split this thing wide open. I was not just a reporter anymore. I was a patriot. And I wasn't going to worry about what Lisa or Dad or any Amish evangelist thought about me. It didn't matter who the Antichrist was, or whether the Four Horsemen were right now riding up Walnut Street. I had a job to do. It was destiny. That's how it felt.

Then I got into the elevator, and Jacqui Johnson got in, too. She smiled, said "Good-morning," and fumbled in her pocketbook for something. My face flushed, and I forgot all about Ali.

"What are you doing for dinner tonight?" I said. *My God! Why did I ask her that?*

Jacqui looked up, dark hair falling over wide, wondering eyes. "I..." she said. But I didn't let her finish.

"How about Marathon On The Square, right after work?" I said. "They've got great pan-seared Norwegian salmon. And New York strip steaks to kill for. We can split the bill...or you can pay the whole thing, since you have seniority here."

She laughed, blushed, and dropped her pocketbook. I picked it up for her. "Yes, I'd like that," she said, smiling. "But...y'all are kidding about the bill...right?"

The elevator door opened. We got out. She gave me a silly little wave. We went to work.

I was euphoric. This was an adventure on top of an adventure. But I kicked myself throughout the day when I thought about how I'd complicated my evening. What had gotten into me? I certainly wasn't thinking about Kahmeel when I invited Jacqui to dine! And what if Wall called?

So what! What was that old saying my dad used to quote? "Damn the torpedoes, and full speed ahead!"

I would just have to excuse myself to go to the bathroom around 6:30. And I'd have to take Jacqui home by 10:00.

Rashid texted me again. I was in the middle of writing a commentary on the situation in Georgia.

A-OK, said the text. I took that to mean that all was well and that everything was on track for the night. Good!

"Ya know," Sutton said to me privately, about half an hour before quitting time, "you'll be covered all around, Matt. More protection than a Prudential life insurance policy. Well…maybe that's the wrong analogy! Ya know," he said seriously, "I'd like to hang out somewhere in the shadows myself."

"Do you think that's wise?" I asked.

"No," he said, with a grim smile. "And so I guess I won't. It's just hard to sit back and wait fer the phone to ring."

"Yeah, I know that feeling."

"The only fear I really have for ya, Matt, is that you'll get distracted somehow."

"Distracted?"

He nodded in the direction of Jacqui's office. She'd been telling everyone about our dinner date.

"Oh!" I grinned. "I'll get her home in time to make her daddy proud."

"She don't live with her daddy!" Sutton smiled. Then he got serious again. "Y'own a gun?" he asked.

"No," I said. "Though that seems to be a popular question these days."

"Com'ere," he said. We walked to a little office that Sutton rarely used. It had his name on the door, but he'd rather pace the newsroom deck than sit at a desk. He closed the door behind us and walked to a small filing cabinet in the corner of the room. He unlocked a drawer and pulled it open. He lifted out a large pistol and held it out to me. I hesitated. "Put yer hand out," he said.

I put my hand out. He put the gun in it.

"It's loaded," he said. "It's legal—though it's registered

in my name, not yers, of course. It's lethal, too, but I think ya know that."

"It's heavy…"

"It's a double-action Smith & Wesson Model 29, 44-caliber Magnum revolver. I named it Harry after Dirty Harry, the cop that Clint Eastwood played in a buncha movies in the 70s. He carried a gun like this. He called it 'the most powerful handgun in the world.' That was no empty boast in its day."

"I don't want—"

"Nobody, I mean nobody, will be followin' ya where ya can see 'em, unless they mean ya harm. Remember that. Anybody who's on our side is invisible. And when they become visible, they won't be chasin' *you*."

"Another friend offered me his gun recently."

"Maybe yer friend knows the city better'n you do."

"I don't know how to—"

"Ya pull the trigger."

I stared at the gun as if it were a bomb.

"Ya don't have to take it," he said, "but if I was you, I would."

I turned it in my hand. "Where do I put it?"

Sutton pulled a shoulder holster from the drawer. "I can show ya how to put it on. It ain't comfortable, but it's concealed. With a jacket on, nobody'll know. Gotta jacket?"

"In the closet by the water cooler. I keep a couple there for interviews."

"Get one."

The weight under my arm was awkward while eating, but I enjoyed myself with Jacqui so much that I almost forgot about it. Almost. It was impossible to put it out of mind for long. I would have taken it off before taking Jacqui out, but I was afraid I wouldn't be able to get it back on.

We talked, and joked, and laughed, and ate more food than was good for either of us. I had a beer, but only one—I

wanted a clear head for my meeting with Kahmeel. Jacqui
drank too much. I'd seen her do that before at holiday office
parties and on the one occasion when we'd gone out in the
past.

She was a lonely girl, I thought, though how anyone so
gorgeous could be lonely I had no idea. But she wasn't
shallow. Sharp, witty, and insightful in political matters, she
was more than a pretty face in front of a TV camera. It was
no mystery that men were attracted to her, but why did she
always throw herself at them? And why hadn't I cared
enough to be a better friend myself?

During dinner, I excused myself as planned and sat for
fifteen minutes in the men's room, hoping for Wall's call. It
never came. "Stomach problems," I explained, when I
returned to the table. But Jacqui was happily sipping her
Amaretto Paradise, singing a little song to herself. I joined in
on harmony.

"Sooo…" she slurred, as dessert was cleared away. She
put her elbows on the table, clasped her hands together, and
leaned her chin upon them. She was happy, pretty,
beguiling, very much at ease. She was also drunk. "Shall we
talk s'more about politics and religion…or maybe sex and
marriage?"

"I vote for sex and marriage," I said, thinking that would
be an interesting talk—to say the least.

"Whichever comes first," she laughed. Then she turned
her smile upside down and declared sharply, "But marriage
sh'come first." A sadness tightened her lips slowly,
wrinkled her brow. A flash of embarrassment crossed her
face, then a look of surprise. Her eyes grew vacant, lost, then
angry. A kaleidoscope of emotions, fascinating—almost
frightful. Did they mean anything at all? "But…" she said,
forcing a crooked smile back in place.

"Yes?" I coaxed, anxious to hear what would come out
of her mouth next.

She sighed. "I've been to see Jumana," she said. "Ali's

wife, you know. 'Course you know Ali's wife… It's hard…"
The lost look returned. "It's hard when those you love are
gone. When those you need are gone. There's so little love in
the world today."

I nodded in agreement.

"Jumana knows she's loved," Jacqui stated flatly. "But
when y'all think somebody loves you…and they
don't…that's hell." She twisted her napkin with her fingers,
staring at it, her chin almost on her chest. "When y'all think
you've found real love at last…and you've signed on the
line…and it goes away somewhere…well, that's almost
like…like dying."

She continued playing with her napkin, watching her
own fingers. She sat like that for a long time, saying nothing.
I didn't know what to do, so I said nothing either. I thought
she was probably too wasted to make much sense. I glanced
at my watch to see the time.

"The Baraki children," I heard her say at last, in a
whisper, as if talking to herself, "are frightened for their
father, but they're well. Jumana's a strong woman. Her faith
community's a very caring one—so different from…from
the men who…who took Ali away." She laid her elbows on
the table again, cupped her head in her hands, and looked
straight at me. "Do you think," she asked, pulling on me
with her eyes, "that bad Muslims don't really believe in
Allah at all? That maybe they're just bad like any other bad
people? Like bad Christians who don't do what Jesus said.
Or bad kids with good parents. Or bad politicians." Her
voice trailed off. She sat awaiting a reply.

I didn't have an answer. Only musings of my own. The
strongest at that moment was, *Who are you, woman?*

Jacqui Johnson at the Bulletin was all business. Business—
and boys. Coy and clever. Calling attention, in one way or
another, consciously and unconsciously, to herself. But here
was the "unplugged" Jacqui. No spotlight. No mic. No
script. Just a woman wondering about matters of life and

love. Heart and soul. God and goodness. A woman reaching out compassionately to another woman worried for her man. A woman bent on comforting young children who were missing their father. That's what women do for women, I suppose—but I'd hardly thought of Jacqui in that way.

"So we're back to politics and religion, after all," I said absently, still caught in my own musings. She was too drunk for real dialog, I thought.

"Oh…" she said, leaning back in her chair. "Guesso." She smiled a crooked smile. "Sorry I got distracted."

She had finished her drink and was eyeing a second bottle of beer that the waiter had brought me. I didn't intend to drink it, but I didn't want Jacqui to drink it either. She'd had more than enough already. She reached for the beer casually, and I pulled it away. She laughed, leaned across the table defiantly, and took hold of the bottle. I unwound her fingers from the bottle's neck. She put her hand on my hand. I removed it.

She sat up straight then, sighed, and frowned in my direction. "Do you believe abortion is a sin?" she asked candidly, unexpectedly.

I didn't want to tell her what I thought. I wondered what she was telling me.

"Why?" I asked.

"Because," she said, screwing up her face in a fuller frown. "Because…no matter what a woman does for a man, sometimes…the man goes away, anyway. And then… But, you live alone, Matt. You should know what I mean."

Loneliness? Is that what she was talking about? No man? No children? And what was this about an abortion? It was more than a random question.

"Ideals are wonnnnderful," she said with emotion. "I believe in ideals. I wanna believe in love—don't you?" Her face went blank. "But…"

Then suddenly she laughed, tossed her hair, and leaned

across the table toward me again. "But...let's talk about sex."

I looked at my watch. "It's getting late," I said, matter-of-factly.

"Eggs...ackly what I mean," she said, putting on a serious face, with a smile in her eyes that was hard to turn away from.

"I'll take you home," I said. "I've got a midnight appointment—an interview, believe it or not—for a very important story."

"You...whaaat?" she said, blinking, not sure of how to take the announcement. "At midnight," she said flatly, clearly disbelieving me, the drink draining from her voice.

"Yes," I said, without explanation. "So we need to get you home now."

"Home," she echoed, with a long sigh and a sad, bitter smile.

I took her to her door, as I had once before.

"I had a reallllly good time, Matthew," she said. "Funny name...Math-yew." She giggled. "I like it, though. Mind if I call you Matt—like I always do anyway?"

I laughed. "I had a really good time, too, Jacqui. I'd like to do it again soon."

She stood up a little taller and looked me in the eyes. "Thank you for the wonderful dinner," she said quietly, inclining toward me, her body softly touching mine. The smell of alcohol—of pineapple, almond, and coconut upon her breath—mingled pleasantly with the strong and wild sweetness of the girl's perfume. It was a toxic brew.

"You will fall over," I said hoarsely, "if you don't go inside right now and go straight to bed."

She started to say something, then turned the key in her door and opened it. She smiled and gave me her silly wave. "Good-night, Matt," she said. "See ya tomorrow...at work."

"Good-night, Jacqui."

I wandered toward my rendezvous, head spinning with the thought of Jacqui Johnson. It was almost 11:00. The night was warm, the downtown fairly active. Cars cruised the avenues, but most folks were walking. Police were everywhere—on foot, parked in alleys, on the streets. They were always in pairs. A couple of SA officers passed me on bikes, their red shirts glowing strangely in the neon night. They were riding the sidewalk and took up more space than they needed to. Seemed to me that they could start trouble where there was none. Soldiers with a badge. Not the best idea for civil law enforcement, but we needed all the help we could get.

I felt safer, saner, stronger…and more solid than I had in weeks. Was it the knowledge of invisible guardians?—and I don't mean angels. Was it a sense of destiny? The blunt acceptance of my role in a story far bigger than me? Or was it Jacqui?

I thought of Cobalt Man. Had he ever existed? Well, of course he had. But maybe he was never that spy that I imagined on my trail. Just a couple of cars that looked alike, a couple of guys who looked alike.

And the girl? Some chick having lunch with her boss. And her boss resembled the other guys who resembled each other. I only saw her once. Couldn't remember exactly what she looked like anymore—not with Jacqui's eyes haunting my mind.

But…

I stopped in my tracks and stared into the window of a bookstore café. At a counter, drinking coffee, was the Hispanic woman I had seen eating at the sidewalk restaurant. Not a doubt in my mind. She was talking with the café attendant, but looked up for an instant, caught my eye and held it. She blew me a kiss, smiled, then went back to her conversation.

I stood where I was, stunned. She didn't look up again. I pulled myself away and hurried down the street in a fog.

A flirtatious reflex? Or a signal.

An impetuous gesture? Or a knowing sign.

Suddenly I was looking all around me again.

I walked the blocks near the Sahara Grill but didn't pass down its street. I bought a coffee from a corner vendor. Lousy stuff, but it sobered me up. Who in the world was the woman in the café? Where was Rashid? When would he contact me?

The phone vibrated. I dug it out. It read, *Good-bye*. Time to meet Khameel!

I cut down Juniper and rounded the corner onto Walnut at Dunkin' Donuts. Half a block to go. Though it was nearly midnight, the street was far from deserted. Downtown Philly on a warm Friday night was a bustling world of its own. You wouldn't know we were sinking into a depression. Money was still being printed, and some folks had plenty in their pockets. Or at least they had government plastic in their wallets. Food, drugs, drink, and dancing could all be bought downtown—and more than that if you knew where to knock.

I wondered where, in this jostle and jangle, Rashid would pop out.

Then I saw him, sitting in Jean's Pork and Beans, three doors away from the Sahara. He was watching for me near the window, and when he saw me, he got up. As he came toward the door, two men rose from a table at the back of the small eatery and hastened toward the door as well. They looked Indian or Pakistani, and their eyes were on Rashid and me. *Anybody who's on our side is invisible. Nobody will be followin' ya where ya can see them, unless they mean ya harm.* On impulse, I pulled the door open to let Rashid out. He was opening his mouth to greet me, when I yanked him outside and pushed the door shut in the faces of the men behind him.

"Run!" I said, whether that was good advice or not.

In an instant, he understood the situation, but he didn't

bolt. Instead he added his shoulder to the blockade and said, "*You* had better run, Matthew, not me! Kahmeel will be in the alley beside the Sahara. Find him now! Run with him wherever he leads! Go!"

I ran. Past the Sahara and into the narrow alley beyond it. Behind me I heard shouting. A crash. A woman's scream. Rashid's loud voice was distinct above the din.

Ahead of me in the dark alley, a door opened and light flooded the passageway. A man stepped outside, the door closed, and darkness wrapped him up.

"Kahmeel!" I said.

"Mr. Clifford!" he replied.

"We've gotta run! I'll follow you."

Without hesitation, he reached into the darkness and found my hand. "Come!" he said, and we dashed down the dim corridor and into another alley that brought us out onto Juniper. There we raced down Juniper to Locust. A black Rolls Royce pulled directly into our path, and a man jumped out.

Cobalt Man! Gun in hand.

I clawed at my jacket for Sutton's Magnum.

Cobalt Man fired—once, twice—then leapt back into his car. The sound of his shots tore the air. I was tackled from behind as more shots echoed in the narrow avenue.

My palms dug into the gravel as I broke my fall. I rolled, and my assailant rolled with me. It was Kahmeel!

Cobalt Man drove his car right at us, then past us. Another gunshot, and his windshield exploded in ten thousand tiny shards. The rising wail of police sirens reached us from streets beyond our sight. Men yelled and women screamed from unseen quarters above us and around us.

Where was Ognobini!? Where were our guardian angels?

Kahmeel was up, pulling me forcefully to my feet.

The sound of screeching tires added to the chaos, and

the headlights of a racing vehicle looped around the corner of Broad Street onto Locust. It barreled toward us at increasing speed, its beams reaching out to hold us where we stood.

Cobalt Man was out of his car again, his gun trained on the oncoming vehicle. Gunfire flashed on both sides of the street. The rumble of the shots followed instantly. Cobalt Man went down.

Something slammed me in the arm and I tumbled violently into the dirt beneath a curbside tree. The speeding car hit someone, and in its lights I saw a body catapulted onto the hard pavement. Kahmeel! The car sped away.

I rose painfully, forgetting the riot around me, and stumbled out into the street where Kahmeel lay. I knelt at his side, put my face close to his. His eyes moved.

"I guess I won't be going home after all," he gasped. Where *was* he going? I was suddenly very afraid for him.

He put his hand in mine and pressed something into my palm. "I won't need this anymore," he whispered hoarsely, "but you might."

A crowd had formed around us. Uniformed policemen. Plainclothes agents with guns. SA cops in red shirts. Rashid, on his knees, taking his brother in his arms, weeping.

I saw red liquid dripping on the street in front of me. My left shirt sleeve was drenched in blood. My own? I was dizzy, dazed, and the sounds around me began to blend into one loud throbbing hum. I saw a woman's face. The woman who had blown me the kiss. Her eyes were intently on mine. I saw her mouth move, but I couldn't hear her anymore. And that's all I can remember.

20
Kazakh Holiday

Far from the urban violence of the City of Brotherly Love, the Irtysh River becomes the Ertis River when it crosses an invisible line separating Russia from Kazakhstan. One hundred miles south of that border, Bradley Wall walked briskly through the ancient woods. His clothes were dirty, but his face was clean and shaven. Even in the wilderness of the Kazakh Steppe, Wall found water to wash with and time to employ his razor in honor of a civilized upbringing.

After two days plodding across the flat grass plains of Pavlodar, the shaded groves of birch and wild apple were a cool and invigorating change of scenery. Birds sang in the branches, flitting through sunlight and shadow in the pillared woods. The musty scent of mold mixed with the sweet perfume of wild berries. Ferrets, badgers, and hares rustled through the undergrowth, seemingly oblivious to the presence of man.

Wall had walked since dawn, climbing higher into the hills, stopping only twice to eat of the bounty of the land — and now the sun was nearing its summit. Straight before him, at an outcrop of bald rock, the forest opened on a brilliant vista of sunlit majesty. Southward and below, a roof of rippling green spruce stretched for miles. Beyond that, lying like a golden sea upon the horizon, were the wild grain fields of Astordau. Somewhere on that boundless steppe was a reed-palisaded lake with a small house sitting solitary on its eastern shore. That was Wall's destination. His hope was that Ali was there—with the man named Imanghari.

He started down the mountainside, watchful as always, hopeful as always, prayerful as always, shifting the pack on his back for the downhill journey. Marching through the northern Eden of Kazakhstan, it was almost easy to forget that the world was filled with treachery, violence, and blood. Passing through a sunlit glade where fallen trees had torn a hole in the forest ceiling, he flushed out a small flock of oriental turtledoves. They rose with a rattle and a whir and fled toward the open skies.

Wall laughed, drifting for a while in memories of a childhood hiking with his dog through the mountains and valleys of southern Wyoming. These weren't the Tetons, and this wasn't Jackson Hole, but God was everywhere. And with a compromised cell phone, there was no one to talk to but God. That was all right with Wall. Sometimes a man needed to walk in the cool of the garden with his creator.

That last phone call to Philadelphia had been a wee bit too long. Kazakhi airspace, like Kazakhi life in general, was heavily policed by the intrusive military government of Ulmes Malashenko. Satellite signals had just as tough a time getting past the government as spies and investigative reporters—even guys with Wall's connections. The government hadn't blocked the calls right away. They wanted to trace them—both ways. They sent men to find Wall, and they alerted their agents near Philadelphia.

Wall's phone was no dummy, though. American tax dollars and Israeli technology had gone into its making, and it knew when the Kazakhis were listening. When the KNB— the Kazakhi special police—burst into Wall's apartment in the Kazakh capital of Astana, "the fox" was four hours gone.

But the phone could still listen—selectively—even if Wall could no longer talk on it. It had one other frequency, and that was tuned to a solitary digital chip invisibly implanted in the back of the left hand of Ali Ahkmed Baraki.

Ali could speak to Wall. Wall could not contact Ali. That was how it was programmed from the start. That signal was elaborately complex—and swift as light. Nobody had intercepted it yet. But that didn't make it any easier for Ali. Not with Imanghari watching his every move.

Imanghari Koval was an Afghan Muslim by birth. His mother was Afghan. His father had been a Kazakhi soldier in the Soviet Army. Imanghari didn't meet his Russian Orthodox father until the dissolution of the Soviet Union. Imanghari was five when he and his mother moved to Kazakhstan and his parents finally married. A decade passed. His mother died giving birth to a stillborn baby girl, and Imanghari found himself the teenaged son of an infidel Kazahk soldier who was seldom home.

Imanghari ran away. He worked for room and board on a farm in the Quraghandy uplands. He joined the army under a feigned name and ran off again. He fished the Zhayyq River and worked the docks in the larger cities along the Caspian. He sold drugs. Then he settled down in Aqtau and made friends in a local mosque.

He joined a fundamentalist Islamic group. It was a local chapter of a larger sect with chapters and leagues throughout the Caucasus and Central Asia—and in other nations around the world. They were working toward international Islamic unification. Even with the recent brutal subjugation of Syria, Iran, and Turkmenistan by the western infidels, they had hopes for a major Islamic upsurge in the days ahead. Things were happening. Greater things were on the way. *Jihad.* The infidels would be defeated. The United States would submit to Islam. Israel would be crushed at last. The imams said so. And Allah promised victory.

Imanghari was part of something significant, something big, something glorious and unstoppable. But he felt lost in the midst of it all. He was lonely. He missed his mother terribly. He missed the close-knit family life of the village he was born in. He missed the mountains of Afghanistan where the stars were brighter at night than anywhere in the world. Why had he never gone back? It was twenty-two years since he'd left Afghanistan, twelve years since he'd run away from home.

He met Ali after the failed attempt on Putin's life.

When Yusef and his disheveled team returned from their botched operation in Moscow's Red Square, they had an American reporter in tow. Imanghari was given guard duty over the prisoner. He saw traces of home in the American's eyes and recognized a familiar accent — even beneath Ali's American inflections. Soon, the two were conversing quietly in the tongue of the Aghan hills.

Nobody had a plan for the American. Yusef's team hadn't counted on hostages. It was a desperate move on part of the men in the Tomb. They killed one of their hostages within minutes of their escape, but Ali had begged for his life in four languages! They saw he was a fellow Muslim. They had no reason to believe he was anything more than a foreign reporter. They let him live. They'd survived a terrifying incident and a harrowing escape together, and nobody especially wanted to kill him now.

They took him out into the hills to film a staged hostage video. They told Ali what to say, but they let him say it in his own words. It was a confused message, but that's what the captors wanted. Their real message was something they worked into the visuals in order to trigger other desired events. After the filming, Ali was left alone with Imanghari for long periods at a time.

As the days passed, the lonely guard and the hapless captive got to know each other well. They found pleasure in one another's company. They shared a common sense of humor and a longing for the homeland.

The hostage asked many questions about Afghanistan,

and Imanghari told him many stories. Torn by a heart filled with conflicting loyalities, Imanghari finally decided that he'd found a true companion. An enemy had become a friend.

Once, Imanghari heard Ali speaking to the back of his hand—and he suspected deeper things of the American reporter. But he had determined to become Ali's ally above all. He confessed his heart, pledged his loyalty, and revealed their present location to Ali (for Ali had no idea where he had been taken). They were in a house in Zhetybay, Kazakhstan, about eighty miles west of Aqtau and the Caspian.

Ali—knowing his own desperate situation and sensing Imanghari's deep and undisguised sincerity—took the young Afghani carefully into his confidence.

"I have a friend in Moscow," Ali told Imanghari, without revealing Wall's name or identity. "He is very resourceful. He could help me if he knew how to find me. If I could get away from here and find a place to hide, he could reach me."

The deep call of unexpected friendship led Imanghari to imagine a daring plan.

"There is a house, far from here, far from everything," he said, "where we could hide and await your friend. It is my father's house. His grandfather built it year's ago. Father took my mother and me there, when first we came to this country. It is a lovely, lonesome, and abandoned place, the only house within a hundred miles of itself. There were ruins of an old barn and other outbuildings. There were no roads. We traveled there by military helicopter. There is a lake. We fished and swam and walked through the tall grasses in the sunlight and the moonlight. It is one of the few good memories I have with my father."

"How far is it from here?"

"A thousand miles."

In seclusion, with Imanghari keeping watch against his

own Muslim brothers, Ali talked to Wall. Or to Wall's phone. At least he hoped so—desperately hoped so. The chip in his hand could be activated only by an infrasonic, hyperthermic image of Ali's right thumbprint. And then it was only on for sixty seconds. The instant it was ready for audio, it would emit a split-second pulse that Ali felt immediately. He had to be ready. He had to be clear. He had to be brief.

He named the region and described the lake and the house and the surrounding territory from the ground and from the air, as Imanghari recalled it. He gave Wall a time frame—three to four days for Imanghari and Ali to reach the house. And he added quietly, so that Imanghari would not hear, "The silversmith on the 20th." It was the 16th when Ali left the message.

A few hours later, a meeting was called for the entire cell. Someone from the Kazakh military would be addressing them. There had been increased talks between the Kazakh cells and agents within the army. Something called "the push" was underway, and "the pull" had to be in place. Imanghari knew very little of the details. In fact, few within the cell were privy to the full plan. The meeting would reveal next steps—nothing more.

It hardly seemed necessary to maintain a guard on the prisoner. He had been loosed from his bonds within a few days of his blindfolded arrival at the house in Zhetybay, but his room was kept locked and it had no window. Someone was with him always during the first week. But Ali had been such a compliant prisoner that now he was sometimes left alone in his room.

The meeting was too big for the house. It would be held in a school a few streets away, a few hours before midnight, when dusk fell. The cell chief didn't trust Ali enough to leave him totally unguarded.

Imanghari volunteered to watch the house, and at the

appointed hour, he settled himself in a chair outside Ali's room. There was nobody in the house but the two of them.

At 10:00 p.m., a man came to the house to give Imanghari an update on the meeting. He found Imanghari reading a book at his post. They smoked a cigarette together, and the herald left. He would return again at 11:00.

As soon as he was gone, Imanghari knocked at Ali's door and opened it swiftly. Ali stood there, dressed in Kazhak clothes, a long thin coat over farmer's pants and walking boots. The coat hid a Russian Ots-33 Pernach automatic pistol tucked in his belt. Imanghari stepped into the room and quickly changed into the clothes of a common rural laborer. He, too, donned a traditional light overcoat. He, too, was armed, with one pistol in his belt and one under his arm in a sling.

With nuts and fruit, and a wallet filled with enough Kazakh *tenge* to buy some food and drink as they traveled, the two slipped out of the house and into the darkness of the streets of Zhetybay. A late night taxi ambled past them.

"We need a ride," Imanghari said, as he sank back into the shadows. "But not in a taxi. And not in a police car. Follow me."

The two men retreated through an alley and headed eastward through the city, careful to stay out of sight as much as possible. The city was patrolled at night by police cars and local urban troops who generally traveled in groups of five or six. The government was constantly suspicious of political and religious discontent, and uniformed manpower seemed to be its answer to everything.

Curfews were seasonally imposed in the cities near the Caspian. Zhetybay was presently not under a midnight ban, but police were always prowling, looking for someone to order around—hoping to find a tourist without a passport, a worker without an ID. For a few *tenge*, the police would look the other way. Without the payoff, they would pack the offenders off for interrogation at the local police station where the price of freedom was highly inflated.

Imanghari took the lead as the two made their way through the city, ducking in and out of alleys, squatting behind bushes and barrels when cars drove by. At a bright-lit cafe near the city's edge, Ali halted for a minute—out of breath. Nearly doubled over with exhaustion, he stared longingly through the steamy windows at a group of contented foreign diners. It was an alluring picture—cozy, colorful, and dreamlike in the midst of the cold, tense reality of their flight. Imanghari was drawn to it too, and the urgency of the hour fell from him for a moment as he joined Ali in silent observation.

The front door burst open. A man and a woman, laughing and stumbling, collided with Ali as they came outside.

"Sorry!" the man blurted, gripping Ali by the shoulders to steady himself.

The woman teetered at the curb, and Imanghari reached out to catch her. "Thank you," she said stupidly, drunkenly, in a sharp English accent.

"London?" Ali asked quietly.

"Manchester!" she said with a slur.

"Silly thing," said the man. "She's got more Liverpool in 'er than anyone I know!"

"Oh, you!" she retorted. Then she giggled.

"Is this your car?" Imanghari asked, nodding to the vehicle parked against the side of the building.

"S'rented!" said the woman, grinning. "It rides on the wrong side of the road!" She laughed again.

"Do you think you can drive...in your condition?" Ali asked the man cautiously.

"Ha!" he answered. "'Course not...but I'm gonna."

"Do you want me to drive you home in your own car?" Imanghari offered candidly. "You will be safer, if you do not mind me saying so."

"Locals!" laughed the man. "Always lookin' for a way to make some coin! But," he said bluntly, in spite of the drink, "you're not Kazakhi."

"Afghani," admitted Imanghari.

"And your friend?" said the woman, making odd eyes at Ali.

"From the States," said Imanghari. Ali nodded.

"On holiday?" she asked. Ali nodded again.

"Well," the man hummed. "I see," he murmured. "Yes," he said suddenly, assertively, "you may drive us home. We're in a house just outside town…an inn of sorts, if you can call it that!" He reached out to shake Imanghari's hand, missed twice, and then climbed awkwardly into the passenger side of the front seat.

"Get in behind the wheel, get in! My name is Richard Sherwood," he said, offering Imanghari the keys. He nodded to Ali to help the woman into the back. "The lady is Judith Hunt. We're here on oil business, since the Peace," he added. "Exxon. Out of Aqtaú. A little Kazakh 'oliday today. A visit to the 'amlet of Zhetybay. Back to Aqtau in the morning."

"In the morning," Judith echoed loudly, sprawled drunkenly in the back seat. Ali found himself pressed uncomfortably against the window.

Imanghari headed out of town, where the pavement soon ended and a thin road of gravel wound through sandy hollows and past genuflecting oil rigs. The wind was strong and constant off the dunes, and it buffeted the car as they drove. Camels crossed the road once, heading toward water most likely. Ali thought of England, thought of home. He might have taken these two Brits into his confidence, found a way out of the country with them. But he had an appointment with Wall—and a friend to run with.

"'ere we are!" Richard announced, pointing to a lonely brick structure up against a brush-covered hill. "Pilgrim's Parcel…or something like it! They've a warm bath, at least.

Pull in by those bushes, will you?"

Imanghari parked the car and got out.

"Thank you, good sirs." Richard rolled out of his seat with a smile. "Now 'ere's a few pounds," he said, digging into his pocket for money. "You can 'change it for *tenge* back in town. Or…hey!" He stood up straighter, his eyes sobering. "How're you blokes gettin' back to where y'came from?" And then he saw the pistol in Imanghari's hand.

"We are not going back," said Imanghari. He got into the car, as Ali climbed over into the passenger seat.

"I'll be blowed!" Richard bellowed as the car pulled away.

"S'rented," said Judith, grinning, rocking on her heels as her hair danced in the desert breeze.

The roads forked constantly, splitting and intersecting with each other, turning from gravel to ground to gravel again. There were few road signs, and sometimes the wind threatened to push them off the road altogether. About an hour later, near a sign that read Prohlada Spring, the car overheated…and stalled.

"Maybe some water from the spring will get us back on the road," Imanghari suggested. The air smelled of hydrogen sulfide and camel manure. The spring was dry. "We walk," said Imanghari, "unless we can catch a camel!"

They walked. The wind was cold.

They cut across the country, avoiding the roads. "In this direction is a village," Imanghari explained. "Beyond it is a famous cave called Kov-Ata. It has a warm lake inside. We can rest there, eat, and wash."

They passed the village on its backside, crossing through sandy fields to avoid being seen. At Kov-Ata, the cave was shut up. A heavy iron gate covered its entrance. Within sight was a solitary hotel, dark except for a light in the first floor office area.

The two companions found a hollow near the cave, out

of the wind, to eat where the sand wouldn't blow in their faces. They drank some of their water and headed out into the desert again.

"I know a man who lives beyond, in the way we are heading," Imanghari said. "We will reach him before the dawn, and he will put us up. We can trust him fully, if he will trust *me*. He knew my father through the army, and so knew my family in Afghanistan. He was there when I was born. He was a doctor then, with the Soviet government—though never a communist. I have been in touch with him a few times in the last few years. He has not approved of my political affiliations, but he loves me. We can sleep at his house during the day and travel again by night."

"The word will go out about us," Ali said, "from the cell in Zhetybay, from their military contacts at tonight's meeting, and from that British businessman. Everyone will be looking for us everywhere. We must find a direct way, quickly, to get to your father's hideaway. Otherwise…"

Imanghari understood.

At a small arid farm, on the edge of a windblown canyon where a stream flowed doggedly through the thin bristled grass, they stopped at a house and knocked.

Though it was the middle of the night, Dr. Erkin Temirzhon opened his door and graciously invited the tired travelers in to take off their boots and rest their weary feet. Erkin roused Aiday, his wife. Candles were lit and tea was served.

"I have seen you three times since you were old enough to run. And you are running again, Bobek Bala?"

"He calls me Baby Boy," Imanghari explained to Ali, "because that was what I was when we met. Yes," he said soberly, turning back to his host, "I am running again."

The men were called to the table where Aiday had laid out refreshments. Dried fruit, fresh grapes and melon, nuts, cakes, and *baursaks*, a traditional flatbread baked with raisins. Aiday poured fermented goat's milk into her colorful Asian teacups. "*Syen ashsinba?*" she asked, smiling.

"Yes, we are hungry, good mother," Imanghari answered.

"*Rahmet sizge,*" said Ali, in perfect Kazakh. He had learned much in his short time as a captive.

"You are welcome," Erkin and Aiday replied in unison.

Erkin prayed a blessing on the meal and served his guests first. When they had eaten, he said "*Bar youkta!*" to his wife — meaning "Go to sleep!" — and he and his guests sat down together by a small fire he had started for their comfort.

"I ask only what I can do to help you," said Erkin, prodding a dry log closer to the flames with an iron poker.

"We need to travel to the plains of Pavlodar, about a hundred and twenty miles due west of the region's capitol, near the border of Aqmola province," said Imanghari. "We need to be there within two or three days."

Erkin stared into the chuckling fire, nodding his head. He was silent for many minutes. He knew of Imanghari's father's house on the plain.

"From Beyneu to Aqtobe by train," he said. "From Aqtobe to Pavlodar by plane. From Pavlodar toward Aqmola by bus or truck...even bicycle. And then you walk. A two-day trip, most likely, if you sleep on the train and in the air. But you must take turns sleeping. And we will have to get tickets ahead of time. Someone in Pavlodar will have to find you transportation north to the plains. I think I can work out that last detail."

"This is dangerous for you, as well as for us," Imanghari lamented.

"There is no life without danger, Bobek Bala," Erkin said, rising to put his back to the fire.

"Do you have a cell phone, father?" Ali asked respectfully, in Arabic.

"And would you call home to America?" Erkin grimly

replied. He recognized Ali's accent. Erkin had once been a well-traveled man. And he had been something more than a doctor. He had played many roles, worn a few disguises. The Cold War had been a time of deep subterfuge, and men of intellect and a profession were pulled at from all directions and by all parties. Sometimes, you didn't know which direction to turn. Those days were over, but the lessons learned were never lost. There would always be wars to fight. And on whose side?

"No," said Ali, lowering his eyes. "Somewhat closer." There was someone in Oral, on the Kazakh border with Russia. A friend of Wall. A man Ali had met but once. "One call could get us the tickets we need."

"One call," Erkin echoed, "could get us more than that— and we'd not like it at all. I must call someone I know first. Then they must get in touch, personally and without a phone call, with the one who can get you the tickets."

"We can arrange that," Ali said. "I hope."

Who can Ali know in Kazakhstan? Imanghari wondered. Another reporter? An American government agent? How could anyone who Ali knew get tickets at such short notice? What kind of pull did he have?

But Imanghari didn't ask. He and Ali were in this together. They had a long and perilous journey ahead of them—one with no sure destination. They had to trust each other.

Erkin called a man in Chapaev, a few miles south of Oral. They had a nice chat about how they used to ride the railroad between Uncle Ravil's hometown and Aunt Bakytgul's summer house. "I wonder what the price of two tickets is these days?" Erkin asked.

They talked about the birds that used to fly over Aunt B's house on their way to the northern mountains. Oh!— what they would give to be young again, lying in the grass by Aunt B's lake, dreaming of flying like the swallows.

They spoke of many other things, and anyone listening

would have heard two old men reminiscing of days gone by. But when the conversation was over, Erkin's "cousin" knew exactly what Erkin wanted him to know.

"He is resourceful and entirely trustworthy," said Erkin when the call was done. "He will contact your man while you sleep today—and tell me so once it has happened. If your man is as good as mine, we'll get you to your train by dusk tonight—with tickets for your flight at the end of the rails. And my man will make sure someone takes care of the last legs of your journey."

"I am very, very grateful," said Ali, deeply moved. Imanghari could only grin.

"*Zhoor youktayik,*" Erkin said.

"Yes, time for bed," Imanghari repeated in Afghan, so that Ali would know what Erkin had spoken.

The host showed his guests to a small room with one bed. The weary fugitives stretched themselves out upon the bed together, wrapped the thick blankets around them like a sleeping bag, and soon were sound asleep. Imanghari snored so loud that Erkin came back to the room and closed the door.

Thursday, July 17.

It had seemed a long day of waiting—but early in the evening, as the sun was descending again in the summer sky, a laborer in an old truck pulled into Erkin's lane. Ali and Erkin went out to greet him. Ali climbed in with him, and they drove away. He had shaved the beard he'd worn for the past two years. His newly-bared skin was artificially toned to match the tan of the rest of his face. A summer cap covered his thick, black hair. A pair of wire-rimmed glasses, with clear, non-prescription lenses, hugged his temples and made him look a different man.

A few minutes later, Imanghari and Erkin got into Erkin's rusted green Lada, a Soviet era car with 200,000 miles on it. "She keeps rolling," said Erkin, as they rumbled down the unpaved road on their way to Beyneu.

Imanghari, too, was transformed. His short-cropped hair was dyed blonde, with tinges of grey around the ears, making him look much older than he was and more Russian than Afghan. That was Aiday's handiwork—she had once been a popular watercolorist. Her impressionistic cityscapes hung in the homes of former Soviet officials throughout Asia. She painted still, on whim or occasion, portraits from photographs, scenes of the desert.

Imanghari's skin was lighter after a long bath in a special dye that gave it a pigment his ancestors never had. He also wore a pair of faux glasses with brown plastic rims. He grinned whenever he looked at himself in the car's side view mirror.

The ride to Beyneu was slow and dusty. A policeman stopped them once to ask for identification. He recognized Erkin by sight. "Doctor Temirzhon," he said, upset with himself, "I did not know it was you, or I would not have interrupted your journey."

"You are doing your job, Toktar," affirmed the doctor, soberly, "and hoping to turn dust into gold for your household in the process. Well, here's a little gold for a hardworking family man," he said, handing the policeman a few *tenge*. "Buy the children some fresh date bread. And bring your wife out to see Aiday sometime. The women need to talk to one another. It is a lonely world."

"Thank you, doctor," said Toktar, beaming. "I am glad I stopped you after all!"

"Bring your wife to see Aiday," Erkin insisted, as he drove away.

In Beyneu, Ali and Imanghari climbed out of their vehicles, many blocks from one another.

"*Sau bolynyz*, Bobek Bala," Erkin said to Imanghari.

"Good-bye to you, too, good father!"

"*Asalaam Aleykum*," Erkin added.

"And peace be with you," Imanghari echoed with a bow.

Alone, he made his way to a location that Erkin had written for him on a scrap of nondescript paper. Ali had similar instructions, and he reached their destination first — a small electronics shop on a cobblestoned alley.

Ali went in and was greeted gruffly by the bearded Kazakh proprietor who was dusting the cheap Chinese goods. There was nobody else in the store.

"*Qayirly kesh*," said Ali. "Good-evening."

The man said simply, "*Iye*," and Ali slipped quickly through a curtain into a back room. A half hour later, Imanghari joined him in the carton-cluttered quarters.

The bearded man closed and locked the door of his shop, and turned a cardboard sign around in the glass of the door. In small red letters (in Russian, Arabic, and Kazakh), the sign read: "Open again tomorrow, thank you."

"*Teesh-tan*," said the bearded man as he entered the storage room where the two fugitives waited. "Be quiet," he repeated in Afghani Pashtu, holding a finger over his lips as he ushered them through another door to a staircase leading to the basement. He followed, locking the door behind him.

"We will speak in Pashtu now," he said, "because you both know it. But very quietly, please. This is my shop," he gestured, tossing his hands in various directions, "and you are my customers. I have received your order, and I will deliver it to you here — all expenses paid.

"My name, as you could have read on the door of my shop when you came in, is Surum bin Vadim. You may call me Surum." He smiled wryly.

"Sit down, please," he said to Ali. He took Ali's picture with a digital camera. "You are next, sir," he said to Imanghari, and took his picture, too. "One moment, sirs," he murmured, as he hooked the camera to a laptop and went to work.

Within minutes, two authentic looking ID cards had been printed, laminated, and handed to the men. The lamination was worn and scratched, giving the cards the look of long use. One was dated 2009, the other 2007. Both had new names for the men, false birth dates, and other details of identification.

"These cards will fool anyone who doesn't know you personally," said Surum bin Vadim. "And they are imprinted with an override barcode to trick the most sophisticated computer. Even most of mine," he said, looking around him.

"Amazing," Imanghari whispered, staring at his face on the card. "Are you a magician?"

"Hardly," Suram replied. "Other than the barcode, the rest is typical."

He opened a weathered leather wallet and pulled out two packages of tickets. He handed the smaller package to them first. "This is for your train, which leaves the station here in Beyneu in about ninety minutes. You will board separately and sit in separate cars. One of you has a sleeping pass for a bunk in any of the economy sleeping cars. The other will sleep in his seat.

"It would be wise not to talk with each other throughout the trip but to make the acquaintance of someone else, preferably — and discreetly — an unchaperoned woman. They are less likely to be agents of any kind, and especially if they are with children. Make no romantic moves, but be friendly. Avoid current events. Talk about the weather, the countryside, your health. Speak well of the government. A quiet and discreet friendship with a woman will make you appear — to others — to be attached."

Imanghari liked that idea.

"Memorize the information on your ID," Suram continued, "especially your name. Invent a likely life for yourself — but make it realistic, and keep it mundane — nothing to attract the attention of anyone who might overhear. Ali, you are dressed as an urban laborer, and your ID says as much about you. Imanghari, you are clothed as a farmer from the Uplands. You have worked on farms in real life — yes, I know this about you — and you will be able speak of farming naturally. Don't draw attention to yourselves with conversation too lively or too loud. And never take off your glasses, even when you sleep. You don't know who will wake you up — or why. You are no longer Ali Baraki or Imanghari Koval — and you must not look like them."

Imanghari sighed. "I have run before, when I was myself, and have escaped those who sought me."

"Do you know this for certain?" asked Surum bin Vadim. "Or did it simply cease to matter, to those who sought you, whether they apprehended you or not?"

Imanghari stared blankly at Surum.

"These are your plane tickets," said the bearded magician, holding out the second packet. "Neither of you is in first class. One is in the back of the plane. One is in the middle. The plane seats one hundred and sixty people, not including first class. It is a three-seater, on either side of the aisle. You both have aisle seats. That makes it easier to get out of your seats when — and if — you need to. No contact with each other. The plane leaves about two hours after your train arrives in Aqtobe. When you get off the flight in Pavlodar, you will go to the address on the other side of the note that brought you to me. Memorize the address and keep the note in a deep pocket, on your person. If you are searched, eat the note! No one must see it. Any questions?"

"Can I use your bathroom," asked Ali. The goat's milk of the night before had caused him pain all day.

The Temir Joli, the national railway system of Kazakhstan, stitched together most of the nation's major cities and all of its ports and airports. At the borders of Russia, China, and Uzbekistan, the rails crossed over and continued under the oversight of those foreign powers. The trains that ran the Temir Joli were Russian built — and fast.

The Beyneu train pulled out of the station at 9:35 p.m.

The boarding went without a hitch. Ali headed for the bunks and left his bag there to stake a claim. He pulled a thin curtain shut—the unofficial sign that his bed was taken—and headed for the dining car. He intended to eat like a bunk-holder. He would speak Egyptian Arabic to Arabs on the train. He would speak an urban Russian slang to others. That was common in the larger cities of Kazakhstan, and he was far more fluent in Russian than in Kazakh. He bought a newspaper, ordered tea and dessert, and sat down at last to rest and think.

Imanghari found a seat and started looking for a woman. He saw only one in his entire car—a striking young mother with long dark hair, her small son fidgeting energetically in the seat beside her. She was sleeping.

Maybe later, he thought.

The repetitious rattle of the rails, the rhythmic rocking of the car, the incoherent hum of quiet conversation—all conspired to close Imanghari's eyes. Half dreaming, half scheming how to introduce himself to the woman in the back of the car, Imanghari drifted off to sleep.

He dreamed of the house on the steppe. The woman from the train was with him there. It was a warm and moonlit night, and the two of them were walking by the lake. Its waters rippled in silver and black, as a soft wind bent the tulips by the shore. Long-beaked pelicans stood silhouetted against the endless grey steppe. "*Delta aman dae?*" the woman asked in Pashtu. "Is it safe here?" A fox barked somewhere far away. And then...there was nothing but the fox.

Imanghari opened his eyes slowly. Something was prodding him—poking his chest. A man was standing above him in the aisle of the train. He held a long metal baton. He poked Imanghari's chest with it again. Another man, in the uniform of a railway security policeman, stood behind him.

"Mr. Imanghari Koval," said the man with the baton, "you are under arrest."

21

Cobalt Woman

Saturday morning, July 19. 4:45 a.m.

I opened my eyes and wondered, *Was it all a dream?*

But it was no dream.

I was on my back in a strange, sterile room. The smell of antiseptic was pervasive. Medical equipment surrounded me. A liquid-filled drip bag hung from an IV stand a couple of feet above my face. My eyes followed the tube from the bag to my body. My left arm was bandaged. And it hurt!

"You were shot," said a man in a chair to my right.

"Kevin?"

"You'll be all right. In fact, you'll be up and out of here later today they say."

"Shot?"

"Flesh wound. No bones. No muscles. Just a nice chunk out of your forearm, and a pint or two of blood. Nothing that any self-respecting cowboy would ever boast about."

"Who shot me?"

"One of the bad guys," said Kevin. "I think."

Bad guys…good guys. "Kahmeel…" I said, remembering.

"He's dead, Matt," said Kevin soberly.

I felt sick in the pit of my stomach.

"Rashid?"

"Mourning. Safe. He was here to see you about an hour

ago. He'll be back. He's got bodyguards, now. A couple of plainclothes Philly cops."

"Cobalt Man?"

"All shot up, but he'll live. They flew him to Hershey Medical."

"Who is he?"

"CIA."

"On our side!" It was hard to believe. I'd been afraid of the man for weeks. "Who were those two guys...those... those Indians or Pakistanis?" I wondered aloud. "They were in Jean's Pork and Beans. They got up to follow us, and..."

"Don't know. Sons of Islam, maybe. Connected to Kahmeel's network in some way, probably. It was one of them who shot you, I hear. They're dead, too. Shot by Cobalt Man. Or by Ognobini's men. Maybe the FBI got them. There were lots of bullets flying."

"Yeah..." I said. "There were." I remembered Kahmeel pulling me down when the shooting began. He may have saved my life.

Kevin leaned toward me. "The seminarians were praying," he said.

"They shoulda prayed harder..."

"You're alive," said Kevin.

Alive! "Sutton... Stein?"

"They'll be in after the sun rises. Jacqui Johnson is around here somewhere. She's been in to see you more often than the nurses. Came with a cameraman the first time and filmed you while you lay here. Anybody who's awake in town, and has tuned in to the news, has seen you snoring."

"Was she sober?" I asked.

"I think so," he said with a puzzled frown.

"Does Dad know?"

"Called him myself. He was asleep. He'll be on his way in the morning."

I thought about Lisa. I didn't want to see her.

"Kahmeel's cell..." I said hoarsely. "We've got pictures.

Rashid can finger those guys. We've got to go after them. What do the cops know? Where's Ognobini? The CIA?"

"They don't report to me, brother," said Kevin. "But the cell hasn't shown up in the news. That's still under wraps. You've made the news, of course—big time! The gunfight was on the late night Bulletin Boards. Then national coverage. 'Midnight Madness in the City of Brotherly Love.' It's being pitched as a drug gang thing. Something the Bulletin was investigating with undercover cops. That's the official spin."

"Why do I feel like a puppet?" I said stiffly. "A shot-up, laid-up puppet!"

Then, for the first time, I noticed a woman seated in a corner of the room. I recognized her face! As she stood up and moved toward me, I recalled the moments before I passed out in the street.

"I had a key," I said slowly, thoughtfully. "Kahmeel gave me a key. Pressed it into my hand before…"

"Before he died?" asked the Hispanic woman at the foot of my bed, taking out a notepad to write something down.

"Yes, but…"

"Matthew Lyle Clifford," Kevin interrupted, rising from his chair, "meet Magdalena Elizabeth Rivera, alias Cobalt Woman, assistant to Cobalt Man, Central Intelligence Agency operative, around-the-clock member of Operation Matt-Watch. She's armed and dangerous, and she's been here all night."

She blushed and nodded. She was very pretty. Dark, thoughtful eyes. Jet black hair braided stylishly behind her head. Professionally dressed, as she'd been when I first saw her sitting with Cobalt Man at the sidewalk café. Lips that would pout if they weren't smiling. Lips that had blown me a kiss on the night I was shot. When *was* that?

"How long have I been here?" I asked.

"About four hours," said Kevin. "It's almost 5 o'clock in the morning. It'll be dawn soon."

"I'm glad to see you're awake at last," said Magdalena Elizabeth Rivera sincerely. "Could you tell me about this key you just mentioned?"

"I…I think that…" I hesitated. Kevin was standing behind Ms. Rivera, frowning and putting a finger to his lips to hush me. For some reason, he didn't want me to talk about the key.

"My memory…it's blurry… It's sketchy, confused… Maybe… No. No key. That was just my waking dreams…my fever…the pain-killer…"

"You said just now, quite clearly," Ms. Rivera insisted, "that Kahmeel gave you a key and pressed it into your hand."

"I…I thought so…for a moment…a minute ago," I muttered. "But…no," I lied, "that was just a dream. But last night was no dream, was it? Running for our lives. Gunfire everywhere. I'd been knocked down twice. Shot once. I couldn't get to my gun…I had a gun."

I wondered where the gun was. I was certain it was not in the closet of my hospital room.

"People were falling," I said. "A car came hurtling toward us. That's when I was shot, I guess. The car hit Kahmeel. I crawled out to where he lay. He said something to me. He took my hand…squeezed it…one last time." Real tears formed in my eyes, rolled down my cheeks. "He's gone. And here I am."

Ms. Rivera wrote in her notebook. She sighed and sat back down. Kevin nodded his head at me, sadly, knowingly.

The door to my hospital room was kept closed. The nurses were not allowed to ask me about anything other than my comfort and my condition. A few visitors would be permitted, but they had to be screened, prepped, and approved. I knew the security was because of the terrorist issue and the Sons of Islam, but I felt like a prisoner.

The seminarians were allowed in around 7:00 a.m. "It's Saturday, guys," I said, grimacing as I tried to move my arm, "but I don't think we'll be doing Bible study."

"Man, this is the *last* time we send *you* out for pizza so late a'night!" Tyrone joked. He leaned over and looked me in the eyes. "Y'okay, Matthew Lyle?"

"I don't know," I said honestly. "But thanks for praying."

"No safe place," Luis reminded me, soberly.

"Safe here, I hope," I answered.

"Dude, you look awful!" said Doug.

"You look pretty bad yourself," I said. "But I'm glad to see you anyway." Everyone laughed but me. It hurt too much to laugh.

"What's for breakfast?" Doug asked. "And where's the coffee?"

"You can have my leftover shredded wheat," I said, "but you don't want the coffee they brew here!"

We chatted. Small talk. Bantered about Ali—questions without answers. Ms. Rivera listened intently. She took notes.

Tyrone read a psalm. They prayed for me. And then they were ushered out by my undercover guardian angel. "Ten minute visits," she said.

"I'm here for the duration, Matt," Kevin piped from his chair. "Special permission—arranged by your boss, Aaron Stein. The guy has connections. I'll take you home, with the oversight of Ms. Rivera here, when they release you."

"Oversight?"

"You'll have twenty-four hour protection as long as you need it," said Ms. Rivera. "Another agent will be joining me in the place of Cobalt Man, as you call him."

"As long as I need it? What does that mean?"

"Until the assignment is completed."

"Which is when?"

"I'm sorry, but I don't know that."

"How long have you been watching me?" I asked.

She blushed again. "I can't tell you that."

"Since that night at Penn Treaty Park?"

"I can't tell you."

It hit me. "You called the cops! Or Cobalt Man did! That's why they showed up suddenly to get us out of the jam with that gang. Where else did you follow me? Lancaster? The Bulletin? Kahmeel's? My own place? What about when I go to the bathroom? Is my apartment bugged?"

She couldn't tell me.

"It was like one of those shootouts in your western novels, Dad."

"Thank God the wound isn't serious, Matt."

"I have thanked him."

"The Lord has a plan for your life, son."

"Is it on his website? I'll check it out when I've got some free time."

"Lisa has been praying for you."

"Tell her thanks."

"Do you need anything?"

"Answers, Dad. Answers for a lot of stuff that's happening. Keep praying for Ali, will you? That's what really matters right now. That, and…" I couldn't tell him about the cell. About Wall. About the bombs—or whatever else was supposed to happen. I didn't *know* what was supposed to happen. And our ten minutes were up.

My TV screen was tiny, but the news was big: spotlight on Georgia.

Putin demanded that the little republic cough up the terrorists that had tried to blow him to smithereens. He had claimed the terrorists were in Khevsuretti, in northern Georgia. Now Russian intelligence (supposedly corroborated by EU sources) had discovered jihadist training camps and fortified caves in the mountains of Georgia's Kentekhi province. Russia said the terrorists were being harbored by the Georgian government and armed by Azerbaijan, Georgia's Islamic neighbor to the east. It was an old line, these Kremlin accusations against Georgia. I didn't believe the tale of Georgian caves filled with fundamentalist Muslims. Besides, the Kentekhi province was predominately Christian.

Romano preached the Peace but pledged solidarity with Putin. EU peacekeeping troops pushed northward through Turkey toward Georgia to close off the border against escaping terrorists. "There must be no more war!" Romano proclaimed. "And there will be no more war if Georgia opens its doors to the Russian expeditionary force and helps them root out the jihadists."

Georgian president, Tengiz Kobadze, railed against the very notion that he was harboring terrorists—especially Islamists. "It is an egregious conspiracy!" he declared. "It is absurd to blame the Christian republic of Georgia for the crazed acts of a small group of Islamic fanatics who are nowhere near our borders. Our own intelligence has traced them to Kazakhstan, on the other side of the Caspian. Russia is howling at the wrong door, and Putin can huff and puff all he wants! He won't get in without a fight!"

I admired that little Georgian! Five feet four inches tall, and all fire!

"And who is Marco Romano to command us to open our borders to Russian tanks?" Kobadze continued, live from Tbilisi. "It is the act of an arrogant bully to take part in such a show of force. For what? To catch a few Muslim monkeys wearing stolen Georgian underwear? This is an undisguised ploy to plunder our house! Putin wants Georgia for himself. He can't stand the smell of freedom. And the European Union is acting a traitor's role in feeding Georgia to the Russian wolves!"

I imagined, for a moment, Kobadze and Romano locked in a dark room together, teeth clenched upon a common bit of short rope, Bowie knives in hand. I'd bet on Kobadze.

"Georgia is an autonomous democracy — a free European nation!" Kobadze reminded the watching world. "We appeal to free nations everywhere! We appeal to the United States, to free-thinking members of the European Union, to all who believe in independence and democracy! Speak up for Georgia! Stand up for Georgia! Do right by Georgia! For here we stand alone against a powerful and unjust aggressor!"

And how long could they stand alone?

The Pentagon and the White House were at odds about Georgia. Our military shook its sabers at Putin. Clay cautioned patience and moderation. The United Nations wet its pants — further polluting Manhattan's East River.

I had my own questions. Why was Romano so committed to Putin's rabid manhunt? Was the Italian premiere so at enmity with radical Islam that he would support the violation of Georgian sovereignty? It seemed more likely that he wanted the EU to keep a close eye and a tight leash on Putin.

Where was Ali on the map? Would he be caught up again in the crossfire? Did these events have anything to do with Kahmeel's "push" or "pull"?

Why was Kahmeel killed?

Who shot *me*? And why?

Where was Wall? Was he still alive?

If this was peace, then bring on the Prince of Peace! Maybe we needed Jesus to come back tomorrow after all.

The news switched from Tbilisi to Brussels, and Marco Romano's grim features filled the screen.

"The Antichrist," Kevin said quietly from his chair beside the window. "We'd better have our hell insurance paid up. Things are about to get very hot around the world."

I said nothing.

Ms. Rivera took notes.

Rashid came to visit, heartbroken over Kahmeel. He wrung his hands. He cried. "Some of the Sons of Islam are in jail, thank God! But not all of them. Nobody has confessed to any conspiracy. The police are doing all they can to hunt down the rest of the cell, but it's all very quiet. They have put me in a hotel. I have two personal watchmen. I have answered a thousand questions—though, I'm sure, not very satisfactorily. Kahmeel is..." he halted. "They have his body... at the police morgue," he said brokenly. "I have no idea what he wanted to tell you. Do you?" He glanced at the corner of the room, where Ms. Rivera sat, pen and tablet in hand.

"No," I said, "I don't."

"No clues? No keys at all?" he asked. *Keys?* Ms. Rivera looked up from her notes.

"Does your mother know about what happened to Kahmeel?" Kevin asked, as if he hadn't heard Rashid's question.

"Not yet..." said Rashid.

"I'm sorry," Ms. Rivera said sympathetically, "but your ten minutes are over."

Kevin was resting in the chair, reading a Bible. Ms. Rivera was watching an historic documentary on the television when a male orderly came to the door. "Agent Rivera?" he said. "You have a phone call at the nurse's station."

As soon as she left the room, Kevin pulled his chair up to my bed.

"It's a post office box key," he whispered, holding it up for me to see.

"Is that—?"

"Yes," he said. "Rashid slipped it to me in the middle of the night. He saw Kahmeel give it to you. Saw it fall from your hand when you lost consciousness. Apparently, in the darkness...in the confusion...nobody else noticed."

"But...."

"Let me talk quickly." He nodded toward the door. "The feds brought everyone here to the hospital, including Kahmeel—he was already gone. Rashid called me, and I came. They let us talk together. He had *this* with him." Kevin held a Bible out for me to see.

"It's a Gideon's Bible that he picked up somewhere in the hospital. He handed it to me—said he was reading Revelation, of all books! When they escorted me to your room, I brought the Bible with me. A scribbled note from Rashid was stuck in the pages of Revelation, with this key, explaining that he'd seen Kahmeel give it to you."

"A post office box," I repeated numbly, taking the key from him. "Box number stamped on it. F-236. There may be a post office close to Kahmeel's apartment, but the downtown offices nearest to where he worked are on Market and on Kennedy. We need to go box shopping!"

"I already have," said Kevin, "while you lay sleeping." He took back the key, and pocketed it.

"Why haven't you said anything to me?"

"First time we've been alone, Matt. Even Rashid doesn't know I've been to the box. He was probing you when he came earlier, hinting to see what you knew, but…"

"You kept it to yourself. My God, man, what did you find?"

The door opened, and Magdalena Elizabeth Rivera came back in. Keith Sutton entered the room behind her, Jacqui Johnson on his heels.

"You'll be out of here by noon, or one o'clock latest," Sutton said, after making sure that I was doing all right. "Ya won't be goin' home after all. Yer goin' to a hotel room. Same digs as yer friend Rashid."

"With Cobalt Woman in tow?" I asked.

Ms. Rivera looked embarassed. Jacqui looked upset. Kevin chuckled humorlessly.

"It's a three bedroom suite," Sutton explained.

"Sweet," I quipped.

"I'll be in a single room," Ms. Rivera explained hastily. "Rashid is in another room. My new partner will sleep on a cot outside your quarters. His name is Earl Benner. I've never met him. He should be here shortly."

"Stein and me'll come and see ya there. Obnobini'll be with us—Jemison, too. We'll have all the time we need to talk, then."

"Am I getting paid for all this?" I asked, half joking.

"'Course y'are," Sutton said, "and so'm I."

"Remind me about Jemison," I said.

"CIA," Sutton said. "Ya met him in Stein's office, when ya met Ognobini and the rest."

"Mr. Jemison is my boss," said Ms. Rivera.

"So," I said, "he's the one who put you on my tail."

"Protection," she replied.

"Front page of the Inquirer!" Jacquie beamed, pushing her way to my side. She set a copy of the morning paper beside me on the bed. The headline read: "Bullets for the Bulletin."

"Clever. They scooped us." I smiled. "In print, at least." The Inquirer was the city's morning paper, our main competitor. The Bulletin didn't hit the streets until evening.

"But the photo," said Jacqui, smiling widely, "is mine. No other journalist has access to you, Matt. Mr. Stein gave the Inquirer permission to grab the photo from our website."

There I was, in pixilated color, asleep in a hospital bed, wired and monitored and with my mouth open in an uncomplimentary gape. "Cute," I said, shooting Jacqui a sarcastic smirk.

"*I* think so," she said quietly, holding me with those gorgeous, lonely eyes.

"Your ten minutes," said Ms. Rivera coolly, "are done."

Magdalena liked me—I think. The feeling wasn't exactly mutual. She was friendly, classy, and pleasant to look at, but I couldn't get used to the fact that the woman carried a semi-automatic handgun and followed people around to make sure nobody killed them. It made it hard to talk to her. I didn't know if she was real. I've never been good at figuring out how women think.

She sensed my distance and tried her best to bridge it. "You are a courageous man, Mr. Clifford," she said outright, shortly after Sutton and Johnson left. "And you are not a puppet."

"Okay," I said, "more like a hamster in a cage. I run. You watch." That hurt her, which I hadn't intended. She was quiet for a while after that. Kevin fidgeted in his chair.

"We are all doing what we can to stop these men," she said finally, staring out the window. Was she complimenting me again? Defending herself? Or both?

Her cell phone rang. "Excuse me," she said tersely. She left the room, closing the door.

"We've gotta get outa here!" I rasped. "Will you help me?"

"What?" Kevin asked cynically. "Why?"

"To follow the key lead. Can't do it here in bed!"

"Well, you'll have to! Besides, I've been to the post office. I've got what Khameel left for you."

"What is it?" I whispered harshly.

"An envelope of his writings. Mostly poems...but there's one in there especially for you."

"We can't look at it here," I argued. "Not with Cobalt Woman in the corner journaling."

"She's on our side, Matt," Kevin countered. "We can trust her. We can trust the rest of them, too."

"Maybe..." *Ali. Wall.* "I've got a charge to keep, Kevin."

"No kidding! And your charge is to stay right here while the pros pick up the pieces."

"No," I barked, pulling the IV needle from my arm. "There are other lives at stake. There's more to this than I've told anyone, even you. Can you help me one more time?" I stood up.

Kevin stood up too, and stared at me wide-eyed. "Are you crazy?"

Probably, I thought. "A bit dizzy," I said. I clawed open the closet and extracted my clothes. I grabbed a plastic bag that held some personal items. Wall's red phone was in the bag. Sutton's pistol was not. I supposed the police had confiscated it. My bloody shirt was also missing.

I stepped into the bathroom. "When Rivera comes back, tell her I had to pee, real bad, and I didn't want to use the bed urinal. I'll talk to her from in here. I'll..."

"She's coming," Kevin said. "And you *are* crazy!"

I locked the bathroom door and started to dress. I heard Ms. Rivera enter. "Where's Mr. Clifford?" she demanded.

"I'm in here!" I said through the door. "Too much to drink. Can't a guy piss in peace?"

She didn't answer me.

"Hey," I said. "These bandages need to be changed. Kinda messy. Could you go get a nurse to redress my arm? I'll be out in a minute."

"You took the IV out," she said flatly. "Why did you take the IV out? I'm buzzing the nurses. Excuse me, Mr. McCarthy, but could you move out of the way? I need to..."

"The buzzer doesn't work," he insisted. "I tried it when you were out. If you wish, I'll go get that nurse for Matt myself." Kevin played his part well.

"No," she said. "No thank you, Mr. McCarthy." She obviously didn't like any of this but didn't know what to do about it either. "I'll get someone to look at his arm and to hook him back up," she said at last, stiffly. "You'd better help him into bed when he's done in there." It was more of an order than a suggestion.

"He's pretty steady on his feet," said Kevin nonchalantly, "and pretty stubborn besides." I knew Kevin was probably smiling then, wryly, out of the left side of his face, stroking his chin.

I heard a woman's sharp sigh, then the sound of high

heels on the tiled floor. The door to the hallway opened, then thudded shut.

I hurried out of the bathroom, without a shirt, one shoe in hand. "Take a look in the hall," I urged, putting on my shoe.

Kevin peeked out. "Coast is clear."

The nurse's station was just around the corner, out of sight of the room. A cop was positioned there. Extra security for Matt Clifford.

We stepped out of the room together and moved quickly down the hallway in the opposite direction.

"Not the elevator," I said.

"Then here!" Kevin shoved open a glass-paneled door.

We hit the stairs running, Kevin in the lead. We descended several flanking flights. That left me weak.

We exited the stairwell at the second floor, and Kevin hurried us down a narrow hall toward the parking garage.

"My car's on this level," he said, as an automatic door slid open to let us into the garage. Twenty yards away, a couple of hospital security guards were talking to someone on a two-way responder. They hadn't seen us, and we didn't want them to. I covered my mouth with my hands so that my labored breathing made no noise. My injured arm hurt terribly.

Between the buzz and the click of the guard's two-way dialog, we heard him say, "On the lookout! Over and out." He cut the call and glanced furtively around.

"We're on the wanted list already!" I whispered from our crouch behind a low-roofed hybrid.

The guards split up, heading toward opposite ends of the garage. They were on the prowl. And what luck!—they had been standing next to Kevin's 2008 metallic green Volkswagen Beetle.

We doubled around another row of vehicles to get closer to the Beetle. Stooping, stopping, crawling, we reached the car unseen. Kevin unlocked it by remote. The guards were hollering to each other, and they didn't hear us open or close our doors. Turning on the power without turning on the engine, Kevin thumbed his window down. From the back seat, he grabbed a Frisbee and flicked it out the window. It sailed magnificently over a long line of cars, struck one on the roof, and then scudded across the concrete floor.

"What's that?" barked one of the guards. As his query echoed in the low-ceilinged room, Kevin fired up and pulled out. The guards shouted. We rocketed past them toward the exit. The Beetle squealed as it spiraled down the ramp. Within seconds, we bulleted past a startled parking cashier, catapulted over a traffic hump, and skidded out onto the Philadelphia streets.

"Godspeed," said Kevin.

"Where're we going?" I cried, turning frantically in my seat to watch the street behind us.

"The Batcave," Kevin shouted.

A police car barreled down the street toward us, lights flashing, siren blaring. We turned abruptly down a side street as the cops sped by on some other urgent errand, thank the stars!

Anxious and watchful, we rolled with the midday traffic through Old City and Society Hill. We crossed Route 95 near the river, and Kevin zigzagged the alleys and avenues that headed us toward the docks. Where Pattison Avenue turns back toward the city, we cut over the railroad tracks and rode a gravel utility road beside a long line of stationary railcars.

When our course was about to dead-end, we turned sharply toward the river onto a strip of crumbling asphalt and headed straight for a bulking, rusted, steel-sided warehouse with hardly an unbroken window on its three-story façade. As Kevin turned his lights on and off in a rhythmic pattern, the warehouse door rolled up like a huge gaping mouth.

We drove right in. Just like Batman into his Batcave!

With a rattle and a groan, the great metal door closed behind   us.

22

Trains, Planes, and Automobiles

Imanghari sat in the center of a circle of interrogation. Four officers stood around him, elbow to elbow. The captain of security sat behind his tiny desk, a smoldering cigarette squeezed between fat, frowning lips. The security room was small, and everyone felt pressed. They jostled one another for space and leaned into their work with a nervous intensity.

Imanghari was not a good liar, but he had a wonderful imagination. His interrogators barely knew the difference between the truth and a lie. They were railroad cops, not special police agents. So Imanghari held his own. While he had been escorted to the room, he had managed to pull Erkin's tiny note from his pocket and pop it in his mouth. It was in his stomach now.

"My name is Abiram al'Kadri," Imanghari insisted. "I am a farmer from the village of Ambi, just west of Temirta in the Uplands. I have been to visit my cousins in Aqtau. My God, a city in the desert! And right on the Caspian! It is so cold there, but so beautiful. So very different from my farm in the hills."

"Who are your cousins?" asked the officer with the metal baton.

"They are on my mother's side," Imanghari declared, flashing a convincing smile, as if engaged in a conversation with a new friend. "My Uncle Zhulduz works at the water-desalination plant. He is a cleanup man. What I do in the barn, he does in the plant—shovels, sweeps, moves things. But he doesn't milk goats."

The officer with the metal baton smiled in spite of himself.

"And he doesn't make much money," Imanghari continued, "but he took me to the cinema twice. We watched an Egyptian comedy and an American Western. I liked the Western!"

The security cops liked Westerns too, and they said so—but of course they had an interrogation to undertake, if the prisoner didn't mind.

"What was the name of the cinema in Aqtau?" pressed the officer with the metal baton. He knew the names of them all and thought that this farmer-imposter would not.

"Mangyshlak Movie House!" Imanghari said enthusiastically. "Four screens. The biggest in the city. Near the botanical gardens. You should see those gardens! It's really amazing what they are growing there. My grandfather used to speak of the terrible, dry deserts of the Caspian."

"Yes," said a skinny guard with a thick black beard, "I know those deserts! Nothing grows there, and not a drop of water to drink for a hundred miles!"

"Like the deserts in the John Wayne movies!" Imanghari exclaimed. "Like the Sahara itself!"

"Colder!" said the skinny guard, his red eyes wide with unwelcomed memory. He shook involuntarily, as if a chill had come over him.

"You have heard of the great Ukrainian poet Taras Shevchenko," Imanghari prattled, warming to his role.

Heads bobbed dubiously up and down, though nobody actually knew of the once-famous poet—except perhaps the captain, whose bushy eyebrows arched, creating a second frown upon his weathered forehead.

"He was exiled to the Caspian deserts in the late 1880s

by the Russian government," Imanghari said.

"The Russians," said a small, stocky guard with a uniform too big for him, "are experts at exile!" The skinny guard whistled through his crooked teeth, a cold, knowing hiss.

"Shevchenko said that the sight of the endless sand and stones would make you feel so dreary that you might as well hang yourself," Imanghari declared.

They laughed. The captain grunted, and shifted the cigarette to the left side of his frowning face.

"Did he hang himself?" asked the small guard.

"No," said Imanghari.

"Look at this!" the captain mumbled impatiently, pointing to a laptop on his desk. He had turned its screen to face the men. On the computer's backlit desktop was a poorly pixilated photo of Imanghari Koval. It had been e-mailed to every police official within the Kazakh state security network. When the Beyneu train captain received it, he printed copies of the photo for all his guards and instructed them to keep an eye on the passengers.

He tapped his laptop, nodded toward Imanghari, shook his head in a slow negative wag, rolled his eyes—and sighed through flared nostrils.

"If you take the glasses off…" appealed the guard with the metal baton. They had already taken the glasses off. Imanghari had been squinting since.

The captain drew a breath through the limp cigarette. It glowed red for a last tired moment and then died. He blew the smoke out through his nose.

"If you pretend that he is not wearing the clothing of a farmer from the Uplands…" offered the skinny, bearded guard. "Or that the clothing does not smell like the clothing of a farmer from the Uplands…" He wrinkled his nose.

"Or that his hair is longer, and darker, and with less grey so that he looks younger than…than Mr. al'Kadri," added the short guard, weakly.

The captain chewed on his cigarette as though it were a piece of taffy.

"When his eyes are closed and his mouth is open and he is lying back sleeping," said the guard with the baton, anxiously, "there is a similarity in the cheeks and the nose and..." He put his baton back in his belt.

"I am Abiram al'Kadri," said Imanghari, emboldened by the captain's obvious skepticism. "Is my ID not in order?" he asked, looking from the captain to the guards and back again.

The guards shifted nervously. The man with the baton coughed into his hands and looked out the window at the passing landscape.

"There has been a mistake—" Imanghari began.

"Mistake?" snapped the captain from behind his desk. "This is a matter of state security, and I assure you there has been no mistake! Vigilance is necessary in every age, and especially in our own. It is no mistake to be vigilant."

The captain turned the laptop back around and stared at it for a long time. He took the damp, dead cigarette from his lips and laid it in an ashtray on his desk. "You men may go back to your duties," he said to the guards, without looking at them. "Keep up your vigil. And be more discerning as you compare the passengers with the photos I have given you." His eyes were steel. His frown seemed to color his face with discontent. The guards saluted and backed out the door.

Imanghari sat quietly in his chair.

"We must be very careful, Mr. al'Kadri, to maintain the unity of the republic. A pair of subversive fundamentalist militants is being sought by the national authorities, and you happen to resemble one of them...in some ways. I am sorry for the trouble we have put you through, but I am sure you understand it is all for the good of the state."

"Yes, sir. Of course, sir," said Imanghari with great flourish. "I know what it is like to have a fox skulking around the farm!

I am only glad to have made your acquaintance—and that of your good men." But he didn't dare get up from his chair. Not without being dismissed. He reached clumsily, fumbling for his glasses on the captain's desk. He put them on, blinked, and smiled awkwardly. The captain, frowning, watched his every move.

Their eyes locked and held. Imanghari lowered his, and the captain rose suddenly to extend his hand. Imanghari stood up, unsteadily, and the two men shook hands. "Mr. al'Kadri, we have about one hundred miles more to Maqat. Should we need your assistance further, I will send a man to bring you. But I think you have served us fully, and I hope the rest of your ride will be a quiet one."

"*Asalaam Aleykum,*" said Imanghari, as he opened the door to let himself out.

The captain nodded. He sat quietly for a long while after Imanghari left. Should he call Aqtau and ask about Mr. al'Kadri? No, he was sure of the matter, so why make himself look foolish in the eyes of the office at Aqtau?

He opened a small wooden box on top of his desk, took out another cigarette, and stuck it between his lips.

Ali made friends of a small boy who had run through the dining car and tripped over his own shoelaces. The little fellow sprawled at Ali's feet and was so embarrassed that he cried. Ali picked him up, told him a few jokes in Egyptian Arabic, and ordered him a glass of chocolate milk.

"You'd best get back to your parents," Ali said, when the boy had finished the last drop and licked the glass as clean as he possibly could.

"I'm with my mother," the boy said, "and she won't miss me right now. She is sleeping."

"Danil!" said a commanding feminine voice. The boy was startled.

"Sleeping?" said Ali with a smile.

The woman was young, but her eyes were old. A touch

of the Mongol steppes was in the shape of her face, the set of her eyes. She was short, pretty, and not afraid to accept Ali's invitation to sit down in the company of a strange man. Her name was Deri Sesin. She was the recent widow of a Russian soldier who died in the first days of the Mideast War. He had been deployed in Azerbaijan. The boy was their only child. Mother and son were on their way back to Russia after a visit with relatives in Kazakhstan.

Ali bought them a late supper, and they ate quietly, thankfully.

"Bombs," she said, pushing aside her emptied plate, "know no borders and they have no soul. They fall from the sky and tear holes in the world. For every soldier they kill, a dozen hearts are broken to pieces which can never be put back together again." She didn't cry when she said this, but she held her son closer. "Danil's name means 'divine justice,'" she said bitterly. "He is four years old."

Danil is a Hebrew name, Ali mused. Staring at the boy, he thought of his own children, safe at home in Cherry Hill, New Jersey. In America.

Safe? He thought of Matt. Wall. Red Square. The last few desperate weeks. Imanghari. The silversmith. The need to escape, to warn his loved ones of the destruction and the death that hovered over the earth like a hawk in the hunt, waiting to fall swiftly and unmercifully upon its prey. He looked around him for a moment, distracted, and then turned his attention back upon Deri.

"What kind of a world has God given us?" she asked, looking out upon the rural miles that ran past them in the blurred and muted colors of summer. "Men are born as helpless babes. They suck at their mother's breasts. They crawl. They walk. They laugh and run and wrestle one another. They love and marry. They smoke and drink and argue about freedom and power and wealth and women. They build things and then they tear them down again. They go off to war as if it is a grand adventure. As if they are immortal sons of the gods, riding their wild horses behind the Great Khan as he sweeps across the globe on his glorious mission to subdue the earth."

Danil climbed out of his mother's lap and under the table in search of a piece of bread that had fallen from his plate.

"And then they die," she said. "And the women are left to raise the sons to repeat the fathers' folly. I'll be damned before I ever let my son follow a man to war!"

"I am sorry," Ali said sincerely. He thought of his wife, Jumana, sitting late at night, alone, watching the news, wondering if he were alive or dead. He felt the hand of little Danil on his knee beneath the table, and his heart was deeply moved.

Sympathetically, almost unconsciously, he reached out to take the hands of the woman sitting across from him. There were tears at the edge of his eyes. She squeezed his hands once, but didn't speak. Her eyes were locked on the world outside their window.

On a parallel track, a south-bound train rolled past them in a long slash of color and a loud metallic drumming that stilled the conversations in the car.

"Soldiers," said Deri Sesin. "Heading south again. President Malashenko, God damn his soul, has ordered the sons of Kazakhstan to an exercise of military display along the Uzbeki border.

"The Peace! What do men know of peace? They hate it! Russian troops are dancing outside Georgia. The pride of Europe is toasting the Turks on their ships in the Caspian. The Turkish army is massing along the Syrian border and crowding the docks at Tarsus. The swords and banners of Uzbekistan are shuffling north to hold a party of military solidarity with the Kazakhs of Malashenko. Break out the cognac!"

"I would not speak so openly of Malashenko," Ali said carefully and quietly, but he admired her spunk and her poetic cynicism. Deri Sesin turned her eyes from the passing train and looked at him intently.

"I am not a Kazazkhi," she said simply, searching him deeper than he knew. "Nor are you," she added.

He opened his mouth, but found no words. She smiled for the first time, and withdrew her hands from his. "We are both seeking something that no man can find," she said. "And what we *don't* want will hunt us down until we are so weary that we cannot run another mile. Then we, too, will die."

"What are we seeking?"

"The freedom to live free."

"Is there nowhere you can go?" he asked, diverting the issue from himself.

"And you?" she said.

Ali wondered at her question. Then he asked, almost stupidly, "Are you Jewish?"

Her eyes flashed, then faded. "I am nothing," she said, "other than the mother of Danil. That is who I am." She smiled again, sadly, but with a strange defiance in her eyes. "And I thank you, perfect stranger, for your kindness and your company."

They sat silent then. That he had struck a nerve, he knew—and that he was riding with a Jewess, he was fairly sure. Danil crawled up beside him and rested his head against Ali's enfolding arm.

Imanghari was back in his seat. The officer with the metal baton had sought him out again, fascinated by the passenger's interest in Western films, and wanting somehow to make amends for the false arrest. The two had already voted for *The Good, the Bad and the Ugly* as their mutual favorite Clint Eastwood Western. Imanghari laid claim to having seen fourteen John Wayne films. The guard insisted he had seen at least seventeen.

"Oh, but have you seen *Nomad?*" asked the guard with

the baton. "It is like an American Western but without the Indians!"

"Yes!" said Imanghari, animated by the conversation. "In 2006, I think. Directed by Sergei Bodrov and Ivan Passer. Filmed right here in Kazakhstan. It won many awards. And my favorite parts are when the Mongol warriors come thundering over the horizon on their horses, ready for the battle!"

"Oh, and another movie I never tire of is *Dances with Wolves*," said the guard. "The actor is an American named Kevin Costner. He plays an army officer who is sick of war." He looked up from the conversation, to see who was near. "And who *isn't* sick of war?" he whispered bitterly.

"I have not seen it," said Imanghari honestly. "The movie, I mean." They had all seen war, close up or far away.

"It is a sad tale," said the guard. "A lonely tale, about a man who doesn't fit among his own. He doesn't really fit anything at all…until he meets a woman. And with her, he can go anywhere."

"Yes…" said Imanghari dreamily, almost forgetting he was a fugitive fleeing for his life, completely forgetting—for a moment—that he was supposed to be Abiram al'Kadri, a farmer from the Kazakh Uplands, married with children. But he didn't give himself away. And while the man with the metal baton was lost in the wilds of the American West, Imanghari stared out the window at the dark blue Kazakh night.

Maqat. Atyraū province. An oil town with streets so full of potholes that they looked like they'd been bombed. No hotels. One petrol station. A hard-working, dirty industrial town that nobody visited for the sake of leisure or pleasure. The train stopped long enough for a few passengers to disembark and a few more to get on. Rail-bound oil tankers choked the terminal. Soldiers crowded the station. Two more military trains were headed south.

Danil was asleep under Ali's arm, head upon his lap. Ali was thinking of Matt Clifford and the Bulletin. He wondered where in the world Bradley Wall was at that moment. He stared at the back of his own left hand. Would he ever see home again? He was strangely depressed, and he wondered how Imanghari was getting along. He thought of Jack Pascov and said, gently, "I have a friend in Israel."

"There is no Israel," said Deri Sesin grimly. "God has not kept his promise."

"But there *is* an Israel," Ali insisted, rising to the defense of the battered little nation on the Mediterranean. Though he was a Muslim, he had a fascination for Israel. "A few more years and Israel will celebrate seventy years of nationhood!"

"No," said Deri Sesin, "Rome squashed Israel with a hard-heeled boot nearly twenty centuries ago. Allah moved into the Promised Land without invitation. The soldiers of Christendom have made periodic, violent incursions. The children of Jacob have wandered the world like they wandered the desert of Egypt. Did God wander with them, even then? No, the stories are only stories. And if God was ever with 'his people,' he died with them at Auschwitz and Dachau. Let Rachel weep!"

The miles rolled by as the train rattled over the rails through the Kazakh countryside. Hills and trees. Windblown sand. Oil wells, peasant shacks, and abandoned factories. And always the trains heading southward, filled with young men in uniform staring out the windows into an uncertain future.

When the train pulled into Aqtobe at 7:15 in the evening, Imanghari had to be awakened. He opened his eyes to someone poking him in the chest with a metal baton.

"Mr. Imanghari Koval," said the man with the baton, "you are under arrest."

Imanghari came wide awake with a look of horror. When the officer with the baton saw Imanghari's terrified expression, his own face fell. "I am so sorry, Mr. al'Kadri!"

he exclaimed sincerely. "I was only joking. A miserable jest!
I beg your pardon, a thousand times."

Imanghari's face relaxed, and he began to chuckle.

"We are in Aqtobe, Mr. al'Kadri," said the guard, upset
with himself. "I thought I would wake you by…but…I have
a horrid sense of humor! Can you ever forgive me?"

Imanghari stood up and actually embraced the man,
he was so happy to be at his destination. Together, they
stepped out of the car onto the station platform. Together,
they chatted as they walked the length of the long train.
When the officer with the baton had pointed out the way to
the taxi station, they embraced once more with genuine
laughter and a sense of sincere camraderie.

"*Asalaam Aleykum,*" said Imanghari, waving and walking
away.

"*Asalaam Aleykum,* Mr. al'Kadri!" shouted the man with
the metal baton.

Amid the bustle of the discharging train, soldiers milled
about the station, awaiting their turn to embark. Two
policemen stood on a raised luggage platform observing
Imanghari bid farewell to his new friend. They heard the
guard's loud parting blessing. Looking together at the photo
in their notebook, they let Imanghari pass as they continued
their watch of the passengers getting off the train.

"I am a married man from another land," Ali said as he
walked beside Deri Sesin and her son through the crowded
railway station. "A good husband, I believe, and a loving
father," he added, lifting Danil into his arms to carry him the
distance from the train to an automatic walkway that moved
them out of the station and onto the sidewalk of a busy city
street. "My intentions in this ruse are honorable. I have
nothing in mind other than a play to get me safely to
Pavlodar."

"And to freedom," said Deri Sesin.

"As Allah wills," Ali said quietly.

"Perhaps he does," she said.

They were both headed to Pavlodar. Their tickets had them on the same flight out of Aqtobe. Their designated seats—remarkably, almost miraculously—were directly across the aisle from each other on the plane. They would pretend to be one family, traveling together. Deri had agreed.

"And you will call him Papa while we are together," she said to Danil. It was the only time she almost came to tears.

From Pavlodar, Deri and Danil had reservations for a flight to Sheremetyevo International Airport in Moscow.

"Small world," Ali said. "I wish…" It was tempting to think of escaping Kazakhstan on the same Moscow flight as Deri, but he knew how dangerous that would be. Not only for him, but for Deri and Danil. He must stick with faithful Imanghari. They must meet Wall tomorrow, on the steppe.

"We all wish," she said.

Ali hailed a taxi, and the three of them bundled inside. A policeman at the curb barely paid them any mind. He was looking for a lone, bearded American to match the picture in his hand

Imanghari saw the taxi pull out. He whistled for one of his own. The sight of Ali with the pretty woman and her little boy pulled at him pitifully. He felt terribly alone—almost abandoned—a feeling that was like an old coat to him, he had worn it so often, so long. But he shook it off. "Home to the farm," he said aloud, squinting into the cloudless sky before pulling the cab door shut.

"Which farm, sir?" asked the cab driver.

"My farm in Ambi," said Imanghari with a laugh. "But I don't want you to take me there. I need a ride to the airport…*then* it is home to the farm."

Aktyubinsk Airport, about two and a half miles south of Aqtobe, was a small terminal with space for five airliners.

But four of those spaces were presently vacant. A solitary Air Astana Boeing 757, loaded and fueled, awaited the green light to pull out into the runway.

Imanghari was settled in an aisle seat near the rear of the plane. Ali had a seat near the wings, directly opposite Deri and Danil. The plane was a three-seater on both sides of the aisle, and only half the seats were taken. Ali moved over next to Deri—the little family appeared cozy and content.

The passengers were an international mix. Ali listened intently to the buzz of conversation. He recognized half a dozen languages, including German and Greek. An Armenian couple sat only a few rows ahead of him. A Ukrainian Jew was already asleep across the aisle, a few seats behind. In First Class (he noted upon entering the plane) were three western European businessmen who appeared to be together. He thought he heard them speaking in Polish. The plane appeared free of police. There were no soldiers. He knew exactly where Imanghari was seated.

The plane took off on time. Once airborne, Ali leaned his seat back and said quietly to Deri, "I am going to sleep. Will you wake me in one hour exactly?"

"Yes, dear," she said without a smile.

"Good dreams, Papa," said Danil, a wide grin on his small face. His mother stroked his hair.

Ali woke to a kiss upon his cheek. He blushed.

"One hour," Deri said. "Would you please take Danil to the bathroom? He has to go."

Ali blinked the slumber from his eyes as he led Danil down the aisle. Imanghari watched him come with bland disinterest. Ali spoke to Danil as they passed. A dark-skinned Kazakhi with his nose in a book raised his eyes to study the father and his son. He smiled and turned the page.

Deri rested her head on Ali's shoulder. Her lips were within inches of his ear. "You are Muslim," she said. "The president of Kazakhstan is Muslim."

"My parents are Afghani," he said quietly, turning his head toward hers. "I was born in America. Raised in a Muslim community near Middletown, New Jersey. A big town in a small state along the shores of the Atlantic Ocean."

"America," she said. Her eyes were closed. She was very pretty, very young. What a strange world it was.

"I love America," he said.

"Freedom," she said.

"I wish…" he began. But there could be no promises. He didn't know if he would make it out of Kazakhstan alive. But if he did, maybe he and Jumana could bring Deri and Danil to America. To freedom. But he dare not say so.

"We all wish," she breathed, and then she was asleep.

In the pocket of the back of the seat in front of him, Ali found a few magazines to read. One was a Kazakhi government tract extolling the virtues of the regime of Ulmes Malashenko.

Elected president in 2011 after the political defeat of longtime president Nursultan Nazarbayev, the anti-Zionist Ulmes Malashenko quickly placed Muslims in key positions of power. Though the nation was a fairly even mix of Orthodox Christians and Muslims, Malashenko tipped the scales toward a closer affinity with the Islamic nations to the south.

Disdaining the political reach of Putin while keeping the lines of commerce and communication open, the Kazakhi president wooed the nations of the European Union with crude oil and enriched uranium for nuclear power facilities. Though Malashenko refrained from public denunciation of Israel, his convictions concerning the Jews echoed those of his political crony, Mahmoud Ahmadinejad, former president of war-battered Iran. Malashenko and Turkish

Prime Minister Gökhan Savas (another avid anti-Zionist) were cousins. The two spent a good deal of time together hunting in the Kazakh hills of Qostanay.

Ulmes.

"He cannot die," Ali said aloud—for that was the meaning of the name *Ulmes*. Deri stirred. She sighed. Ali almost turned to kiss her forehead. He smiled at himself. *I am a wanted fugitive,* he told himself, *who must thank Allah for every blessing in his life.*

Imanghari sat awake and dreamed of the house by the lake.

Without incident, the 757 landed in Pavlodar. It was 11:17 p.m.

Ali and his small clan disembarked with kind words for the attendants and thanks to the pilot. Making their way through a crowded terminal filled with military men and their families, they found a quiet corner in which to say their good-byes.

"Good dreams, Papa," said little Danil—and Ali broke. He got down on his knees and wrapped his arms around the little boy. "Why are you crying, Papa?"

"Tears are a gift," Ali said. "And I give you mine. They bind our hearts and heal our wounds. And I think they make us stronger."

Deri was crying too, but she wiped the tears as quickly as they came. Ali picked Danil up and placed him in his mother's arms. Her fingers found Ali's sleeve and held it for a moment.

"I have your e-mail address and your residence address in Krasnogorsk," he said. "I am sorry that I cannot give you mine. As soon as I am free…" His hand moved to his heart. "I will contact you. Allah send his peace to you. Allah send his angels."

Deri held her son close. "Peace," she echoed, lips drawn tight.

"Thank you for trusting me," said Ali. "For helping me

in the way that you have." Deri's eyes held his. He wanted to kiss her, but he restrained himself.

"Freedom," she said, forcing a smile, wiping her eyes again.

"Take this," he said hoarsely, putting money in her hand.

"No," she said, refusing it. "You need it more than I do. I have my husband's death allowance. And the apartment is paid for by the state. There are others who help me when help is needed. You are alone. I…am not."

"Then I must go," Ali said. He placed his hand upon Danil's forehead in silent blessing. Then he kissed the boy's head, said "Good-bye, Divine Justice. Good-bye, Deri Sesin," and hurried down an escalator toward an exit for the street.

Imanghari clambered off the plane and looked for Ali. He knew he could not be seen with him, but he hoped to follow him somehow. The directions Erkin had written for him had long been ingested, digested, passed out, and flushed down the toilet. He hadn't memorized them. He had no way to know how to find his contact.

But Ali was nowhere in sight. Imanghari searched the terminal twice, bathrooms included. Once he thought he spotted Ali, but it wasn't him. Young soldiers were everywhere. Mothers and sisters and girlfriends and wives were weeping. Then he saw the woman and her son. Did they know about him? Would they trust him? Could he risk speaking with them.

"Please forgive my intrusion on your refreshment," said Imanghari. Deri and Danil were eating a small supper at a table in the terminal's food court. "But I am a friend of…of the man whom you were sitting with upon the plane."

She recognized Imanghari from the plane ride—and the train ride, too—but who was he really? The kind stranger had said nothing about a traveling companion.

"He is my husband," she said simply. "He is taking care

of business elsewhere in the terminal at this moment. And I have never met you."

"A friend of Papa?" said Danil, smiling.

"I know he pretended to be your husband," Imanghari said carelessly, desperately. "I would have found a wife or a girlfriend myself if I could have, but I got myself arrested instead. Oh!" What if he upset her, and she called for security? He would be arrested again! "Please," he pleaded quietly, passionately. "He is the only friend I have in the world at the moment—a wonderful man—and I have pledged myself to him, to help him escape. If he didn't tell you about me, it was for love of me, so that if he were caught, I would not be caught with him. We have run across half the country together, and our running is not done. We had instructions on where to meet—a common destination in the city, but traveling separately to avoid detection. I lost my instructions—ate them actually—on purpose, to keep from being discovered." He threw his hands up, in spite of himself. "This must seem terribly ridiculous to you, but…"

"To help him escape," she repeated softly.

"Yes," said Imanghari weakly.

"I believe you," she said. "But I have no idea where he went. Only that he has gone out of the building on the north side of the terminal. That is all I know."

"Thank you," said Imanghari. "*Asalaam Aleykum.*"

"Peace be to you, too."

"Good dreams, friend of Papa!"

Imanghari hit the street, searching up and down with his keen eyes. Ali wasn't there. Road signs pointed to the city, but Imanghari didn't know if the city was his destination. The rendezvous could be anywhere. His instructions were forever gone. He should have read them thoroughly when he received them, should have memorized them fully. Why hadn't he? What a fool he'd been!

Running away was his specialty. But running into the

forest in search of a single tree, with no light and no map and no sense of direction whatsoever? "I am lost!" he said aloud.

Perhaps he could take a taxi into town. Hire a man to drive him around while he looked for Ali anywhere, everywhere. "No," he said to himself. "Ali will not be anywhere and everywhere. He will be somewhere, hidden, waiting for me. And if I do not arrive, then he will come back looking for me. And so I am not lost, and I am not going to get lost. I am going to stay right here…and wait!"

The night was cold, and Imanghari was dressed for it. But it was warmer inside. He could get himself something to eat and settle into a comfortable seat near the doors where Ali had exited. From there, he could watch for his friend.

I am Abiram al'Kadri, Imanghari rehearsed, as he headed back into the terminal. *I am a farmer from the village of Ambi, just west of Temirta in the Uplands. I have been to visit my cousins in Aqtau.*

He hurried back to the food court. The woman and her child were gone. He bought himself a sandwich and a soda, and ambled nervously toward the exit. The terminal had emptied somewhat, and it was harder to blend into the crowd. He looked for a bathroom, and there on a bulletin board outside the restrooms was a poster of himself! And one of Ali.

Numbed, he entered the men's room and studied himself in the mirror. He didn't look like Imanghari Koval. And so he *wasn't* Imanghari Koval. *I am Abiram al'Kadri, a farmer from Ambi…*

A new wave of soldiers arrived. Another flight was on its way to move them south. Airport security was thick. Warily, Imanghari took up his post by the northern doors.

Something big was up. There were too many soldiers for a mere show of military bravado. A major initiative was underway—connected in part, Imanghari knew, to the work of his cell and its networks. Before Malashenko, the army had smoked out the cells. With Malashenko in power, the army was looking to the cells for a political alliance that served Islam in a straightforward way.

Islam was not dead as a world power. The Prophet fought for Islam until his own death. His successors fought in his place. No defeat was ultimate. Iraq and Afghanistan were tied to the Peace, but the Muslim cause still lived. Syria and Iran were down and out, but not Islam itself. For Islam was the truth of Allah. The prophecies must be fulfilled. The Mahdi—the Muslim messiah—must still come. Islam would cover the earth as the snows cover the high Kazakh mountains—fully, finally, forever.

But was that the world Imanghari wanted to live in? Was that the world his father had fought for? A world held in the stranglehold of Sharia?

What *had* his father fought for? Communism? The Soviet Union? Liberty? A future for his children?

What was liberty? Surely it was more than running and hiding. Surely it was more than planting bombs and then running some more. When did the running end? When all your enemies were dead?

Who was the enemy? The policeman with the metal baton? Ali the Afghan? These were enemies who had become friends.

What of the enemies of Islam—Israel, the United States, Putin, Romano?

Where was his father now? How was he involved in this military maneuver?

Though the years and the miles had separated Imanghari from the man whose blood flowed in his veins, Imanghari thought about him often. It was a strange contemplation, fraught with guilt and pain and longing. His father had not been cruel. He had simply been an utter stranger to the world within Imanghari's soul. And so Imanghari had run away and never gone back.

He was running still. What would his father say if he knew?

Where had Ali gone? Would he come back to the airport looking for him? How far was it to the house on the lake? How would they get out of the country? Would Ali and his friend take Imanghari to America? Would there be bombs there, too? What about the silversmith? The 20th was the day after tomorrow!

"Sir," said the man in the uniform. "Can I help you?"

"Oh, thank you," said Imanghari pleasantly. He had not seen the security guard approaching. "I have been waiting for some time for my brother to come and get me. I flew in from Aqtobe around 11:15, and I'm sure he'll be here shortly."

"You have been sitting here for over an hour," the guard stated flatly. "There is no loitering allowed. Once your business in the terminal is complete, you must leave the building within a reasonable time."

"He is late for me, yes," said Imanghari, "but might I not wait a few minutes more?"

"I'm sorry," said the guard, without emotion. "But I have given you one hour. There are benches outside. Have you called your brother? Is he on his way?"

"Yes, I have called," lied Imanghari, "and he is on his way. It is warmer in here of course, and—"

The guard gestured impatiently. Imanghari got up reluctantly. The door opened by itself as he approached. He shivered at the cool, damp breath of night that touched him as he walked outside.

Rather than sit on a cold stone bench, Imanghari paced back and forth on the airport portico, passing in and out of the orange glow of the overhanging lights. It was well past midnight. His cell phone was dead, the battery long since depleted. He had no way to recharge it.

A security police car pulled up to the curb as he paced. It

moved as he moved, stopped when he stopped. A loud crackle sent a momentary shock of alarm through him, followed by the amplified voice of an officer of the law. "It is past the hour of curfew," said the man in the car through the loudspeaker on his roof. "If you have business in the terminal, go inside. If you have no business in the terminal, you must go inside elsewhere. The streets are closed. You are in violation of curfew. This is your only warning. Thank you."

"Thank you?" Imanghari snapped, staring in disbelief at the car beside him. The policemen hadn't even put his window down. Like prodding cattle! Let the man get out of the car and *then* ask him to move!

Imanghari looked back toward the terminal doors. The guard who had evicted him was standing there, frowning.

Where to go?

Imanghari threw up his hands in a gesture of frustration, and set off immediately across the parking lot in the direction of town. A residential street was within sight. The police car followed.

"What do you want?" Imanghari grumbled to the headlights behind him, but he didn't look back. "I'm going home, all right? My brother didn't come for me, and I've got to walk home. Curfew be damned!"

The car pulled up alongside him. The loudspeaker crackled. "You are in violation of curfew, and you must go inside."

"Put your window down!" Imanghari growled, his finger against the windshield.

"I can hear you," said the patrolman from inside his car.

"I live on the other side of town!" Imanghari said. "I was waiting for my brother who has been delayed. The terminal guard will not let me wait inside. You will not let me wait outside. What am I to do but walk home? Will *you* give me a ride?"

The window came down. "Where do you live?" said the

policeman, sympathetically.

"The…uh…Gaukhar Commons," said Imanghari. The name was on a billboard at the edge of the parking lot—a housing project advertisement.

"That is quite a distance," the policeman affirmed. "Get in the back seat. I will take you. My shift is over."

"Your shift is over," echoed Imanghari as he climbed reluctantly into the cruiser. What had he gotten himself into?

"How long have you lived at the Commons?" the policeman asked as he turned his car toward the city. "They are very new homes, and I have wondered what they are like."

"Oh, they are very nice, I hear…all things are nice when new," Imanghari said. "But I do not live there myself. My brother has just moved into one of the apartments, and I am staying with him for a few days before going home to my farm in Ambi."

"You look like a farmer," the policeman noted. "My father is a farmer. But you are a long way from Ambi."

"I have been in Aqtau, working with the horticulturists at the botanical gardens. We are making many things grow that never grew there in the desert before."

"Aqtau! Is it cold?"

"Very much so!"

"My name is Ulzhan Kuandyk. I patrol the parking lots."

"My name is Abiram al'Kadri." *And I am lost.*

Two men in a rusty pickup truck saw Imanghari get into the cruiser.

"That is him," said the driver. "Keep your eye on them. Remember those taillights. Make sure you note which street they enter first."

Without stopping, he did a wide loop in the airport parking lot, pulled out onto the exit lane, and sped toward town in pursuit.

23

The Batcave

Kevin got out of the car. I just sat there, staring.

The warehouse we'd driven into looked like a movie set for a science fiction film or the technical development department for an undercover intelligence agency. Maybe it was an indoor junkyard, a private flea market...or, as Kevin had said, the Batcave!

A couple of cars were up on lifts. But they weren't just cars. They were artistic automotive creations—futuristic vehicles that looked like they could fly or swim or (with a little imagination) travel through time.

Long tables stretched in front of me covered with an orderly collection of hardware of all shapes and sizes. Electronic components. Computers and monitors. Metal spools with cable, wire, rope, and chain. Light bulbs in boxes and buckets. Various tools were hung on hooks, in neat procession, all around the tables.

Light fixtures of a dozen kinds were attached to the high ceiling. But the only light in use was a large hanging sphere of snow-white brilliance that chased the shadows from every corner of the massive room.

The walls were painted a deep golden yellow.

The wall to my left was plastered with posters, photographs, and pages ripped from magazines and newspapers. A large bulletin board was fastened to the wall, covered with handwritten notes.

The wall to my right was a showcase of gadgetry, shelved in sections that allowed for items of all kinds: ancient radios, old TVs, phonographs, coffee makers, microwave ovens, sewing machines, kerosene heaters, telephones, typewriters, cash registers, toy trucks, and gumball machines—a flea market mogul's delight!

Against the back wall was a side-by-side lineup of dozens of identical army-green filing cabinets, each drawer labeled. Above the cabinets were bookshelves stretching toward the ceiling, filled with books, each volume straight, labeled, and organized for reference.

The whole place was one big, fascinating workshop—a remarkably ordered cosmos of creativity.

Then I saw the remarkable creator of this cosmos.

He was Korean, and his face was one big smile.

Out of the car and on my feet in the middle of the warehouse, I shook hands with Sam Wong Lee.

"Sam boards at my house," said Kevin, "in a couple of rooms on the third floor. He's the younger brother of Paul Yong Lee, another boarder at the McCarthy Hotel. Paul and his wife and kids take up the whole second floor. Paul's the guy trying to unwrap the files we copied from Khameel's hard drive—the guy who broke into the Pentagon's computer system, a man with a cyber-mind who dreams in digital and speaks JavaPerl as a second language. And Sam here is a pack rat inventor who works with his hands." Sam's smile morphed into a grin full of perfect teeth. "Dr. Seuss in 3D. Thomas Edison on steroids. Anything you can make or break, Sam can re-envision, remold, resurrect, and recharge. He makes flying robots out of transistor radios."

"Well…almost," Sam said. His grin grew wider, if that were possible.

"The Lees are Christians," Kevin said, "members of the

Renewal Presbyterian congregation, the same church I attend."

In spite of the mass of miscellany that covered the tables in the center of the room, the floor was immaculate, uncluttered, and swept clean. Brooms of varied shapes and sizes stood next to a fleet of vacuum cleaners in a corner. A collection of dust pans of different shapes and colors hung upon the wall, like pictures in a gallery.

I noticed that all the windows that appeared broken on the outside were framed and sealed from the inside with a second, solid sheet of tinted glass. Sam saw me staring.

"No pigeons in my rafters!" He laughed. "Nothing but light comes in the windows. And no light goes out, and very little sound."

"What is all this?" I asked, astounded.

"My shop," he said.

"How long have you had this place?"

"Three, four years maybe. My brother Paul and I bought it from the city. A rusted shell, the place was trashed. I turned a lot of that trash into sculptures. There's a gallery upstairs. I can show you."

"Another time, Sam," Kevin said. "We've got some urgent business, and we need your help."

"Urgent?" Sam asked.

Kevin turned to me. "We've got to add another mind to the brain trust, Matt. I'll vouch for Sam. We need him badly."

"For what?" I blurted.

"Safe haven, for one thing," Kevin answered sharply. "I gave in to your claustrophobic frenzy and played Great Escape with you. Now we're fugitives! Trust me—we need Sam."

"Okay," I sighed.

"Three things, Sam," Kevin said, striding toward the only table not stacked high with gadgets. "A clean desk, a fast car, and permission to pick your brains."

"And I could use a shirt," I said.

"How fast does the car have to be?" Sam asked.

"Real fast," said Kevin, "but the car comes last."

Kevin strode back to his VW and pulled a briefcase out of the trunk. From the briefcase, he extracted a manila envelope. From the envelope, he pulled a disheveled, dog-eared stack of typewriter paper.

"This was in Kahmeel's post office box," he said, handing it to me. "This is what he wanted you to have. Poems. Lots of them. And one just for you."

I sat down on a bench at the table and picked slowly through the papers. Kahmeel's poetry, typed on his old typewriter!

 Love poems. Nature poems. Free verse about Hogback Mountain in Oregon, about the lakes and the trees and the cool summer breeze. All of it very well written. Kevin read over my shoulder. Sam sat down on the other side of the table, watching us.

Poems about cats. A poem for Rashid. One for their mother. Prayers. Koranic verses. And then, "Look at this," I said, setting one poem aside from the rest.

It was titled LIBERTY. Handwritten in the top left corner, were the letters "M.L.C." — my initials.

"That's you, Matt," said Kevin. "That's the one."

"Puzzles in poetry," I sighed. It had been hard enough to figure out Ali's cryptic clues — and he knew me like a brother. Kahmeel hardly knew me at all.

"Kahmeel is telling us something," Kevin said. "He died trying to get this to you."

"He typed it up like this so that it couldn't be traced to him on his computer," I said.

"He hoped to live…to go home again," said Kevin. "But he wanted to make sure we knew the information that he was afraid to tell us to our faces. He trusted us to figure it out. Let's get on with it!"

"Figure what out?" asked Sam.

"Where the bombs will be planted," said Kevin, looking at Sam. He shoved his hands in his pockets and stared up at the ceiling. "Where they may already be planted…all over the city."

"Bombs!" Sam coughed.

"Bombs," I echoed.

The poem, in four stanzas, neatly typed and without error, was this:

In the city, the city, the city of love,
*   where brother and brother abide,*
Secrets are hidden although they are bidden
*   to come out and say where they hide.*
The mountains they call me, they woo me away
*   from the shadows that weigh on my soul.*
The secrets, they whisper in words that are key
*   to the pieces, and then to the whole.*

On the wings, on the wings, on the wings of a dove,
*   I would rise and fly west on the wind,*
But I cannot fly free if I don't help them see,
*   for the conscience is slave to the friend.*
Some men like to push and some men like to pull,
*   but my soul, it is neither and none.*
It is gentle and meek and it kisses the cheek
*   like a breeze in the warm summer sun.*

In the city, the city, the city of hate,
*   where brother and brother have dared,*
Are the seeds of dark dying, of wailing and crying,
*   of plotting that's long been prepared.*
The bell has stopped ringing, the hall where they prayed
*   is as silent as death at the dawn.*
And the founder stands tall and he stares with blind eyes

at the graves lying cold in the lawn.
A phrase was once coined that "Dead men tell no tales,"
  but that's not always true of the dead.
Some shout, and their words are a thousand to one
  where the blood of the ages runs red.
Oh! I long for the summers where fathers and mothers
  still live, laughing long in their play.
Where never is heard a discouraging word…

"And the skies are not cloudy all day," I quoted, though the words were not on the paper.

"He didn't finish it!" Sam declared.

"Yes, he did," said Kevin. "The artist in him left that tired old verse out. Let's not get hung up on it. He was simply letting the reader imagine the end…and the end was out west, where Kahmeel's heart has been all along."

"So…what's he saying?" I complained. I hated these games. Life and death hung on our interpretation of the verses, and how could we ever know the mind of a dead man?

"Don't fry any brain cells," Sam said quietly. "I've got just what you need to figure this thing out."

"What?" I threw my hands in the air. "Have you invented a séance machine that can speak to the dead?"

"I wouldn't dare such a thing," Sam said, unmoved by my sarcasm. "I have a computer program that my brother Paul and I worked on together that might just be able to read between the lines. You'll have to give me some first thoughts, though. Break the poem down as much as you can yourself…naturally."

"Naturally!" I said acidly.

"Yes," said Sam, unruffled. "First natural impressions. First thoughts. Like finding shapes in clouds. What do you hear your friend saying…naturally?"

"Go ahead, Matt," Kevin urged me. "Give it a shot. I'll join you in it."

"Well…okay," I mumbled, looking at the poem again. "The first verses…that whole section about the city. He's obviously…well, it seems obvious…"

"Natural," Sam said, smiling.

"Yeah, natural," I echoed cynically. "He's talking about Philadelphia," I declared. "The city of love where brothers abide."

"Makes sense," Kevin said. "And brother and brother are Kahmeel and Rashid."

"And the hidden secrets, and all that, is about when we were trying to get Kahmeel to tell us about the bombs."

"And he wants to go home, back to Oregon," Kevin added. "But he can't go home—like he says in the next stanza of verses—until he tells us those secrets. His conscience won't let him fly away west without giving his friend—that's probably you, Matt—the clues we need to uncover the secrets ourselves. To find the bomb locations… or the main headquarters of the cell."

"And the mountains that woo him," Sam said, "are the mountains back home in Arkansas."

"We already said that," I fussed. "And it's Oregon, not Arkansas!"

"Of course," said Sam, smiling.

"He just wanted to go back, dammit!" I shouted. "The whole poem is full of that longing. He just wanted to go home and…" Angry tears stung my eyes. I wiped them away.

"Did he know the Lord?" Sam asked Kevin.

"I don't think so," Kevin said bleakly.

"What the hell difference does it make right now?" I blurted. "He's still talking to us, isn't he?"

"The push and the pull," said Kevin deliberately.

"Of course I saw that!" I said. "It jumps right out. But what can it possibly mean?"

"The push and the pull means something to Kahmeel," Kevin said, "even though we don't know what. But I think he's using that phrase poetically to tell us something about himself, not about the push and the pull. Something about what he's *feeling* about the push and the pull. He's saying that he's no longer—or probably never really was—a man who hated America. He isn't a man who wanted to kill people for a religion he only half believed. He isn't a man given to the violence that the Sons of Islam plotted."

"He's a poet," I sighed.

"Yes," Kevin agreed. "So what about the third stanza?"

"The city of hate," Sam reminded us.

"Same city," I said. "Our city. But now Kahmeel is talking about the haters—the terrorists…"

"And the brother and brother are still Kahmeel and Rashid, daring to break loose from the cell," said Kevin.

"Or maybe they're the brothers *in* the cell, daring to do whatever they've plotted to do," Sam suggested, diving into the poem with us.

"Either way, it's about the bombs," I said. "The bombs! Darkness and dying, wailing and crying!"

"The seeds are the bombs," said Kevin. "Bombs have been planted in the city, like seeds."

"And now," Sam said. We looked at him, but he was simply waiting for us.

"Now, the poem gets harder to figure," I groaned.

"Don't try," said Sam. "Impressions…naturally."

"Maybe we won't need your séance machine after all." I smiled bleakly. He looked disappointed.

"The bell that stopped ringing is the Liberty Bell!" Kevin got up and started to pace. Sam grabbed a notepad and wrote down Kevin's thought.

"Independence Hall?" I wondered. "Where they prayed? During the days of the First Continental Congress they prayed before every meeting. For wisdom, for…"

"Those damned—!" Kevin stopped pacing. "Punching us in the gut! Hitting the symbols of our freedom…our faith! If they bomb those places, they'll stir up a hornet's nest for sure!"

"If there are any hornets left to stir up," Sam said.

"We can figure this out." I was hopeful. "Kahmeel laid it all in the lines. The founder is William Penn, and he stands tall upon old City Hall. He's got blind eyes because he's a statue!"

"The graves he stares at," said Sam, "are — "

"Are in the church cemeteries scattered around town," said Kevin. "You can see the old churches from the observation tower in City Hall. Maybe he's writing about the graveyards where some of the nation's founders are buried. He seems to be pinpointing heritage sites."

Sam wrote it all down.

"Dead men tell no tales," I pondered. "What's this about? Did he know that he'd die? But that doesn't make sense. This — "

"Coined!" Kevin interrupted. "Back up a minute to *coined!*" The Mint, the Franklin Mint, and the Philadelphia Federal Mint!"

"Man! They're going to blow up every — "

"No," said Kevin, "they're not. God wouldn't be giving us all this so that we could watch the city blown to high heaven."

"God?"

"Yes, God," said Sam and Kevin as one.

"Dead men tell no tales!" I recited, returning to the poem. "Kahmeel is saying that's not always a truism. Some dead men 'shout', and 'their words are a thousand to one where the blood of the ages runs red.'"

"How do dead men shout?" Kevin asked.

"Through their poetry," I said.

"No," Kevin argued, "that's not it."

"Okay, their deeds shout," I said. "Their reputations shout. Revolutionary war heroes? A battlefield somewhere? Where the blood ran red?"

"Blood of the ages," said Kevin. "That's more than a battlefield."

"Was there a battle in the city?" I asked. "A massacre?"

"Time out!" said Sam. "You're trying too hard. Not natural. Time for my secret weapon." He reached under the table and pulled open a drawer. I expected some mad-scientist contraption with a lever wired to a lightning rod. What I saw was a cheap laptop. And it wasn't even an s-com.

Sam flipped open the laptop and started typing. Kevin and I moved over to his side and watched.

"This is a program that thinks naturally," Sam said. "I dreamed it up, and Paul programmed it. I call it Googolution. It's like a sentient Google after a couple of million years of natural evolution. It figures stuff out without giving itself a headache. Never locks up either."

"That's not evolution, Sam," Kevin quipped. "That's intelligent design."

Sam typed Kahmeel's lines about the dead men in one text box, and then typed a question in another: *What does this have to do with Philadelphia?*

"Does it give you a mile-long list of possibilities?" I asked.

"Oh, no," said Sam, "that wouldn't help answer our question at all! It will think about it and give us a natural answer. Sort of a train of consciousness thing. A few thoughts, that's all."

"Thoughts!"

"But we forgot to pray!" said Sam.

"Pray?" I said.

"To ask God for wisdom, as the Bible says," he stated. "If any of you lacks wisdom, let him ask of God, who gives to everyone generously and without reproach, and it will be given to him. But let him ask in faith, without doubting, for the doubter is like a wave of the sea, driven and tossed by the wind. That person must not expect to receive anything from the Lord—"

"Go ahead and pray, Sam," said Kevin with an impatient wave of his hand.

Sam laid his hands on the computer and prayed that God would give it wisdom. I was thinking right then that if any man was unstable in all his ways, it was Sam Wong Lee!

As soon as Sam said "Amen," he typed a final command and said "Amen" again. The computer made a noise that sounded very much like a man humming in private contemplation. "My brother's idea," Sam said. And then it began to talk. I'd heard plenty of computers talk before, but this one spoke with human inflection and sounded like a real person.

"It took us awhile to program all the vocal possibilities," said Sam, talking at the same time as the computer, "and to merge them with the proper syntax in the order that the brain usually processes conversation and solves problems. But it's very cognitive, and I think it sounds pretty natural."

"Yes," I said, stunned. "But I didn't hear much of what it said to us. Can you play it back?"

"Oh," he said. "I'm sorry. I got carried away with telling you about it. No, I can't play it back."

"Sam!" spat Kevin.

"But I can ask it the same question again. It won't give exactly the same answer, naturally. Any more than you or I would if we were answering a question the second time. But it will think about it much the same way."

"Then ask it!" I urged.

He asked and we listened as the computer said, "Dead men speak volumes...at the public library. And there are many branches of the Free Philadelphia Library all over the city and out into the suburbs. But which one are we wondering about, I wonder. There is Andorra. There's Blanche Nixon—that's the Cobbs Creek Branch. There's Bushrod and Bustleton. Hmmm. What about Chestnut Hill? Or could we be talking about that grand old Philadelphia Public Library downtown on Liberty Street?

"But, you know, as I think about it—how could I have missed it? It's *pictures* that paint a thousand words. And pictures are all over the place—well, mostly on the walls at the Philadelphia Art Museum. They depict the ages and the blood of the ages. War and other messy happenings of all kinds. Prometheus having his liver plucked out by an eagle. Christ dying on the cross. Rock of ages. Blood of ages. Blood is red. Red and yellow, black and white, all are precious in His sight. Red, yellow and blue…the primary colors. So many paintings from so few colors! Well, well…I'd sure love to go to the Art Museum one of these days. It's been a long time."

And then it stopped. Sam wrote down "art museum."

"Weird!" I said.

"Brilliant!" Kevin said.

"Natural," Sam said, smiling. "I can ask it again if you wish."

"No, no—I think we've got enough! I'm calling Sutton. We've got to stop the bombs!"

"Your phone won't work in here," Sam said. "And don't call from outside unless you want to be traced." He opened another drawer and pulled out an old black rotary dial telephone. "Here…use my own line."

"You're kidding me," I said.

"Paul hardwired it to a transmitter disk we have on the roof. The signal bounces off a series of orbiting telesats and finds its way back into the city government's computer system. Then it hooks up with their phone system and enables me to call all over the world. It doesn't cost them anything, and they don't even know the calls go out—or come in. The signal is 'guarded,' Paul calls it. Don't ask me how it works. Paul's the digital whiz, not me."

"You can call all over the world?" I wanted to meet this Paul. I wondered if he could take apart my red phone and figure out how to connect me with the Sleuth.

"I've called my folks in Korea a few times—excellent phone reception. Other than that, I just call friends around town, and sometimes I call out for pizza and Chinese."

"Well, I've got to call the Bulletin!" I said.

I dialed up Sutton.

"Where in tarnation are ya?" Sutton hollered.

"Hiding for the moment," I said.

"Ya wanna get yerself killed?" He was angry. "They took my gun from ya and gave it back to me, so ya don't even have that. Tell me where y'are, and we'll send the right kind of protection right now!"

"No," I said. "I've had a taste of the 'right kind of protection.' Got a bullet through the arm. Kahmeel is dead. And my own private bodyguard—Cobalt Man—is lying in intensive care at Hershey Medical Center. I'm not sticking my head back out for a while."

"What's yer game, Clifford? This is nuts. I—"

"The bombs, Mr. Sutton!" I shouted back at him. "We know where they are…where they're going to be!"

"Jeepers Christmas, Matt! Are ya sure ya haven't been workin' with Ognobini all along…? Or maybe S.H.I.E.L.D.? Tell me what ya got! No…wait! Let me get Stein and we'll conference this call."

The phone was silent for a moment and then…

"Matt," said Aaron Stein sternly. "What do you have?"

I told him about the key, the post office box, and Kahmeel's poems. "I wish they'd given us a clue about Ali, but nothing we can figure out," I said. "Are you recording this?"

"Yes."

I read him the poem about Philadelphia. "It has my initials on it—this was meant for me, for us." I told him our thoughts. "I'm going to write this story up from where I am. I'll e-mail the files through to the Bulletin. Give me the okay and I'll get on it right now. Then you can run it on the Boards as soon as Ognobini or Jemison—or whoever!—gives you the go-ahead. What do you think?"

"I think you're an amazing fellow, Matt Clifford," said Stein passionately.

"The 007 of the journalistic underground!" piped Sutton.

"Start on your story, Matt," said Stein. "We'll contact the right folks to start on the bomb trail. But I'd feel much better knowing where you are. What makes you so sure you're safe?"

"Have you traced this call yet?" I asked.

Stein chuckled. "We've tried. I turned on the ferret as soon as Sutton put me on the call. You could be on Mars, I guess. No coordinates showing on our end."

"Then I'm safe."

24
Chase

The Pavlodar Airport police cruiser was a Russian Lada Oka 2525—a small hybrid built for local travel. When it rolled off the assembly line in Togliatti on the banks of the Volga, it had a high-tech engine that ran on a mix of ethanol, gasoline, and solar-generated electricity. The battery could be double-charged by plugging the vehicle into a normal household outlet overnight. It didn't have much power. It didn't have much speed.

Security officer Ulzhan Kuandyk was a handyman mechanic who preferred carbon-monoxide emissions and the exhilaration of acceleration. He saved up his money and replaced the hybrid engine and its transmission with a 20th century imported Ford V-8 and four-on-the-floor. On his days off work, he drove to an abandoned military airstrip outside Pavlodar. There, he pretended he was a race-car driver. That little Oka could do 175 kmph by the time it was halfway down the runway. But lately, the old pavement was crumbling, and it wasn't safe to race there anymore. Instead, Ulzhan Kuandyk imagined the streets of Pavlodar were a professional automotive obstacle course.

"You drive very skillfully," Imanghari commented nervously as the Oka sped down the near-deserted city streets. "Is there no speed limit in Pavlodar?"

Ulzhan glanced at his passenger in the rearview mirror.

"I am a policeman," he said, "on a mission to deliver an abandoned farmer to the comfort and haven of his brother's home. Nothing will get in my way! No one will catch up with me."

"I'm not in that much of a hurry," said Imanghari, "that we need to break the sound barrier."

"I normally don't go this fast," Ulzhan admitted, "but we are being followed."

Alarmed, Imanghari turned to look out the back window. About half a block behind them, keeping pace with the racing cruiser, was a large pickup truck. Its distinctive oval lights stared at Imanghari like two Asian eyes. Its toothy chrome grill, flashing orange in the glow of the cruiser's amber taillights, grinned malevolently. "Who is this?" Imanghari wondered aloud.

"It is not the city police," said Ulzhan. "They don't drive pickup trucks. And if they did, there would be lights and sirens and lots of shouting over loudspeakers. The whole town would be looking out its windows. I don't know who it is. But he will not catch me! Ha! Hold on!" He spun left onto a one-way street. Putting the car through its gears, he shot down the avenue like a lightning bolt.

"We will die," moaned Imanghari, sinking into his seat.

"He is fast!" belted Ulzhan. "He is behind us still! What a contest! Ha! I have not had such fun in years! Brace yourself, Mr. al'Kadri!"

The Oka nearly spun in a circle, as Ulzhan braked and turned and barreled into a narrow alley that bounced them along for several blocks before spitting them out again onto a wide boulevard. Ulzhan hit the big street burning rubber. "We have cut their strings!" he bellowed, as the V-8 coughed blue smoke and fired the little car down the street like a cannonball.

In spite of himself, Imanghari poked his head up to spy out the street behind them. He saw headlight beams on buildings about two blocks back, then oval eyes swung his way as the truck leapt out of the alley and angled itself to follow.

"It is a rocket, not a pickup truck!" Ulzhan declared. "So I will call in anti-aircraft fire! I have friends on the police force, working late." He punched a button on his dashboard and the Kazakh state radio came on. "Wrong one!" He punched another button, and the city's police frequency was engaged. That was what he wanted…but all he heard was static. He punched it again. Static. More buttons. Only static. He shut it off.

With an oath, Ulzhan pivoted the Oka into another alley, this one dirt and gravel. Dust rose behind him like a storm cloud. The alley angled up a hill and through a small woods, where it widened—then ended suddenly at a wooden gate before a graveyard. The Oka splintered the gate, but the gate cracked the car's windshield. "Ah!" Ulzhan cried. "A month's wages!" But he didn't stop. A narrow grass lane went straight through the cemetery, where another wooden gate blocked the way out.

Ulzhan slammed on the brakes, leapt out, kicked the second gate until its lock snapped, threw it open, then jumped back into the car and sped away.

"They plowed right through the cemetery," said the driver of the pickup truck, his windshield streaked with dust and mud. "I guess we'll do the same."

"He tried to connect to city police," said the passenger, fiddling with a small laptop strapped over his legs. "I blocked that. Now let's *really* scare him."

"Can you engage his radio from here?"

"Yes, but I think we're out of range. We've got to get closer again. But we don't have to see him anymore to know where he is. When he turned on the radio, I locked in an electrosonic link."

The truck lurched forward, pulling out of the graveyard. "Down the hill, and north," said the man with the laptop.

He had a city street grid on the desktop. A tiny yellow icon moved across the map. "They are on Abalsha Street, about a half-mile ahead of us. Ah!—I've got a stronger signal now. I think we can do this."

"Just get him to pull over somewhere soon," said the driver, "before somebody pulls *us* over! This guy is a maniac!"

The radio came on inside the Oka. Loud static. Ulzhan punched it off. It came on again. He punched it off again. It came on a third time, and he couldn't turn it off. "I must have damaged something crashing the gate!" Ulzhan shouted over the static.

"I am permanently emotionally damaged!" Imanghari yelled from the backseat.

Then the static stopped, and a commanding voice came loudly through the sound system: "This is the police of the KNB! Pull over now. You are being tracked via satellite. The truck that is following you is an unmarked bomb-squad vehicle of the Committee of National Security. If you do not pull over now, other vehicles will be dispatched to apprehend you. Your vehicle is one of dozens in the city that has been rigged by terrorists to explode at 2:00 a.m. this morning! We must disarm the bomb in your trunk. We must do so now. Pull over immediately!"

Ulzhan screamed, braked, veered off the street, and ran the Oka into the center of an empty lot beside a darkened office complex. Frantically, he threw off his seatbelt, stumbled out of the car, and ran for cover behind a large tree. Imanghari followed.

"My Oka!" gasped Ulzhan, staring at the little blue vehicle in the middle of the concrete lot. In his imagination, the car was exploding in a ghastly—and expensive—shower of fire.

"My life!" groaned Imanghari, standing behind the horrified security guard.

The pickup truck rolled into the lot, and two men got out. They were armed. Imanghari wondered if he should run. "My Oka…," blubbered Ulzhan.

"Come out from behind the tree," said one of the armed men. Imanghari stepped out. Ulzhan crawled.

"My name is Abiram al'Kadri," said Imanghari, taking out his ID card. "I am a farmer from the uplands. I have been working in the gardens at Aqtaú and am on my way home to Ambi. I arrived tonight in Pavlodar on a flight from Aqtobe. My brother lives in the city. This kind policeman was taking me to my brother's house when you began to follow us."

The driver took Imanghari's ID. "Come to the truck for a moment," he said.

"What about the bomb?" Imanghari asked.

"There is no bomb," the driver said quietly in Imanghari's ear. "And Ali is waiting for you."

Imanghari's head came up sharply. He looked back at Ulzhan who was weeping on his knees.

"Get in the truck," whispered the driver to Imanghari. "We'll take care of this policeman."

"You won't hurt him," said Imanghari sharply.

"No."

The two men from the truck moved swiftly to the Oka, holstered their weapons, and opened the trunk. One man turned on a flashlight. The other took some tools from a utility belt he wore. The two of them hovered over the trunk, leaning carefully into its confines.

"Done!" declared the man with the tools, hoisting a small metal box out of the trunk and carrying it toward the pickup.

Ulzhan got to his feet. "Is it…safe?"

"You may drive your Oka home," said the man with the metal box.

"May I see your ID?" asked the man with the flashlight.

Ulzhan produced the card. The man with the flashlight

looked it over and thumbed some text into his cellpod.

"You're a very good driver," he said, as he handed back the card. "And you almost lost us. It is a good thing for you—and your friend—that we were able to break into your radio. And that you obeyed us so swiftly."

"Thank you!" said Ulzhan. "For saving me—for saving my Oka. And for the compliment about my driving," he said, standing up taller. "Do you think that the government could replace my windshield?"

"No," said the man with the flashlight. "I suggest you go home, Mr. Kuandyk."

"What about Mr. al'Kadri."

"He is afraid to get back in your car. And so, perhaps the government can afford to give him a ride to his brother's."

"Will this be on my record?" Ulzhan asked nervously.

"There will be no speeding violation reported, if that's what you're worried about," said the man with the flashlight, smiling grimly.

"Thank you!" said Ulzhan with a deep sigh.

The man with the flashlight got into the pickup truck. His companion was already in, with Imanghari in the middle of the seat. As Ulzhan leaned wearily against his tired Oka, the truck drove away.

"What was in the metal box?" Imanghari asked.

"Cuban chewing tobacco," said the man to his right, grinning. "I took it out of my coat pocket and pretended to find it in the trunk. It might kill me someday, but at least it won't explode."

"How did you know where to find me?"

"We didn't," said the driver. "But when you hadn't arrived at the rendezvous, and an hour had passed since your companion had come, we were sent out to look for the lost Mr. al'Kadri. We headed to the airport first. You were just getting into the Oka. We certainly didn't expect a car chase!"

"My name is Abiram al'Kadri," mumbled Imanghari. And then he laughed wearily.

"My name is Ulyanov," said the driver, extending a laboror's rough hand in formal greeting.

"And I am Sabalak," said the man on Imanghari's right, brushing a mess of shaggy black hair from his eyes.

When the pickup truck arrived at the safe house on the north side of town, Imanghari and Ali were gratefully united. It was 1:45 a.m. on the 19th of July.

"We'll get very little rest tonight," said Ali. "A few hours, and then we travel out of town to Zhanatlek. The men who rescued you will be driving us in their pickup. You'll ride in the back this time, and so will I…covered with a tarp."

"First class at last!" quipped Imanghari.

25
House by the Lake

The truck was washed up and gassed up. The tires were checked. Two mountain bicycles were tied town tightly in the truck bed. Strapped to each bike in special tubes were water bottles, food provisions, a set of collapsed and compressed rough-road bike tires, a small packet of wrenches, and a compact, hand-operated tire pump.

A backpack for each of the bikers was filled with high-energy victuals, a solar water purifier, an inflatable pillow, a secure Israeli solar communipalm phone, a multi-purpose utility knife, and a forty caliber semi-automatic Israeli Jericho 3000 pistol with silencer. The backpacks were locked in a wooden box against the back of the cab.

"Wait a minute," said Ulyanov, opening the box back up. He unzipped the packs and pulled out the guns and the phones. "You two should carry these at all times," he said. "Your pockets are big enough."

Ali and Imanghari got into the truck bed and lay down on their backs on a firm foam mattress. They put on face masks, each with a breathing tube. A light metal frame was placed over them and secured to the truck bed. A thin sheet of plywood was set on top of the frame, snug against the truck bed walls on either side. It had holes in it for the breathing tubes. A coarse-hair blanket was spread over the plywood false floor—with slits in it corresponding to the breathing holes. The bikes were laid flat on the blankets. A couple of sleeping bags and other camping gear were packed in and strapped down around the bikes. Then a white tarp was pulled tightly over the entire bed and fastened securely. The tarp could repel rain, but it breathed. The men beneath it all would have a safe and fairly comfortable (though tightly confined) trip through the Kazakh countryside.

Ulyanov and Sabalak would be riding in the cab—supposedly on their way to a bike and camp excursion in the uplands. If anyone stopped the truck, a quick look under the tarp would reveal the gear these men needed for their wilderness getaway. Nobody could see the other two men hidden beneath the false floor.

"Did you go to the bathroom before we got in?" Ali asked Imanghari.

"Yes," said Imanghari through his breathing tube. "All praise due to Allah."

It was not yet dawn when the truck pulled out of Pavlodar. The early morning ride to Zhanatlek was a bumpy one, but Imanghari slept.

Ali lay awake, replaying the last few weeks—and the last few months—in his analytical mind. He thought of home. He dreamed of freedom. He wondered what Deri Sesin and Danil were doing this morning.

His own children would be getting ready for bed. It was nearly eight o'clock in the evening in New Jersey. How he longed to be tucking them into bed himself, singing silly songs, giving good-night blessings, holding them… holding them.

Jumana would be doing the dishes or getting her clothes ready for the next day. Maybe she was combing her hair in front of the mirror, humming in that tuneless way of hers. Surely she knew he was alive. Surely she prayed while she hummed. What did she say to the children when they asked about him?

The gang at the Bulletin would have all gone home, finished with their news biz for the day. What was the Bulletin saying about events in Georgia—about the kidnapping of Ali Ahkmed Baraki? What was Matt writing about the troop movements in Kazakhstan and Uzbekistan?

Had Matt ever heard from Wall? Had he seen the video? Had he figured out the message? Had he met Rashid? Had Wall's intelligence information been correct? Was there really a terrorist cell in Philadelphia plotting death in partnership with other cells throughout the world? Would Matt be able to flush it out? Would the agency protect him? Would he be able to stop the silversmith? Who *was* the silversmith?

How connected were these cells? How efficient? How well-supplied? Imanghari's cell was linked to cells throughout Asia and Europe—apparently linked to the Sons of Islam and Rashid's own brother Kahmeel. But there was more to all this than an underground network of scattered jihadists. There had to be. Since Ali had become involved with Wall and the agency, he'd seen too much to ever again think of politics in terms of independent national agendas. Self-seeking personal agendas, yes. The world had shrunk remarkably in the decades since the Second World War, and those with the power to realize their own agendas were allied with others in power across the globe.

And in the Middle East? Since the war ended, a move-ment was growing for international disarmament. But the present Peace, Ali knew, was as fragile as an eggshell.

Would the world achieve a global peace? Would it find a united economic solution? And if it did, what kind of a world would it be? And who would run the show once the world was "one"? Who would be in command? Who would be "king"?

Who was in command *now?* That was the pressing question. Who was really in command, deep in the heart of all that was boiling?

Ali prayed. He could chant the traditional Muslim prayers by rote, but those prayers often didn't reflect his heart. So he simply talked to Allah. He knew Christians who talked to God as if they were talking to their father. In fact, that's how Christians thought about God. That's how Bradley Wall thought about God. Wall was a remarkable man.

Wall thought the world was coming to an end...soon. And Ali didn't disagree. He could feel the social seismic tremors. He could see the coming global landslide. He just didn't know what to think about it, what to do about it. He and Matt had talked some about that, but that was in another life, another world — or so it seemed.

The truck stopped briefly from time to time.

Sabalak came to the back once and spoke to the men quietly, telling them to lie still and to be silent. Apparently, they were filling up at a petrol station.

At last, after an especially long, jostling ride without an intermission, the vehicle came to a halt on a downhill slope. Birds were singing somewhere as both of the truck doors slammed. Ali and Imanghari heard the tarp being stripped back, then the sound of baggage being pulled off the false floor. The blanket was removed, and cool air seeped into their quarters.

"We've come in for a landing, men." It was the voice of Sabalak. "We're ten miles west of Zhanatlek. It's 10:30 in the morning. We hope you have enjoyed your ride."

The clatter and creak of boots on plywood was followed by a flood of daylight as the false floor was lifted.

The lake wasn't as far from the end of the road as Imanghari had remembered. But it was half that far, at least, and they had to get there on bikes. There were paths through the steppe, and they made good time at first.

Their communipalms had GPS capability, but the signals might also be tracked and traced so they'd been warned against using them for guidance. They had a satellite map printout to follow instead. Imanghari pointed to the blue splash in the midst of the white miles. A tiny dark square sat on the eastern shore of the blue splash.

"That is the house," he said. "We should be there by sundown, if not sooner."

"I don't think I've ridden a bike for more than five miles in the last ten years," Ali moaned. "If we get there by sundown, I'll probably be crawling. My bike will be somewhere back along the trail. Why do they make these seats so skinny. My butt's bawling already!"

For a while, the main path was a well-trodden hiking trail, flat and easy to ride. But after the first hour, it narrowed into a passage for the adventurous only. And then it closed up altogether at a wide marsh.

"This is not on the map," said Imanghari.

"It has to be," Ali said. "That isn't a hand-drawn map. It's a bird's-eye photograph, taken yesterday, they said. It shows what's really here. We must have passed a turn-off somewhere."

"Yes." Imanghari stared at the printout. "There is a trail heading north that we missed completely."

They swiveled their bikes around and walked them back the way they'd come. There were no landmarks to identify the trails, no signposts, few trees.

"Antelope dung." Imanghari bent down over the trail. "And animal tracks heading back and forth from the marsh."

They followed the tracks away from the water and into the tulips near a small grove of flowering apricot. Beyond the grove, the antelope trail widened enough to allow them to get back on their bikes and ride.

"We are back on the map," said Imanghari as they peddled.

The steppes were full and magnificent in flower. The distant hills were so filled with brilliant red tulips that they looked like a prairie on fire. Skinks and geckos scurried off the trail ahead of them. Rat snakes lay sunning. Buntings, larks, and warblers dived and dipped among the flowers and the wild wheat. Doves rose occasionally in anxious curiosity at the unfamiliar sound of human traffic. High above, a hawk rode the wind. Higher still, and farther off, a cabal of Egyptian vultures circled lazily in the late-morning sun.

"There was a steppe cat in the hills beyond the house," Imanghari recalled. "It cried at night when on the prowl—a frightening sound! But father called it the 'song of the steppe,' and he made up words to sing along. Always after that I imagined the cat was singing. And that took the fright away—the thought of a wildcat singing!"

They stopped to rest from time to time, and more often as the long day brought them closer to their destination. Much of the time, they had to walk their bikes upon the overgrown trail. By late afternoon, Ali's legs had all but given out. The insides of his thighs ached sharply. He could hardly climb back on his bike, even when the path was passable.

They lay down beside a small pond where a long-eared hedgehog came out of his den, ignoring them completely as it ambled to the pond to drink. They drank some of their own water and ate a small lunch.

Then Ali slept, and Imanghari sat and watched the world around him. The surface of the tulip-pocked pond was bright blue with the clear summer sky. The air was cool, the sun was warm. Wheateaters flew out of the fields and skimmed the pond for insects. A ferret slithered into the water for a swim, disappeared among the bobbing tulips, and climbed back out on the far side.

"We've got to go on," Imanghari said finally, rousing his companion.

They walked the rest of the way, pushing their bikes beside them, sometimes ahead of them, through the wild wheat. It was dusk indeed when the path opened up into a natural grassy meadow beside a still, dark lake. Across a narrow spit of water, stood a square two-storied house, black against the far-off mountains. Its windows were shuttered, but a single, small rectangle of glass in the narrow front door reflected the fast-fading light of the western sky.

Imanghari laughed. He dropped the bike in the long grass and ran along the lakeshore toward the house. Memories came flooding. He was a child again, walking with his parents by the magic waters. But sorrow fought with joy as he recalled his mother's death. How was it possible that she was gone? Why was life filled with such loss and longing? Who had given death such power that it could so fully and finally separate those who loved one another? And why should an empty old house pull such conflicting feelings from his soul?

A shadow moved at the window in the door. Was it his own reflection? "There's someone in the house!" gasped Imanghari.

26
Reunion

Wall saw them coming. He had been there for hours. He'd found the house closed up, locked up, and shuttered. But that was a momentary inconvenience, not a deterrent. He picked a lock at the back of the house, let himself in, found a chair, and pulled it to the portal at the front door. There he waited, cleaning his gun and watching the sun go down over the azure lake.

It had not been easy to find the place, sitting solitary as it was in the midst of the wide, wild steppe. But Wall trusted in an old proverb that had led him to many a destination harder to discover than this one: *The steps of a righteous man are ordered by the Lord.*

He didn't consider himself especially righteous, but he knew that his sins were paid for, and he believed that God would take him wherever he wanted him to go. So far, even in a world filled with violence and war, that was Wall's take on how life had turned out.

He saw Imanghari running. Ali was striding through the grass behind him. Wall stood up and lifted the chair away from the door.

Imanghari stopped and stared. Someone was in the house! He pulled at his pocket to find his gun.

The door opened.

Imanghari lifted his pistol.

Wall shouted, "It's Wall! Bradley Wall. And you are Imanghari Koval and Ali Ahkmed Baraki!"

"All praise due to Allah!" Imanghari shouted as Ali let out a wild whoop.

Imanghari watched in tired astonishment as Wall came out of the house, walked toward Ali, and embraced the man as though the two were brothers. They stood that way for a long quiet moment, then Wall stepped back and laughed.

"Thank God!" he said. "Thank God!"

Imanghari wanted a fire in the cold house. He wanted to see the room lit up with the dancing flames that he recalled from many years ago.

"Not in the fireplace," Wall cautioned. "It will send up a signal that anyone can see for miles around."

"But there is no one for miles around!" Imanghari argued.

"There's always somebody somewhere whom you don't want sniffing your stuff," Wall said. "I can make us a smokeless fire out among the rushes, if you wish. At least we'll have a warm meal."

They settled in the wild lawn by the lake and ate their little supper as the stars started winking in the ebony expanse. Ali took care of the introductions, first telling Wall about Imanghari and his cell, then telling Imanghari a selective history of Wall.

Ali and Wall compared notes carefully, discreetly, because of Imanghari's presence, but completely. Imanghari was fascinated.

"How do you know all these things? Governmental secrets. International intrigue. You sound like my cell captains. Who are you, really? News reporters? I don't think so! 'My name is Abiram al'Kadri. I am a farmer from the uplands.' Not really. And who are *you*?"

Ali laughed. Wall did not.

"We *are* news reporters, my faithful friend," Ali said.

"But we are also patriots. Americans. Agents of a dream of freedom, but strangers here in a land where freedom has only been a dream. And we must get out of this land—alive. You want to go with us, don't you?"

"Yes, I do," said Imanghari. "But my dream is of a land south of here, where my mother's father tends sheep on a rocky hill. I don't know if I understand your dream. But it calls me, and I will follow you."

"All hell is going to break loose very soon," said Wall grimly. "Right here in this land. We'll be caught in the middle of it if we don't run fast and smart. Let's get back into the house and talk about it. Bring the bikes inside, too."

In the kitchen of the old house there was a wooden table with three chairs around it.

"One for Papa Bear," said Ali. "One for Mama Bear, and one for Baby Bear. It's an old German folk tale," Ali explained to Imanghari, "but every American child knows it well."

"I was the baby bear here," said Imanghari thoughtfully.

He found an old lamp in a cupboard and a bottle of lamp oil. So they had light. Wall hung a couple of ragged towels up over the window at the door to keep the light in.

"Nice communipalms," Wall noted, nodding at the men's phones. They had taken them from their pockets and placed them on the table with their guns.

"Compliments of the agents in Pavlodar," Ali said

"Whose agents?"

"I don't know," Ali admitted. "But they served us well! They were contacted through Dr. Erkin Temirzhon, an old friend of Imanghari's—and no friend of the Maleshenko regime!"

"I've heard of Temirzhon," said Wall. "A good man and a friend of freedom. Old connections to the agency. God was looking out for you."

"The agency?" Imanghari asked.

"Your lifeline," said Wall. "And that's all I'm going to tell you about it." He turned to Ali. "Can I mess with that phone of yours?"

"Sure."

Wall took out his own phone. "Compromised," he explained. "This is how I talked to your friend Matt, but too many Kazakh ears were listening. This little bugger can still hear your backhanded comments, though—and without interception."

Wall winked at Ali. Ali held his left hand up, fisted. Imanghari looked at them both, fascinated.

"I'm going to do a little work on these phones while we talk," said Wall, "to see if I can reprogram either your phone or mine. And maybe, Lord willing, we can get through to Matt again—just once. Then I'd like to look at Imanghari's phone and program some more security into it. We need to make a couple of calls inside Kazakhstan, if we can. There is so little time!"

"The 20th," Imanghari said darkly, "is tomorrow."

"The silversmith," said Wall, looking Imanghari in the eyes.

"What do you know about the silversmith?" asked Imanghari, surprised.

"What do you know about the 20th?" Wall asked in return.

"It is something called 'the pull,' for one thing," Imanghari answered slowly. He was not used to telling secrets to strangers. But this stranger was a savior—or so he must believe.

"I do not know what the pull is exactly," he continued, "except that I am sure it is related to the troop deployments we have seen all along our way. The meeting between the military and my cell on the day that Ali and I ran away— that was a briefing about 'the push and the pull.' *Jihad* operations and military diversions.

"I know no details because we fled while the meeting

was going on. But it is going to be big. It is a blow against the peace treaty. It is meant to turn things around for Islam in the world. It is going to hit the Zionists hard. But I can only guess. We were never told more than we needed to know for our own particular missions."

"Tell me what you know about the silversmith," Wall insisted.

"America." Imanghari said the word as though it was holy. "Whenever I have heard of the silversmith, there was talk about attacks against America. I do not know what. I do not know where. I am sorry," he said, staring at the tiny flame within the lamp.

Sorry that he didn't know. Sorry for America. Sorry for the Americans who sat at table with him. Imanghari kept his eyes upon his own hands on the table.

"You seem to know more than I do, Mr. Wall," he said. "Do *you* know who the silversmith is?"

"The silversmith is not a man, I think," said Wall openly. "It may be a communications post of some kind. A command center. Or a cue, a signal. We're not clear on it. But we've heard the connection between the silversmith and the 20th…and America—and I've prayed for revelation."

"While I was a captive," said Ali, "I listened intently to every conversation I could hear. I heard some talk of the silversmith and the 20th, and that's why I passed the phrase along to you, Brad, in my call to you before we fled the cell. But most of what I heard was old-fashioned sectarian bigotry. Anti-Zionism. Anti-Americanism. Curses against Christians and crusaders. A lot of hatred from a lot of confused men. Damn this *jihad!*"

"Ali!" said Imanghari, alarmed. "Allah calls for *jihad!*"

"Not the *jihad* we have seen!" Ali fired back. "Suicide bombs in grocery stores. Beheading journalists. Death threats against novelists and cartoonists. Human shields. Missiles fired indiscriminately into playgrounds and neighborhoods and…"

"Actually," Wall said quietly, "that *is* the *jihad* Allah calls for. That is how Mohammed lived. That's what Mohammed's book says."

"That's not how I read it," said Ali, coolly—though he knew that Wall was right. History was clear on Mohammed. And the words of the Koran were clear enough as well.

Wall popped open the back of his phone and extracted a microchip.

"The 20th," he said absently, inserting the chip in a small program port on a fat retractable ball point pen.

"What *is* that thing?" Imanghari asked, his eyes wide.

"It's a pen," Wall said, "and more."

He pressed the button that normally pushes the ballpoint out of its casing. Instead, the pen sprung open into a three-pronged instrument with a double-sided lens between the prongs.

"It's called a Tri-Pad," said Wall. "A mini-computer on three legs. Really cool. Israeli, of course."

He set the Tri-Pad on the table and snapped his fingers once. The lens blinked, projecting an image of a keyboard on the tabletop in front of Wall. *"Voila!"*

He snapped his fingers twice, and the lens blinked again. A stream of light shot out in the opposite direction, throwing the image of a computer screen upon the far wall. It had a photo on its "desktop," but it was blurred.

Wall placed his fingers on the projected keyboard, typed the word *focus*, and tapped the image of the Enter key. The picture on the wall became clear. It was a young boy sitting with a dog on the porch of a rustic log house.

"That's me," said Wall, "at home in Wyoming. I was about eight, I think."

He typed some more, his fingers tapping lightly on the wooden table top. A series of schematic drawings came up on the projected desktop.

"This is the program diagram for my phone," he said. "I'm hoping to reconfigure the signal so that it's insulated against detection and intrusion. There's a code matrix that I know that might work, but I'm not a techie. All I really want is one good shot across the world to Matthew Clifford, God help me."

"Where did you *get* that?" Imanghari wondered, still staring at the Tri-Pad.

"Radio Shack," joked Wall without smiling. "The push and the pull—we've picked up on that phrase for quite a while now," he commented, while typing his code. "From many sources—inside and out. We're working on it...all the time, all over the world. We've followed tracks and bagged some big boys. Squeezed some of their stone hearts until they bled, without getting anything that really helps us know where to focus our firepower."

"That's amazing," Imanghari said, watching Wall work. "A ball point pen!"

"I've got my own thoughts on the push," Wall continued. "The push was the miscarried Putin hit. Or at least stage one of the push was Putin. Ali and I were at that little party in Red Square because we knew something was up. I had connections and I got us invited. Didn't know we'd all get shot at. Didn't know it was a play on Putin's life. Didn't know Ali would get dragged off, chained up, and browbeaten. Thank God nobody knew of Ali's deeper connections."

"I took good care of your friend Ali Ahkmed Baraki," Imanghari said defensively.

"Yes, you did," Wall said sincerely, looking up from his work to affirm Imanghari. "Thank you. You've risked your life for Ali. I trust that I can repay your good with good."

"He needed a friend," said Imanghari simply. "I needed one, too."

"You're a true friend, Imanghari," Ali said. "I'm amazed that we're sitting here in your father's house. I hope that you and I will be friends forever, and I'm sincere in that."

He looked to Wall then. "It's so good to see you, Brad,"

Ali said. With a sigh, he leaned back in his chair and watched the shadows shimmy on the ceiling.

"Somebody wanted Putin out of the way," Wall said, eyes back at his work, "and that attempt on his life wasn't a personal vendetta by anyone in Imanghari's little club."

"You are correct," said Imanghari. "It was part of the big plan—perhaps part of the push, as you suggest. Though, as I said, I do not know the big plan."

"I know something about that plan," said Wall. "It's big all right. And it's coming down soon…maybe tomorrow, across America, across the world." He stopped typing. "The 20th," he repeated.

"Putin was supposed to die," Ali said, vividly recalling that afternoon in Red Square. "But he didn't. So he's being played right now, isn't he? And I don't think the game has changed much even though he's still in it."

"We know this is bigger than Putin," said Wall. "Much bigger than bullets and suicide belts. But we've got a chance. I sense it. At least for Philadelphia. I've prayed that we can stop things in Philadelphia. If Matt has read your clues right, Ali, then we can save one city at least…and maybe more."

He stopped typing altogether.

"There! I think I've got it."

He pulled the chip from the program port. He popped open Ali's communipalm, took out its microchip, and inserted his own.

"God, bless America," he prayed. He looked at the men sitting with him at the table. "But even if we save Philly, we can't save Georgia."

"Georgia?" Ali asked. "What's happening in Georgia?"

"Putin says that's where *you* are, along with the men who captured you, and a whole colony of terrorists like Imanghari's recent gang."

"Putin says so?"

"Marco Romano says the same thing."

"Romano!"

"So, they're laying siege to the little republic," Wall said. "And they won't be satisfied with anything less than rolling into Tbilisi."

"The push! Georgia is the push," Imanghari said suddenly, loudly. "I think so," he added tentatively.

"Maybe," Wall said thoughtfully. "But Georgia's not the tinderbox. It may be firecrackers and smoke bombs—a deliberate diversion from the real show—but I think it's mostly an *hors d'oeuvre* on the menu for world conquest."

"World conquest?" asked Imanghari. "By Islam?"

Wall didn't answer.

"Are we really near the end?" said Ali.

Wall sighed. "I pray for the peace of Israel," he answered. "I want desperately to talk to my friends in Jerusalem—and your friend Jack Pascov—to warn them to find a deep foxhole to hide in. But they may know more than I do."

He sighed again, sharply. "These are the days that Jesus called 'the beginning of sorrows.'"

"Is Isa Jesus?" asked Ali. "Is Jesus coming back?"

Imanghari sat astounded. He had never heard a Muslim ask a Christian such a question.

"Isa is not the Jesus of the Bible," Wall said. "Wrong book."

Ali laughed ironically. He'd previously told Wall about his religious nickname. "Shall we call Matt now?"

"Can't," said Wall. "It's got to be 5:30 in the morning here so that it's 6:30 in the evening over there. There's a signal grid. I've got to avoid the Kazakh cyber searchlights. It's like running for the fence at a prison camp. You have to wait for the spotlights to swing away…the guard to change…the wind to blow in the other direction. Our IT guys have the time targeted. Don't ask me how. I only know it's got to be as they say. So I can't call until 5:30 tomorrow morning."

"When you call, it will be the 20th here and…"

"And it will still be the evening of the 19th there."

"So what's next?" Ali asked gravely. "What's supposed to happen next, according to the Bible prophecies?"

"Well, Jesus *is* coming back," said Wall. "But before that, more headlines."

"Headlines?" echoed Imanghari.

"Tomorrow's headline," Wall suggested, spreading out his hands dramatically. "Front page of the Bulletin. I'll let you scoop me for once, Ali—in theory, at least. Big letters. All caps. GOG OF MAGOG KICKING DUST ON ROAD TO JERUSALEM.?

"You're serious," Ali said grimly, "aren't you?"

"I'm not a knee-jerk doomsayer, Ali," Wall said. "There are six, seven, maybe eight million soldiers massing at the Kazakh-Uzbek border. For what? Push-ups and a military parade? No. I've seen battle plans, orders, maps. Saw some just hours before the KNB came knocking on my door in Astana. A PDF file was sent to me anonymously. It came from inside Kazakhstan—through our sources. But I've been sniffing this out for a long time."

"You came to Astana after Red Square?" asked Ali.

"I came down here to look for *you*, but I also came to find out why the Mohammedan warriors of two nations were planning a picnic over their backyard fence."

He leaned across the table to look more fully into the eyes of his companions. The light of the oil lamp painted his rugged features with exaggerated shadows.

"Here's what I think," Wall said. "From the Kazakh-Uzbek border, they're headed straight to the Caspian—Tajiki and Kyrgyz troops, too. Then it's several fleets of ships to the northwest corner of Iran. Then two or maybe three lines of armor and infantry moving through Iraq, through Jordan, and into Israel.

"And out on the Caspian are some ships just itching to pitch some missiles into Israel—baby nukes, a jump ahead of the troops. A nice little prelude to invasion. Turkish troops and tanks are coming down through Syria. There've been a few million armed Turks garrisoned along Turkey's southern border for a couple of weeks. Turkish ships are out on the Mediterranean.

"A couple more armies will be moving in, to back them up, from Sudan and Libya. Airpower from Libya. Sudanese warships on the Red Sea. Russian ships have been there a long time already. Russia will train its guns on any EU vessels that get in the way. Arms and oil are on the way from Russia. Putin's factories are cranking out war machines day and night right now. He's in on this, though that shootout in Red Square wasn't on his datebook, I'm sure! That was someone else's ad lib."

"Whose?" fired Ali.

"Yeah, whose?" echoed Wall. "That's what Putin wants to know. That's what we all want to know. Georgia is taking the rap for Imanghari's cell mates, but it's a bad rap. Georgia's the scapegoat for someone else's sin."

"Gog of Magog?" queried Imanghari, puzzled by the name.

"The Hebrew prophet Ezekiel wrote about him," Wall said. "Ezekiel's prophecies are in the Hebrew Scriptures—that's the Old Testament of the Christian Bible. Ezekiel was seeing all the way to the end of the world. We're living it now."

"Maleshenko!" said Ali suddenly, bitterly.

"No," Wall countered bluntly. "Not Maleshenko—he's a key player, but he's not the boss. The guy in charge of this battering ram is Gökhan Savas, Prime Minister of Turkey."

"Gökhan Savas is Gog of Magog?"

"Magog?" asked Imanghari again, fascinated, strangely frightened.

"Ancient Scythia. Present-day Russia, Kazakhstan, Uzbekistan, and Turkey all wrapped up into one."

"But what's going to happen?" Imanghari pressed.

"War on Israel, nothing less. Ezekiel wrote it down—and God told Ezekiel. The world gets to watch. And Israel wins—again! Do you believe it?"

"No, I don't," said Imanghari flatly. "Israel is sitting on its hands right now. Its guns are not loaded. And not even the European Union could stop such an all-out assault. Not in time to save the Zionists."

"Don't you worry about war-weary little Israel," Wall declared. "Zion will come out of the fire on its feet. It'll be David against Goliath, déjà vu! I've no idea what kind of pebbles he's got in his sling, but he's got God on his side whether he knows it or not. And that's all he needs." Then Wall was silent for a minute—and nobody spoke. "But Jews will die," he said. "Gentiles, too."

"Gentiles," wondered Imanghari.

"Anyone who's not a Jew," Ali explained wearily.

"But we won't be sitting here in this house when the fireworks start," Wall said. "We'll stay the night and move out in the morning."

"What about America?" asked Imanghari.

"Collateral damage," said Wall bitterly. "Terrorist acts will keep the United States busy putting out fires at home. I pray we can stop some of it. But I can't call Matt until the dawn."

"What does our government know?" asked Ali. "What is it doing about it right now?"

"It knows more than I do," said Wall bitterly. "But what it will do, I don't know."

"America is a nation divided," Ali stated bluntly.

"Yes," Wall said. "It is."

"The end of the world," Ali mused.

"Not yet," Wall said. "The end is not yet—though it's going to look like it! And I could be wrong about tomorrow. I could be wrong about a lot of what I just said. I *hope* I'm wrong. But the danger all around us is very real."

"And very big," said Imanghari.

"Let's get some sleep," Ali said dejectedly.

"In shifts," Wall added.

"Nobody is out there!" Imanghari whined.

"We've got to make sure Nobody *stays* out there!" Wall said. "You take the first shift. I'll take the second—and I'll work on that other phone during my shift. Wake me in two hours."

It was cold in the house on the steppes.

Imanghari found some matted blankets in a pine chest on the second floor. He spread the largest on the kitchen floor to soften their bed for the night. He gave two more to Ali and Wall, and saved one to wrap around himself while he sat watch.

He went outside briefly to pee, then came back in and positioned himself on a chair near the door.

He tied back the towels on the window so that he could see the lake, the steppe, and the ever-reaching heavens above the horizon.

Ali could not get comfortable. His legs ached, but he knew sleep would come. He was so weary.

"Who's behind all this?" he whispered quietly to Wall. "Who's pulling the strings? Who's orchestrating this terrible scenario? The risk is too great for Turkey to go to war against Israel in the face of the Peace. Even with a coalition of the armies of Kazakhstan and Uzbekistan. Even with Sudan and Libya as allies. Even with Russia on their side. China won't sit still. The nations of Europe will pounce as soon as the first assault is over and they catch their breath. Clay will send America back into the fray. So, what's the purpose? What's the prize? Who's to gain? Is it simply to wipe Israel off the map?"

"Demons drive men who follow Mohammed," Wall said.

"I don't want to believe that," Ali sighed. "But I believe it anyway," he whispered.

"Demon-possessed men live for a prize that doesn't exist."

"But they believe the prize exists," said Ali. "They believe that Isa will come back and destroy all infidels. That Islam is destined to rise from the grave and subdue the earth."

"Yes."

"They believe that any price is worth paying to strike an enemy and cut off his head. Any blood is worth spilling as long as it is spilled for Allah. If a man can't be good enough to earn heaven, he can be bad enough to purchase it with the blood of an infidel."

"Yes," Wall said thinly, his eyes closed.

"They have misread the Koran," Ali said. "They have read the wrong verses. They are crazy—or demons themselves."

"Jesus…shed his own blood…so that crazy men…would not shed the blood of others," slurred Wall, almost asleep.

"My heart is darker than the steppes around us!" Ali whispered.

"Jesus…is the light of the world," said Wall. Ali could barely hear him.

"The world is full of devils," Ali muttered. "And the devil has friends among men. Who are they, Brad? Who are the demon-driven at the top of the ladder? Where's the hidden Hitler in this terrible story you've narrated?"

A sharp cry arose in the fields outside, a sound like a woman in distress.

"A corsac fox," said Imanghari from his chair by the door. "Now that is a shriek that could *never* pass for singing!"

Ali sighed heavily and slowly fell asleep to the sound of Bradley Wall snoring at his side.

It was the middle of Ali's watch. The rest were soundly sleeping. Ali was about to wake them just before he heard it.

A woodpecker? Not on the Kazakh steppe!

Automatic gunfire? No, too steady…and getting louder, closer. It woke Imanghari first, but Wall was on his feet before the Afghan could unwrap his blanket.

"Helicopters!"

They could see them in the distance, flying across the steppe in their direction.

"One for Papa Bear, one for Mama Bear, and one for Baby Bear," Wall counted bleakly, peering out the window.

"Kazakh military," said Imanghari, joining his companions at their little porthole. "What are they doing out here?"

"Looking for us, probably," said Ali. "Though you'd think they'd have better things to do today."

"The 20th!" said Imanghari.

Wall checked his phone. It was 5:22. "We can't get out of here now. It isn't dark enough any longer. They can see any movement on the ground from where they are. But once they land…"

The copters were about a mile away, flying low over the lake from its farthest end, creating a wind wake as they came. The sky was pale yellow in the east.

"There is a second-story exit in the back of the house," said Imanghari, remembering. "It has an outside staircase."

"Right!" said Wall. "I was on those steps yesterday. They're safe. And the door is now unlocked." He grinned. "That's how I got in here."

"Maybe the copters will fly right by," said Imanghari. "But if they land, they are likely to set down on the grass in front of us. From there they might not see anything behind the house."

"The wheat is high within a few yards of the back of the house," Wall said. "There are animal paths through the fields, leading up into the hills. There are fox dens and larger holes for hiding. We'll run together. If we time this right, we can get out of here while they're setting down."

He put on his pack and pulled out his gun.

"Buckle on your packs. Open that cellar trap, Imanghari. Put the bikes down there, guys! Throw the blankets in there, too. Put the lamp back in the cupboard. They're hovering over the lake! How many men in those flying machines? Don't move those towels away from the window!"

Imanghari pressed closer to the curtained pane in the door, staring hypnotically at the helicopters hanging above the water in the early morning light, like monstrous mechanical hummingbirds. The noise of the great machines was thunderous. The water beneath them heaved and rolled. Birds scattered and fled.

"How many men?" Imanghari heard Wall ask again. But his attention was riveted by a dark, familiar visage in the copter closest to the house.

"They're going to land," shouted Ali. The noise of the helicopters shook the house.

"It's 5:28!" Wall shouted in Ali's ear. "We've got to move upstairs! I've got to call Matt!"

Ali headed for the stairwell.

"Imanghari!" Wall yelled. "Let's go!"

But Imanghari didn't move. He was like a statue, standing still and staring out the window. He had even pulled the towels back further.

"They're coming down!" he yelled.

Wall yanked him away from the door. The noise of the copter engines and the whirling blades sent tremors through the building. It felt as if the earth was moving.

"What are you doing?" Wall cried. "Upstairs, man! Upstairs now!"

Imanghari shook him off. "There are at least a dozen men," he yelled, a strange look in his eyes. "And one of them…is my father!"

"What?" shot Wall.

He looked toward the door.

"Don't go out there! We've got to get away from here now!"

It was 5:29. Imanghari wasn't moving.

Wall bolted for the stairs without him, vaulted them two at a time.

Ali was out the second story door and on the back landing. "Where's Imanghari?" he shouted.

"I don't know!" yelled Wall. "We've got to run!"

"Without him?"

"Go!"

The two men scrambled down the steps and ran for the field behind the house. Wall punched a button on the reprogrammed communipalm.

They found a path through the wheat, and Wall pressed the phone to his ear. He heard it ring faintly on the other end. He shouted for Ali, who was only a few strides ahead of him.

As Ali turned his head, Wall caught him and pulled him into the tall grain and forced him to the ground.

"Here!" he said, slamming the phone into Ali's hand. "I'm going back for Imanghari."

He rolled over, jumped up, and tore back toward the house.

Imanghari came out of the upstairs door, looked wildly about him—and saw Wall. He barreled halfway down the stairs and jumped the rest. He hit the ground running, while behind him a man bellowed a warning. It was a voice that had haunted his dreams for years.

"Halt! Halt!" shouted Colonel Ivan Koval of the Kozakh Air Command. "You cannot get away!"

Ali lay in the wheat, breathing heavily, listening to a phone ring on the other side of the world.

27

The Silversmith

The afternoon went quickly. I managed to push Ali and Wall out of my thoughts, and I nearly wrote a book. Kevin napped on a couch in a comfortable corner that functioned dually as a compact dining room and a reading area. Sam tinkered at his benches while keeping an eye on his laptop for the ongoing news in Europe. I wandered back and forth from my writing and Sam's laptop.

Sam had a refrigerator-freezer hidden inside an antique wooden ice closet. It was stocked with plenty of cranberry juice and Mountain Dew. On a remarkable convection oven, disguised as an old coal stove with classic flat-top iron burners, Sam made us bacon, lettuce, and tomato sandwiches for supper. And he cut open a watermelon for dessert.

I had written all that I could pull out of my weary head, and I was getting anxious to hear from Sutton. It was almost 6:30.

And then I heard a faint familiar sound coming from Kevin's car!

I ran to the Beetle, flung open the back door, and scrambled in. I could see the little green light blinking inside the hospital bag as I tore it open. Red phone in hand, I said, "Hello?"

The phone was silent.

"Wall?" I asked anxiously.

I heard a crackle, then, "Matt! It's Ali. Can you hear me?"

"Ali!" I cried.

He sounded a world away…and, of course, he was. I don't think he heard my reply. He spoke again. "Matt! Matt Clifford?"

"Yes, yes! I hear you, Ali!" I yelled. "Where are you? Are you safe?"

"The signal isn't good, Matt. It's broken up."

"I can hear you," I spoke more deliberately. "Where are you?"

"On the run," he answered. "In Kazakhstan. Somewhere in the northern steppe. Brad Wall is with me. And another friend. Pray for us, Matt! There are soldiers after us!"

I heard shouting in the background. What was going on?

"Your video, Ali," I said loudly. "It has helped us much!"

"Did you meet Rashid?" he asked frantically.

"Yes."

"Praise be to Allah!"

"We're cracking the cells. CIA, FBI, all kinds of undercover manpower. Some of the terrorists are in custody. Some are dead."

"Who is dead?" He couldn't hear me clearly.

"Some of the terrorists." I didn't tell him about Kahmeel.

"Good!"

"But the bombs," I pleaded.

"It's today, Matt!"

"Today?"

"The silversmith on the 20th! You've got to find the silversmith. It's a code name or a command center. A communications cell. Something to do with the bombings. And it will happen today — the 20th!"

"It's still the 19th here," I yelled into the phone. "Do you hear me?"

"Yes!" he affirmed. "You've got time. But there's no time here! Troops moving to the Uzbek border — millions there already. It's a massing of both Kazakh and Uzbek armies. They're going to attack Israel! Call Jack in Jerusalem. Call my wife. Tell the kids I love them all dearly and…"

Israel! "But the Peace…"

"They've got Brad! I think they see me!"

"Got Brad! What do you mean?"

I heard Ali yelling in another language—Arabic or Kazakh. Men were shouting, arguing. Indistinguishable noises came across the miles.

The phone went dead.

"It's Ali!" I yelled, rolling out of Kevin's car. "He's in Kazakhstan! Soldiers attacking! They got Wall. Caught him or…I don't know! Damn!" I pounded my fists on the top of Kevin's car.

"Matt!" Kevin shouted, grabbing my arms. "Settle down." I could hear Sam praying loudly, in English and Korean.

I sat down on the floor, my back against the VW, and buried my face in my hands. "Ali said to pray," I whispered.

Kevin prayed.

Sam prayed.

I said, "God help them. Please help them," over and over until somehow I couldn't say anything at all.

And then it seemed that I couldn't hear anything either. I felt like I was alone in a soundproof room, drugged, exhausted. But the panic had lifted, and a tired euphoria— an unnatural sense of peace—settled in my soul instead. And I knew—*knew*—that Ali was all right. That Wall was alive. That nothing terrible had happened after all. But how could that be? I wanted to argue with this impossible revelation, but I thought of the silversmith instead.

I got up, unsteadily. Kevin was staring at me. Sam was sitting at his worktable, bent over his laptop, praying still.

"I'm okay," I said, wiping my eyes with my sleeve. My nose was runny. I felt dizzy. "Ali's okay, too."

"I…thought so," said Kevin slowly, still staring at me.

"Russia is moving on Georgia," said Sam from behind his laptop. "It's on the news."

"The beginning of sorrows," Kevin said.

"It's the 20th over there," I said. "But *we* have time. A few hours before it's the 20th here. We've got to find the silversmith. Ali says so."

"The silversmith!" Kevin smacked his hands together. "Like the message on Kahmeel's computer!"

"Russian tanks are rolling across the border," Sam said. "Pushing the Georgian army back. Russia's going in with planes, too. They've hit Tbilisi, the capital! It's smoking like a bonfire. This isn't a hunt for Islamic terrorists—this is an invasion. They're going after President Kobadze. They're going for the jugular. They're going to bleed Georgia dry!"

"Where's the European Union?" shouted Kevin, lurching toward Sam's computer. "Taking a crap out on the Black Sea?"

"They won't just sit there," I said. "They can't. They've got to back up the Peace. Threaten Moscow with a military strike. Anything!"

"Actually," Sam reported, pointing at his laptop, "Romano is screaming bloody murder. He's calling Putin a criminal, a back-stabbing warmonger, and a two-faced opportunist of the worst kind."

"Words!" said Kevin. "What's he going to *do* about it? Take out Putin himself?"

We stared at the images streaming over the Internet.

Romano was livid about the actions of the Russian army. He swore grave political consequences. The European Union had already called for immediate economic sanctions. Other world leaders were decrying the invasion. Clay—ever the dour diplomat—warned of a suspension of diplomatic relations. China condemned Putin soundly and threatened military reprisal if Russia dared to step outside the bounds of the defunct Soviet empire.

I picked up Sam's secure line and called the Bulletin.

"Mr. Sutton?" I said, when I heard his voice.

"Watchin' the news, Matt?" Sutton fired.

"Yeah," I said. "We see it."

"Tell me where y'are! We'll send an armored car if ya want one!"

"No," I said. "Not yet."

I told him at last about Wall's phone. About the calls with Wall. About the message in Ali's video—directed specifically to me. About how I'd met Rashid and Kahmeel. About Ali's call, the silversmith, the Kazakh army. About Wall's intuition about Israel.

"Who'd be crazy enough to attack Israel now?" Sutton asked. "The Pentagon knows about the Kazakh and Uzbeki movements—and you can bet the EU and Israel do, too! We all know Turkey's been flockin' along its southern border. But Savas and Malenshko would be outa their minds to start somethin' up again."

"I don't know, Mr. Sutton," I said wearily. "All I know is that Ali's still out there, with Wall, and that Jack's sitting in Jerusalem. And that we're not done with our work here yet. We've still got bombs to hunt up in Philadelphia."

"Found a bunch already, Matt. Saved the Liberty Bell from the scrap heap! Saved the Philly Mint from cashin' in its chips! Rounded up more of the Sons of Islam. You've done it, boy! You and yer own private underground— Bradley Wall, of all guys! And now Ali on the phone. You've busted this thing wide open, cowboy. It's time to come back to the ranch."

"Not yet," I said. "We don't know what's happening to Ali—or to Wall. We don't have the silversmith...or at least we don't know that we do. There's more to the bomb plot than what we've uncovered locally. If bombs are set for other cities tomorrow, then maybe the silversmith is key to stopping that, too. Tell Ognobini everything I told you. And don't worry about me. Don't try to find me. I've got to dig into this last mystery."

"All by yerself, Matt? Ya need protection!"

"Sorry, Mr. Sutton," I said. "I'll call you soon." I hung up the phone.

Sam's Googolution talked to us some more.

"*Hi-Yo Silver, away!* The Lone Ranger was a silversmith, you know. He owned a silver mine…made silver bullets. Rode a horse named Silver. Had a faithful Indian friend named Tonto. Tonto means fool, idiot, or blockhead in Spanish and Portuguese—Italian, too. But Tonto was no fool! And he wasn't a white man playing a red man, either. He was a genuine Native American actor named Jay Silverheels. Silver, silver, everywhere!

"But…this has nothing to do with Philadelphia, does it? I'll bet you think I'm running down a rabbit trail! Well, I'm not. I'm just thinking. I like to think.

"Paul Revere! Now there's a silversmith worth thinking about. 'The red coats are coming, the red coats are coming!' Henry Wadsworth Longfellow wrote a wonderful poem called 'The Midnight Ride of Paul Revere.' Let me quote a few verses:

> *One if by land, and two if by sea;*
> *And I on the opposite shore will be,*
> *Ready to ride and spread the alarm*
> *Through every Middlesex village and farm,*
> *For the country folk to be up and to arm.*

"Great idea!" Googie jabbered on. "Lanterns hung from the steeple of Old North Church in Boston to let folks know where the invading British soldiers would be coming from. One lantern if the Redcoats were coming by land, two if…well you get the idea. When the signal was given, Mr. Revere rode through the dark of the night to warn the country folk of the danger to come. I haven't ridden a horse in a long time. In fact, I can't remember the last time."

The computer actually sighed, and then went silent.

"Got all that?" Sam asked.

"The machine is crazy!" blurted Kevin. "But I think it told us something."

"Told us nothing!" I argued.

"Old North Church," said Kevin. "Is there an Old North here in town?"

"We're looking for churches again?"

"I just asked Googie about Old North," said Sam.

"Old North," the machine mused. "There's no Old North Church in Philadelphia. There's the Old Swede's Church over on Columbus Boulevard and Christian Street. It's called Gloria Dei now, and it traces its roots to the church on Tinicum Island that was dedicated in 1646 by the distinguished missionary, Johannes Campanius. His translation of Martin Luther's *Small Catechism* is the very first book published in the Algonquin language and..."

"Forget about Googie!" I said heatedly. "Let's use our own heads on this one."

"His work among Native Americans was the first attempt by anyone in the original thirteen colonies to spread the Gospel among the native people," the computer continued.

"A blockhouse at Wicaco, now South Philadelphia, was renovated for worship in 1677 and totally re-renovated—is that a word?—in 1999. It's the oldest church in Pennsylvania and a National Historic site. But, you probably know all this. No, there's no Old North Church in Philadelphia."

"Okay!" I said. "There's no Old North in Philly! Now..."

"Now Boston is a different story—if you want to *hear* a different story," said Googie.

"I do not!" I said.

But Googie wasn't finished.

"The enduring fame of Boston's Old North began on the night of April 18, 1775, when the church sexton, Robert Newman, climbed the steeple and held high two lanterns as a signal that the British were coming. This fateful event ignited the American Revolution. The little details are important, that's why I mention them. Oh…and Old North in Boston is now called Christ Church."

"That's it!" Kevin shouted. "Christ Church! Shut it down, Sam. "

Sam shut it down. "There's a Christ Church here in town," he said.

Kevin jumped to his feet. "What do you know about it, Matt?"

"It's one of most historic churches in the nation," I said. "George Washington attended there. Betsy Ross. The Continental Congress worshipped there. It's got several signers of the Declaration of Independence, and of the Constitution, buried in its graveyard."

"It's still an active church," said Sam. "I went there to hear a friend preach last summer."

"Is it a bomb site?" Kevin wondered.

"It's…" I hesitated. "Oh, who knows what it is!"

"Is it worth considering that it might be the communication site?" Kevin asked. "The signal tower of the silversmith?"

"The steeple is almost two-hundred feet high," I said. "You can see it from all over the city."

"But you don't have to hang lanterns in it to send signals," said Kevin. "Not if somebody is holed up there with communications equipment."

"It seems ludicrous to consider lines from a Longfellow poem," I complained, "especially suggested by a computer! But…I'm caught by that bit about being on 'the opposite shore' ready to spread the alarm. That could be across the ocean on another shore. A signal going out around the world. If the bomb plot is worldwide, then the 'country folk' getting up and arming themselves could be terrorists in each nation rising up to detonate bombs and shoot up police stations."

Kevin looked like a dark cloud about to spit lightning.

"Some freakin' terrorist," he muttered violently, "could right now be sitting in the heart of an historic house of Christian worship, in the very center of the nation's first capital, waiting to hang out his lantern to signal the minute men of Mohammed to rise up and kill in the name of Allah."

"It's possible," I said.

"Let's go!" spat Kevin, clapping his hands together in finality.

"Church shopping?" I asked.

"It paid off last time!"

"I'll call Sutton."

"Not now!" Kevin ordered. "Call him on the way." He turned to Sam. "We need that car."

"The fast one?" Sam asked.

"The fastest!"

It was a jet black 2008 Ford Edge...originally. Now it was a souped-up, super-calibrated, computerized rocket on wheels. Sam had reconstructed an interior that seated two people only. The dashboard looked like the controls on a spaceship, but actually contained simple meters and gauges for fuel, speed, engine heat, and global positioning.

Sam brought the Edge down from its lift.

"Registered, licensed, inspected, fueled up, and ready to go," he said.

Sam gave me a hooded jacket and a baseball cap.

Kevin borrowed a dark T-shirt and a pair of sunglasses. He tied his own shirt around his waist.

We didn't want to look like ourselves. Cops of all kinds were seeking us all over the city. And those were just the good guys.

We climbed into the Edge and strapped up.

"I've programmed the GPS for Christ Church," Sam said. "The car will talk to you — in natural inflection, of course — and you can talk to it, too. Its name is Alfred. It doesn't ramble like Googie, but it's a good conversationalist. You can ask it directional questions or anything at all about downtown landmarks. Paul programmed it to know all that.

"You can ask it what kind of vehicles are driving a block ahead of you or behind you. It will know that, too, if there are cameras stationed nearby. Alfred can read and interpret images picked up by the city's video surveillance system—and the city's traffic signal grid.

"Alfred can change a traffic light if you ask it to. If it talks too much, you can tell it to shut up, and it will. To get it to talk again, just say, *Alfred*."

As soon as Kevin started the motor, Alfred said (in an impeccable British accent), "Welcome to the Batmobile. Good to see you. I'm glad you've buckled up—we don't move otherwise. Wait for the door to open."

"Shut up," said Kevin.

The door opened in front of us. We pulled out of the Batcave. Sam waved good-bye. Alfred was silent.

"You hurt its feelings," I said.

Kevin knew the way to Christ Church, and we rode through town as quickly as we could. When traffic snarled, Kevin spoke to Alfred, and Alfred started talking again.

We asked it which streets were most congested. It knew.

We asked it where police cars were sitting or driving. It knew.

We asked it which lights were going to turn red or green next. It knew.

We asked it to change one red light to green, but it refused. It saw a car coming which we hadn't noticed, and it kept our light red in order to avoid an accident.

I called Sutton. I told him where we were going—and why. I asked him to send the cavalry.

"Blast it, Clifford! What are ya doin', tryin' to head the bad guys off at the pass by yerself?"

"Just doing my job, Mr. Sutton. I'm an investigative reporter!"

"I guess y'are!" he admitted. "And I guess I'd be where you are if I was you. But until the feds get there—and I'm pointin' 'em straight at ya—be careful, Matt!"

From the time I called Sutton, it took us ten minutes to pull into the church parking lot behind Neighborhood House next to the Arden Theater. It was almost dusk. We ran to the doors of Christ Church. They were locked.

Kevin led us back into the courtyard where we could check the church windows for light. The interior of the sanctuary was dimly lit to showcase the classical arched windows of one of the nation's most beautiful eighteenth-century structures.

"William Penn's baptismal font is in there," I said. "Sent here in the late 1600s from a church in London."

"There's a light on inside the steeple," said Kevin, pointing upwards. "There, above the tower, in that little louvered window."

I could barely see it.

"That's not an office area," he said. "It's probably a landing on the stairwell to the bell tower. Maybe a storage closet. Maybe the headquarters of the silversmith."

"This place is wired," I noted. "There are cameras on the poles right behind us. And on the church itself. A security system. Alarms and strobes."

"It must be turned off—or there couldn't be anyone in there. They've disarmed it. And that's just fine with me." Kevin pulled his phone. "I'm calling Sam," he said.

I wondered when the feds would arrive. I was anxious. The evening was warm. I wanted to take my coat off. I couldn't see very well with the hat pulled down over my head.

"Hey, Sam!" said Kevin to his friend in the Batcave. "Can you talk to Alfred from where you are? Good! Give me the low-down on the police out here: cars, foot traffic, anything within a mile of Christ Church. Anybody running in this direction. Any groups of two or three headed this way in a hurry. Any...whoa!"

He elbowed me while he was listening and whispered, "Alfred is talking to me over the phone. Sam hooked up a 'conference call."

He listened for a couple of minutes, then said "Shut up!" to Alfred, "Thanks!" to Sam, and "Come on!" to me.

I followed him to the foot of a tall sycamore.

"Boost me up," he said.

The lowest branch was ten feet over our heads. Other branches stretched skyward like the crooked steps of a giant stairwell. One long branch spread out over the roof of the church.

"Where are you going?" I asked.

"Up the tree."

"People'll see you! The cops'll come."

"No cop cars within ten blocks, according to Alfred. But they're coming. And some folks on foot are scurrying in our direction seven blocks south of here. We've got five minutes, maybe eight or nine, before the feds arrive. Get me up there, will you?"

"You're going on the roof?"

"To knock on the silversmith's door."

"Crap!" I said, and I locked my hands together to let Kevin step into them. "You're heavier than you look."

He hugged the tree trunk, and I lifted him higher.

"Now stand on my shoulders," I said. "Can you reach it yet? Ow! Don't kick my ears, you lug!"

Kevin had his hands over the lowest branch. It was thick as a trunk itself. I took the toes of his shoes in the palms of my hands and pushed upwards. He pulled while I pushed, and suddenly I felt his weight lift.

In less than a minute, he was up the tree, on the roof, and out of my sight. I ran back to the courtyard where I could watch him. I thought I saw something move behind the louvered window on the steeple above him. Or was it the shadows of the trees themselves upon the church's spire?

The window was about five stories off the ground, near the base of the steeple. The steeple stood on top of a tall brick tower. Kevin would have to scale the tower to reach the steeple. That alone looked impossible. Not only was there nothing to hold on to, but the roof of the tower overhung its walls by several feet. Nobody could scale that, not without rope and tackle or some kind of ladder. But he was already partway up the tower, straddling one corner where the walls met. There, the brick construction afforded handholds on either side.

He shifted to one side, moving carefully away from the corner and toward a high arched window in the center of the tower. His toes were pressed tight to a ledge of brick—it couldn't have extended a few inches from the wall—as he reached for the sill of the window. When he had it in hand, he reached still higher, using the louvers as rungs to pull himself up onto the windowsill itself. The window was taller than Kevin. Its strong louvers could serve as a ladder to reach the eaves.

But to get onto the roof itself, Kevin would have to lean out from the window, grip the overhang, let go with his feet, and do a full-bodied pull-up through thin air. If he fell, it was a twenty-foot plummet to the slanted roof of the sanctuary. And that wouldn't be the end of it. He would certainly roll from there to the edge of the roof, and then it was a free fall to the churchyard. It could easily kill him.

I wanted to yell at him, tell him to forget it. He wasn't Spider-Man! He wasn't a cliff climber. He was Kevin McCarthy, freelance electrician, my best friend—and I wanted him to come back down. But coming down seemed just as impossible, from where I watched, as climbing higher.

He was up under the eaves, crouched in the louvers of the tower window, hands pressed against the wooden overhang above him. He worked his hands toward the roof's edge and gripped it. There was a small lightning rod bolted there. He took that in one hand, the roof in the other, and up he went, pulled higher by tired muscles, sheer Irish stubbornness, and some invisible thread from heaven.

On the roof of the tower, he had plenty of room to stand. Straight and dark against the whitewashed wood of Christ Church's famous spire, he was at the level of the window with the light.

Kevin's climb had taken about three minutes, but it seemed like an hour to me. What happened next was so fast that I yelled out loud in spite of myself.

Kevin knows karate. I had never seen him use it. He took it up after losing his basketball scholarship to a busted ankle. He became a black belt, and taught it for years. That was a long time ago, but I guess you don't forget that stuff.

He kicked the window, and the louvers broke. Glass broke, too. He kicked it again. The shirt that had been around his waist was wrapped around his left arm. He was going in, feet first. Maybe he *was* Spider-Man.

He had something else in his right hand. His gun!

I didn't see what happened next, but Kevin told me later.

Two men were inside, one an Arab, the other an Australian. It was a small utility room, as Kevin had imagined, on a stair landing. It had a small table and two chairs. The light he had seen was the combined luminescence of a desktop computer and the power tubes of an ancient radio set.

The men were completely surprised.

When the window on their hideout exploded in upon them, the Arab fell backwards out of his chair. The Australian, who was standing, lunged for a pistol that was lying on the table. But he hardly had it in hand when Kevin swiveled and kicked again. The Australian was knocked into the table, scattering equipment in all directions. The gun flew from his hand and slid toward the door. The Arab picked it up. Bullets are faster than feet. But Kevin also had a gun. He fired first.

"Lord Jesus!" he cried. "I've killed a man!"

28

A Genesis of War

I heard the gunshot and ran for the doors of the church, banging on them, pulling at them.

A hand gripped my shoulder from behind. Another grabbed my arm, wrenching it behind me. In an instant I was on my knees, and a voice I'd heard somewhere before said, "Matthew."

I twisted my head to see him.

A short dark man was smiling a lopsided smile, but his eyes were hard and his grip was iron. "George Ognobini," he said, to remind me.

There were men behind him, guns in hand.

"Kevin McCarthy is in the steeple!" I rasped. "The silversmith! There's been gunplay!"

Ognobini's men were inside in a flash, but George stayed outside with me.

Other agents arrived. Ambulances. SA cops. City police. They set a yellow tape perimeter to hold back the gathered onlookers. I saw Cobalt Woman stepping through the crowd.

"He climbed," I said to Ognobini, massaging myself where he had gripped me. I was glad he hadn't pressured my wounded arm. "Climbed up to the steeple from the outside."

"Incredible," said Ognobini, eyeing the spire high above us.

Within minutes, the Australian came out, handcuffed and escorted, head down, face bruised and bloodied, eyes defiant, one arm dangling.

An agent carried out a box of equipment from the steeple room. Shortwave radio parts—nothing high-tech at all.

Kevin emerged next—somber, silent. I could see he wasn't injured. Not even a cut upon the arms that had passed through the shattered window. He found me immediately.

A larger knot of police began to form at the door. A medical emergency crew pressed past us and entered the church. I looked at Kevin, a question in my eyes.

"One man down," he said ruefully.

"The daredevil feat of Philadelphia's own Kevin McCarthy was *right on time*," Jacqui Johnson declared for all the world to hear. "In a spectacular act of heroism that would make the Navy Seals proud, this local independent electrician and black-belt Karate expert scaled the steeple of historic Christ Church, broke in on two men intent on bombing our city, and stopped them in the act!"

The silversmith signal was aborted.

The "lantern" was snuffed before it had a chance to shine.

We busted the cell—completely.

Not a single bomb went off in Philadelphia. We found them all—an even dozen. Confessions confirmed the number—corroborated by evidence gathered from the apartments of the cell members.

I watched the coverage on a TV in a room at Hahnemann University Hospital on Broad and Vine. The cops had sent me back to my bed, and they weren't going to let me get back up until the doctors (and the feds) said I could.

"The terrorists in the Christ Church tower were part of a

larger local terror cell called the Sons of Islam. Eleven members of the Sons of Islam are in custody," Jacqui continued. "There were fifteen men involved in all. Three have confessed. Four of them are dead."

Photos of the four appeared on the screen. Two of the dead were the men who had fired at Kahmeel and me on the night we ran. One was the man shot by Kevin. The last was Kahmeel.

"With us here today, to tell us more, is CIA operative Morton Stanley," said Jacqui. "Thank you for joining us, Mr. Stanley."

An African American in a dark suit and a trim grey mustache faced the camera from his office in the Central Intelligence Agency headquarters in Langley, Virginia. "You are quite welcome, Jacqui," Stanley nodded. "In regard to your city, the scheme of the Sons of Islam was horrific. In regard to our nation and our world, the Sons of Islam was the essential hub of a much larger conspiracy of terror. Philadelphia was to be the first strike. The birthplace of American freedom—the Eden of modern democracy throughout the world—would have exploded in a display of deadly fireworks. The men in Christ's Church steeple were then to send a signal to other cities, other nations. Bombs would go off like ripples in a pond. Philly first, then cities close by, then another ripple…on and on around the whole world."

"How were they going to signal other cities, Mr. Stanley? Tell us about their equipment."

"Remarkably, the silversmith communication initiative was not some new solar technology, digitally coded to deflect detection. It was a simple strategy of Cold War spying, utilizing carefully selected shortwave radio frequencies. Very effective. Very quiet. Almost invisible, as we say."

"A much larger conspiracy? But who? Who is behind it all?" Jacqui asked, facing the camera.

How can it be that nobody knows? I wondered. Not even the Sons of Islam—at least not the three who talked.

My own little circle of intelligence had some clues, but no solid answers. Through Ali, Wall, and Rashid (as well as a myriad of sources accessed by the various American intelligence agencies involved in the operation) we knew about terror cells in Russia, Kazakhstan, Turkey, and several other scattered nations.

But how were they connected? How were they coordinated? Who called the tune? How did this fit with other troubling rumblings internationally? Lots of guesses. No clear enemy to go to war against.

Yes, Philly was saved, but bombs went off in the wider ripples anyway! The bigger picture must have been plotted to proceed no matter what happened locally.

I heard the news and saw the pictures from my bed. I thumbed the controls from one channel to the next as the terror unfolded. I could imagine the frenzy in the newsroom at the Bulletin. That frenzy was evident on every network I turned to.

World News Now. ABC 7 in Washington D.C. A disheveled Maureen Bunyan, obviously called out of bed in the middle of a summer's night dream.

"At 12:30 this morning, only twenty-five minutes ago, a bomb exploded near the top of the Washington monument," Bunyan announced, her voice cracking.

"Broken chunks of white marble and twisted pieces of the national icon's cast-metal cap fell at its base and were scattered for a great distance over the lawns and pools of the National Mall. There was no one in the monument when the bomb went off, but several people present in the Mall were injured by the hail of debris. Firemen report the monument's stairwell charred halfway down."

Behind Ms. Bunyan, a live-feed image of the famous

landmark showed it eerie and tall in the bright beams of the emergency spotlights, blasted and blackened at its top, smoking like a giant industrial chimney.

Weekend Today. NBC's Studio 1A at Rockefeller Center, Manhattan. A very shaken Lester Holt.

"Terrorist bombs have torn through the tunnels of the New York Subway system, killing hundreds, wounding hundreds more," the nerve-wracked Holt announced. And no wonder he was shaken!

"Explosions have also shattered buildings at Rockefeller Plaza, where I am speaking to you now. Studio 1A, where I am sitting, is untouched—but it looks like a war zone just outside my windows."

Good Day Chicago. FOX 32, Chicago. Anna Davlantex, wide-eyed and weary.

"The Willis Tower in downtown Chicago, known around the world as the famous Sears Tower, was bombed this morning at 12:35. Dozens were killed in multiple explosions on several floors. The Skydeck, a spectacular glass balcony affording a breathtaking view of Wacker Drive and the Chicago River, has been…" She hesitated, visibly upset. "It has been totally destroyed."

Video of the destruction played on the screen.

Fires burned in the upper stories of the familiar structure. Firefighting helicopters swarmed around the bomb-battered central tower of the tallest building in the western hemisphere, shooting fire retardant into its darkened face. Smoke poured from hundreds of shattered windows.

I flipped to *FOX News National.* Stories and images from around the country were relayed in fast-motion sequence.

In San Antonio, Texas, the stones of the Alamo were blasted to rubble.

At Gettysburg Battlefield in Pennsylvania, the Visitor's Center exploded and burned to the ground. On the battlefield itself, the largest and most famous landmark in the park—the State of Pennsylvania Monument—lay in ruin, its carved granite panels irreplaceably shattered.

At Mount Rushmore in South Dakota, Theodore Roosevelt was missing half his face.

On an Indian reservation in Arizona, the local post office—not much larger than an outhouse with a porch—erupted like a miniature volcano, spewing mail into the sky where the hot winds caught it up and flung it out into the desert.

Smaller bombs went off in smaller towns throughout the nation.

The bomb strikes in America, though not simultaneous, took place within an hour's time. During that same hour, bombs went off around the world.

The Eiffel Tower was hit, the Great Sphinx, the Taj Mahal, the Leaning Tower of Pisa.

Car bombs tore up residential neighborhoods in Europe. Ancient universities were visited by terror and flame. Historic churches were reduced to piles of brick, stone, and shifting ash.

The Vatican was hit. The Basilica of St. Peter sustained major damage to its Renaissance sanctuary.

In Israel, both the Knesset and the Israel Museum were bombed.

In Nepal, Buddhist monasteries were destroyed.

In China, terrorists were caught in the act of planting bombs in the Forbidden City.

Civil war erupted in Costa Rica and Honduras.

Suicide attacks killed world leaders in South America and Africa—many of them Christians: Bomani Wa Banda of Malawi, Moses Adeyemo of Nigeria, Carlos Gomez-Garzon of Colombia.

Poland's president narrowly escaped an explosion that pulverized the presidential office.

"Murder and Mayhem!" Stein exclaimed, sitting with me in my hospital room in the middle of the night. "Never in all my days could l have imagined..." he choked. His face was set like flint, his hands were locked upon his lap. "There's no clear pattern to it all, other than historic locations targeted and national leaders in the crosshairs."

"Countries with Islamic governments have taken the lightest blows," I noted, "while democracies—especially those with a heritage of freedom and Judeo-Christianity— have been hit the hardest."

Stein nodded. "Few nations have been left untouched, but America and Israel have been hammered the heaviest," he agreed, staring out the window into the night. "But who is the enemy? What is his name? Where are his armies? How do we fight back?"

"Islam?"

"Mohammed is dead. Who can say which of his children are responsible for this madness? Who could possibly coordinate such a comprehensive blitzkrieg? Who could handle so many packs of 'mad dogs', as Romano calls them? What are they after? And who is running at the head of the wild packs? No petty desert warlord!"

"If this is the Push," I said, "God save us from the Pull!"

The global response was chaotic, confused, and combative.

Nations, states, and communities bumped heads and tangled arms and legs in an effort to mobilize missions of mercy, organize national defense, and identify and track down the perpetrators.

Romano called for global solidarity and a final, deep purge of the jihadist underground. The EU pledged money for emergency relief. Clay called for men and women of all faiths to pull together and pray for peace. Raul Castro locked Cuba's borders and went on an internal manhunt. Putin used the attacks as further justification for Russia's move on Georgia.

Riots broke out spontaneously in England, France, Spain, and Italy, with mosques being burned in religious retaliation. Nigeria, Senegal, and Ghana, where national leaders had been assassinated, scrambled to stabilize their governments.

The South American Defense Council of the Union of South American nations mobilized troops to increase regional security.

Egypt railed against Saudi Arabia. The Saudi kings railed against Egypt.

In Israel, the Knesset called for suspension of the disarmament clause of the Peace in order to reorganize Israeli national defenses. But Brussels said, "No! Put your hands back in your pockets. The EU's got your back."

When Stein left, I couldn't sleep. I couldn't turn off the TV. And as the night crept toward day, spokesmen for various terror groups, headquartered in hidden enclaves in undisclosed nations, began to contact media outlets to claim responsibility for the bombings.

Al-Aqsa Martyrs Brigade, Takfir Wal Hijra, Salafia Jihadia, Muslim Brothers, Gamma Islamiya Egipt, Al Fatah, Tabligh al Dawa—and, of course, Al Quaida—all laid down their calling cards.

Other scattered groups—some previously at odds with each other—crawled out of the shadows to shout, "We did it!"

Familiar jihadist leaders—and men nobody had ever heard of before—flashed their faces on the Internet. Some of the leaders were internationally sought criminals, some were new kids on the block. But they all raised their hands. And some of them seemed totally surprised at the presence of the others in the *jihad* room.

It appeared that this coordinated conflagration was not one in which these scattered jihadists had covenanted together in any way. So, who was the mastermind? Who was calling the shots?

While countries around the world fought the fires in their own front yards, few were watching as the nation of Georgia went up in flames.

Putin's sham terrorist hunt had become a brutal battering of the Georgian military and an undisguised subjugation of the Kobadze government. As Russia marched through Georgia, foreign journalists were rounded up, locked up, and silenced. Only a few evaded the Russian net. Those few told the rest of us the story. Those few became the messengers of war.

The Georgian army fought valiantly, but it couldn't stand against the Russian juggernaut.

Within hours of the invasion, Russian bombers had destroyed every major military facility in the country. Power was down. Railroads destroyed. Airports closed completely. Cities and towns were taken over in swift succession. Whole provinces were under Russian domination.

Russian tanks had advanced within fifty miles of Tbilisi when president Kobadze realized that no help would be coming from a world reeling from international terror.

When Putin's tanks entered the city, Kobadze walked out of the presidential palace, alone, to meet them.

Dressed in traditional Georgian attire, an Orthodox cross around his neck, an ancient Georgian sword in hand, he stood at military attention, facing the approaching armored column. From a Russian personnel vehicle, an officer stepped forward with a pistol to take him prisoner.

Kobadze bowed, stood straight again, raised his sword in an obvious gesture of martial invitation—and thrust the Russian through. Immediately, a machine gunner in the nearest tank opened fire—and the president of Georgia died in the streets of Tbilisi, sword in hand.

I had to watch this all from bed!

To lie there all night in a hospital bed and do nothing while the world went to hell was worse than being shot at.

At last, at dawn, surrounded by medical professionals of various colored uniform and garb, after signing a dozen forms and charging my stay to the government, I was released from my confinement and told that I could go.

George Ognobini moved me in his casebook from Level One Surveillance to who-knows-what. The CIA signed off, too, apparently, and Magdalena came to see me briefly.

"You are a courageous man," she said again. "And you are not a puppet."

"And you're a courageous woman." I returned the compliment, popping open the closet to extract my things.

"Just doing my job," said the girl with the gun. She blushed and dropped her eyes for a moment.

"I guess I'm not a security priority anymore, now that the Sons of Islam are busted," I said. "But with everything else going on around the country, professional phantoms like you have plenty to do."

I pulled my wallet and my little red phone out of the hospital bag and pocketed them.

"I haven't been a very grateful client, have I?" I smiled awkwardly. "Well…thanks for watching out for me. You and Cobalt Man have made my life very interesting in the past couple of weeks. Of course," I said, less flippantly, "you may have saved my life, too."

She just looked at me. She tapped her notebook with her fingernails and looked at me.

"Is he going to be okay?" I asked.

"I don't know," she answered. "He was unconscious when they took him to Hershey Medical and he's unconscious still."

"Is he married?"

"Yes."

"Kids?"

She nodded another yes.

"When you see him," I said, "when he wakes up, tell him I've been thinking about him. Tell him 'thank you.' And tell him I'd like him to get in touch with me through the Bulletin. Of course," I said, smiling, "you guys can track me down *anywhere!*"

She stared at me for another long moment, then said abruptly, "Good-bye, Mr. Clifford."

She stepped toward me lithely and kissed me on the cheek.

She was gone before I could say another word.

I called Sutton. I wanted to bolt back to the Bulletin, but Sutton wouldn't let me.

"Don't worry 'bout yer column this week! I'll write it myself!" he said. "As for yer own chapter of this story, we'll give ya a special section when yer back on yer feet."

"I'm on my feet now, Mr. Sutton."

"Then go home and lie down!"

"I want to run! I want to work!"

"You can write a thriller at yer kitchen table, and we'll run it in pieces like a serial," he joked. "Seriously, Matt, ya gotta lay low and get well. That arm wound ain't a cat scratch!"

"But what about Ali?" I complained.

"We're on it," he assured me. "There's folks on the ground over there with noses like bloodhounds and gadgets that take up where the noses leave off. Very little happens in the world that someone else ain't watchin' or listenin' to."

"Even in Kazakhstan," I wondered.

"Apparently so."

The doctors said I needed a couple of days of bed rest at home. As if I could rest!

But I went back to my apartment. Kevin drove me. It was seven o'clock on a Monday morning when I unlocked my door to let us in. Turning the key, I noticed that my hands shook and my legs were weak. "Maybe I need sleep, after all," I said. "I'll check my e-mail, take my meds, and hit the hay."

"Good idea!" said Kevin. "Turn off the phones, turn off the Mac. Take some of that stuff they gave you to knock you out. Get ten or twelve hours of sleep. You need it! I've got to get some work done and make a dollar. I'll come by at the end of the day to see how you're doing."

"Thanks, Kevin. I appreciate you—more than I can say."

"That goes both ways," he said. "Hey, can I grab a glass of orange juice before I go?"

"Make some eggs and toast, too, if you want. There's instant bacon in the fridge."

I threw my bag on the couch, shuffled into the bedroom, sat on the edge of the bed, pulled off my shoes, and said, "E-mail."

The MagicMac flashed on and opened my account. It was crammed with notes from worried well-wishers. I stared at a few, including one from Dad and one from Bethany, then decided to save the rest until I woke up later.

I saw one from Lisa but left it unopened.

I was about to tell the Mac to shut down when I heard the opening notes to "Tradition," a song from the old Broadway musical *Fiddler on the Roof.* Jack Pascov skyping—from Jerusalem!

"Pascov!" I commanded the Mac, and it connected us, crisp and clear.

"You are well?" he asked, a troubled look upon his face and no *shalom alechim.*

"I don't know," I said, "but it's good to see you."

"I'm glad to be able to see you," he said strangely, and fell silent. His eyes were red, his appearance disheveled. I heard voices, like a crowd at a football game, distant, indistinct, with sharp shouts interspersed. Something was going on outside Jack's apartment in the streets. Or was he in his apartment at all? The room behind him didn't look familiar.

I tensed. "What's happening, Jack? Terrorists? More bombings? You okay?"

"Missiles, Matthew," he croaked. "Jerusalem is on fire."

29
How Long, O Lord?

"Jerusalem…on fire," I echoed numbly. "My God!"

The picture went bad. Jack all but disappeared.

"Jack? Jack?"

"Still here," he said. "The connect is lousy. I tried maybe fifty times to get through to you."

"So good to hear you, Jack! What…what's the news?"

"There was a direct hit in the Old City," Jack recited wearily. "A conventional warhead, but groundhog nukes have been falling, too. At least one of them outside the Old City. They dig in deep when they hit and go off underground like an earthquake! It's horrible. Parts of the Old Quarter are rubble! I had some warning—not about the missiles, but about the armies that are on their way. I got out of my place. Took a duffle bag of clothes and my grandfather's gun. But nothing else. Siggy's with me."

"Put him on," I said.

Siggy stuck his head in sight and waved a tired hand.

Kevin came into the room with me, a plate of bacon and eggs in hand. He stared at Jack and Siggy without speaking.

"I'm in Haifa," Jack continued. "Tried over and over to get a connect to the Bulletin. Transmission is terrible. There've been a few missile hits in Haifa. It's bad, it's bloody, but nothing like Jerusalem. I've been running the streets. Finally connected with Sutton, but only for a few minutes. He told me what happened to you."

He was silent for a breath. "I've been worried about you," he said.

"Worried about *me?* What about *you!* And what armies? What armies are coming? What's Israel doing?"

"The Turks are rolling through Syria. Uzbeks and the Kazakhs are headed this way—hundreds of thousands of them...millions, probably. Haven't you heard? Haven't you seen?"

Kevin went out into the living room and turned on the TV. The news was full of violence and war. A world gone crazy!

"The Turkish border is about five hundred miles from Israel," said Jack. "That's like New York City to Washington D.C. and back again—it's a jaunt. The Uzbek border is around sixteen hundred miles away. That's the distance from Philadelphia to...to Denver.

"They've been moving toward us for quite a while. Troops could be here in ten to twelve hours—by midnight maybe.

"They'll take ships across the Caspian, of course. Trains and trucks and tanks through Iran and Iraq, through Jordan and Syria. Planes are coming at us from carriers out on the Mediterranean. Turkish carriers, we think. They were already out there, of course, because they've been part of the European Union since March. How the Turks are pulling this off with the rest of the EU patrolling the waters, I don't know.

"Our own satellite recon has been messed with—maybe a strat-nuke or something big going off way over our heads. But we've reestablished satellite video. The pictures are coming in of the damage on the ground...and the enemy advances. We see troops and planes coming up from the south, too. From Africa—Sudan, and maybe Libya. Even from within Iran—where we thought jihadist forces were disintegrated—a full-blown militia has emerged from the mountains. It's horrifying, Matt, watching the armies crawl across the miles toward us like a storm front…like an evil cloud covering the earth. It's our worst nightmare played out in broad daylight. God help us!"

"He will," said Kevin, back in the room again—and he began to pray for Jack, for Jerusalem, for Israel.

He prayed against the enemies of Israel. Against the missiles and the bombs, the bombers and the boats. Against the armies marching from the north and from the south.

He prayed in English and in some other language I had never heard. It sounded like Hebrew, but I don't think it was.

When Kevin was done, Jack murmured, "Thank you." And he meant it. "Israel can't fight back," he said darkly. "Tabeel called for complete re-mobilization, but with what? We've given up all our weapons—and all our military installations are under the command of the EU Peace Force. EU soldiers are getting hit the same as everyone else here. Who would have thought it? So soon after the Peace! My God, if they throw everything they've got against us, we're history! If it was man to man, they've got us outnumbered ten to one."

Just like Wall had said.

"So what's the EU doing? Tabeel and Clay? Egypt? Britain? Italy?"

"Tabeel is calling anyone who'll listen. We didn't expect what happened, but we knew something was coming, apparently. Israeli intelligence, like God, never sleeps! But on the ground here, EU forces are running around like chickens with their heads cut off."

"What about the anti-missile defenses that are still active? What about those silos in the Negev?"

"Some defenses are up, but not enough. They were being reprogrammed with EU protocol for EU oversight. I wonder if anybody there knows how to open the silos now. Anti-aircraft working overtime though, with Israeli gunners under EU command."

"If the silos were open," I said, "all those Arrows could take down the incoming Shahobs!"

"Things look better in the air than on the ground," Jack said. "Anti-ballistic fire is flying over our heads from EU ships on the Mediterranean and from EU sites in Saudi Arabia and Afghanistan. So the sky's full of EU missiles intercepting Arab missiles.

"The EU has drones flying recon from aircraft carriers on the Caspian and doing bombing runs. They're heading for those damned Turkish ships and in many other directions. They've got live fighter flights up there too, but it's hell for our seasoned pilots to have to sit on their hands down here and curse the Peace."

"What're you gonna do, Jack?"

"I'm going back out to the streets, Matthew—Siggy and me. I'm still a reporter. We've still got our cameras…our phones. Maybe we can't connect to Philly from the streets, but we can film what's happening. I can write it down. That's my job. To be the eyes and the ears and the mouth of the truth."

"Jack," I said, "have you heard from Wall?"

"Not since…not since he contacted me to play dumb about his contact with you."

"He's with Ali," I said.

"Alive!" Jack cried.

"I hope so," I said huskily.

"Don't stop hoping, Matt," he pleaded. He was quiet for a moment. "I've got to go now."

"Jack," I said, "please take care of yourself!"

"I'll try! But you better take of yourself, too, *goy!*"

I stumbled into the living room and stared at the TV. Shocking. Sickening. Numbing.

I turned it off—turned everything off and sank into the couch next to Kevin, dizzy, my mind reeling.

Lisa's Facebook messge, from the 4th of July, echoed in

my head. *Do you think the peace won't last? And what will happen to us if it doesn't?*

I thought about her dream. The Four Horsemen of the book of Revelation pursuing us to the edge of a raging river. Pressing us into the dark waters. Somehow, that's how I felt. Watched by spirits. Pursued by spectral warriors on horseback—like the terrifying mounted Nazgul of Tolkien's epic fantasy. Chased up against a flood that can't be forded—like Moses at the Red Sea but without that magic staff. The Sunday school stories had happy endings. Where was ours?

"The world's on fire, Kevin. What *will* happen to us? What's going on?" I didn't even look at him. My questions fell on the carpet in front of me.

"A world at war," he said quietly, "and we've got to choose sides. A world coming to an end, and we've got to stand strong."

The doorbell rang. Kevin went to the window to check the front-door mirror. "It's Doug."

Kevin unlocked the main door with the buzzer button, and within a minute Doug was out of the elevator and barging into my apartment.

"Matt, I'm glad you're home!" he said, out of breath. "I figured you'd be here because of what happened and…" He stopped when he saw I wasn't alone. "Kev! What are you doin' here? It's a…it's a workday, isn't it?"

"Hardly a normal one," said Kevin.

"Hardly," Doug admitted flatly. "The whole country… the whole world…is falling apart around us."

He sat down heavily upon the recliner. "We closed the store for the day—maybe longer," he said. "Maybe forever. No business anyway. Clay bailed out Target, but there weren't any stimulus dollars for Rittenhouse Hardware.

"And the bombs. And Israel. Jesus has to come back soon! I was bitching about it this morning at home. The kids were crying, and Caroline told me to shut up or get out of the house until I got my head on straight. So," he glanced around the room, "I came over here." He looked at me. "I've been praying for you, Matt," he said meekly. "You look a little pale. How are you?"

"I'm a little pale," I said, smiling optimistically. I felt like crap.

"Work's down everywhere, Doug," said Kevin bluntly. "If the store closes, don't be too proud to beg a job in the hardware section at Wal-Mart."

"Yeah, right! They're gonna hire *me* when they can pay some high school kid minimum wage? When the government is giving them a dollar on every five bucks they're paying to employ Mideast vets? I might as well try to sell toilet plungers door-to-door!"

"Not a bad idea," said Kevin.

"Or join the Marines!" Doug added.

"Not a good idea," Kevin replied.

"God's judging America," Doug said bitterly. "And we've got to reap what someone else's sin has sowed! Why doesn't Jesus just take us outa here and get it over with. Burn it all up. Start it all over."

"Soon enough," sighed Kevin. "But not until it gets much worse."

"What could be worse than Jerusalem in flames and bombs going off in Toys R Us?"

"Going to hell," said Kevin.

"The whole world's going to hell!" Doug shouted. "I've got a brother up in the mountains in Colorado. I'm thinking about moving out there and waiting for the rapture.

"There's just no way out of this hole! Voting won't do any good. The system's busted. Washington just prints money and throws it to the wind. Even if you've got money, there's nothing solid to invest in. China's got all the gold. And if you have something nice, the gangs will break it or steal it. If you own a cheap rental property, you have to let gays live there. If you kick about that, you end up in court with some lisping lawyer calling you a faggot-hater. Then they fine you a couple thousand bucks and make you kiss the lawyer!"

"In this life," said Kevin, "we'll have tribulation."

"Not me!" shot Doug. "I didn't sign up with God to go through tribulation. Hard times are hard times, but…"

"Kevin thinks this is it—Tribulation, day one. And we're still here," I said to the floor and to Doug and to myself.

"No way!" Doug argued. "You're all screwed up if you buy that baloney, Matt. What's wrong with you, Kevin? We need some hope—not negative confession. Why do you talk like that? I thought you went to a good church. Don't you read the Bible?"

Kevin sighed. "I'm sorry about your job, Doug," he said.

"Yeah! Change the subject when it gets hot! Show me in the Bible that Christians are going through the Tribulation, and then maybe I'll shut up…like my wife says I should."

"Chill out, Doug," said Kevin. There was pain in his voice and steel in his eyes. "I just killed a man," he added flatly.

"You wanna rough me up, too?" Doug stood up angry. "You wanna grip it up over Jesus coming back? You can't back your bad doctrine, so you wanna pull the karate thing on me?"

"No," said Kevin quietly, evenly.

The two men stood staring at one another.

Doug was riled, tense. Kevin hardly moved.

"I don't want a fight, Doug. What I'm telling you is that I just killed a man. With a gun. Blew his brains out."

Doug's eyes widened, his mouth opened and closed without words.

"I had to," Kevin rasped. "I think I had to. To save others. Maybe…maybe just to save *me*. Or maybe because I was pissed off at the freaking terrorists because another man died trying to save us all."

"Save us all," Doug echoed blankly. "You mean… Jesus?"

"No, you idiot," said Kevin, blinking back tears. "I mean Kahmeel! I'm hurting real bad right now—right here!" He thumped his chest with a fist. "So I don't need to hear you whining about your busted piggy bank. And I don't need any argument about when Jesus is coming back! But..." Both his hands were fisted. "But we sure as hell need to hold on to Jesus!"

Doug sat back down.

"I'm sorry, Kev!" he blurted. "I'm upset about a lot of things, too." He hung his head. "I misunderstood you."

"Obviously," said Kevin, wiping his eyes with the back of his hands. He sat down on the couch himself.

"Sorry," Doug said again, soberly.

Tears slid down Kevin's cheeks.

My heart was aching, heavy, weighed down, and so very troubled about so many things, so many people. The wars that were raging and the darkness that was rising. The confusion, the questions, the cares of my own heart. But more than that.

Something of my own sin lay heavy in me, too. I wouldn't have called it that, but that's just what it was. A cold, bitter burden, somewhere deep within me. Deep and ancient and chained to me like a rusted iron anchor. And it made me feel old—infirm, unsteady, unable to prop myself up on my own two feet. I needed to cast it off somehow and climb out of the pit to stand on something solid.

Faith. I needed faith. Faith like the rock beneath Kevin's feet that kept him standing no matter how high or troubled the waters roiled around him.

"Doug," I said, after we'd been sitting silent for a while. "No offense, man, but do you think you can handle it if Kevin shows us where he gets his take on the end times?"

"Can I handle it?" he said, his voice rising. Then he laughed wearily. "I don't know. Probably not. But I can promise to leave if I can't. I'm good at walking out, if nothing else."

I handed Kevin a Bible from a shelf above the TV. He stared at it blankly for a long moment.

"Okay," he said at last, sitting up, blinking at us through red eyes. "Here's the quick take. Try to follow me."

He held the Bible up but didn't open it.

"The prophet Daniel was given a vision," he said. "He saw through the ages up to the end of the earth. He saw history unfolding in seventy 'weeks' that represent various eras and events. Daniel's final week—his seventieth—is the seven years prior to the second advent of Christ. I think we've just stepped into the front door of Daniel's last week—at the beginning of the final seven years before the Second Coming. The eleventh hour, as Tyrone would say."

"Final seven years," Doug grumbled. "My pastor says Jesus is coming right before those seven years. Or rather that we'll be raptured then, and Jesus will come back at the end of the seven years."

"Oh?" said Kevin with a tired smile. "He's coming back twice?"

"No, no. He'll rapture us," Doug shot back. "Nobody'll see him then, but we'll be taken up into the clouds to meet him. Then the Antichrist is revealed and the Tribulation begins. But the church is outa here! And then Jesus comes back, big-time."

"That's typical pretribulation doctrine," Kevin quietly agreed, "but that's not Bible. Nowhere in the Bible is there anything about a secret rapture or an invisible return of Christ. The whole earth will see him when he returns, and he'll gather his faithful from the four corners of the earth at that time. That happens at the end of the Great Tribulation. Then God pours out his wrath upon the earth. Armageddon happens. And it's over."

Doug was going to protest, but he saw my face and held his tongue.

"According to your pastor's timeline," Kevin continued, "you and Matt and I are already left behind."

"No way!" Doug fired. Then he was silent for a moment, thinking. "You mean," he said, "you think the attack today is…?"

"Gog of Magog."

"Gog has to be Russia!" said Doug. "It says so in Ezekiel. I've always heard—"

"Gog is a man. Magog is a nation," Kevin interrupted. "And Kazakhstan and Uzbekistan might as well *be* Russia. They're former Soviet states—still tight with Russia even though they don't trust Putin. Kazakhstan has been selling enriched uranium to Russia for three or four years before Maleshenko took power. They all want to see Israel destroyed. Whether Russia's in the vanguard against Israel or not, you can bet Putin's in the cheering section. Meanwhile, Russia's just added Georgia to its territorial portfolio. And there're some other nations mentioned in Ezekiel as part of the assault on Israel."

"Yeah," said Doug. "Meshech and Tubal…and Gomer."

"Wrap 'em up together, and you have modern day Turkey," said Kevin.

"Ethiopia?"

"That's Sudan," said Kevin.

"The ancient country of Put?"

"Libya."

I was riveted. These were the nations right now moving on Israel. Was this really the Bible coming true?

"So who's Gog?" Doug asked, agitated.

"Ezekiel says he's the chief prince of Meshech and Tubal. In today's politics that makes him the Prime Minister of Turkey."

"Gökham Savas!" I blurted.

"Well!" said Doug, aghast, getting up and walking to the window to look out at the sky. "Maybe today."

"He's not coming back today, Doug. And not tomorrow.

Jesus said he's not coming back until the gospel is preached in the whole world for a witness to all nations. Then the end will come. That's his own words."

"Yeah, but he can come any day, can't he? He's God. He can come back when he wants to."

"Where's that in the Bible?"

"The Bible talks about him coming back in the wink of an eye."

"Yeah, that's how sudden it happens," said Kevin. "But as for *when* it happens, Jesus talks about coming back after the Great Tribulation."

Kevin flipped the Bible open to the gospel of Matthew.

"Immediately *after* the tribulation of those days," he read, "shall the sun be darkened, and the moon shall not give her light, and the stars shall fall from heaven, and the powers of the heavens shall be shaken. And then shall appear the sign of the Son of man in heaven. And then shall all the tribes of the earth mourn, and they shall see the Son of man coming in the clouds of heaven with power and great glory. And he shall send his angels with a great sound of a trumpet, and they shall gather together his elect from the four winds, from one end of heaven to the other."

He closed the Bible. "Nowhere in this book does it say he can come back any day."

"There's been over two thousand years of 'any day,'" I noted.

"And still nearly sixty-five hundred people groups who have never heard the gospel," Kevin added. "The book of Revelation talks about a great multitude of people from every nation, tribe, and tongue, standing before God's throne in heaven. These are people who have 'washed their robes and made them white in the blood of the Lamb.' These are Christians."

"So what's the point?" Doug asked.

"Well, look here." Kevin fingered the Bible open again and found some verses in Revelation. "It says here that those people 'came out of the Great Tribulation.' They were Christians, from every people group on earth, alive during the Great Tribulation. And that means the church goes through the Great Tribulation in order to finish preaching the gospel to every tribe before the Second Coming."

"Jesus said he'd keep us from tribulation!"

"Come on, Doug! You accuse *me* of not reading the Bible!" Kevin sat up straighter. "Jesus flat out said, 'In the world, you'll have tribulation.' Paul wrote to Timothy that 'Those who live godly lives in Christ Jesus will suffer persecution.' Jesus started out the Sermon on the Mount by telling us to rejoice in persecution. He said that people would revile us, slander us, hate us, kill us, drag us in front of kings. He said we'd be treated like he was treated! And how did they treat him? They whipped him within an inch of his life and then nailed him to a cross. So why do we expect some special protection from trials and tribulation?"

Doug shrugged heavily and scowled more heavily still.

"The apostle Peter was crucified upside down," Kevin pressed. "Tradition speaks of the martyrdom of all the original apostles, except John—and Judas, of course, who hung himself. The apostle Paul was executed in Rome. The early church was bitterly persecuted. Dragged out of their homes, challenged to renounce Christ, fed to lions, torn apart by wild dogs, burned alive as human torches in the garden of Nero. They were forced to worship in hiding, in underground catacombs.

"Were they yelling 'Foul!'? Did they threaten to sue Jesus for breach of covenant? Did they whimper about being 'left behind'? Or did they hold on to Jesus' promise that 'those who endure until the end will be saved'?"

I was rattled by Kevin's words. They reminded me of things I'd studied in history.

"The persecution of Christians during the first three centuries was terrible," I commented. "The church actually believed it was in the Great Tribulation and that Nero, and then Decius, and then Diocletian were the Antichrist."

"That's right!" said Kevin. "And Luther thought the turmoil of the Reformation was the tribulation and that the Pope was the Antichrist. The saints of days past weren't looking for the rapture to yank them out of here. They were standing firm in the faith while looking for Jesus to return. Like John wrote in Revelation, they overcame Satan 'by the blood of the Lamb and the word of their testimony.'"

"And they loved not their lives unto death," Doug said, quoting the rest of the verse by heart.

"Martyrs," Kevin declared.

"I don't get it," I said. "It's like the historic church had one doctrine of the last days, and the American church has invented the pretribulation rapture as an extension of the American dream."

"Almost," said Kevin. "But America doesn't hold the patent on pretrib thinking. That belongs to Great Britain. It started there, around 1830, took hold in certain circles in Canada and America—and then spread. Today, there are hundreds of thousands of our brothers and sisters who sincerely believe it. It is the 'pop doctrine' of the end times and so widely believed that few people know that before 1830 hardly anyone even considered a pretribulation rapture."

"What?" Doug coughed. "Paul taught it! Jesus taught it! John taught it!"

"Nope," Kevin countered. "They taught a post-tribulation, second coming rapture, not a pretribulation rapture."

"I don't believe it!" said Doug. "Where do you get this stuff?"

"Church history, church doctrine through the ages, the Christian preachers of nineteen centuries. Anybody can check it out if they bother to read," said Kevin. "My pastor teaches it, too." He handed Doug the Bible. "The rest is in there," he said.

Doug stared at the book in his hands.

"Well, the Bible does say that people will suffer for Jesus sometimes," he admitted sullenly. "But why would God make the whole church live through the worst time the world will ever know?"

"Because the world needs to hear the gospel," Kevin replied. "We're the light of the world, aren't we? Isn't that what Jesus said? A city that is set upon a hill cannot be hidden, right? When the days are darkest, that's when the light is needed most. Christians through the ages have risen up to love their neighbors in the midst of terrible times. God's not going to take his people out of the world during the time the world most needs what we've got!"

"He's coming back soon," Doug said, shaking his head morosely.

"Why did Jesus come in the first place?" Kevin asked. "To seek and save the lost, right? He said that people don't need a doctor unless they're sick. The whole world is sick and getting sicker! As the Father sent the Son, so the Son sends us. This is Sunday school simple, Doug. This is our calling—to be salt and light in the midst of a crooked and perverse generation."

"God is going to pour out his wrath upon his own church—his precious bride?" Doug glowered. "Is that what you're telling me?"

"No," Kevin said. "That happens only to a wicked, hard-hearted remnant of humanity, for a very brief time, right after Jesus comes back for us."

"Not the way I heard it," said Doug.

"Unpack your bag, brother. Put on the armor of God. Get ready to fight the good fight of faith. Prepare your heart for whatever comes—peace, persecution, or Pilate."

"That's looney!" Doug argued. "I'm counting on Jesus saving my neck, not on the Antichrist cutting off my head."

"Maybe you should worry more about the souls of those around you," said Kevin flatly.

"So what about *my* soul?" I heard myself ask. They turned toward me.

"Get saved," said Doug.

"I know what the Bible says," I protested. "That I'm a sinner like everybody else in the world, and that Jesus died to save me. Shed his blood to pay the price for my salvation so that I don't have to pay the price myself…in hell. I know all that. I memorized John 3:16 in youth group. 'For God so loved the world that he gave his only begotten Son, that whosoever believeth in him shall not perish, but have everlasting life.'

"But what does that do for me now? Give me goose bumps? Make me dance and talk in tongues? I don't understand this 'born again' thing. I know that Jesus spoke about it. I know he was talking about a new spiritual life, but what I've seen in too many churches—and in a whole lot of Christians—doesn't look like transformation. It more like a religious initiation into God's Club."

Doug stared at me dumbly.

Kevin nodded grimly.

I continued. "Walk the aisle. Kneel at the rail. Have some deacon lay his hands on you and recite some holy incantation that you repeat out loud to make sure God hears you. Then, bingo! You're in. If it doesn't seem to take, come back next week and try it again. Then tap your ruby slippers together and repeat positive mantras, read your Bible every day, make sure you come out to the God Club meetings every Sunday morning and Wednesday night, and pay your dues—ten percent of your paycheck in the offering plate from gross, not net.

"Put in a few bucks more, with a 'cheerful heart,' of course, if you want special perks—like pooling your money to bet on a ball game at work. Or buying a lottery ticket. You might hit the jackpot, who knows?"

I threw my hands in the air. "What's all that got to do with following Jesus?" I said.

"You can't forsake the assembling of the saints," Doug quoted soberly.

"And who are the saints, Doug?" I asked. "Who are the saved?"

"Actually," Kevin said, "what really matters is humbling yourself and trusting Christ with all your heart. Loving him with all your might and all your mind. Learning about him. Getting to know him. Doing the things he said to do. Walking with him. Holding on to him, no matter what."

"How do you know he's real?" I asked candidly. "How do you know you're not just talking to the wind? Not just all hung up over the words of an old book?"

"You wouldn't ask that if you were saved," said Doug.

"Maybe he would," said Kevin. "Maybe I ask those questions sometimes, too. Don't you?"

"No," said Doug, "I don't."

"Well..." said Kevin, "I guess your faith is stronger than mine. Sometimes my heart condemns me and my head confuses me. But there is no condemnation for those who are in Christ Jesus, and God is greater than my heart."

I was standing in front of the darkened television. Kevin looked up at me intently. "But I do have an answer to your questions, Matt," he said. "I do know he's real. I do know I'm not talking to the wind. I know who he is, and I know who I am. He's my Father, I'm his son. He hears my prayers, and he answers them. He lives within me and wakes me each morning with a purpose so real that sometimes the smell of heaven is stronger than my coffee."

"I believe you, Kevin," I said.

"Then believe God, too," he challenged.

"I do," I answered, "but I don't. Not like you."

"You're not me, thank God. Believe him like you!"

"How do you know when you really believe?"

Kevin was quiet for a long moment. Then he said, "He tells you."

We turned the TV on and watched a world on fire.

We huddled on the couch, the three of us, horrified, paralyzed by the images that flashed before us.

At times, I dozed. The medication dulled my senses, closed my eyes, and shut me down. In those moments I dreamed sad, troubled dreams.

Awake or asleep, Wall's little red phone was in my hand.

Meet the Authors

MARK AMMERMAN was born into an artistic, literary, Christian family. For as long as he can remember, his passion was to put words and pictures together on paper. His earliest published works were cartoons in his father's small town newspaper. His mother was a published poet. His sister Kris (who edits a roofing industry trade magazine) says, "The ink is in the blood."

Mark is an internationally published author and illustrator whose historical fiction novel *Longshot* was chosen by the American Library Association's *Booklist* as one of the Top 10 Best Christian Fiction novels of the year 2000.

Mark's published writing includes history, biography, historical fiction, Bible stories for children, newspaper and magazine journalism, and materials for equipping Christian leaders. He has illustrated books for many of the nation's largest publishers, and his cartoons have been featured in newspapers, books, and magazines in the United States, South America, and Europe.

Mark enjoys hiking and biking with his wife and children, playing tennis, listening to surf guitar music, writing songs and singing, theological conversation, and reading western novels at bedtime.

Mark and his wife Terri live in Lancaster, Pennsylvania, where Mark is pastor of Grace Evangelical Congregational Church, an historic inner-city congregation which has been serving the city of Lancaster for 170 years. Mark and Terri are foster and adoptive parents with five children of their own and three grandchildren.

You can visit Grace Church online at: gracesunday.com.

E. MICHAEL RUSTEN grew up in Plymouth, Minnesota, a suburb of Minneapolis. God drew him to himself at a Billy Graham crusade when Mike was a junior high boy, and life was never the same.

Mike is an avid Christian historian, theologian (specializing in eschatology and the book of Revelation), and Scholar-in-Residence at Bethlehem College and Seminary in Minneapolis, Minnesota. At Bethlehem, Mike is the director of the college's Degree Completion Program.

Mike has written four books (two with his wife Sharon.) His *One Year Christian History* for Tyndale House Publishers (a book in which Mark Ammerman was a contributing writer) is a bestseller. Mike has written for *Decision, Christian Bookseller, The Bookstore Journal, The Freedom Report, Journal of Psychological Studies*, and *Minnesota Medicine*.

His academic credentials include a B.A. *magna cum laude* from Princeton University, M.A. from University of Minnesota, M.Div. from Westminster Theological Seminary, Th.M. *summa cum laude* from Trinity Evangelical Divinity School, and Ph.D. from New York University where he wrote his doctoral dissertation on the book of Revelation. Along the way Mike also attended Dallas Theological Seminary and Jerusalem University College.

After finishing his classwork at New York University, Mike served as the assistant pastor at Calvary Memorial Church in Orono, Minnesota. Then God opened the doors for him to become the owner of Cascade Lodge near Grand Marais, Minnesota, which Mike operated with his father-in-law as a Christian resort. During those years, Mike started Morning Star, a Christian greeting card company. It grew to be listed in the Inc. 500, and Mike was elected to the Board of Directors of the Christian Booksellers Association.

After selling the resort and the greeting card company, Mike became involved in electoral politics, serving as the National Coordinator for the Freedom Council, the predecessor of the Christian Coalition. In each presidential election from 1988 to 2000 Mike was on the campaign staff of one of the candidates for president. During that time Mike also served for three and a half years as director of adult education at Church of the Open Door, a church of 6,000 now located in Maple Grove, Minnesota.

Mike and Sharon live in Minnetonka, Minnesota. They have two grown children and four grandchildren.

For more on Mike's many insightful thoughts on Revelation and the Bible, visit howthebiblefitstogether.org.

Acknowledgments

Mark and Mike wish to shout out a heartfelt "THANK YOU!" to Marlene Bagnull for the energizing affirmation, personable humor, seasoned advice, persistent prayer, and roll-up-her-sleeves help she lavished on us in the final stages of publication.

In spite of a flooded basement, a plague of computer software glitches, and deadlines of her own, Marlene (and her husband Paul) gave us the time and encouragement we needed to complete *PUSH* on schedule and with the polish and punch it now has. Marlene's unflagging commitment to help Christian authors "write His answer" is praiseworthy and unmatched in Christian publishing today.

Marlene helps Christians self-publish affordably but professionally through Ampelos Press: writehisanswer.com/ampelospress. Check out her other ministries at writehisanswer.com.

She is the founder (in 1983) and director of the Greater Philadelphia Christian Writers Conference. For information about this annual conference go to philadelphia.writehisanswer.com.

Since 1997 Marlene also has been directing the Colorado Christian Writers Conference—colorado.writehisanswer.com.

AN EXCERPT

Eleventh Hour • Book Two

PULL

GOG OF MAGOG

MARK AMMERMAN
with E. Michael Rusten

BRIDGE STREET BOOKS
LANCASTER, PENNSYLVANIA

Excerpt
Eleventh Hour · Book Two
PULL

Marco Romano generally stayed up late. Sometimes he didn't go to bed until 4 o'clock in the morning. On nights like that, he slept until exactly 8:30 a.m., and woke up refreshed. If he slept more than six hours in a night, he was sluggish upon rising—and he hated being sluggish. A ten-minute supplemental nap during the afternoon (and early evening if he had no appointments), powered him up as well as a full night's sleep for a normal human being. Marco Romano was certainly human—but no one could accuse him of normality.

Brilliant, driven, able to multi-task as if he were a trinity of personalities, Romano was an able administrator as well as a spell-binding orator. Those who worked closely with him had seldom known a man so cool under pressure, so able to lead with grace and wit. But his heart could be stone, his words sharp steel. His personal staff was glad to go home at 5:00, to let him work late—and alone.

He was buried so deep in his thoughts that at first he didn't hear the phone. When the hum broke through his muse, he slowly turned his face from the computer screen, a puzzled, troubled frown upon his pale brow.

The line was secure, private, a "gate-keeper" line. All calls were screened and qualified before being sent through to the Italian premiere. This was a line for the chosen few—and no others. He squinted at the monitor above the phone.

No name appeared. No bio. Something was wrong with the I.D. system. But he would take the call.

He cleared his throat, swallowed a mouthful of cognac from a glass which he had at hand, and pushed the respond button on his phone.

"General Marco Romano speaking," he said graciously. "I am honored to receive your call."

"General! Ah, yes! They call you that, don't they? And why not? You *are* a general, a military mammoth, a tactical genius on the battleground...or in the background, or in the underground for that matter! A hero, yes, and a savior. The gifts of God are irrevocable, Romano! I envy you—though my own destiny is glorious and assured!"

Romano recognized the man immediately. The voice was one in a million. Romano would know it in a crowded room. He'd heard it in many a crowded room during the Peace talks. "Savas! How did you get...?"

"Your phone number? You gave it to me once! And I talked myself right past your clever checkpoints. You told me how to do that too. You were drunk at the time. That doesn't happen to you often, bless the Prophet and his angels—peace be upon them! But...here we are."

Romano recovered himself and sat up in his chair. His eye went to the cognac glass. His mouth straightened in a grim, angry line, but his voice was smooth, pleasant, leading. "And to what do I owe the pleasure of this personal conversation with the Prime Minister of a nation at open war with Israel?"

Savas laughed loudly, freely.

"I called to say I love you! After all, my dear General, we have you to thank for our excellent advantage here in the Middle East. If was you who lobbied so passionately for Turkey's inclusion on the European Council. And if it were not for your Peace, signori Romano, I should not have dared to saddle up and ride my war horse toward Israel. But because of you, we are praising Allah while shooting Jewish doves from the sky, skewering Jewish pigs on the ends of our lances, singing and dancing our way toward Zion—poor, doomed Zion!"

Romano was silent. Savas! The architect of this horrific breach of the recent Peace. The man at the helm of the alliance against Israel. The supposed kingpin of the international terrorist attacks. Should he talk with him? But the line was secure—and what better way to know the present mind of this Turkish madman—this Gog of Magog, as some called him?

"Are you enjoying the fireworks, Marco? Pretty colors all over the world! And in your own backyard—that grand old church in the Vatican! A pity that your little pope doesn't do a better job protecting his prize properties."

"You will not win this war, Savas," said Romano, coldly.

"You are ridiculous, Romano. Hilarious! Brilliant! Beneath that malevolent mask of yours, beloved General, is the grin of the Grand Jester!" Savas laughed again, uncontrollably. "The Peace!" he wheezed, catching his breath. "They laid down their swords and shields! Thank you, General Romano! If I could, I would make you king of the world."

"You will die, Savas."

"Tomorrow at dawn, we crush Zion. Come and see, Romano. I have more horses. You may ride beside me into the unwalled villages of Israel. Like your Christ rode into Jerusalem so many years ago—according to your fables. But this time not on a carpet of palm branches, but over the bodies of the Zionist swine. Men, women, children… chickens, cows, dogs—it's all the same. Allah is happy tonight. Ha ha!—do you know that Allah laughs? Yes, I have heard him."

On Romano's own phone! Past the "gate keeper." Past every safeguard. All the way from Baghdad. Romano knew where the man was, because he was watching the war like a hawk. The whole world was watching. But the Italian premiere had better eyes than most.

"Angels, Marco. I talk with angels. Wouldn't you like to talk with angels? Come and see me. I'll introduce you to them!"

"You will die, Savas."

"No, no, Marco. Not Gökhan Savas. I will be taken up to Paradise…after the war…like the Prophet—peace be upon him. Tomorrow we crush Zion. Then the Mahdi returns to earth, and all the infidels will die. You will die, Romano, not I. Allah laughs. "

Savas tittered giddily, took a deep rattling breath, and then continued. "Three more days, and then the Night of Power, the anniversary of the first divine revelation which came to the Prophet—peace be upon him—in the cave of Hira. Yes, three days more and I will be taken up to talk with Adam, Abraham, and Moses. Gabriel will go with me, to show the way. I only wish I could stay to see you all bow. To watch your heads roll, your blood flow—glorious *jihad!*"

"You are where?" Romano wanted Savas to say so himself. The conversation was recorded.

"Baghdad. On a white horse, Romano. Prancing in the streets where Mohammed's grandchildren danced—peace be upon him—when Baghdad ruled the Muslim world. Are you coming? You should be here, General. To see the dead and dying. You should make the pilgrimage. Allah might be merciful toward you. Haw! Allah laughs. Can't you hear it?"

Romano heard the laughter of the madman. He saw him laughing, too. On a sat-screen on the wall beside the phone. It was world-class Chinese technology. Chinese satellite videography. Funded by American dollars—by Wal-Mart and K-Mart and K-Bee Toys. Color images, all the way from the stratosphere to a wall screen in Rome. Blurred images because of the drought and the dust and Iraqi winds, but amazing images nonetheless. Close up—very close. *The horse is white*, Romano noted. *And the idiot is talking to me on a cell phone!*

"You will die," Romano said once more, then he cut the connection. "And I will kill you," he said when the line was dead.

CONNECT
with Bridge Street and its authors

Quantity copies of PUSH are available
at a discount

Contact us through
eleventhhourpush.com

Also available through amazon.com
and other online stores

If PUSH has raised questions about the End Times,
Mark Ammerman and Mike Rusten
may be available to speak
to your church or organization.

E. MICHAEL RUSTEN has been writing and speaking on
Revelation and the End Times for decades. His Revelation
seminar is an enlightening experience of biblical exegesis,
impartation, and inspiration. Mike's doctoral dissertation (at
New York University in 1977) was on the book of
Revelation. His study guide *The End Times: Discovering What
the Bible Says* (WaterBrook Press/Random House 1997) is
part of the series of Fisherman Bible Study guides.

MARK AMMERMAN preaches weekly at Grace Evangelical
Congregational Church in Lancaster, Pennsylvania. A gifted
communicator and singer/song-writer, his perspective on
the Bible and our times is informed by 40 years of Christian
ministry, 35 years of marriage and family life, a lifetime in
the Church of Jesus Christ, and a precious legacy of multi-
generational faith.

Mike and Mark can be contacted through
the Eleventh Hour website at eleventhhourpush.com

www.ingramcontent.com/pod-product-compliance
Lightning Source LLC
Chambersburg PA
CBHW060138260626
47160CB00001B/34